# CONTEST OF HEARTS

"Molly, please," Sam pleaded, "I only want to help you. I want Foley off that ranch and out of your life!"

Shaking with anger, Molly stood up and faced him defiantly. "You're so used to running things around here you think you can run me too!" She unbuckled the riding skirt he'd presented her, let it fall to her feet, then kicked it aside. "This skirt is just one more attempt to control me, and I won't have it!"

Sam spun to face her. "I swear by the saints, Molly Brannigan, I'll—"

"You'll what?" she challenged him. Then, clad only in her blouse and pantalettes, she turned and stalked upstairs, daring him to follow.

*Also by Kat Martin*

MAGNIFICENT PASSAGE

Published by
PAGEANT BOOKS

# DUELING HEARTS

KAT MARTIN

PAGEANT BOOKS

Publisher's Note: This is a work of fiction. The characters, incidents, and dialogues are products of the author's imagination and are not to be construed as real. Any resemblance to actual events or persons, living or dead, is entirely coincidental.

PAGEANT BOOKS
225 Park Avenue South
New York, New York 10003



Cover artwork by Pino Daeni

Printed in the U.S.A.

First Pageant Books printing: March, 1989

10 9 8 7 6 5 4 3 2 1

*To my dad, now gone, who gave me such a wonderful love of the Old West; and to my red-haired grandmother, whose split leather skirt, like Molly's, I still have.*

# Dueling Hearts

# Chapter One

*April 29, 1875*

The first shot whizzed harmlessly above his head. The second pinged loudly against a granite boulder, hurling splinters of rock through the crisp mountain air.

"Take cover!" Sam Brannigan shouted, his deep voice cracking across the pass. In a single quick motion, he swung his stiff leg over the buckskin's rump and pulled his Winchester from the scabbard behind the cantle. Crouching low to avoid the second series of gunshots, Sam made a dodging run into the safety of the rocks. He cocked his rifle and began firing, while his brother, Emmet, and Buck Redding, the bullwhacker, ducked into the boulders beside him, leaving two riderless horses and eight teams of oxen pawing the earth nervously in the din of gunfire.

"What do you make of it?" Emmet asked Sam. The rifle shots grew more sporadic, but pinned them down just the same. The oxen lowed and fought the heavy yokes around their necks, but the attack was clearly directed at the men and not the animals.

"Can't tell yet," Sam answered, another shot just inches above his head forcing him to crouch lower. Bits of shale flew from a shot near the brim of Buck Redding's black felt hat.

Cautiously raising himself up, Sam scanned the rocks above the pass for any sign of their assailants. Nothing. "By the saints, I wish I could get a fix on whoever it is. From the way the bullets are hitting, I think it may be just one man moving after each shot. Get ready to cover me. I'll circle around and come up on him from behind."

Emmet Brannigan nodded. Adjusting the red kerchief around the thick girth of his neck, he steadied his Henry in the crevice of a rock, the brass receiver reflecting a ray of sunlight. As Sam started to move, several more shots rang out, forcing all three men to flatten themselves against the sun-warmed granite.

Emmet grinned conspiratorially at his brother. "Lucky for us. Whoever the bastard is, he's a mighty poor shot."

Sam's hazel eyes darkened, his vision searching the line of boulders across the pass. "Or a damned good one." Lifting his worn felt hat, the band stained with the sweat of a year's hard work, he raked a hand through his dark blond hair, then settled the hat low across his brow.

"Start shooting, but don't hit anything. I want to find out who's up there—and why."

Used to following Sam's orders, Emmet nodded and squeezed off a round, careful to overshoot his target, but firing the shots close enough together to prevent any return gunfire. As he watched his brother's tall figure dart among the rocks, his muscular body moving with the sureness of a fine cutting horse, Emmet smiled. Only the slight stiffness of his brother's bothersome knee affected the grace of his motion. Every few seconds, Sam's blue checked shirt flashed between the boulders, the barrel of his rifle glinting a darker metal blue.

Emmet and Buck continued their cover fire until Sam disappeared into the dense copse of sugar pines that darkened the slopes of the nearby hills. Each hoped Sam would find the assailant before their limited supply of bullets ran out.

Lying on her stomach, her rifle propped in front of her, Molly James molded herself against the granite boulders beneath her. A flurry of bullets whizzed just above her head. It appeared the men below were not shooting to kill, but the constant gunfire forced her to remain where she was. It was not what she had planned.

From her location at the top of the pass, she had spotted the tall bearded man moving through the woods to her right. It looked as if he had fixed her position and was circling around to cut her off.

Molly slid four more shells into the magazine

of her carbine. She had to move, and move fast; and bullets or no bullets, it had to be now.

Taking a breath to steady herself, Molly raised up on the rock, fired two well-placed shots that blasted jagged chips near the heads of the men below, slid off the boulder, and began a dodging run toward a new position and fresh cover. She was counting on her speed and agility, and her slight size, which enabled her to squeeze through the narrowest crevice. Her snug men's clothing gave her mobility and a partial disguise.

Molly raced around the back of the boulder, determined to get a fix on her pursuer, but stopped short when just ahead she spotted a pair of muscular thighs in blue denim breeches. Heart pounding, she spun on her heel to run, but strong hands caught the material at the back of her shirt, stopping her in midstride.

As she whirled to face her adversary, her floppy-brimmed hat prevented a good look at the blond man's face. She saw only his narrow waist, and a glimpse of his ham-sized fist, before she felt a jolt of pain in her jaw and was hurled backward over a fallen log. Landing heavily in the dirt several feet away, she rolled once and slid to a painful stop against the trunk of a tree, gasping to replenish the air knocked from her lungs and fighting the tiny swirling circles that finally swept her into unconsciousness. . . .

Sam Brannigan reached his quarry just moments before his brother and Buck Redding raced up beside him.

"Tarnation, Sam!" Buck exclaimed. "It's a woman!" Thick masses of shiny, flame-red hair tumbled across two full breasts clearly evident beneath a white cotton shirt that disappeared into denim breeches. A wide leather belt surrounded her tiny waist.

Sam knelt beside the unconscious figure and checked the pulse throbbing evenly at the base of her slender throat. "I tried to pull my punch when I realized the fellow's size, but I guess it wasn't enough."

"I guess not," Emmet agreed a bit ruefully. Dropping to one knee beside his brother, Emmet pulled away the floppy hat, which still covered part of the feminine face. More heavy red hair cascaded from beneath the hat, where she had haphazardly tucked it out of sight.

Sam marveled at the wild, disheveled appearance of the small young woman in breeches. Her skin looked smooth and clear except for the smattering of freckles that dotted the bridge of her slightly upturned nose. A wide, generous mouth outlined by full red lips curved upward in what might have passed for a sleepy smile. She was pretty but not beautiful, small but full figured, not dainty or petite. He guessed her years to be less than twenty.

Sam had never seen a woman dressed in men's clothing; it was a sight to throw any man a bit off track. But it was more than her appearance that intrigued him. There was something about her: a raw sensuality, a compelling recklessness that ebbed from the girl's very pores. As his eyes traveled from her mouth to the rounded curves of her body, Sam felt a tightening in his groin.

"Who the hell is she?" he asked, beginning to feel peevish as he eyed the purple bruise on her otherwise flawless skin. He'd never hit a woman before, and the deed set none too well with him now. "And why the hell was she shooting at us? Buck, fetch me a wet cloth, and make it snappy. I want the lass awake, and I want some answers."

Buck nodded and left to do Sam's bidding.

"My guess is, the girl's Molly James," Emmet said. "Ain't many round these parts got redder hair'n the Jameses. She's about the right age. Besides, I heard Molly was back at the Lady Jay."

As Emmet picked up her carbine, Sam lifted the girl in his arms and carried her to the shelter of a shady pine. Propping her against the rough bark of the trunk, he accepted the damp cloth from Buck, and placed it across her forehead.

"If it is the James girl," he said, "why would she be shooting at us? We've been using this pass without any trouble for years."

As if on cue, the girl winced and groaned. Her big blue eyes fluttered open, their roundness giving her a look of vulnerability.

"You!" Fighting a wave of dizziness, Molly groped for her rifle. It was nowhere to be seen. More circles swirled before her eyes, and she sank back against the tree to ride the sensation out. Pushing her tangled mass of hair away from her face, she eyed the three big men standing over her. Damn! How had she let this happen? Watching them, Molly thought they looked more worried than dangerous, and resigned herself to capture. "What are you planning to do with me?" she asked, hoping she sounded more courageous than she felt.

"I think it's you, lass," Sam said, "who'd best be answering the questions." Sam's Irish brogue became more noticeable when he grew angry or flustered, or was taken a bit off guard, and the disarming young woman who stared at him through a fringe of dark lashes was causing an array of those emotions—and then some.

"You're Molly James?" he asked.

She nodded, wincing again with the pain in her jaw as her head moved. Sam felt an instant surge of guilt.

"I'm sorry for hitting you. If I'd known you were a woman . . ."

"You owe me no apology, Mr. Brannigan. I'd have done worse to you if our positions had been reversed."

Surprised at the girl's honesty, Sam raised a thick blond eyebrow. He was beginning to get angry again. "Maybe you'd be kind enough to enlighten me, Miss James, as to why you were shooting at us?"

"I wasn't shooting *at* you, Mr. Brannigan," Molly replied, drawing herself up to a sitting position against the trunk of the pine. "If I had been, you'd be dead. I was shooting *toward* you. I was sending you a message."

"Oh, really, Miss James?" Sam felt torn between amusement at the girl's self-confidence and annoyance at her audacity. "And just what message might that be?"

"That this pass belongs to the Lady Jay. That neither you, Mr. Brannigan, nor any of your clan is welcome to use it any longer."

Thus far, Sam had been proud of the self-control he'd exercised. Now he felt a rush of fury through his veins. "This land belongs to the Cedar Creek Ranch and always has. My father allowed your father the use of the pass in order to keep the peace. Before he died, I'm sure he regretted the gesture." Sam's grip tightened on his Winchester until his knuckles turned white. Fighting for time to regain his composure, he turned his attention to the bullwhacker.

"Take those logs on up the pass, Buck. Our little *neighbor* has delayed us quite long enough."

"I'm as good as gone, boss," the driver said. The heavily laden wagon was already past due at the sawmill still several miles away.

Buck hurried toward the rig and climbed aboard the massive conveyance with its ten-foot wheels. Its heavy load of logs required eight teams of oxen and a fairly even roadbed. These logs were destined for Truckee, the closest town. Others were transported via a log flume, which carried the timber closer to the logging railhead on the eastern slope of the mountain.

"Emmet, you'd better go with him. I'll see that Miss James gets safely home. I'm sure we'll have a few things to . . . *discuss* along the way."

Emmet smiled at the forced casualness of his brother's even tone. Sam was furious and fighting hard to control his temper. Only the little lady's diminutive stature and obvious charms were saving her from the full measure of Big Sam Brannigan's wrath.

"Mr. Brannigan," Molly cut in, looking pointedly toward Sam, "I assure you I have very little to *discuss* with you. I believe this land belongs to the Lady Jay. I have taken steps to legally establish my claim. In the meantime, you may take your timber to the mill by way of the main road."

Sam frowned. "What do you mean, *legally establish?*" He felt the heat at the back of his neck as it reddened to the color of his already flushed face.

"See you back at the ranch, Sam," Emmet called out as he mounted his bay. "Unless you think you'll need some help."

Sam ignored his brother's grin as Emmet turned his horse to catch up with Buck's slow-moving team. The flash and snap of the bullwhip cracking above the great beasts' heads rang in the distance, along with the muttered oaths that were the bullwhacker's trademark.

"I mean, Mr. Brannigan," Molly continued, "that I have filed a lawsuit claiming this land as part of the Lady Jay. I believe I'll win, so you may as well get used to going around my land right now."

"Your land! *Your land!*" Sam could barely control his outrage. "My father owned this ranch before yours even came West."

Molly remained calm. "My father bought this strip of land when he purchased the Lady Jay. It's clearly set out in the deed."

"The deed to Cedar Creek also describes this land, as I'm certain you know. It's been a bone of contention between the Jameses and the Brannigans from the beginning. Your father and I had an understanding. We agreed to the mutual use of the pass. It seemed the best way to solve the problem."

"My father is dead, Mr. Brannigan. I'm the owner of the Lady Jay now. In the future, you'll make any agreements concerning the ranch with me."

Sam eyed the spunky redhead who sat calmly beside him. Part of him admired her for having the courage of her convictions, another part wanted to throttle her for the trouble she seemed determined to brew.

"I was under the impression the Lady Jay was being sold. I have tendered an offer to purchase it through your father's solicitor. Is this some sort of trick to try to drive up the price?"

Molly twirled a pine needle with exaggerated nonchalance. So this was Sam Brannigan. She'd heard about him all her life and had seen him once or twice when she was a little girl, though she barely remembered him. Seeing him now, a handsome giant glowering down at her, she found it incredible that she had forgotten him. Even in his carefully controlled fury he was a glorious specimen of a man. Standing at least four inches above his brother, Emmet, who was a big man in his own right, Sam had thick blond hair and hazel eyes, while Emmet was dark haired and dark complected. Throughout Sam's tirade, Emmet had remained calm; he seemed to regard the whole affair as amusing. Emmet reminded Molly of a great gentle bear. Sam Brannigan was a lion.

"I assure you, Mr. Brannigan, none of this is a trick. I intend to run the Lady Jay. There's good timber on this strip of land. I plan to restart the logging operation."

Molly knew a great deal about the Brannigans. She'd made it her business to know. Her father used to tell her, "Know thine enemy. Never underestimate him." She had plans for the Lady Jay, and those plans included a confrontation with the Brannigans, lifelong rivals of the Jameses.

"*You're* going to run the Lady Jay?"

"That is correct, sir."

"By yourself?"

"Precisely. I intend to hire competent help, but the decisions will be made by me."

"What in God's name makes you think you can handle a job like that?"

Molly watched the set of his jaw, the way he clenched his fists. He'd shoved back his hat, exposing more of his thick blond hair. Not really blond, she observed. More of a golden color, like the mane of the lion he resembled. A finely trimmed beard ran along the edge of his jaw, and even his mustache couldn't hide the angular lines of his finely carved cheekbones.

"I don't *think* I can do it, Mr. Brannigan. I *know* I can." She wasn't about to reveal that she had as many doubts as he did.

Sam fought against the hearty bellow of laughter the girl's words evoked but lost the battle and broke into a wide grin. He was hard-pressed to control another deep rumble as he thought of the woman with the wild, flame-red hair who believed she could run a ranch the size of the Lady Jay—a spread almost as big as Cedar Creek.

"You may laugh all you like, Mr. Brannigan. It won't change a thing." Molly struggled to her feet, her head splitting with the force of consecutive hammer blows. She'd delayed her departure as long as she dared.

"Any further conversation you wish to have will be conducted through my attorney." Though she fought against it, Molly swayed as a fresh wave of dizziness washed over her. She swallowed hard, determined not to lose consciousness again. A show of weakness at this point could cost her dearly. But her feminine instincts could not deny the physical strength and beauty of the man, nor the unusual stirring he caused in the pit of her stomach.

Before she could take a step, she felt Sam's big hands surround her waist and turn her to face him. She braced her palms against the front of his checkered shirt. Even through the rough material she could sense the strength and power in him, feel the rigid muscles of his chest beneath her fingers. A tiny shiver raced up her spine.

"Looks like I hit you even harder than I thought," he said.

She flashed him a weak smile and stepped away, keeping one hand braced against him to steady herself.

"Every worthwhile endeavor involves risks, Mr. Brannigan." She wondered at the slight limp she had noticed in his stride. It didn't seem to hinder his movements, yet she was curious about the cause. She'd find out, she told herself. Before this was over, she intended to know *everything* about Sam Brannigan.

"I think I'd better get back to the ranch," she said. Beads of perspiration popped out on her forehead, and another wave of nausea rocked her. Not only did her jaw hurt, but an egg-sized lump was forming at the back of her head.

"Is Angelina there?" Sam asked, and Molly eyed him suspiciously. Doubtless the Brannigans knew as much about the Jameses as she knew about them. They'd been neighbors, if one defined the term loosely, for almost twenty years.

"It's her day off. She's at her sister's in Truckee."

"What about Joaquin?"

"Rounding up strays."

"Well, who the hell *is* there?" Sam asked irritably.

"Just some of the new hands. What business is it of yours, anyway?" She wanted to pull away, but reason dictated that she remain calm. There was no need to make a fool of herself any more than she already had.

"I think you may have a slight concussion. I'm not about to leave you with a batch of new cowhands." Although he was playing the gentleman, Sam groaned inwardly, cursing the bad luck that had saddled him with a cantankerous female, albeit a damned attractive one. "I'll take you back to Cedar Creek. Lee Chin can watch you till the doctor says you're well enough to go home."

The girl lifted her chin, prepared to do battle, it seemed. Evidently common sense prevailed, and she nodded resignedly. Sam eyed the ugly purple bruise on her jaw and cursed himself again. In his anger, he'd been deceived by her clothing; now he was paying the price. Damn! A woman in breeches. What would they think of next?

"Where's your horse?" Sam picked up the girl gently, and headed down the hill. She felt so small and slight in his arms, he wondered at the daring it took for a woman her size to attack three seasoned men.

"He's grazing behind those boulders. He'll come when I call him."

A cool wind fluttered the leaves at his feet, and they crunched beneath his boots as he carried the girl along. Strands of glistening red hair wrapped around his neck and teased his cheek. Ignoring the stiffness in his knee, Sam moved purposefully. He'd grown used to the inconvenience. He was lucky he could walk at all.

Gilgamesh, Sam's big buckskin, waited patiently in the shade of a tree, his braided reins draped carelessly about his neck. The big horse had long ago been cured of his need to be tied.

The girl put two fingers in her mouth and blew a shrill whistle. Heavy hoofbeats pounded against the earth, and a gleaming black gelding, ears alert, nostrils testing the wind, thundered into the clearing. He stood as tall as Sam's horse—well over sixteen hands.

Eyeing the size of the woman in his arms, Sam looked at the horse in amazement. He wondered how the devil the girl reached the stirrups, since they hung no lower than the tall horse's belly.

"That's El Trueno," she told him proudly. " 'The Thunder.' I raised him from a colt. Joaquin and I trained him together."

"He's a beauty, all right." Sam ignored the girl's uncertain look and continued walking toward his own horse. The buckskin outweighed the black by several hundred pounds. Gil's thick neck, massive head, and wide shoulders were well muscled, easily carrying Sam's heavy weight, but the two horses stood even at the withers. Mindful of her stunned expression, Sam swung his light burden onto Gil's back.

"Why can't I ride my own horse?" she asked peevishly.

"I'm not taking any chances." He swung up behind her, ignoring the stirrup and using only the horn for assistance. "You might black out again, fall off your horse, and have me arrested for assault." Her *harrumph* and the straight set to her small shoulders did not go unnoticed. Nor did the gleam of the sun on her flame-red hair or the smile on her pretty face.

It was a long ride to the Cedar Creek Ranch, especially when sitting so close to a man like Big Sam Brannigan. With each step the horse took, Molly felt the corded muscles of Sam's chest rubbing against her back, though she did her best to keep her distance. One arm circled her waist, not really touching her but positioned there to control the beast and keep her from falling.

It was a strange sensation, being held in a man's arms. Even when she was a child her father had never held her, or even hugged her. His affection had been guarded at best. She'd been kissed, of course, by her beau in Chicago. But he hadn't really held her—at least not for any length of time. She found kissing not unpleasant, but not all she'd hoped for, either.

From a few feet behind Sam's buckskin Trueno whinnied softly. Molly knew the horse would follow them wherever they went. She loved the big black gelding. True stood tall and proud, and his loyalty was matched only by Joaquin and Angelina, the Mexican couple who had helped raise her since the age of seven, after the death of her mother.

The day her mother died was the only time Molly had seen her father show emotion. "You might as well know right off," he'd said, coming to stand beside her out at the corral. "Your mama's gone." He wouldn't even look at her. "Dead and gone. Just like she was never here." Then he'd wept like a child.

Molly had cried, too, for days it seemed. Until her father stormed into her room, gripped her arms, and jerked her off her tiny bed.

"Stop it!" he'd screamed. "I can't stand to hear it. Not one minute more!" So Molly had sniffed, wiped her eyes, and turned her grief inside. She'd never cried again.

Sam turned the big buckskin onto a smaller trail, which led toward Cedar Valley. "How long have you been back at the ranch?" he asked, breaking into her thoughts.

"About two months."

"I'm surprised our paths haven't crossed before now."

"There's been a lot to do. Most of the hands have quit. I'm trying to hire men now, but it isn't easy."

"I'm sure it isn't," he agreed smugly, knowing that few men would work for a woman.

They crossed a mountain stream, the quiet, bubbling sound soothing her tightly strung nerves. The same stream crossed part of the Lady Jay. She and her mother used to picnic beside it.

Molly stiffened slightly, pulling away from Sam's hard chest as a hazy image of Colleen James came to mind. Unlike her own fair complexion, her mother's skin had been dark, her hair blue-black. But Molly had inherited her mother's small size and full bosom, as well as her round blue eyes.

Her father had loved her mother with a grand passion. Molly well remembered how protective he had been, the way he'd worried every time her mother went riding, or took a trip into town without him.

"I'd best go with you," he'd say. "You never know what might happen. Besides, it gives us more time together."

Molly thought of her mother often, thought of how different her life would have been if her mother had lived—*if Shamus Brannigan hadn't murdered her.*

As always, the disturbing memory sent a slight shudder along her spine.

"Are you cold?" Sam Brannigan's deep voice rumbled across the silence in the forest. "I've got a jacket in my saddlebags."

"No. No, thank you, I'm fine."

"Feeling better?"

"Yes, much better. I was just thinking about the past. It's been years since I've been in this part of the country. I didn't realize how much I'd missed it until I returned." Why was she telling him that? It was certainly none of his business. Besides, she was sure he couldn't care less. He probably disliked her as much as she did him. Or at least as much as she wanted to.

"You were in school," he said, conversing in an even, inquisitive tone that encouraged her to continue. "In the East, if memory serves."

"Yes. I left when I was thirteen. Boarding school in San Francisco till I was sixteen, then finishing school in Chicago. Father wanted me to have the finest education." She sensed his skepticism in the changing set of his shoulders. "You don't believe that, Mr. Brannigan?"

"There is little your father ever said or did that I believed, Miss James. But you and I are neighbors, for as long as you remain at the Lady Jay. What happened between our families is past. It's a painful memory for us both. I, for one, would rather not dwell on it."

Molly did not reply. Things were not as simple

for her. She'd thought of little else since her father had been crushed to death by a huge timber that had toppled backward as it was being felled.

She wished she could have cried for him.

Instead, she'd read and reread the wire, then packed her bags and headed West. She'd made up her mind years ago to return to the Lady Jay just as soon as she finished school. But there always seemed to be one more course her father wanted her to take, one more school to attend. "You want to please me, don't you?" he'd written.

It was the thing she wanted most in life, no matter how long it took. But she'd never really succeeded; at least he'd never said so. Maybe making a success of the Lady Jay would compensate for her past failures.

The buckskin stumbled, jolting her against Sam's chest.

"Trail's a little steep through here," he remarked.

"It's beautiful." Molly glanced at her surroundings as they rode along. Massive ponderosas towered above the trail amid huge granite boulders. "I don't think I could ever grow tired of this."

"Then I guess we have one thing in common."

She smiled. "I've always loved the pines. I think of them as the lords of the forest." The western pines grew to a height twice that of the eastern variety, some of them reaching two hundred feet.

"They're special, all right. I hope you remember that, if you're crazy enough to start logging again."

Molly bristled. "Are you implying my father didn't?"

"I'm not implying anything, Miss James. I just believe it's important to use good judgment."

Molly's temper cooled a little. She believed wholeheartedly in conserving the land, though few others did. Surprisingly, it appeared Sam Brannigan felt the same way.

A blue jay darted from one of the branches, causing the buckskin to dance sideways. A muscle tightened protectively in the huge arm around her, and Molly smiled again. Everything out West, it seemed, grew to immense proportions.

# *Chapter Two*

"I'M FEELING much better," Molly told Sam as his large hands lifted her from his horse. "I really think I should go on home."

"Sorry, Miss James. You started this little war, now I'm going to finish it. I want the doctor to take a look at you, and in the meantime we can have our little *talk*."

Molly ignored the sarcasm in Sam's deep voice

and continued walking beside him toward the wide front porch. The ranch house was an impressive two-story log structure that had been built years ago by Shamus Brannigan, Sam's father. From upstairs, dormers watched the yard while the first floor was lit by wide-paned windows.

Sam opened the thick plank door, and Molly brushed past him into a large living area. It was a man's house, from the rustic log walls to the thick log trestles overhead. Stone floors led to corridors off each end of the room, and a wide staircase pointed upstairs. It even smelled like a man—woodsy, kind of like smoky pine. Sam had that same clean smell; she'd noticed it as they'd ridden toward the ranch.

Molly let Sam guide her across the floor. The pain in her jaw had about disappeared, but the lump on her head still ached fiercely. Though she'd enjoyed the chaos her little episode had caused, she was beginning to wonder at the wisdom of the endeavor. She hadn't expected Sam to be such a reasonable man—if, indeed, he turned out to be. It was hardly the picture her father had painted of the Brannigans.

Sam motioned her to the huge leather couch stretched in front of a great stone fireplace. She sat down, feeling a little awed by the size of the room. But then, everything about the Brannigans had awed—or infuriated—her for years.

Sam eased her back on the couch, methodically removed each of her boots, then covered her with the woven Navaho blanket that had been draped over the back.

"Lee Chin!" Sam called, and in seconds a Chinese man with a long braided queue down his back entered the room on noisy wooden shoes.

"Yes, Mr. Sam?"

"Our guest, Miss James, has had an unfortunate accident. Send someone to fetch Doc Weston. In the meantime, bring me a damp cloth."

"Yes, sir, Mr. Sam. Right away." Slightly bent at the waist, the Chinese scuttled from the room, only to return seconds later with the wet cloth.

"Miss James and I have a few things to discuss, Lee. When we're finished, I'll let you take over."

Lee Chin bowed and left the room. Molly smiled, liking the little man immediately. His face had taken on an almost paternal expression when he saw the bruise on her jaw.

Sam helped Molly lift her thick mane of hair, then slid the cloth beneath the bump at the back of her head. As big and powerful as Sam was, Molly felt no fear of him; something about the way he cared for her spoke of his concern. Though she knew he was furious about the shooting incident, she felt cosseted and secure in his nearness. Inasmuch as he was the head of the family that had destroyed hers, the thought was far from comforting.

"You know, Miss James," Sam began, "that was a damned fool thing you did out there today. You could have gotten yourself killed."

Molly scooted to a sitting position on the couch. "I quite agree with you, Mr. Brannigan."

"You do?" Sam looked surprised.

"Most assuredly. Had I any idea what a sensible antagonist you'd be, I would simply have ridden in and delivered my message in person."

Sam's temper receded a little at the respectful tone of her voice. A slight smile curved his lips.

"Thank you for the compliment, Miss James, but I'm afraid you may be speaking a little too soon. You and I both know it's ten miles farther to the mill by the main road. My oxen can't haul timber that far." His eyes narrowed, and all trace of humor fled. "I intend to keep on using that pass, just as we always have."

Molly remained undaunted. So far, she'd had much better treatment from the Brannigans than she'd believed possible. She certainly didn't expect the man to yield to her demands on the first attempt.

"In that case, Mr. Brannigan, since you've been so chivalrous today—aside from hitting a lady in the jaw—I shall be good enough to return the favor. You may use the pass until the case is settled in court. Then I'll expect you to abide by the law."

Sam's hazel eyes flashed his disbelief. "You are giving me *permission* to use the pass? *Permission* to use my own road?" First he chuckled, then his whole body shook with the force of his deep laughter.

Molly relaxed against the couch, casually flipping several thick strands of her red hair over her shoulder. Long ago she'd learned to control her emotions, and the skill had come in handy on more than one occasion.

His laughter finally under control, Sam stared

at her. "You are truly something, Miss James. Tell me, just what will you do in the event you lose the case?"

"I shan't lose, Mr. Brannigan."

A muscle twitched in Sam's jaw as his anger surfaced again. "You know, Miss James, this little act of yours is about to go too far. The Cedar Creek Ranch and the Lady Jay have been using that pass for years. There is no reason we can't continue just as we are. You have plenty of other timber land, so why the sudden urge to settle the dispute?"

Molly raised her chin and glared at him, forcing herself to dwell on the lonely years in a distant boarding school, the neglect, the loss of a mother's love. "Your father murdered my mother, Mr. Brannigan. I want any connection with your family severed once and for all. I want what is mine, what my father built for me—every acre of it!"

"You mean you want revenge."

Molly felt a twinge of unease at the look of cold fury on Sam Brannigan's face. "In a manner of speaking, yes."

"And what about my father?" he said. "My father rotted in jail for a crime he didn't commit. My father died because of *your* father's false accusations!" His voice softened to a deadly calm. "But unlike you, Miss James, I don't live in the past. Cedar Creek is my life, my home. My brothers and I have worked hard to make it into the success it is today. I want no trouble with you. What happened wasn't your fault or mine." He took a steadying breath. "But if trouble is what *you* want, Miss James, by God I'll give it to you! All you can handle and then some!" He clenched his fist, his face flushing as red as Molly's hair, his nostrils flaring in anger.

"Lee Chin! Come sit with Miss James." He turned his hard gaze in her direction, and Molly felt the first prickle of fear, tiny needles in the pit of her stomach.

"Good-bye, Miss James," Sam said softly, his voice belying his fury. Turning his broad back to her, he strode from the room. The screen door slammed against the frame, signaling his departure.

Untying the horses from the hitching post in front of the house, Sam's long strides carried him swiftly to the corral where he led Gil and the girl's big black to water. Anything to calm his raging temper. The last thing he wanted was to dredge up the whole sordid mess again. The Jameses and the Brannigans. It had taken years for the gossip to die down. Years for his family to be accepted again into polite society. Emmet had a wife and two children. Sam's youngest brother, Peter, was just graduating from Harvard Law School. Peter had plans for a career in politics. The Brannigans were building an empire, and an empire needed leaders. Peter, with his easygoing personality, unblemished record, and ethics, would be a natural.

Now his brother's first case would be defending the Cedar Creek Ranch in a land dispute with the Lady Jay. If the pass were not essential to the logging operation, Sam would give in to the girl's demands just to keep the peace. But dammit, it was! Besides, the idea of being bested by a woman wearing breeches galled him. A woman's place was in the home, bearing children, taking care of a husband—at least he'd always thought so.

His mother had believed that. Lorna Braelorne Brannigan had been the sweetest, gentlest, kindest woman Sam had ever known. She'd met his father on a cattle boat bearing emigrants from Ireland to America. They'd fallen in love and married as soon as the long, terrible voyage was over. In the fifties, Shamus brought his wife to California searching for gold. Found a bit of it, too. Not much, but enough to buy some land and start the Cedar Creek Ranch.

Sam was ten when his mother died birthing Peter. By then she'd given Sam a respect for women he'd carried all his life. He believed they were special. He couldn't stand to see a woman cry, couldn't stand to hurt a woman. It was part of the reason he'd never married. He'd never met a woman he could be faithful to—not for a lifetime, anyway. And the idea of infidelity, of lying to some sweet lass, kept him a bachelor. He had his lady friends, but he never led them on, never promised them marriage. That way they'd never be hurt.

As for himself, he had the ranch to keep him busy. Whenever he got lonely, he just worked a little harder. Besides, he had Emmet, and Emmet's family, and Peter to worry about. He certainly didn't need to be burdened with a wife as well.

Sam swung open the corral gate and led the buckskin inside, then did the same for the black, careful to keep them separated: Gil might not take kindly to a corralmate, and Sam didn't want to risk marking the black's sleek coat.

He had to admire the girl's taste in horseflesh. He had to admire her guts, too. Few men would go up against a Brannigan. Molly James was something, all right. She had Colleen's eyes and figure—some figure, at that—but the hair and audacity were all Malcolm James. Mal had been ruthless, an overbearing tyrant. Was Molly as ruthless as Mal? She was a fool—of that, Sam had no doubt—and foolish enough to believe she could run the Lady Jay.

The thought calmed him a little. Soon she'd realize how futile it was to try to do a man's job. Maybe then she'd go back where she came from, and the lawsuit would be dropped. He hoped so.

For everyone's sake, he hoped so.

Molly left Cedar Creek several hours later, without waiting for the doctor. She pretended to be asleep till Lee Chin went to work in the kitchen, then she slipped out the front door. By then her dizziness had faded completely, and the pain in her head had eased as well. She knew if she hurried, she'd be home before dark. And Joaquin would be back by nightfall.

Molly led True from the corral and swung into the saddle without using the stirrup. If a Brannigan could mount that way, she could too. She noticed her carbine had been replaced in its scabbard. So much for the menace she'd hoped to present. It was obvious no one took her the least bit seriously. She smiled slightly. Just wait until they were served notice of her lawsuit. They'd be forced to take her seriously then.

Molly's eyes scanned the corral, noticing Sam's buckskin was still penned, but the man was nowhere to be seen, thank God. One round at a time with him!

Her father, too, had been a big man, about as tall as Emmet. Molly got her red hair from him—and her temper, though for the most part she'd learned to control it. Even though they had never been close, Molly wished her father were still alive to teach her how to run the Lady Jay. Without his guidance, it was going to take every ounce of her willpower, every particle of her determination to operate the ranch successfully. When she had arrived home, most of the hands had left, thinking the land would be sold. Only Joaquin and Angelina remained, and old Torger Johnson up at the logging camp. Since her arrival, Molly had spent every waking moment with the two men, grateful for their knowledge and assistance.

Joaquin was a vaquero. There was no better man to run the cattle concerns, but he knew nothing about logging. Torger knew the logging business better than any man alive. But he was not a foreman and didn't want to be. He'd been her friend since childhood, taught her the logger's art, spent endless hours teaching her about the forests, explaining the woodsman's techniques. Now, she thanked him for his endless patience. It was her knowledge of a man's world that just might give her a fighting chance.

Molly nudged True forward. Skirting the barn, she rode across the creek and into the woods. She knew the mountains so well, she needed no trail. Before she'd been sent away to boarding school at age thirteen, she'd roamed every inch of the area. After that, there had been summers at the ranch till she was sixteen, but for the past three years she hadn't been allowed home. Her father wanted her mind on her studies, Angel's letters had suggested. Her father had been too busy to write.

Crossing a barren ridge, True expertly picked his way down the narrow path on the rocky slope. Molly could see men working a herd of cattle in the fields beyond. They'd be winding up the day soon: The horizon was beginning to redden. Molly grinned broadly. The sky was just about the color of Sam Brannigan's face when she'd told him she intended to claim the pass. He had some temper, that one, yet she'd also sensed in him an underlying gentleness she hadn't expected.

An hour's ride put Molly in front of the gravel lane that led to the main house. The ranch was originally named the Vagabond, but Mal James had renamed it the Lady Jay, in honor of his wife, Colleen James.

Molly was surprised to see a buggy sitting

empty in front of the house. Since she'd arrived two months ago, she'd had no visitors. And after her altercation with the Brannigans today, she didn't feel very social. Riding straight to the barn, she unsaddled True, grained him, and rubbed him down. As soon as she was finished, she headed up to the house. She hoped the unknown visitor wouldn't be staying long. She certainly wasn't dressed for company, and the throbbing in her head had returned.

Angelina opened the back door in greeting. "*Chica. ¿Donde estuviste?* You have company." Angel reached a chubby hand to Molly's chin, lifting it to scrutinize the purple bruise on her jaw. "What happened to you?"

"I . . . I had an accident," she said evasively, then changed the subject. "What are you doing back here so soon? I thought you wouldn't be home till tomorrow."

"I got lonesome for Joaquin." Angel grinned broadly. "Where did you say you went today?" Returning to her cooking, she twisted off a circle of dough from the butter-slick loaf on the table and began to flatten another tortilla between her thick palms.

"I was over at Cedar Creek. I met our neighbor, Sam Brannigan." Molly watched Angel's reaction. Rolls of fat on the small woman's chin jiggled as she chuckled aloud.

"Our neighbor is some man, eh, *chica?* Maybe I should have warned you."

Molly smiled. "Maybe you should have. I'm afraid I didn't make a very good impression. I told him we'd be claiming the pass."

Angel clucked and frowned. She shook a plump finger at Molly. "I have told you to stop this nonsense. The past is over. Let it rest. Sam Brannigan is a good man."

"Who's visiting?" Molly asked, again changing the subject. She knew exactly how Angel felt about the lawsuit. Angel had never been one to withhold an opinion.

"Oh, *sí,* I forgot. Your uncle Jason is here."

"Uncle Jason? Is Aunt Vera here, too?" She didn't wait for an answer. Eager to see her aunt and meet her new uncle, she dashed through the kitchen toward the parlor. The house was much smaller than Sam's big house at Cedar Creek, the furniture more delicate: spindle-legged Queen Anne tables, mahogany Chippendale chairs, a Windsor rocker, a carved walnut, tapestry-covered settee. Dainty lace doilies, a remnant of her mother's handiwork, kept the dust from the tables.

As Molly rushed into the parlor, a tall man dressed in black got up from the settee. When he eyed her dirty shirt and breeches, the smile of greeting on his handsome dark-skinned face quickly turned to a look of dismay.

Molly took one look at his stunned, wide-eyed expression, and suppressed a note of laughter. Why did men find it so astonishing that a woman should work in practical clothing?

"You must be my uncle Jason," she said, carefully controlling her voice. "I'm really happy to meet you. Aunt Vera wrote and told me about you. Where is she?" While extending her work-roughened hand, she glanced around the room in search of her aunt's freckled face. Though her uncle seemed a bit unsettled by her appearance, he brought her fingers to his lips in a show of gallantry.

"I'm honored to meet you at last, Miss James."

"Please call me Molly," she said. "Where's Aunt Vera? Isn't she with you?" She couldn't wait to see her. Though Aunt Vera had never been to California, she'd visited Molly several times at Mrs. Finch's Finishing School in Chicago. They'd begun a tentative friendship Molly had hoped would grow. A little over six months ago, Molly had received news of her maiden aunt's marriage, and hadn't heard from her since. Molly supposed the older woman was adjusting to her new life and had been too busy to write.

"Please sit down, Miss James," Jason Foley said. He'd regained his composure, and now a solemn expression rested on his well-formed lips.

At the serious note in his voice, Molly did as she was told.

"I regret to be the bearer of grim tidings, but I must tell you that three weeks ago your aunt was killed in a terrible accident. I would have wired you, but since she and I had already made plans to come west, I thought it better to tell you in person."

Molly felt a wave of despair. "Aunt Vera's dead?"

"I'm afraid so."

Molly clasped her hands to keep them from

trembling. Her uncle's hand covered hers in a show of sympathy. Molly had only begun to know the frail woman who was her aunt, but Vera James Foley was her father's sister, her last living blood relative. Now Aunt Vera was dead, and Molly James had never felt more alone in her life.

"I know how hard this is for you," her uncle was saying. "First the loss of your father—and now this. Believe me, I too have suffered. I loved your aunt very much. We had such a short time together."

Molly glanced up to find tears welling in her uncle's clear black eyes. Her own eyes remained dry. She wished she could cry as he did, but felt only a dizzying numbness. For the first time, she noticed the white swatch of cloth just beneath his chin, which contrasted with his dark skin and the even darker black of his somber suit.

"Are you . . . are you a preacher?" she asked, dumbfounded.

"Why, yes, didn't your aunt tell you?"

"No. No, she didn't. She was probably afraid my father would find out. He would have disapproved of her marriage to a Protestant. The Jameses have been Catholic for generations."

"When your aunt and I fell in love, she converted to my faith. In mourning her loss, that was the one thing that made it all bearable."

He turned away, brushing a tear from his cheek. She wished she could share in his display of grief. Instead, she sat quietly staring at the hands folded carefully in her lap. Though the reverend appeared a pious man, there seemed to be something very odd about him—something that warned her to beware.

"How did she die?" Molly asked softly. Only part of her wanted to know. The other part wished she'd awaken to find all this a bad dream.

"There was a fire at the boardinghouse where we lived. It was terrible. Terrible." He pulled a kerchief from his pocket and wiped his eyes. "I'm afraid I find it too upsetting to talk about."

"I understand." Molly had the strangest feeling his grief was not as sincere as he would have liked her to believe. Rising from the settee, she fought to calm the pounding in her head and the slow thudding of her heart. "Thank you for coming to tell me in person. I hope you'll consider staying awhile. I know my aunt would have wanted us to become acquainted." The polite words she was saying seemed to come from somewhere far away.

"I'll stay here, of course. Now that your aunt is dead, I'm your legal guardian. I've come to help you tie up the loose ends of your father's estate. Once the ranch is sold, we'll both go east together."

Molly's head came up. "Go east together? I'm afraid I don't understand. After you and Vera were married, I had understood that Father had arranged my guardianship with you. But I understood that only to be a formality. Surely you don't think I intend to sell the Lady Jay?"

"But of course, my dear. What other avenue is open?" He rose to face her, and she noticed again what a handsome man the Reverend Foley was. He stood tall and well proportioned. His clothes, sober as they were, fit perfectly. Wavy black hair, short and well kept, crowned a distinguished face marred by few signs of age. Only the silver strands at his temples betrayed his years. Through her confusion she thought what an odd mate he seemed for her maiden aunt.

"I intend to run the Lady Jay myself," Molly answered, her voice still sounding distant.

"Molly, dear, that's quite absurd. A young woman cannot possibly manage a ranch of such immense proportions. I'm afraid I must forbid it." He eyed her speculatively, an odd light in his eyes.

"You don't understand, *Uncle* Jason," Molly said, beginning to get angry. "I own sixty percent of the Lady Jay. I presume that since Aunt Vera is no longer alive, you own forty percent."

"That is correct."

"Then you see that it is I who make the decisions. I who will manage the ranch." *At least for two years,* Molly thought. There were a number of strict provisions set out in her father's will. Most important, she had to make a profit within two years from the date of her father's death. She must live on the ranch for twenty of the next twenty-four months, unless she married. But either way, making the profit was essential. Her father never believed she was serious in her desire to run the Lady Jay, but he'd given her a chance. For that, she would always be grateful.

"Of course, my dear. Although I am your guardian, I didn't mean to imply—"

"I'm sure you're just upset and tired, Uncle Jason, as I am," Molly interrupted. "We've both had a long day. Now, if you'll excuse me, Angelina will show you to your room. Dinner's at seven, though I believe I'll just have a tray in my room."

"Of course." Jason Foley graced her with the briefest of bows, his expression inscrutable. "We'll talk again in the morning."

For the first time, Molly felt older than her nineteen years. The burden of making the ranch a success was tough enough, but that was a challenge she looked forward to. What she didn't need was problems with her uncle.

# *Chapter Three*

✦✦✦✦✦

MOLLY HAD RISEN before the sun. The Lady Jay needed attention, and she wasn't in the mood for another session with her newly discovered uncle, at least not first thing this morning. The ranch was worse than short-handed. Today, the few men she had would be rounding up strays for branding. And Molly was determined to do her share of the day's work, and prove to the men she could be a pretty fair hand herself.

Sitting astride her horse, Molly lifted her broad-brimmed hat and blotted the perspiration from her forehead with the back of her hand. Almost noon. Since the men were working some distance from the cookhouse, Angel would be hauling out a load of grub in the back of the wagon. Molly was starving, but it looked as though she was going to miss the meal.

She urged True over the rise. For over an hour she'd been following a trail of hoofprints and broken branches. One of the bulls had strayed from the herd. The lure of the heifers usually prevented a bull's wandering—unless there'd been an accident, so Molly was sure something had happened to the bull. As she dodged a tree limb and rounded a granite outcropping, the bull's soft bellow drifted across the clear mountain air. Molly's heartbeat quickened. The sound was weak and distorted, coming from just over the next ridge. When she crested the hill, the reason bacame obvious. Satan, her lead bull, had gotten himself trapped in a mud bog. He was buried neck-deep in the dark brown ooze.

Molly reined True up beside the big bull, who did little more than bawl his discomfort. His fight to free himself had long ago exhausted him, and now he waited patiently to die. Floating shadows, like leaves in the current of a stream, drew Molly's attention skyward. Overhead vultures circled the massive bull, whose head lolled against his shoulder, then sank nose-deep in the thick, dark mud.

Molly freed the stiff rope coiled against her saddle and shook out a loop. Whirling it above her head till it hummed, she dropped it expertly over the big bull's head, where it rested atop the mud. Satan made no protest, but Molly was forced to repeat the task several times just to get the animal to lift its powerful head far enough out of the mud for the loop to slip around his neck.

She dallied the rope around the horn and urged True forward. Used to working cattle, the stout horse set his back to the task. The bull's long neck stretched and he bellowed loudly, but other than a slight rocking motion, he made no attempt to budge.

Molly's next tactic took a little more imagination. Riding the black around a tree, the rope still tied to the horn, she used the tree as leverage—a sort of a block and tackle system. The black strained, and the rope sang against the bark of the tree. Still no luck.

Her third attempt took masterful creativity, Molly told herself, and a powerful will to succeed. Reining up and dismounting, she sloshed into the mud. On the first step, she sank to her knees, went belly-deep on the second, and wondered for a moment if she and the bull would both end up food for the vultures. In slow, determined steps she reached the bull's side and looped the rope around the beast's massive hindquarters. She was determined to succeed, if it took the rest of the day . . . and then some.

Forgetting his hunger, Sam Brannigan crested the hill between Live Oak Ridge and Cedar Valley astride his big buckskin gelding. It was the time of year for rounding up strays and branding cattle, and he enjoyed working with the hands, enjoyed the exhilaration of hard physical labor. It was time to sign the Double-C name to a new batch of calves, and he was rounding up the cattle from his eight-thousand-acre ranch.

A gust of cool air ruffled the thick strands of blond hair curling at the nape of Sam's neck, and he was thankful for the gentle breeze in the heat of the day. The wind carried the sound clearly this time, telling Sam he was practically on top of the distressed animal. He'd been searching for half an hour, certain, from the creature's plaintive moans, it was in some kind of trouble.

Urging the buckskin forward, and rounding a granite boulder that marked the entrance to a near-dry water hole, Sam came upon the bull . . . and Molly James. Taking in the scene at a glance, Sam broke into a wide grin. He curled a booted foot around the saddle horn as he watched the girl try to free the bull. He wouldn't let her struggle long, but just for a moment he'd enjoy the fun.

Molly positioned herself behind the great beast, both hands and a shoulder shoved firmly against his rump.

"Pull, True! Pull!" she ordered, and the big black gelding leaned into the task. The rope stretched taut, the saddle strained, and the big horse pawed and snorted as the weight of the bull met that of the horse. Molly felt the bull's powerful haunches quiver and strain beneath her hands. Even the bull, it seemed, was beginning to get the idea. His pink tongue lolled, and his eyeballs rolled back in his head, exposing the whites of his eyes as he fought to make his legs move. He stepped forward, but only far enough to make Molly lose her footing and slip to her armpits in the mud.

"Damn you, Satan!" she swore, spitting the gritty muck from her mouth and sloshing it from her forearms. "Can't you do any better than that? You're going to die out here if you don't do something!"

"Need some help?" Sam Brannigan rode down to the edge of the bog, rope in hand, shaking out a loop.

Molly wanted to say no, that she didn't want to be indebted to a Brannigan, didn't need his help—or anyone's. But the bull's life was at stake. Some things were more important than family pride.

Sam didn't wait for an answer. Skillfully he threw the loop over the bull's head. Molly slogged through the mud and pulled it snug around the animal's neck. When she glanced up, she saw that Sam was using the same technique with his big buckskin that she'd used with True, putting a tree between horse and bull for leverage.

"He looks pretty weak," Sam said. "If this doesn't work, I'll join in your little swim. We'll get him out one way or another."

Molly felt a wave of relief at the big man's words. He was willing to help, no matter what the price. The notion surprised her. "Thank you, Mr. Brannigan," was all she said.

Molly put her shoulder to the bull's rump, and this time, when True pulled, he had help from Sam's buckskin. The two horses pulled in unison, and the bull began to move. Slowly at first, then faster. Molly was straining with all her might, giving the animal the last measure of encouragement he needed to make the trip to safety. She didn't anticipate his leap from the bog, didn't think he had the strength for such a move.

All she knew was that one minute she was pressing against a solid wall of flesh, the next she was drowning in a pool of mud, her mouth full of the thick, gritty substance, groping in the mire to regain her balance.

Sam was laughing heartily, when, coughing and gagging, Molly broke the surface of the bog. Careful to keep his eyes averted, but grinning all the while, he busied himself with freeing the bull, then seeing to the buckskin and the black as Molly sloshed to shore.

She was covered with mud from head to toe. Only her eyes shone like two huge blue platters in the gritty blackness.

"You think this is pretty funny, don't you?" she sputtered. She felt leaden with the weight of the mud—and she wanted to kill Sam Brannigan.

Sam stopped coiling his rope and turned to face her. Beneath his blond mustache, an unabashed smile curved his lips. His eyes danced with devilment. "Yes, Miss James, I do."

"Well, it isn't!" Molly slumped to the ground dejectedly, wiping the mud from her face and scraping soggy handfuls of muck from her clothes. She set to work squeezing the black ooze from the single braid that hung at her back. Then, against her will, she started to laugh. At first just a giggle, then a chuckle, then a full, throaty peal. The laughter bubbled from her throat, shook her small frame until her sides hurt. Sam walked up beside her, his own laughter hearty and seemingly without end.

"At least you got your bull out," he reminded her, helping her to her feet.

She spit mud, wiped her eyes, and broke into another fit of giggles. "*We* got the bull out, Mr. Brannigan. And I'm in your debt. Now, if you'll excuse me, I'm going upstream to clean this mud off." Without further comment, Molly led True around the boulder and, clothes and all, waded into the stream. Sinking below the surface, she let the swift current carry the first load of mud away. She broke the surface of the water with a sigh of relief, then ducked her head again.

The stream wasn't deep. Even at the center, the water reached only above her waist. Molly unlaced her heavy braid and eased back down in the stream. Floating on the surface, she allowed the cool water to cleanse her hair, enjoying the feel of the current moving the thick strands around her face. Playfully she ducked under several more times, and, finally satisfied, waded to shore. Sam was standing near the edge of the water as she climbed onto the bank.

"God, that feels good," she told him, feeling ten pounds lighter. Sam said nothing. "I feel like a new person again." Still no comment. The silence pulled her attention in the tall man's direction, and she realized Sam Brannigan was staring at her like a starving man eyeing a steak dinner. The look in his hazel eyes, more of a smoky green today than the dusty brown of their last meeting, sent a shiver from her scalp to her toes. Her heartbeat quickened, and breathing suddenly seemed her most important task.

"Mr. Brannigan," Molly said as she approached, beginning to worry that something might truly be wrong with the man. "Are you feeling all right?

Sam Brannigan was waging a war with his tongue. He wanted to speak but couldn't trust the sound of his voice. Molly James taking a bath, even fully clothed, was perhaps the most sensuous display of femininity he had ever seen. The already revealing denims were molded to the rounded curves of her bottom; the shirt strained against full breasts where small circles darkened the shirt around each peak; her unbraided hair hung in dripping ripples to her waist; and her round blue eyes, thickly fringed, reflected the color of the stream. Beads of water cascaded down her smooth cheeks.

Sam felt a tightening in his groin and longed to take the woman right there on the bank of the stream.

"Mr. Brannigan?" the soft voice said again, with a note of alarm.

Sam cleared his throat and turned away, determined to control his voice and the desire he was feeling. "I'm sorry, Miss James," he apologized, regaining his control and turning again to face her. "I'm afraid my thoughts were elsewhere." The words came none too easily. "There's a lot of work to be done this time of year."

"I understand completely. And I want you to know how much I appreciate your help with the bull. I don't believe I could have managed without you."

Sam fought to keep his eyes on her face. One quick glance, and his control would snap. "I'm sure you'd have managed somehow, Miss James," he told her, a little too gruffly. "I'd better be getting back to work." He mounted his horse, then waited for the girl to mount hers. When she approached the black, she swung into the saddle using only the horn, then glanced at him triumphantly. He fought back a smile. She grinned impishly, apparently delighted he'd noticed her prowess with the horse.

"I, too, have a long day left, Mr. Brannigan," she said, "but again I thank you." She started to ride away.

"One more thing, Miss James," he called after her.

She reined up.

"It's none of my business, but sooner or later those clothes of yours are going to get you in trouble. I'd advise you to get back into a nice simple dress and stay there. Somebody's likely to take those breeches of yours as an invitation. You may find one of these cowhands tougher to deal with than your bull."

Molly felt the fire rush to her cheeks. "You're right, Mr. Brannigan, it *is* none of your business.

But for your information, I'm certain most men would find a woman much more desirable in a *nice simple dress* than covered with dirt and sweat and wearing a pair of denims."

It was Sam's turn to grin. He eyed her round posterior above the cantle of her saddle and the high curves of her breasts.

"That, Miss James, tells me you may know how to throw a rope, but you have one helluva lot to learn about men. Good-bye, Miss James." He touched the brim of his hat, whirled his horse, and rode away, chuckling to himself all the way back to the ranch.

Molly shepherded the big bull back to the valley, though there was little necessity. Satan was more than happy to be free of the bog and on his way back to his harem. By the time Molly reached day camp, the grub wagon had already gone and the men were back at work, but Joaquin spotted her and rode his palomino mare over to her. Seeing her in such disarray, Joaquin's thin face, with its angular lines and high cheekbones, broke into a wide grin.

"I knew your appetite would bring you back sooner or later, *hija*," he told her, calling her "daughter" as he often did. "I have saved some *pan* and cheese for you. If you are going to match wits with Satanas, you had better keep up your strength."

Molly accepted the food gratefully. "Thank you, *Padrino*," she said. She called him her "godfather" for want of a better word. He and Angelina had practically raised her. Molly and Joaquin had spent more time together than she'd spent with her real father.

Joaquin was a vaquero, first-born son of one of California's oldest families. Once, the Sanchezes had been wealthy, but after the discovery of gold, the greedy *Norte Americanos* had driven the Sanchez family, along with hundreds of others, off of their land. The courts were not sympathetic to the *Californios'* plight. Americans believed in Manifest Destiny. Settlers had every right to establish themselves on land meant to become a part of the United States.

The Sanchezes, like dozens of other Californios, were displaced, forced to find employment wherever they could. Joaquin had worked for Malcolm James for over fifteen years. He was the *segundo,* the second in command of the Lady Jay.

Joaquin lifted his wide-brimmed sombrero and ran a hand through his glistening still-black hair. He eyed Molly's slightly damp clothes and disheveled appearance. "I am not too sure who won the encounter, you or *Satanas.*"

"I think Satan would still be in the bog if it hadn't been for Sam Brannigan," she told him truthfully, taking another bite of the flat Mexican bread. "He came along just in time."

Joaquin smiled, exposing a flash of white against the dark skin of his weathered face. "Señor Brannigan has a way of doing that. He can smell trouble like a stallion sniffs a mare on the wind. What did you think of the big gringo?"

"He's big, all right. He doesn't seem a bad sort, but I won't be hasty in forming that opinion. He's still a Brannigan, and Papa always said they weren't to be trusted."

"As I told you many times, *hija,* your father's judgment was often clouded when it came to our neighbors. I have found the Brannigans to be a fine family, though I never said so while your father was alive." Joaquin's mare jerked at her rein and began to paw the ground, impatient from standing so long. "Do not let the past blind you to the future."

Molly nodded her understanding. Both Joaquin and Angel believed the long feud with the Brannigans should be ended, and part of Molly agreed. The other part felt she could have no peace until she won some concession from the Brannigans for all the hurt and loneliness they'd caused her. And, she rationalized, controlling the pass and the land around it would add needed profits to the Lady Jay.

"Someday I'll see justice done," her father had often said. "Someday I'll make them pay." The year Shamus Brannigan had spent in prison before he died was hardly enough. Mal vowed to someday find a way to settle the score.

Now Mal James was dead, and Molly had claimed the James Pass as part of the Lady Jay, which she truly believed it to be. She'd hired a lawyer from Sacramento City, and she meant to win her suit. After the pass was rightfully hers again, she'd decide what to do about the Bran nigans. Until then, she had other, more pressing matters on her mind.

"I must get back to work," Joaquin said, interrupting her thoughts.

Molly nodded. "I'll head over toward Sugar Loaf summit," she said. "Bound to be a few strays down near the river."

*"Si, hija."* Joaquin grinned again, his smile crinkling the skin at the corners of his dark eyes. "Try not to get lost this time."

Molly smiled back, waved, and headed toward the distant mountain. There were hours of daylight left.

Molly was ravenous by the time she headed home. She'd done a good day's work, but the lonely nature of the job left plenty of time for thinking. Although she had briefly considered the problem of her guardian, her thoughts returned again and again to Sam Brannigan. He'd looked entirely too attractive today, with his broad shoulders and lean hips. She remembered the way the sun had glinted off his golden beard, while the breeze had ruffled the blond hair below his broad-brimmed hat. Just the thought of his imposing presence as he sat astride his thick-necked buckskin took her breath away. She'd been able to hide her interest from Joaquin, but, unfortunately, not from herself.

What a cruel master fate could be, she thought. A Brannigan, head of the family who'd destroyed hers, attracted her as no man ever had. But Sam Brannigan was not what she'd expected. She sensed an honesty about him, a sincerity that was rare among men. Her father had portrayed Sam as an evil, scheming man, a troublemaker—and a womanizer. Though Mal had said Sam was seven years younger than her mother, Sam had fancied Colleen, a thought Molly found repulsive. An image of her mother's clear blue eyes, her smooth dark skin and flashing smile held a special place in Molly's mind. Was it true that Sam had desired her? Made advances toward her, as Shamus had done? Sam didn't have the look of a man like that, but Molly hadn't had enough experience with men to be sure.

So far there had been only one special boy in her life. Richard Anthony. He was tall, sandy-haired, and handsome—and back east he had pursued her endlessly. He'd begged her to marry him—to stay in Chicago where he was going to take over the family business. But the Lady Jay had been more important to Molly, and she'd told him so.

He hadn't given up, though Molly had warned him repeatedly that his suit was useless. She'd spent hours with Richard—even kissed him—but she'd felt none of the excitement one look Sam Brannigan's hazel eyes could stir. Richard was a boy, young, adoring, sweet. Sam Brannigan was a man. For the first time in her life, Molly realized she was a full-grown woman.

*"Por Dios,"* she swore, lapsing into the Spanish that came as naturally to her as her native English. Why did it have to be him? Of all the people on God's green earth, why did she have

to find herself attracted to a Brannigan? She guessed it probably didn't matter, anyway. Except for his strange behavior at the stream, he'd hardly paid her any attention. They barely knew each other. Surely she was making much ado about nothing. Thinking about it, Molly decided that was the best way to keep it. She wanted nothing to do with a Brannigan, especially not Sam.

# *Chapter Four*

MOLLY ENTERED THE house through the kitchen. Angel was again busy slapping dough into round, flat tortillas. Each rhythmical movement shook the wide girth of her hips and jiggled the huge mounds of her breasts. *"Óla, Chica. ¿Que pasa?"*

*"Nada interesante,"* Molly answered, pulling a steaming tortilla from the stack beneath a warm cloth and popping it into her mouth. "I did see your friend Mr. Brannigan today. He helped me pull old Satan out of a mud bog up near Live Oak Ridge."

"Ah, then something interesting *did* happen. Something interesting always happen when Señor Sam is around." She grinned knowingly, then moved to stir a batch of chile verde, which simmered on the cookstove. Her chubby hands moved with a grace one wouldn't expect from a woman her size. "Señor Sam is a handsome hombre, no?"

"He's all right, I guess." Molly tried to look unimpressed, but her mind fought an image of the big blond man with the wide shoulders and the hungry look in his eyes. What had he been thinking? she wondered for the tenth time that day. Then, chiding herself, she steered her thoughts in another direction. "How did you and Uncle Jason get along today?"

Angelina rolled her black eyes skyward, as if in silent appeal. "He is a strange man, your uncle. He read his Bible all morning. He asked me at least five times when you'd be home. I think he wants to convert you."

Molly laughed aloud. "God forbid." The door opened, interrupting her laughter, and the doorway was filled by the tall reverend's dark-haired presence. He took in her sweaty, disheveled attire in an instant and, raising his nose in a gesture of disdain, motioned her forward.

"Hello Molly, dear, I believe it's time we had a talk."

This time it was Molly who rolled her eyes. She winked at Angel and followed him from the room.

"Please sit down," he instructed her, pointing toward the settee. Molly obliged him. The Bible lay open on top of the knee-high rosewood table. "I know things have happened rather suddenly. That you have lost your father and your aunt Vera, both in a very short time. But Molly, dear, you must begin to accept what has happened. God and I are here to help you carry your burden."

"I appreciate that, Uncle Jason, truly I do, but I'm really all right. I've come to terms with their deaths. I just want to put all the sadness behind me." Molly nervously twisted a strand of her shiny red hair, wishing they could discuss something other than bereavement, wishing too that this strange, judgmental man had never come west. Then she straightened her shoulders and faced her uncle squarely.

"I'm sorry I wasn't able to visit with you today, and I hope you aren't finding life too dull in the house. But I have a ranch to run. I'm afraid that has to come first."

"But that's just the point, my dear." Jason sat down close beside her, picked up her hand, and patted it solicitously. "A woman shouldn't be concerned with such things. Running a ranch is a man's business. You should be thinking of marriage, of a home and family."

Molly stiffened, irritated that he was sitting so close to her and was patting her hand like a child. She began to feel her temper flare and fought to keep it under control. She knew she should respect her late aunt's husband—he was her guardian. "I want to run the ranch, Uncle Jason. I like what I'm doing. I'm not ready for marriage. I'm quite content just as I am."

Her uncle's face reddened. "I'm trying to be patient with you, Molly. I'm trying to understand. But I'm your guardian. Your father entrusted you to my care. I can't have you making a spectacle out of yourself. I forbid it! Look at you." His eyes raked her. They seemed to darken as he appraised her, and Molly felt a current of something she didn't quite understand.

"You look like some sort of heathen," he snapped. "You let your hair go wild, and those clothes—they're not proper; they're not fit for a young lady to wear. You're supposed to be in mourning. What will people think?"

Molly could barely control her voice. "I don't care what people think. I have a closet full of *proper* clothes. I can't very well brand steers in them, or haul timber to the mill. This ranch has to show a profit—you know that as well as I do. Up until my father died, it always did. As to my time of mourning, I've been mourning my father ever since my mother died. That's quite long enough. I intend to live my life as I see fit. I won't let silly prejudices stand in my way!"

"Molly, you are going to learn to obey me, one way or another. I'll let that outburst pass this time, but in the future, you're going to have to learn to control yourself."

Molly held her tongue. Jason Foley could make her life miserable for the next two years—and even after that, he'd still be her partner. "All right, Uncle Jason. Whenever I'm here, I'll wear a dress. But while I'm working, I have no choice except to wear something practical. That's the best I can do."

Jason glared down at her, his dark eyes flashing. "I guess that will be acceptable for now," he conceded. "We'll talk about it again another time."

Just then Angelina bustled into the room, and Molly could have kissed her for the interruption. She wasn't sure how much longer her temper would hold.

"Dinner will be ready soon, *chica*. You had better get washed up."

Molly smiled, knowing the buxom woman had purposely come to her rescue. Angel loved Molly like the daughter she'd never had, and Molly felt a special love for Angel. But somehow it wasn't the same as having a real mother's love.

"We'll be right in, Angel," Molly told her, suddenly recalling how her father had frowned on her closeness to both Angel and Joaquin.

Rising from the settee, Molly turned to her guardian. "You'll have to excuse me, Uncle," she said. "I'd like to slip into something more *proper*."

"Of course, my dear." His voice was deceptively calm. Their earlier discussion might never have been.

Molly lowered her chin in deference to his authority and left the room. But she could feel Jason Foley's odd dark eyes boring into her back all the way down the hall. It wasn't easy to understand why her aunt Vera had married the man, except that she'd been lonely. He was handsome—charming, when he wanted to be—but God, what a bore! Any way she looked at it, the next two years would be trying at best, especially with Jason Foley on the scene.

* * *

Sam Brannigan finished the last of his breakfast of eggs, thick slabs of ham, and homemade biscuits, and pushed away from the massive dining room table.

"You want more coffee, Mr. Sam?" Lee Chin asked, hovering over him.

"No thanks, Lee.

"You goin' with us, Sam?" Emmet called from the doorway.

In answer, Sam tossed his napkin onto the table and rose from his chair, the sound grating on the hardwood floors. "I'll be right there, Emmet. I'll work on the ledgers this evening. It's too nice a day to be cooped up inside." His long strides carried him quickly to where his brother waited, hat in hand.

"That's for damned sure," Emmet agreed. With their usual easy camaraderie, the two brothers headed toward the front door, arriving just in time to see a man on horseback ride into the yard.

"Who do you suppose that could be?" Emmet asked.

"I think we're about to find out," Sam said.

The man dismounted and tied his horse to the rail, moving almost furtively in Sam's direction. He was dressed in a dark gray suit, and wore tiny round spectacles and a bowler that seemed a bit too small.

"I'm looking for Samuel, Emmet, or Peter Brannigan," the man told them.

"I'm Sam Brannigan."

"Then these are for you." He handed Sam a sheaf of papers, tipped his hat, and returned to his horse without another word.

Sam didn't have to read the official-looking documents to know what they were. It was all he could do not to wad them into a ball and hurl them into the dirt.

"What is it, Sam?" Emmet asked, shoving his hat back.

"It seems our little neighbor is as good as her word. She's going ahead with the lawsuit over James Pass."

"Damn! Them Jameses never were nothin' but trouble."

"Let's go," Sam said, striding toward his horse. They both swung into their saddles, but Sam reined the buckskin away.

"Ain't you goin' with us?"

"I'll catch up with you later. First I want a word with Miss James."

Sam recognized Molly's round bottom before he caught sight of her face. Mad as he was, it was all he could do to keep from smiling. Wearing her breeches, she was bent over the rim of a feed barrel, trying to scoop up the last of the grain. Her wriggling posterior made a charming spectacle as Sam quietly dismounted, leaving Gil to graze on a bit of grass beside the barn, and started moving in Molly's direction. He'd taken only a few steps when one of the hands walked up beside the barrel, wearing a lopsided grin that said he was enjoying the sight as much as

Sam. The difference was, the cowhand did what Sam only thought about doing—he cupped a handful of Molly's behind and gave it a gentle squeeze.

Molly's head cracked against the barrel as she came up, her face flushed beet red. Whirling on the cowhand, she caught the man's satisfied grin. For a moment she seemed at a loss for words. Her fists were clenched, her breathing fast and uneven.

"Would you like me to defend your honor?" Sam asked, his voice laced with amusement.

Molly flicked him a glance, noticing his presence for the first time. "You always seem to be around at the right time to see me look foolish, don't you?" Not waiting for an answer, her hand came up and cracked across the cowhand's face, leaving a red print in the shape of her fingers. The cowhand's grin withered.

"I need you, Stevens," Molly informed him. "If I didn't, you'd be out of a job. But you ever touch me again, I'll make do without you. Now get on your horse and get up to Live Oak Ridge. I'm sure Joaquin will find something useful for you to do besides indulge your lecherous desires."

The cowboy stormed off. He mounted his horse and rode out of the barn at a gallop, Molly staring after him, still furious.

" 'Indulge your lecherous desires'?" Sam teased.

"I'll thank you to stay out of this, Mr. Brannigan."

"I warned you about wearing those breeches."

Molly's face flushed even redder. "What I wear is none of your concern. What are you doing here, anyway?"

As he recalled his business with her, Sam felt his temper rise. "I was served notice of the lawsuit this morning. I thought you'd be anxious to know your little attack is progressing just as you'd planned."

"I wouldn't call it an attack, Mr. Brannigan. I'd call it justice, long overdue."

"Justice, Miss James? Is it *just* for my family to suffer for something that happened almost thirteen years ago? Is it *just* for you to cause trouble for innocent people?"

"I won't discuss this with you, Mr. Brannigan. I told you that before."

"And I told you, Miss James, if it's trouble you want, I'm just the man who'll give it to you. I'm warning you once and for all, let the matter be."

Without answering, Molly just spun on her heel and walked into the barn. Sam's eyes were drawn to the sway of her hips as she moved, and against his will he remembered the sight of her wriggling bottom bent over the rim of the barrel. Despite the slap, he almost envied the cowboy.

Jason Foley seated himself in a stiff-backed rocker facing the hall. His hand trembled slightly as he opened the Bible he held in his lap. Each of his encounters with his niece had ended in disaster—for him as well as for the girl, and now Jason was more shaken than he cared to admit. Vera had told him of Molly's wild, disarming beauty, but he hadn't anticipated the effect she would have on him.

Though he tried to deny it, part of him craved a woman like Molly. Maybe it had something to do with his childhood. His father had had scores of women like that. Wicked women, who slept with him even while his wife was still alive.

Jason's mother had been a beautiful, pious, God-fearing woman, and Jason had loved her dearly. After she died and Jason had grown up, he'd married a woman much like her. He and his first wife, Elizabeth, had been happy enough—except in the marriage bed. There, Elizabeth had at best been dutiful. She hated making love; she felt it was dirty. Jason spent agonizing days and nights dreaming of the wild, sinful women his father had known. The very women he was trying to reform.

When Elizabeth Foley died, Jason had been devastated. He missed her terribly and felt guilty for his traitorous thoughts. Some years later, he'd met Vera, another pious woman. She'd shown some interest in the marriage bed; still, he yearned for a woman with passion—a woman who would do wild, forbidden things to his body. Six months after their marriage, Vera was dead, and again Jason was riddled with guilt—and now there was Molly James.

Thumbing through the pages of his Bible, Jason searched for familiar words, trying to find strength, and solace from his thoughts. Turning to Hosea 2:2, he began to read: " . . . *For she is not my wife and I am not her husband; And let her put away her harlotry from her face, and her adultery from between her breasts, lest I strip her naked and expose her as on the day when she was born."* The woman was indeed of a wicked nature—it oozed from her very pores. Molly was the kind of woman who led pious men astray, the kind he'd spent his whole life preaching against. Her willfulness infuriated him. Her clothing was sinful.

Every time he saw the girl in her "work clothes," as she called them, it was all he could do to keep from tearing the offending garments from her all-too-enticing body. Thinking of her uncommon beauty, her wild sensuality, he felt himself harden, and cursed the vixen for the power she held.

God protect him, it was his duty to save her sinful soul. He was certain he could—he was one of the Lord's chosen ones. He'd always had the power to convince others—God had given him the gift. He'd see to Molly James's willfulness, show her the way to salvation one way or another.

Jason thought of the circumstances that had brought him to the Lady Jay: his marriage to Vera James. God had given him the means to bridge his lagging finances and continue with his life's work. And, in his own way, he had cared for Vera. She'd been a good woman.

But the Lord worked in strange ways. Vera's death would be the means for Jason to continue his work. His late wife's inheritance would ensure his return to the East, where he belonged. He wanted to found a church on Long Island, wanted to carry God's word there.

Money was the key.

Jason had to convince Molly James to sell the Lady Jay by whatever means he could find.

Thankful for God's wisdom in leading him to Vera, Jason thumbed through the tissue-thin pages of his Bible. He read verse after verse, seeking the message that would guide him. He had no doubt of his eventual success. The Lord was on his side.

During the past month, Molly had been able to hire a skeleton crew of cowhands, at least enough to manage the cattle operation for the present. She'd need more men when it came time for market—and God only knew where she'd find them—but for now she'd get by.

Needing no more hands himself, Sam Brannigan had sent over several men who'd applied for work at Cedar Creek. Molly was stunned at the gesture. He was probably trying to soften her into dropping the lawsuit. After their last confrontation, he knew she meant business. Or was it something else that had motivated him?

She only wished she didn't make such a spectacle of herself every time he was around. She found it infuriating that he had witnessed her humiliation by one of her own men. What on earth had he been thinking? Every time she recalled the way his hazel eyes had raked her, her heart began to pound. With an exasperated sigh, she shoved the thought aside. She had more important things to do than think about Sam Brannigan!

She needed to concentrate on getting the Lady

Jay to show a profit—and solve the problem of her strange uncle.

Molly spent as little time with Jason Foley as she dared. In his presence she was always careful to wear dark-colored dresses and act demure. But time and again, she'd run into him in her work clothes and his mouth would narrow to a cold, thin line, and that odd light would come into his eyes. She wished he would give up his ideas of guardianship and return East. But he did own forty percent of the Lady Jay, and legally he had a right to stay on her land. However, there was no denying his presence made her uncomfortable.

Restarting the logging operation was now her top priority, and not an easy task. Loggers were a strange breed. Many were wild, reckless vagabonds: men with no real homes; most without wives or children. They lived for the danger and excitement of the woods, and for the most part were fearless, waging a constant battle against death. The woods of California and the Northwest claimed the life of a logger every other day, but lumber was a precious commodity, demanded by the tremendous expansion of the West, and profits for both logger and owner could be enormous. Molly intended to claim her share.

The problem was how to find a crew willing to work for a woman. She thought of hiring them in her uncle's name, but decided his pious demeanor would be an even worse handicap. If she could get a foreman, a "bull of the woods," as they were called, and an independent bullwhacker with his own teams of oxen, other men were sure to follow.

In the *Truckee Republican*, Molly had spotted a small article mentioning a loggers' festival up near Sierraville. She knew the festival would be a bawdy gathering of men who pitted themselves against each other in various logging events: chopping contests, pole climbing, birling, a bucksaw team competition, and others. They were rowdy, drunken events—and a perfect place to hire the crew Molly so desperately needed.

Tomorrow was the day of the contest. And Molly planned to attend in search of her crew.

Sam Brannigan swung his long muscular legs over the edge of his four-poster bed and onto the colorful braided carpet that warmed the floors of his room.

"Sam," Lillian Rose spoke softly into the darkness, her crystalline voice sweet and cajoling. "Come back to bed, it's still early."

"It's a long way to Sierraville. I don't want to be late."

"Are you sure I can't come with you?" Sam felt a slender finger glide along his spine. Several silken strands of her pale blond hair tickled his shoulder as she leaned forward.

"We both know you'd hate it, Lilly. The great outdoors is not exactly your cup of tea."

Lilly sighed. "No. I suppose you're right."

Sam felt her lips grazing the back of his neck. She'd surprised him by coming out to the ranch last night, instead of waiting for him to come to her house in Truckee. She'd been lonely, she'd told him. And Sam had been damned glad to see her. He'd needed some female companionship, needed to ease his need. Images of the luscious little redhead who owned the Lady Jay had left him with a case of the discomforts, and strung his nerves taut as a fiddle.

"Will I see you Saturday?" she asked, her tongue taking the place of her lips against his flesh.

Sam chuckled softly. "Keep that up and you're going to *see* me again right now." Even in the darkness, Sam knew she smiled. She didn't want to make love again. Lilly's appetites were mild in comparison to his. The way he'd been feeling when she arrived, she'd had more than she could handle already. But she liked being in control, liked the power she held over men.

Sam liked their casual relationship, the sex without entanglements. It suited them both, and had for the past two years.

He turned and kissed her lightly on the lips, his large hand cupping her supple, upturned breast, his thumb teasing the nipple. "Lee Chin will have breakfast ready by the time you're up and dressed."

"You're always so thoughtful, darling."

"And you, Lilly, are always so obliging." While Lilly snuggled her slender body beneath the covers, Sam dressed in his denims and pulled on his boots. After his night of lovemaking, he felt relaxed and in high spirits. He looked forward to the day ahead.

* * *

Molly rose early, even before Angel, saddled True and a horse for Torger Johnson, and headed toward Pitch Camp. Old Torger had grudgingly agreed to escort Molly to the contest and do his best to help her get a crew. Cresting the rise, she dropped down into a cedar grove, then spotted the deserted camp and Torger, still in his long johns, splashing water on his beard-stubbled face. As she rode into camp he looked stricken, and dashed into the bunkhouse. He came out wearing worn canvas breeches and a red flannel shirt, though the day promised to be warm.

"You ought to be ashamed, Miss Molly," he said in his slight Norwegian accent, "catching a man in his underwear. You got no shame."

Molly just laughed.

"Man can't get a minute's peace," Torger grumbled. "You ought to be asleep, like other young ladies your age."

"You know me better than that, Torger." She grinned at his discomfort.

"Give me a chance to scrape the whiskers off my face, and we'll get going." Without waiting for permission, he returned to the basin of water beneath a broken chunk of speckled mirror and slipped open his straight-edged razor. Rubbing a meager amount of soap on his lightly freckled face, Torger proceeded to shave. When he finished, he poured the water over his unkempt, sandy brown hair, and, gurgling loudly at the chill, washed the remaining soap away.

Torger was a tall man, though he was beginning to stoop a little. Molly knew his parents had immigrated from Norway to work the pine forests of Maine. When the forests began to disappear, Torger went West. It was the sort of tale common among men of the logging camps. Wherever forests grew, men from all over the country migrated in that direction. After Molly's father died, Torger had only remained at Pitch Camp as a courtesy to Molly. But loggers were social creatures. They loved the wild camaraderie of the camps, and Molly knew that Torger wouldn't stay much longer. Not without a crew.

Molly scanned the camp. It seemed empty and forlorn without the bustle of the timbermen. Usually there was such a stampede of men and equipment, grating saws and clanking metal, Molly could scarcely hear herself think. Listening to the stillness that gripped the camp now, she sighed. Somehow, she had to convince the timbermen at the festival to work for the Lady Jay. She had to make the ranch profitable again, the way it was before. The thought of returning east with her uncle made her stomach roll. She'd take in laundry before she'd go east again! Filled with renewed purpose, Molly straightened in the saddle, continuing through the dense pine forests on the road to the festival.

# *Chapter Five*

✦✦✦✦✦

MOLLY NEVER REALLY reached Sierraville. After a three-hour ride, Torger left the road and headed down into a meadow, skirting the town.

The loggers' meet was being held near Jenkin's Flat: a wide green meadow bordered by a stand of pine; a stream blocked by a splash dam on one side; and a craggy rock face above a granite scree on the other. Logs were collected behind the makeshift dam, then were eventually floated on down to the mill.

As Molly and Torger approached, the meadow echoed with the sound of ringing axes and the hum of saws. Sweaty, laughing men were everywhere. Molly noticed a few ladies present, though most remained somewhat removed from the milling throng of men. Kegs of German beer sat beneath shady pines, and tables were laden with foodstuffs: hearty platters of beef and chicken, corn and potatoes, homemade breads, pies, and cakes.

"Each camp provides food for the meet," Torger told Molly. "To the loggers, food is as important as wages—as long as the pay is fair and on time."

Dressed in her breeches, with her hair pulled into a single thick braid that hung down her back, for a while Molly moved unnoticed among the men. They'd been drinking since sunup, and the contests were well underway.

"Oh, Torger, this is going to be great fun!"

"I still do not think you should be wearing men's trousers," he grumbled. "You are not a little girl anymore. It is not the way for a lady."

"Torger, how am I going to get a crew if I come dressed as a lady? They'd say no for sure, and you know it!"

"They will say no, anyway," Torger predicted glumly.

"We'll see about that." Molly marched stubbornly in the direction of the bucksaw competition. She stopped several men along the way, asking questions about the identity of the contestants, looking to find a bull of the woods and a bullwhacker. Mentally she noted the names as she reached the event.

"Hello, Miss James." Sam Brannigan's resonant voice startled her as he strolled casually up beside her. Molly felt her heartbeat quicken as she glanced at his handsome, bearded face.

"Why, hello, Mr. Brannigan. You know Torger."

"Of course." The two men shook hands.

Sam eyed her masculine attire. "I see you still haven't learned your lesson."

"She listens to neither of us," Torger put in with a scowl, and Molly scowled back at him.

"As I told Mr. Johnson, I'm here to hire a crew. I am not concerned with my femininity."

"But they are," Sam replied, indicating the men who eyed her round posterior and shapely legs. He'd watched the girl since she first approached the flat, surprised that he felt the same stirring in his loins as he had before. After his night with Lilly Rose, he'd felt relaxed and content—until the feisty little redhead had arrived.

"I'll thank you, Mr. Brannigan, to let me worry about my clothing," she retorted. "It seems you men spend more time worrying about my attire than I ever have. Now, may we drop the subject?"

"As you wish, Miss James."

She flashed him an uncertain glance, as if she wondered why he'd do anything she might wish. What was it about her, Sam wondered, that made her different? Special, somehow. Sam wasn't sure, but her effect on him was always the same—a cross between amusement, frustration, and fury. Since he'd spotted her this morning, he'd hardly been able to keep his mind on his conversations.

"Have you ever seen a bucksaw contest?" he asked.

"No, but I'm looking forward to it."

"Mind if I join you?"

"Would it matter if I did?"

"Probably not." He flashed her a boyish grin.

Molly couldn't help but return his smile. "Pretty used to getting your way, aren't you?"

"Yes, I guess I am."

When they reached the site of the bucksaw event, Molly saw two sweaty, shirtless men, standing on opposite sides of a three-foot section of log. A second two-man team waited tensely beside another fallen log. Hands gripping their bucksaws, feet braced a few feet apart, the loggers stood ready and waiting for the shot that would signal the start of the contest.

The onlookers grew silent, each spectator's attention riveted on the two teams. Then the thunder of the pistol was blotted out by the shouts of the crowd. The men sawed back and forth feverishly, perspiration running in glossy rivulets down their muscular backs, the corded muscles of their arms straining with effort. It was essential each man work in perfect rhythm with the man across from him. Not only strength, but timing as well was crucial to success.

As the log split apart with a heavy thud, another cheer went up, and Molly found herself caught up in the excitement.

"Terrific!" she breathed. "Absolutely terrific!"

"The pole climb is next," Sam said. He seemed pleased by her enthusiasm. Molly caught the hint of a smile as he walked beside her through the milling throng of men.

They stopped at the edge of a circle of spectators. Two tall trees, towering a hundred feet in the air, had been stripped of branches. Beside each tree, two men in calked boots strapped climbing irons to their already cleated footgear. A leather strap spanning the girth of each trunk provided some measure of safety.

The object was to climb the pole as fast as possible, ring the bell mounted at the top, then shinny back down the pole to the ground, ahead of the man on the other pole. Making the climb was difficult enough; arriving at the bottom again still on one's feet was even more so. And a fall from the hundred-foot height could kill a man if he became overzealous and tried to descend too fast.

Again a gunshot sounded. Molly's blood, already quick in her veins, pumped even faster. A small man in a red-striped shirt was the underdog. His opponent, Jumbo Reilly, was one of the largest men Molly had ever seen. With his heavy thatch of brown hair, bushy eyebrows that raised or lowered depending on whether he smiled or frowned, and a thickset body bulging with muscles, Jumbo looked as if he could easily defeat his opponent.

The two men dug their calks in, flipped the leather belt up several feet, climbed to that level, and repeated the process, all in what seemed a second's time. Without realizing what she was doing, Molly began to cheer for the smaller man.

"I used to be one of the best," old Torger whispered proudly in her ear. She could barely make out his words for the din around them. "No one could beat Torger Johnson."

Molly grinned delightedly, her eyes glued to the men nearing the top. Then she heard the sharp echo of the ringing bells, and the men were away, their muscular legs haphazardly slowing their crashing descent to the ground.

Molly felt a wave of relief as the two men reached safety. Jumbo Reilly had won. "I bet you could still give 'em a run for their money," Molly whispered to Torger.

Torger beamed at her praise. Approaching his sixtieth year, he was still a fair hand with a saw and an ax, and one of the best river pigs—men who rode the logs downstream—in the mountains. He'd thought about entering the rolling contest today, but his rheumatism was ailing him again, and he wasn't in the mood for another week of suffering.

Torger glanced around him. For the second time, he realized Molly was drawing attention. Several men had lewd expressions on their faces as they eyed her snug blue denims. Torger felt his temper boil. He'd been afraid something like this would happen, and if he was too old to roll logs, he was far too old to be brawling with men half his age.

"Miss Molly, I think we ought to forget this whole idea," he cautioned, seeing the circle of men growing bigger by the moment. Torger just hoped Sam's presence would keep the men in line.

"Don't be silly, Torger," Molly argued. "We just got here. I haven't even started making my rounds."

Torger groaned and remained where he was, convinced in minutes he'd be mincemeat, as the number of men continued to increase. Sam seemed to eye the whole episode with amusement.

"Excuse me." Molly tugged at Jumbo Reilly's sleeve as he passed through the crowd.

"Yes?" The lumberjack turned to face her, taking in her femininity and her diminutive size in a single glance. "What can I do for you, little girl?"

"I believe, Mr. Reilly, you've just ended a stint as bull of the woods for a crew over near Tahoe City."

"So?" Jumbo countered brusquely.

"So, I'd like to hire you."

Jumbo's eyes widened. Sam Brannigan kept his face carefully blank, but now Molly was sure she saw amusement in his hazel eyes.

"Hire me!" Jumbo said, between chuckles. "Hire me! And just who the hell are you?"

"My name is Molly James, Mr. Reilly. I own the Lady Jay. I intend to reopen the logging operation."

Jumbo fought for control. "You and who else?"

"My uncle owns part of the ranch, but you'd be working for me."

Jumbo's laugh, joined by a chorus of hearty laughter from the other loggers, echoed across the meadow until Molly wanted to scream. Instead, using every ounce of willpower, she remained calm.

"Sorry, little girl," Jumbo finally said, "I'm not interested. Now, if you'll excuse me . . . "

"I'll pay you ten percent more than anybody else and provide separate quarters." The latter was a prestigious extra few camps offered.

"Sorry. Not interested." He tried to brush past her, but she stepped in front of his path, the top of her head barely reaching the middle of his chest.

"What would I have to do to get you to work for me?" she demanded.

Jumbo Reilly broke into a toothy grin. "You'd have to beat me in the chopping contest—and even Big Sam ain't gonna do that!" The men laughed heartily and, ignoring her look of fury, shoved their way toward the next event.

Sam grinned broadly. "Maybe she *can* beat you, Jumbo! I intend to!"

Hearing Sam's words, for a moment Molly forgot her purpose. "You're going against him in the chopping contest?"

"What's the matter, Miss James? You're convinced you can run an entire logging operation—why is it so hard to believe I can beat Jumbo Reilly?" Without waiting for her reply, Sam began to follow the men.

Molly walked along beside him, hurrying to keep up and feeling a thrill of excitement. This was going to be something! The sun, though still high, was beginning to roll westward on its journey to the sea. The preliminaries were over, and the next round of events would decide the champions of the day. Only the best men had made it this far.

When they reached the designated area, Sam unbuttoned his shirt and tugged it from his breeches, leaving his muscular body bare to the waist. Molly sucked in a breath at the disturbing display of taut flesh over muscle. Jumbo Reilly, his face split wide in a toothy grin, followed suit. His massive body was white beneath his shirt, leaving only his forearms, neck, and face brown from his work in the sun. Sam's tanned skin seemed endless, and Molly found her eyes helplessly fastened on the line of his breeches. A niggling suspicion he was tan all over finally forced her to glance away.

"Well, Jumbo," Sam called over to his opponent, "think this is going to be your year to beat me?"

"Sam's been the unbeaten champion for the last five years," Torger leaned down to whisper in Molly's ear.

Her eyes grew round. "He beat Jumbo Reilly?"

"Jumbo's only gone against Sam once—last year. Sam won, but Jumbo swore this year he'd be champ. Heard he's been practicing somethin' fierce."

"Loggers, take yer places," came the call, as Sam and Jumbo lined up in front of two pine stumps, each more than two feet in diameter. The trees had been topped ten feet above the ground. The trick was to be the first to chop through the thick trunk. Sam picked up his felling ax, hefted it a couple of times, and, with a quick glance toward the red-haired woman standing excitedly beside Torger, readied himself for the competition. If he'd had any doubts about winning, they fled the moment he saw Molly James's delighted smile. Jumbo Reilly didn't have a chance.

"Ready," came the starter's even tone. Then the gun was fired. Molly shrieked with excitement as she watched the two big men swing the double-bitted axes against the wood. She could hear the heavy ringing blows even above the throng of cheering voices. In minutes the two men's muscular torsos were covered with sweat. Corded muscles bunched across Sam's tanned back, and the thick muscles on his arms bulged with his effort. His teeth were clenched as each solid blow rang against the tree. Many of the men cheered for Sam, but an equal number urged Jumbo on.

Halfway through the girth of the log, the men were almost even. Then one of Sam's strokes hit lightly, and Jumbo edged ahead. Two more solid blows rang out, digging into the flesh of the trees, and Sam was once again even.

"Come on, Sam, you can do it!" Molly cried out, caught up in the excitement and unable to stop herself. Sam heard her, and his handsome face broke into a broad grin, while his strokes, harder and surer than ever, cut through the last remaining inches of tree trunk.

A roar went up from the crowd as the starter lifted Sam's sweat-covered arm in victory. Molly danced around with elation, then began to curb her enthusiasm. What in the world was the matter with her? She should have been rooting for Jumbo; the Brannigans had won too many victories already. A bit sheepishly, she watched Sam approach. Jumbo walked up beside him and extended a meaty hand.

"Next year, Sam! There's always next year."

Sam shook Jumbo's hand good-naturedly. "I couldn't have done it without Miss James cheering me on."

Molly felt her face flame, but fought down her embarrassment. After all, she'd only been carried away by the sport of the competition.

"Well, Mr. Reilly," she said, turning toward Sam's opponent and hoping to use Sam's victory to her benefit, "now that Mr. Brannigan has beaten you, how about coming to work for me?"

"Nice try, little girl," Jumbo replied. "I'd be willin' to work for Sam here. Sam's the one who beat me, not you. But don't feel too bad. Maybe next year *you* can enter the chopping contest!" He guffawed loudly, joined by his group of beefy supporters. "Now, if you'll excuse me, I got to get ready for the birling match. Even if Sam could roll a log, he'd have a devil of a time beatin' me in that!" He clapped Sam on the back and started to walk away.

"Wait just a minute," Molly broke in. "You say you're in the log-rolling contest?"

"Yes, ma'am. I been champion the past two years." His wide grin pulled his bushy brows apart.

"How would you like to make a little wager on the outcome?" Molly asked innocently.

"You don't think Billy Jakes can beat me?" He seemed incredulous. Sam just watched with an amused smile.

"No, I don't," Molly assured him.

"Then who would you be bettin' on?"

"Me, Mr. Reilly. If I win, you come to work for me."

Jumbo's guffaw cracked across the clearing. "You! You know how to roll logs?"

"Torger taught me. But of course if you're afraid . . ."

"Afraid?" Jumbo's face darkened with fury, and for a moment she feared she might have pushed the logger too far. "Afraid of a tiny little girl tryin' to act like a man? Not very likely, missy."

"Excuse us just a minute, Jumbo." Before she could stop him, Sam grasped her arm and tugged her none too gently outside the circle of men. "It's none of my business, Miss James—"

"If it's none of your business, why do you insist on giving me advice?"

Sam smiled dryly. "Let's just say that although you're a James, and although you have a lawsuit pending against Cedar Creek, I'd hate to see a *lady*"—he said the word with a hint of sarcasm—"make a fool of herself in front of every logger from here to Seattle."

"I'm here to hire a crew, *Mr.* Brannigan. Whatever that takes is exactly what I'll do. Now, if you'll excuse me—" She elbowed her way back toward Jumbo and extended her small hand. "Best two out of three. Do we have a bet, Mr. Reilly?"

"Wait a minute. What do I get if you lose?"

She glanced at him uncertainly.

"I'll tell you what," he suggested, before she could answer. "You win, I go to work for the Lady Jay. You lose and I git a kiss. How's that for fair?"

Molly heard Sam's groan, and it stiffened her resolve. "You have a bet, Mr. Reilly. Shall we go?" The loggers went wild. They surrounded Molly and Jumbo, escorting them across the meadow toward the pond behind the splash dam. Drunken catcalls and lewd remarks followed in their wake. The smallest man in the group loaned her his calked boots, which were still a size too big, and fought to stifle his grin as she laced them up.

Molly was beginning to regret her impulsiveness. She was a darned good boom man—she and Torger had spent hours during the hot summer months contesting each other on the infuriating logs—but since she'd been home they'd only played the game a couple of times. Her balance had come back easily, but Jumbo Reilly was an expert. She was worrying her lower lip, wondering what her best tactic would be, when she heard Torger's Norwegian-accented voice near her ear.

"The only chance you have is to use his weight against him. Let him defeat himself. You haven't the strength to outlast him; let him think he is winning, then let him beat himself."

Molly smiled up at Torger's lined face and caught a glimpse of Sam Brannigan's handsome one. She couldn't decide if the look he was wearing was one of amusement or worry.

"Gentlemen, may I please have your attention," the starter said. "We have a special event today. Jumbo Reilly, the current champion, will go against Miss Molly James of the Lady Jay Ranch." The rest of his speech was drowned out by the wild laughter of the lumberjacks.

"There's still time for you to come to your senses," Sam warned quietly, with a dark glint in his eyes. "No one really expects you to go through with it. Just tell Jumbo you didn't mean it." It was obvious Sam disapproved of her strategy, and she was tempted to agree with him.

"Thank you for your concern, Mr. Brannigan. I assure you, I can take care of myself." With a bravado she didn't feel, Molly turned and walked stoically out on the log.

"You'd best get them pretty red lips a yours puckered up, little girl," Jumbo Reilly taunted as he followed her.

His enormous weight tilted the log precariously. Molly wished fervently there'd been some other way to get a crew. Even this might not work, and all she'd get for her troubles would be a soggy ride back to the Lady Jay.

"Ready," the starter said, and the gun went off.

Molly heard Jumbo's deep laughter and the cheering of the men as the massive log began to whirl beneath her feet. It had made only a few revolutions when Jumbo made a sudden movement, and the big log not only spun but bucked and dipped below the surface. Before Molly knew what had happened, she found herself gasping for breath in the cold water of the pond. Her ears were filled with water, so the shouts of the crowd sounded more like a muffled roar. God, this was going to be even harder than she'd expected!

Still sputtering, she grabbed Jumbo's beefy hand, and effortlessly he pulled her back on the log. Torger's words rang in her ears. *Let him beat himself.*

"Bet still on, little girl?" Jumbo asked with such an arrogant smile she was infuriated. She'd lasted only seconds. No one would have any faith in her now, and she'd never get her crew. She could see Sam Brannigan standing near the edge of the pond, but still couldn't read his expression. He did not approve of her actions, that much was clear, but there was an undercurrent of something else she couldn't quite fathom.

"Bet's still on," she assured Jumbo.

When the starter's gun went off this time, Molly was ready. She cleared her mind of all but the feel of the log, the roll and pitch, the dip and sway of the wood in the water. Jumbo tried every trick he knew, using his weight and strength remorselessly, till with a final great effort he spun the log in just the manner she'd been hoping for. Molly did exactly as Torger said, letting Jumbo's own weight work against him—and Jumbo Reilly splashed like an oversized toad into the waters of the pond.

Hoots and hollers of approval thundered through the crowd. Molly was jumping up and down so excitedly she almost knocked herself off the log. With a look of triumph, she glanced at Sam Brannigan, whose astonished expression filled her with a fresh surge of joy.

Then Jumbo Reilly climbed back on the log. His face, until now jovial and smiling, was a bright-red mask of rage, and his jaw was set in a line of fury so tight Molly felt a shudder of fear run the length of her. The man was so tense with anger Molly wondered if he'd be able to control the log at all. His temper was a factor she hadn't counted on, but she couldn't back down now.

"Are you ready, Miss James?" he ground out through clenched teeth.

Molly could only nod. Her knees were already shaking, and the gun had not been fired. When the start did come, it was all she could do to keep her mind on the log, her glance from straying to Jumbo's furious face. The log whirled and bucked and whirled again, but Molly's balance remained sure. She stole another quick glance at Jumbo's angry features, noting the set of his heavy brow—just before she tumbled into the pond.

His large hand was not there to help her out a second time. Molly was forced to slosh to the shore under her own steam, and soggy and tired as she was, it was no easy task. Jumbo waited on the bank, surrounded by his admirers. She wondered where Sam was, then saw him in conversation with Torger, his back to her as if she didn't exist.

For a moment, all she could think of was how glad she was the contest was over. She untied and tugged off her borrowed boots and was standing barefoot when she felt two huge hands surround her waist. She turned to stare into Jumbo's triumphant smile.

"I won, little girl," Jumbo said, a picture of joviality again. "Now how about that kiss?"

Molly swallowed hard and closed her eyes. Jumbo's thick lips seemed to encompass half her face. They were warm and wet, but not unpleasant; his breath tasted of tobacco and beer. The kiss went on endlessly, and Molly finally began to struggle, pressing her small hands against his still-damp chest. Jumbo held her easily. Molly was beginning to worry that he'd never release her, when the big logger suddenly let her go.

"That's enough," Sam warned, his hand biting into the flesh of Jumbo's mighty bicep. "The lady's paid her bet."

For a moment Jumbo stiffened, and Molly feared there might be a fight; then, as Sam released his hold on the big logger's arm, Jumbo smiled and turned to the men surrounding them.

"The lady was a damned good sport and a damned fine river pig. If her offer still stands, I'll be happy to be bull of the woods for the Lady Jay!"

A cheer went up from the men. Sam Brannigan smiled down at Molly with admiration. Dazed, she spoke a few final words to Jumbo, authorizing him to hire a crew and urging him to report to Pitch Camp as soon as possible. Then she and Sam headed toward the horses, Torger having gone on ahead.

"Well, Miss James, I can't say I approve of your methods, but I have to admire your results." Sam chuckled softly. "You know, for a minute or two, I actually thought you were going to win."

Molly grinned conspiratorially. "Oh, but I did win, Mr. Brannigan. I got my crew, didn't I? And we both know one thing for sure—no crew would be willing to work for a bull of the woods who'd been bested by a woman. Good day, Mr. Brannigan." With that, she turned and walked away. She heard Sam Brannigan's hearty laughter all the way to her horse.

# *Chapter Six*

✦✦✦✦✦

MOLLY RETURNED HOME that evening exhausted but content. She had her crew, or at least she would as soon as Jumbo Reilly hired them. Torger had returned to Pitch Camp, grumbling all the way about the unladylike spectacle she'd made of herself, but secretly she knew he'd been pleased with the skill she'd shown against Jumbo and was happy to have the loggers returning to camp.

Molly grained True, finished rubbing him down, then headed toward the house, hoping to change into a dress before her uncle saw her and made another rumpus.

When she arrived at the supper table he was all smiles, and Molly rolled her eyes heavenward in silent thanks that she'd been able to sneak in unnoticed. It was getting harder and harder to play the lady in front of her uncle.

"Well, Molly, dear, don't you look lovely this evening." Jason's approving glance slid over her simple brown cotton dress with its white collar and cuffs. She'd twisted her braid into a modest knot at the back of her head. He smiled at her in that strange way of his, and she wondered at his thoughts.

"Thank you, Uncle." She let him seat her, then himself, while Angel brought in the food—steaming tamales, frijoles, the usual tortillas, as well as a platter of spicy chicken.

The reverend swallowed hard as the pungent

odor of chile peppers filled the room. "My dear Mrs. Sanchez, night after night you serve us the same sort of thing. Am I to understand you only know how to cook these . . . these Mexican concoctions?"

"Sí, Señor Foley. They do not please you?" Angel looked crushed.

*"Please me?* Surely you jest? This is the most vile form of punishment my stomach has ever been forced to endure!"

Molly shifted in irritation. How dare her uncle criticize Angel's cooking? When Molly had been East, how she had longed for Mexican food!

"Tomorrow I'll hire one of the ladies from church to cook in the evenings—with your permission, of course, my dear." Jason glanced at Molly for approval, but she sensed it was only an afterthought. And she knew that any protest on her part would be futile.

"Certainly, Uncle," she replied stiffly. She'd make this concession to keep him happy. Perhaps if he were allowed to make all the decisions about running the household, he would be too busy to be concerned about what she was doing to the Lady Jay.

Angel set the platter of chicken down a little too hard, spilling some of the thick red sauce onto the tablecloth, then spun on her heel and marched her mountainous body out of the room. Molly would try to soothe her ruffled feathers after dinner.

"Molly, dear," Jason began, "several ladies from town stopped by today. It seems they heard there was a new preacher in the valley and wanted to wish me welcome. They spoke of a social to be held at the Cardwell House this Saturday night. I think it would be a fine opportunity for us to get acquainted with some of our neighbors."

Molly lifted her brows in surprise. "I wouldn't have thought you'd approve of dancing."

"I'm a Methodist, Molly, not a Baptist. I see nothing wrong with partaking of God's pleasures—as long as it's done with moderation. Of course I'm still in mourning, but you, my dear, as you so emphatically pointed out, have mourned quite long enough. I think the social would be a good chance for you to meet some young people your own age."

Jason watched his niece carefully. The ladies' timely arrival had sparked an idea. If her guardian couldn't control her, subdue her wildness, maybe a husband could. What Molly James needed was a man who would put her in her rightful place—heavy with child and at home where she belonged.

The deed would take careful planning: The man would have to be someone Jason could manipulate, someone who would demand Molly give up running the ranch. Someone who would want Molly to sell the place. And he would be rid of the sweet temptation she presented, which seemed stronger every day.

The dance was a perfect place for Jason to start his search. It might be difficult, but it was worth a try. It was important he separate himself from this wicked woman.

Molly spun the idea around in her mind. She hadn't been dancing in ages—not since she'd left Chicago. But her father had been dead for months, and Molly refused to succumb to the pressures of society. If Jason Foley was willing to let her go, why should she pass up an opportunity for some good old-fashioned fun?

"I believe you're right, Uncle. Maybe it would be a good idea to get acquainted again. I'd be delighted to accompany you to the social Saturday night."

Molly smiled, and wondered at the satisfied smile she received in return. But there was something about Jason Foley that made just about everything he did seem a little suspect. Molly shook the sensation off and continued eating the delicious chicken.

Saturday arrived almost too soon. Molly had worked so hard all week, she'd forgotten the dance completely until her uncle reminded her about it on Saturday morning. Then Molly began to get excited.

She quit work early, bathed, and with Angel's help carefully arranged her thick red hair: a crown of ringlets on top of her head, the sides pulled back and fixed with her mother's seed-pearl combs, the rest left loose to curl down her back. She selected a blue silk gown just a shade darker than her eyes and a pair of matching kidskin slippers. Beneath the gown she wore her best lacy chemise, corset and petticoats, pampering herself for the first time since she'd come West. She'd worked hard these past few months—she deserved an evening of fun.

The only drawback was the two-hour ride into town with her uncle. She certainly wasn't looking forward to that. Whenever they were together, he looked at her so strangely, and often sat far too close to her for comfort. But she might see some of her old grammar-school chums, friends she hadn't talked to in years, so the uncomfortable ride would be worth it. She'd rarely been to town since her return to the Lady Jay, just gone in to pick up supplies or pin notices to the board in front of Lewison's Dry Goods Store that she was looking to hire a crew. Tonight was really the first chance she'd had to see old friends.

Molly arrived at the dance only a little the worse for wear.

Jason had been talkative at first, discussing his plans for the future, the church he intended to build. Then he'd grown silent, brooding, it seemed to Molly. She'd been relieved when they'd finally reached Truckee and headed for the hotel.

The Cardwell House, a two-story brick building, sat on Front Street across from the railroad station. A dance had been held in the hotel dining room every Saturday night for as long as Molly could remember. Sanctioned by several churches, the social, as the dance was called, was always well attended by Truckee's most prominent citizens.

Molly let her uncle help her from the wagon,

being careful not to get her full skirts caught in the wooden spokes. Jason had grudgingly approved of her gown, though he'd remarked that it exposed a little too much of her neck and shoulders. He staunchly refused to acknowledge the gentle swells of her bosom the dress also fashionably revealed.

Within minutes of Molly's arrival with her uncle, the ladies from the Methodist Ladies Auxiliary captured Jason, so Molly was left on her own.

"Molly James!" Sadie Williams, once her best friend though two years younger, rushed up to greet her, her dainty brown ringlets bobbing with every step she took.

"Sadie!" Molly hugged her friend, already glad she had come. "I thought you were still in boarding school."

"I just got back a few weeks ago," Sadie told her. "I've been meaning to drop by the ranch, but you know how I am about visiting." Sadie hugged her again. "Oh, Molly, it's so good to see you."

"It's good to see you too. You look so . . . so . . . grown up!"

Sadie's bow-shaped mouth lifted seductively as she smoothed imaginary creases from the bodice of her pink ruched-silk gown. "I am grown up, Molly. I'm engaged to be married. Come on, I'll introduce you to my fiancé."

Molly followed the tiny girl across the room. The tables and chairs had been moved to the sides, leaving plenty of room for dancing. A large crystal punch bowl filled with lemonade dominated a cloth-covered table, and platters of spicy meats and delicate cakes sat beside it. The three-piece band had begun to play a slightly too-fast version of a waltz, and the dance floor began to fill up.

"Molly," Sadie said, her round cheeks glowing with excitement, "this is Clive Beasley, my fiancé. Clive, this is Molly James."

Molly extended her small gloved hand, and Clive gallantly pressed it to his lips. A tall, thin young man, Clive glanced at Molly only briefly, then returned his attention to Sadie, an unmistakable look of adoration in his eyes.

"When we were children, Molly was my best friend," Sadie told him, then paused midsentence as a handsome dark-haired man approached.

"You've been holding out on us, Clive." The tall man eyed Molly boldly, a slight rebuke in his tone. "Where did you find this lovely creature?"

"She's a friend of Sadie's," Clive explained hastily, and Molly wondered at the stranger's powerful presence. "Her name is Molly James."

"Miss James, my name is Michael Locke. I'm pleased to meet you. Might I have the pleasure of this dance?" It was more of a command than a question, and Molly accepted the proffered arm with a hint of a smile.

"Are you new to Truckee, Miss James?" asked Michael Locke as he unerringly whirled her about the floor. His steps were strong and sure, just like his features.

"On the contrary, Mr. Locke, I've lived here

nearly all my life. I've been away at school most of the time for the past six years, though."

"How unfortunate for the rest of us," he said with a slight smile. "Are you home for good?"

"Why, yes, I am. And you, Mr. Locke? Are you one of Truckee's finest?"

"I'm with the railroad. I've been living in Truckee for the last two months. I'm negotiating some land sales for a feeder line. After the transaction is complete, I usually relocate. Now that I've met you . . . I may reconsider."

Molly wasn't certain if his words were the customary gallantry, or something more. He was attractive—indeed, dashingly so. But there was something intimidating in his manner. Something that put her off more than a little. He clasped her waist a little too tightly, held her a little too close.

"Would you care for some punch or a breath of air?" he asked as the dance came to a close. His immaculate navy-blue suit set off his firm jawline and the dimple beside his mouth.

"I believe my uncle may be looking for me," she lied. She started to step away, but the sound of deep, familiar laughter pulled her attention to the door. Sam Brannigan stood in the entry, his frame nearly filling it. Molly felt a such a rush of warmth, she worried that someone might notice her high color. With a bit of difficulty, she forced her gaze away.

"Are you certain you won't dance just one more time?" Michael pressed.

She started to say no, hoping Sam might ask

her, then she noticed the blond woman clinging to his arm. The woman was tall and graceful, elegant and willowy, with the most achingly beautiful face Molly had ever seen. Her creamy skin above her apricot gown glowed like moonstones in the lamplight.

"I . . . I suppose one more dance wouldn't hurt." Molly let Michael lead her onto the floor, silently thanking God that this handsome man stood beside her.

"I saw you looking at Mrs. Rose," Michael said.

"Mrs. Rose?"

"Why, yes. Mrs. Lillian Rose, the woman with Sam Brannigan."

Molly was having trouble concentrating on the rhythm of the dance. She was glad it was a slow, simple box-step. "She's lovely. One would have to try hard *not* to notice her." The woman's glossy blond hair, swept up fashionably above her slender ivory neck, gleamed like palest gold.

Molly tried to sound casual. "Is her husband here? I don't remember a Mr. Rose, but maybe if I saw him . . . "

"Unfortunately for Mr. Rose—and fortunately for Mr. Brannigan—Willard Rose is dead."

"I see." And Molly did. Molly saw tall, golden-haired, broad-shouldered Sam Brannigan leading the graceful blond widow Rose onto the dance floor and understood that there had never been two people more perfectly suited than they. Sam's suntanned features and golden beard offset the widow's pale, gleaming locks and creamy skin. As they danced, she saw how perfectly they fit together: Lillian just the right size for Sam's tall frame, Sam making her graceful height seem dainty as few men could. Except for Sam's slight limp, the couple seemed pure fluid motion.

Molly released a sigh of resignation and let Michael Locke whirl her around the floor, but the fun of the dance had ended for her the minute Sam Brannigan stepped into the room.

"Good evening, Miss James." Sam's deep voice spun her around. She'd been dancing with Clive, then begged off from Michael, wanting to catch her breath. Standing near the punch bowl, she'd been wondering if Sam Brannigan had even noticed she was in the room. As she glanced up to meet his hazel gaze, she felt her heartbeat quicken and cursed herself for the effect the man always had on her. He looked exceedingly handsome in his dark brown western-cut suit and crisp white shirt. Gleaming brown kidskin boots peeped from beneath his tailored trousers. She caught that same clean, woodsy scent she'd noticed before.

"Mr. Brannigan. I saw you come in. It's nice to see you again." How inane she sounded. She could bet the beautiful widow would have had something much more charming to say.

"You look lovely tonight," he said, "though I almost didn't recognize you in something other than breeches." His amused smile sent bright heat to her cheeks.

"I assure you, Mr. Brannigan, I have the same

feminine nature as any other woman—whenever I have time for it."

Sam's eyes swept her from head to toe, lingering a bit too long on the curves of her breasts. "I see no reason to doubt that, Miss James."

Molly smiled shyly. She was trying to think of something gracious to say in response when the elegant widow arrived with a flourish of apricot skirts.

"Sam, darling. I've been looking all over." She glanced at Molly almost as an afterthought. "Who's your little friend, darling?"

*Little friend.* Molly was torn between hating the woman for her condescending attitude and wishing she could crawl into a hole.

"Mrs. Rose, may I present Miss James. Molly is the owner of the Lady Jay."

"How nice," Lillian said, dismissing her with the briefest of smiles. "Sam, I really think I need some air. Won't you take me outside?"

Sam nodded curtly. "If you'll excuse us, Miss James."

Molly noticed the way his large hand rested casually at the widow's waist as her graceful steps carried her away.

"So you met the widow Rose," Sadie whispered conspiratorially, joining her beside the punch bowl. "She's Sam Brannigan's mistress, but for God's sake don't repeat that. It's a forbidden subject in Truckee. Everyone's afraid of Judge Egan, Lilly's father. You remember him, don't you? He's the short, stocky man standing over there." She pointed to a heavyset man in an expensive-looking black broadcloth suit. "He's a big landowner, and very influential in Congress."

Molly stared at the judge, but her mind was still numb from her friend's revelation. She knew Sadie was still rambling on, but couldn't catch her friend's words.

A second wave of shock washed over her. The woman was Sam's mistress! His *mistress!* Everything her father had said about Sam Brannigan was true. He was a womanizer of the worst sort. Here he was carrying on an affair with the judge's beautiful daughter and didn't even have the decency to marry her. He'd probably had designs on Molly's mother, just as her father had always said. Molly felt sick at the thought.

"I don't think we should be discussing this, Sadie," she said, wanting desperately to change the subject. She hoped she had controlled her features as well as she usually did, and hadn't revealed her shock.

"You already knew, didn't you?" Sadie speculated. "I can tell by your face. You weren't surprised at all."

Molly smiled inwardly. She hadn't lost her touch. Now, she just wished the evening would end, so she could get back to the ranch and bury herself in her work. She'd been attracted to Sam from the first, and it had been a fool's errand. God, what an idiot she was.

"Dance with me?" Michael Locke extended his arm. This time Molly grasped it thankfully. Smiling at Sadie, she let Michael lead her onto the floor.

* * *

Sam Brannigan watched Molly James dancing with Michael Locke again—as she had so many times Sam had lost count. The man was a four-flushing rogue, and Sam hated to see even a James get involved with a man like Locke—or at least so he told himself as he tried to calm another blast of heat at the back of his neck. It seemed every time Locke eyed Molly with that wolfish gleam in his eye, Sam felt his temper rise.

The little redhead looked stunning this evening—far beyond anything Sam would have expected. Her hair glistened like rubies, and her full breasts peeked tantalizingly above her gown. Sam was tempted to agree with her, after all—she did look more seductive in the voluminous folds of the gown than she had in the more revealing breeches. Well, at least equally seductive, he amended, chuckling to himself.

He'd introduced her to Lilly, and the lovely widow had barely graced her with a smile. Lilly, he was sure, hardly noticed Molly's existence. But that was to be expected. Lilly was holding court this evening, as she did wherever she went. The men in the room were her subjects—admiring her delicate, pale beauty as if she were a goddess—and Sam sometimes wondered if Lilly might believe it herself.

Sam had known Lilly since she was a child. Judge Egan, Lilly's father, was a close personal friend of his. Willard Rose, a man her father's age, had doted on Lilly; he'd built her the beautiful Victorian mansion she lived in at the edge of town, and given her everything she wanted.

Lilly had never loved Willard, she'd told Sam on several occasions; but then, Lilly had never really loved anyone.

The widow Rose wanted to remain happily uninvolved, and that suited Sam just fine. She kept her life private, and her father's powerful position helped assure there'd be no gossip.

They'd spoken of marriage only once, Sam's sense of honor requiring he at least discuss the matter with her. Lilly just laughed in that tinkling manner of hers and said he was being silly, she'd already been married and never wanted to suffer the experience again. Sam had felt a tremendous sense of relief, and been happy to continue just as they were.

"Sam," Lilly said, sidling up to him and running a slim finger along the bearded line of his jaw. "Be a darling, won't you, and get me another punch."

Denny Boswell jumped up to do her bidding instead. "I'd be honored if you'd let me, Mrs. Rose."

Sam just smiled, excused himself, and walked away. He and Lilly had an arrangement, one that didn't involve possessiveness on either side. Neither asked what the other did, even on their occasional trips out of town.

Molly leaned her head back against the rough brick wall of the Cardwell House, glad to escape the heat and noise of the dance; it was still warm outside, though the sun had descended hours ago. But it was cooler out here on the porch, and the summer breeze was refreshing. The porch hung over a tiny stream that ran behind the hotel, and Molly could hear its clear, sweet babbling. It reminded her of the lilting voice of Lillian Rose.

"Mind if I join you?" Sam's rich, deep cadences performed their usual magic, and her heartbeat quickened. Molly glanced around, searching for the widow.

"She's dancing with your friend, Mr. Locke." He rested his hands on the railing, his eyes fixed on the stream.

Molly made no reply.

"Enjoying yourself this evening?"

"I suppose so."

"Suppose?" He turned to look at her, and the moon lit his neatly trimmed beard and glistened on his thick golden hair. Molly thought how much like a Viking he looked.

"I . . . I have a lot to do at the ranch," she told him. "I shouldn't have come."

"Don't you think you deserve a little fun once in a while?"

She'd said those same words to herself, but watching Sam Brannigan in the arms of the beautiful Lillian Rose was not Molly's idea of fun.

"I suppose so."

"I don't believe I've ever seen you quite this uncertain, Miss James."

His teasing look stiffened her spine. "You're right, Mr. Brannigan. I guess I'm just tired. Right now, I'm quite sure I'm ready to go home. If you'll excuse me . . ." She tried to brush past him, but he caught her arm, raising goose bumps on her flesh.

"I'd watch out for Locke, if I were you. He's had a good deal more experience with the opposite sex than you have. You might find yourself in over your head."

Molly's temper flared. "And just how would you know how much experience I've had, Mr. Brannigan? As usual, this is none of your business. How I handle Mr. Locke is my affair, not yours. I suggest you worry about Mrs. Rose's reputation instead of mine!" As she tugged her arm free and swept into the hall, she could have sworn she'd seen him smile. Heading toward the dining room, she fought to control her temper. Of all the unmitigated gall! The man didn't seem the least concerned about the widow's reputation, so why the devil should he be concerned with hers?

Without a backward glance, Molly went searching for her uncle, promising herself she'd put Sam Brannigan from her mind once and for all.

"You know, Reverend Foley, having you as her guardian is the best thing that could have happened to that girl."

Standing in the corner of the room, Jason found himself cornered by Harriet Lewison. The rotund lady was the wife of J. L. Lewison, one of Truckee's most prominent merchants. She was also Truckee's most notorious gossip, so no matter how distasteful Jason found her personally, he intended to milk her interest in him for all it was worth. The more he could discover about his niece, the better.

Harriet rolled her gray eyes skyward. "Her father practically let her run wild after poor Colleen was murdered."

Jason's interest was further piqued. "You know, Mrs. Lewison, I've been wanting to discuss that matter, but I needed to find someone who would hold our conversation in the strictest confidence. Do you suppose you would entrust me with the facts of the matter? I believe it would be in Molly's best interest if I understood all the ramifications of that unfortunate event."

Harriet fairly beamed. "Oh, Reverend, I quite agree." She glanced around, then pulled the reverend deeper into the corner. "It happened when Molly was seven. No one really knows the whole story; each man's version was completely different. But Malcolm James said Shamus Brannigan lured Colleen out of the house with a note saying Molly was hurt. Molly had gone off with that Mexican man . . . oh, what's his name?"

"Sanchez?"

"Yes, that's it. Anyway, Colleen believed the note. When she got to the old line shack where Molly was supposed to be, Shamus was waiting. He forced himself on her—I won't go into detail; it's enough to say Colleen's body was only partially clothed when the sheriff arrived. . . . Well, Mal walked in on them, and during the struggle to save Colleen, Shamus pulled a gun. The gun went off, and Molly's mother was killed."

"Dreadful," Jason said, shaking his head. A lock of his dark, curly hair fell over his brow, and Mrs. Lewison spied it, blushing like a schoolgirl. Jason smiled, thankful to God for his handsome features, which always worked to his—and the Lord's—benefit. "But you said there were two sides to the story?"

"Yes." Again Harriet glanced around. Seeing the crowd engrossed in the music and no one heading their way, she continued with her story, and Jason could see she was enjoying every minute of it.

Harriet leaned even closer. "Shamus Brannigan said Colleen was planning to divorce Mal. That he and Colleen were in love. He claimed Mal found them together and shot Colleen in a fit of temper, but the jury didn't believe him. It was Shamus's gun, you see, and Colleen was a Catholic. After all, you know how those Catholics are about divorce. And Mal was so grief-stricken, it was nearly impossible not to believe him. Still, since there were no other witnesses, and the note Shamus was supposed to have sent never materialized, there was some question in the jury's mind. They sentenced Shamus to three years in prison for manslaughter, but he died of the fever a year later."

Jason Foley sighed, finding the story disquieting. No wonder Vera had refused to discuss it. And no wonder Molly was the woman she was. "I thank you so much, Mrs. Lewison. The whole thing is terribly sordid and certainly best forgotten, but I believe the information will help me understand dear Molly a little better."

"Yes, the poor child was quite distraught. Mal paid her no attention at all after Colleen died. Most of the time, she was left to rattle around the house all alone. Eventually, he sent her to boarding school. She's only just recently returned—but then, you know the rest."

"Yes. Thank you, Mrs. Lewison." He brought her chubby fingers to his lips and smiled at the tiny gooseflesh his kiss aroused.

"Uncle Jason." Molly's warm, throaty voice, a little breathless, interrupted his thoughts.

"You know Mrs. Lewison, my dear."

"Why, yes. Of course." She nodded in the graying woman's direction, then returned her attention to her uncle. "I'm tiring a bit, Uncle Jason, and we still have quite a ride home. Would you mind terribly . . . ?"

"You're quite right, my dear. Shall we say our good-byes and be off?"

She nodded and accepted his arm. Tonight she looked even more beautiful than usual, her flame-red hair framing the sensual curves of her cheeks and lips. Jason felt a tug in his groin, and cursed her for the vixen she was. Few women had affected him as his niece had. He knew it was her untamed nature, the recklessness that lurked just below her surface calm, and her sordid heritage. As hard as he fought against them, images of her beneath him, her legs spread, her red hair flowing over the pillow, burned across his mind. He knew her allure was evil, and he fought against it.

At the dance, he'd spent much of his time visiting with men who might be potential suitors. But the more he'd visualized these men with Molly, the less he'd liked the idea. She was getting under his skin and he knew it, but he couldn't seem to help himself.

She was a temptress—the devil's own—and somehow he had to exorcise the demon in him she threatened to unleash. Steeling himself to the emotions she stirred, he escorted her toward the door.

# *Chapter Seven*

MOLLY SPENT THE next week hard at work. Each morning she rose before dawn and headed for Pitch Camp, or left with Joaquin and the cowhands for the range.

She spent less time with the lumberjacks, worried her presence might make Jumbo Reilly's job more difficult. The cowhands were easier to manage. They worked for Joaquin: She was just a woman Joaquin allowed to tag along. Molly didn't mind. All she cared about was making the ranch profitable—and forgetting Sam Brannigan.

Today, she decided to work in the barn. The rest of the men were out with Joaquin, and Angel had gone to visit her sister, as she did every Thursday. Jason Foley had ridden into town, thank God. The man was getting on her nerves a little more every day. The only man she found more infuriating was Sam.

Pretending the pile of straw she worked over was Sam Brannigan's backside, and brandishing the pitchfork with a little more zeal than necessary, Molly glanced up to see Sam himself, astride his big buckskin, riding in her direction. She couldn't make out the tanned face beneath his broad-brimmed hat, but his muscular frame was unmistakable.

As she watched Sam dismount, Molly leaned the pitchfork against the side of the barn and blotted her damp forehead with the back of her hand. She wished she'd neatly braided her hair instead of just tying it with a ribbon at the back of her neck. Then, glancing down at her faded denims and threadbare work shirt, she laughed inwardly at the thought. Fixing her hair would have done little to improve her appearance.

"Good afternoon, Miss James." He eyed her breeches with his usual disapproving glance. "Hard at work as always, I see."

"What can I do for you, Mr. Brannigan?" Though she kept her tone businesslike, as Sam walked nearer Molly felt the thump of her heart against her ribs. When he stood beside her, she realized again just how big he was—and just how attractive.

"For starters, you can call me Sam. We're neighbors. I hope eventually we're going to be friends."

"That's doubtful, Mr. Brannigan," she informed him, deliberately ignoring his request. "I doubt you'll be feeling overly friendly when you're hauling your logs that extra ten miles to the mill."

Sam stiffened. "Maybe you shouldn't work so hard, Miss James; it seems to put you in a terrible temper. I came to return your comb. It is yours, isn't it?"

Molly lifted the beautiful seed-pearl comb from his wide, outstretched palm. "Why, yes, it is. Where did you find it?"

"Just outside the Cardwell House. Earlier in the evening, I noticed you were wearing it."

Molly felt a little guilty. It had been nice of him to ride all the way over just to return her comb. "Thank you. It was my mother's, and I was afraid I'd lost it." She turned the delicate comb over in her hand, admiring the way the sunlight danced on the lustrous pearls. "It means a lot to me. Father never wanted me to wear it. The memories of my mother were just too painful, I guess."

"I'm sure they were," Sam replied with a bit of cynicism Molly didn't miss.

"From what my father told me, you had quite an eye for her yourself." Molly couldn't believe she'd actually said the words. Sam's courteous manner changed so abruptly, Molly almost winced at the expression of fury she saw on his face.

"Your mother was a beautiful and charming woman. At seventeen I looked at her no differently than any number of men. If your father told you anything else, he was a liar."

Molly felt her own temper surge at the slur against her father. "My father said you were a womanizing rake, Mr. Brannigan. And I believe I agree with him."

He towered above her, his hazel eyes so dark they seemed almost black. His jaw was set, and the cords on his neck strained with his effort at control. "As I said before, Miss James, you have a lot to learn about men."

"I think you'd better leave, Mr. Brannigan. If you need to speak with me further, you may contact my lawyer, Henry Thompson."

"You're determined to make trouble, aren't you? Determined to dredge up the whole sordid mess." He grabbed her arm and shoved her up against the barn. "If you were a man, I'd beat some sense into you."

Molly's temper heated to the level matching Sam's. She refused to back down to a Brannigan, now or ever. "Go ahead, Mr. Brannigan. If you're anything like your father, manhandling a woman should come easy for you!"

Sam's control snapped. "Why, you unfeeling little wench. You're as cold and heartless as your father. Maybe you belong in those breeches after all!" His lip curved menacingly. He took in her anger, the rise and fall of her bosom beneath her threadbare shirt. "Then again, maybe there's some trace of woman inside that tantalizing body of yours."

Reaching behind her, he circled her waist with his arm and hauled her against him. Bringing his mouth down cruelly, he slashed his lips across hers, punishing her, hurting her as she'd hurt him. Molly struggled against him, felt his muscles bunch, felt the heat of his mouth, then the wetness of his tongue as he forced her lips apart and thrust between her teeth. She wanted to hate him, wanted to lash out at him, hurt him, but instead she felt a bitter regret for the harsh words she'd spoken and a warmth in the pit of her stomach. Against her will, her lips parted even more and Sam's tongue moved deeper, beginning to tease instead of force.

Shifting her wrists above her head, he continued his assault. His lips, no longer cruel, felt warm and full and wonderful. He smelled woodsy, and his short-cropped beard brushed against her cheek. Still he kissed her, exploring her mouth, tasting her, exciting her. When he released his hold, Molly slipped her arms around his neck and clung to him, knowing if she let go, her knees would buckle. She heard him groan as his mouth moved to the place behind her ear, then his lips trailed kisses along the side of her throat.

When he covered her lips again, Molly could barely think. His hands were wound in the thick mass of her hair, which was now freed from its ribbon. His chest pressed against her so tightly she thought she might be crushed beneath his weight. But she didn't care. She felt his hands roving down her back to her waist, then dipping lower to cup her bottom and pull her even more solidly against him. The tender kisses Molly had known before had never prepared her for this. She was drowning in liquid fire, feeling achy and shivery and uncertain. She hated it—and she loved it.

Sam was fighting the flames scorching his

soul. He'd wanted the girl for weeks—ever since he'd seen her at the stream. He'd known it would be like this . . . but he hadn't really believed it, because nothing he'd experienced had ever felt like this. He wanted to take her right here beside the barn, wildly, passionately, as he now believed she wanted, too. Her breath betrayed the coppery taste of her desire, not sweet and warm, but hot and wet and wanton. God, how he wanted her.

Kissing her deeply, Sam unbuttoned the front of her shirt. He slipped his hand inside to caress her smooth skin, his fingers straying to the hard bud of her nipple. He felt her tremble, heard her groan, then she stiffened and tried to pull free.

"Stop! Sam, please!"

She tore away from him, her eyes a luminous blue. She kept backing away, shaking her head as if she understood none of what had just happened.

"Molly, I'm sorry," he told her, watching her with a feeling of regret. "I didn't mean for this to happen."

"Don't say it." Still she backed away. "Don't say anything more . . . please."

"Molly, listen to me."

"No! I don't want to hear it! Just go away and leave me alone. Go back to the widow. Go anyplace you want, except here."

Sam watched her, fighting the hot tremors still coursing through his blood. As if reading his thoughts, her eyes traveled downward, and her face flamed red.

"Oh, God," she whispered, turning away.

He wanted to go to her, wanted to say something that would comfort her, but he was afraid he'd only make things worse. As passionate as she'd been, Molly appeared to be an innocent. "I'm sorry," was all he said.

Settling his hat across his brow, he headed toward the big buckskin standing a short distance away. He'd give the girl some time to sort things out, then he'd be back. There were a great many things to settle, and he intended to do exactly that. He was determined to end the feud between the two families, determined to set things straight . . . and now, determined to have Molly James.

Molly's heart finally resumed its even beat as Sam rode out of sight. Good Lord, what had gotten into her? She'd never let a man kiss her like that—never even wanted one to. But every time she thought of the way he'd touched her, his intimate caresses, his wide, tanned hands, she felt a surge of fire in her blood. Richard Anthony had never made her feel that way. For that matter, *nobody* had ever made her feel that way.

She was glad she'd asked him about her mother; she felt sure he'd told her the truth. For some reason, his honesty comforted her. Then the image of creamy skin, gleaming pale blond hair, and the delicate features of the widow Rose came to mind.

Molly groaned at the thought. Why hadn't she fought him? How could she have made such a fool of herself? He was probably laughing at her all the way back to the ranch. Molly sighed aloud and picked up her pitchfork. This time, when she attacked the huge pile of straw, she pretended it was the slender widow's backside she stabbed with her tines.

She'd been working only minutes when the sound of heavy footfalls echoing inside the barn interrupted her. Laying the pitchfork aside a second time, she walked into the darkened interior to investigate, wondering if one of the hands had quit work early. As her eyes adjusted to the dim light, she spotted her uncle's somber, black-haired figure and her heartbeat thudded uncomfortably.

"Uncle Jason . . . when did you get back?" She prayed it had been after Sam had gone, but as she focused on her uncle's face, she dreaded his reply.

"I returned in time to see your lewd display outside. I returned in time to see you make a spectacle of yourself with that . . . that . . . heathen! I returned in time to put a stop to it once and for all!" As he spoke, he circled her, putting himself between her and the door, and Molly felt a coil of fear in the pit of her stomach.

"It wasn't what it seemed, Uncle. Mr. Brannigan just lost his temper, that's all. He didn't mean it. He apologized before he left; you . . . you must have heard him."

"It is not Mr. Brannigan's conduct I'm concerned with, Molly—it's yours." Though he spoke quietly, his anger was there in the set of his shoulders, the tension in the lines of his face.

When he moved beneath a ray of sunlight piercing a split in the wall, Molly caught the glitter of fury in his eyes.

She'd have to brazen it out, bluff her way by him. He was moving closer, herding her into the corner. What in God's name did he intend to do?

"I . . . I'm sorry, Uncle. I regret what happened just as much as he does," Molly tried to explain. "I assure you, it won't happen again."

He kept closing in on her, getting nearer, forcing her back to the wall, leaving her no escape. "Just what do you intend to do?" she asked nervously, noticing the odd light had returned to his eyes.

He smiled tightly. "I intend to rid you of your demon lust. I intend to show you the means to your salvation. Punishment is God's forgiveness."

Molly glanced around, seeking a means of escape, knowing a confrontation was her only avenue. Then she saw the whip.

Inching closer, Jason pulled the buggy whip from behind his back, showing it to her as if it were some sacred object. "I've tried to be patient with you, Molly, tried to make you understand. You refused to heed my warnings, and look where it's led you. It's time someone disciplined you, Molly. It's not too late for you to change. I'm the hand of God. I will mete out your punishment in His name, and you will be forgiven. Turn around, Molly. Turn around and accept God's will."

Molly stood frozen, unbelieving. The long, thin whip loomed above her, dancing like a cobra in a macabre ballet. This couldn't be happening. It was a nightmare, a terrible dream. She shook her head slowly from side to side; then, seeing the look of cold determination in her uncle's glittering black eyes, she broke free of her trance. She tried to rush past him, but he gripped her arm, his fingers biting into her flesh. He dropped the whip and slapped her hard across the face with the back of his hand, hurling her into the straw on the floor of the barn.

She could taste her own blood, smell the musky animal odor of the barn. Panicky now, she climbed to her feet and again tried to bolt past him. His second blow sent her spinning to the ground, her head cracking against one of the wooden stalls. She felt dizzy, and her head throbbed fiercely—then she felt the first sting of the lash.

"Accept your punishment, Molly. Learn from it. You don't have to be a wanton. God will forgive you." The lash cut through the air, and Molly rolled onto her stomach, raising her hands over her head to protect her face from the slicing blows. Each slash burned across her back, and she clenched her teeth against the pain. Twice she tried to grab the whip, hoping to pull it from Jason's hands, but got only a stinging slice for her efforts. She was afraid to stand up, afraid her dizziness would overwhelm her, leave her unprotected against the blows. Again and again, the thin leather whistled through the air to land with unerring accuracy on her back. The worn fabric of her white cotton shirt was no protection at all; the whip sliced through fabric and skin with equal authority.

"Repent and God will forgive you. Repent and you will be saved."

The lash sang and cut, and Molly realized the cries in her throat were echoing off the walls of the barn. They only seemed to drive him on.

She had to get up and fight him. She had to, but she couldn't. Her head was spinning with pain and fear.

"I'm God's right hand, Molly. I've got to save you." More strokes slashed her, and waves of pain threatened to drown her in agony. The whir of the whip echoed in her ears, followed by the slap against her flesh and her own pain-filled moans. Again and again, until she knew her skin was a patchwork of blood and cloth. *Would he never stop?* The bile tight in her throat, Molly waited for the onslaught to cease and realized it already had. When she turned toward her uncle, he had already gone.

Pain engulfed her. Trembling all over, terrified he'd return to beat her again, Molly staggered toward the pasture. If she could get to True, she could escape. Escape! The word drove her on like a beacon of light in a storm. She swallowed hard, put two fingers between her dry lips, but couldn't make a sound. *True. Please, True, where are you? I need you, boy. Please come to me.* She clutched the railing and fought another wave of dizziness, then she opened the gate and tried to whistle again, but still no sound would come.

Then True was there, snorting and blowing as if he sensed her fear.

She was too weak to saddle him, too terrified of her uncle's return. Using all the strength she could muster, she climbed the heavy wooden gate and slipped onto True's back, looping her arms around his neck and locking her fingers together. True moved out of the pasture stepping briskly, sensing something was wrong, yet letting her guide him with her arms and knees.

She headed him across the meadow toward the rise. She knew her destination—there was only one place she would go for help. Sam. Sam would know what to do. Sam would help her. *Sam. Sam. Sam.* She repeated the word like a litany—chanting his name, believing that he would help, that he would care. She didn't stop to question her feelings; she didn't have the strength. She listened to the voice that spoke Sam's name and blotted all other thoughts from her mind. She clenched her legs tighter around True's sleek belly as he climbed the rise. She would take the shortcut. The terrain would test her, but the time she would save would be worth it.

She could feel the blood on her back beginning to congeal. She felt the dense throbbing in her head, and knew her lip was split and swollen. How could this have happened? How could her aunt have married a man like that? But then maybe her aunt had never discovered the kind of man Jason Foley really was.

She thought of Sam, of his gentle concern, even when he was angry. Sam would never hurt her. Sam would help her. She laced her fingers tighter, fighting the dizziness that threatened to unseat her. As she closed her eyes against a bout of nausea, the hazy image of a huge golden lion, snarling and snapping, threatened her, but she wasn't afraid.

Then the lion became Sam, and he was holding her, soothing her. True stepped into a hole, went to his knees, and nearly lost her balance. She knew she wouldn't be able to mount him again. The trail seemed wrong somehow. Had she gotten lost? Had she closed her eyes and missed a familiar landmark, a turn in the forest? She couldn't last much longer. She'd hit her head harder than she thought; the pain in her head hurt worse than her back. Unconsciousness beckoned, promising relief from the pain, the aches in her arms and legs, her fear of the unknown.

She should have stayed on the main trail, she thought. Someone would have found her. Joaquin would be looking as soon as he discovered her gone. The old trail was never used; few even knew it existed. The steep canyons and rocky crags could hide her body for days, maybe even weeks. She swallowed the bile in her throat and urged True on. She'd make it somehow, and then she'd deal with Jason Foley.

In a blinding flash, the thought of Foley owning the Lady Jay tore through her mind, and she clenched her teeth and hung on harder. Foley would not defeat her. No one would defeat her. Dropping her head onto True's mane, she headed along the narrow, steep trail and prayed to a different God than Foley's that somehow she would reach Cedar Creek . . . and Sam.

"Well, lad, it's good to have you home again." Sam clapped his younger brother on the back as he stepped into the massive front room of the Cedar Creek ranch house.

"It's good to be back, Sam. Believe it or not, I've missed you two."

Emmet stepped forward and caught the slim young man in a big bear hug. "You're looking fit, boy."

Peter Brannigan smiled. He'd enjoyed these last few years in law school, but it always felt good to be home.

"I thought you weren't coming in till tonight," Sam said.

"My meeting in Virginia City got canceled, so I came on home. Figured it was a good chance to check up on both of you, make sure you're taking care of my interests properly. After all, I'm the family's new financial advisor, aren't I?"

"You sure are, boy," Emmet assured him. "Know you'll do a fine job, too."

Peter smiled. Actually, Sam would continue to make the decisions, just as he had for the past ten years. And Peter would have it no other way. Sam knew the ranching and timber industries backward and forward. He'd built Cedar Creek into the empire it was today. But Peter was a full-fledged lawyer now, and he'd make sure the family's interests were protected, see that there were no loopholes in any of the myriad contracts and legal documents Sam signed each year. He would be an asset to the family, Peter was sure of it. He knew Sam was proud of him.

Harvard had been Sam's idea, and it suited Peter's goals perfectly. He liked city life. Sam and Emmet were country boys, though Sam was far better educated than Emmet. Peter planned to open an office in Sacramento City—close to his brothers and the ranch, but in a city sophisticated enough to suit his tastes. And Sacramento was the capital of California. Peter knew Sam hoped he'd enter politics, and the thought appealed to Peter more than a little.

"You just make sure those Easterners don't take advantage of us poor old country boys." Emmet grinned at Peter, and Peter grinned at Sam, who lounged, smiling, against the back of the wide leather couch.

"I could use a little help with my bags," Peter said, moving toward the door. Sam and Emmet eagerly moved to help him. Peter watched his oldest brother thoughtfully as he reached into the back of the buggy and effortlessly hoisted out two huge leather bags. Sam had been like a father to him, since Peter had only been nine when Shamus died in prison. Sam had returned from the war two years later, shocked to find the ranch in financial trouble and his father dead. He'd taken the reins immediately, saving the ranch and earning his two brothers' love and respect.

"Lee Chin is cookin' up a storm," Sam said, bursting through the door with the baggage. "Says he needs to fatten you up some."

"You certainly haven't gotten fat." Peter playfully poked Sam in the ribs. "I thought by now the widow would have you married off, and you'd be fat and happy."

Sam's smile faded. "Not a chance, lad. You know I'm not the marrying kind. I leave all that to Emmet."

Emmet chuckled, his thickset body shaking with mirth as he, too, piled the floor high with bags. "You wouldn't be sayin' that, Sam, if you had a wife like Patience. Woman like that keeps a man warm in winter—and smilin' all the time!"

Sam laughed heartily. "Unfortunately, Emmet, there don't seem to be any women like Patience left."

"You've got that one right, Sam," Peter agreed.

"You and the kids *are* coming over for dinner?" Sam said to Emmet. "If you don't, we'll be eating leftover pork ribs for a week."

"That cinches it. You know how Emmet Junior loves Lee Chin's ribs."

"Speaking of little Emmet," Peter said, moving back toward the door, "I've got something for him in my satchel. It's still in the buggy."

"Come on," Emmet said, "I'll help you fetch it." The two men skirted the already huge pile of baggage blocking the entry and headed outside.

Sam's chest swelled with pride. He was lucky to have such a family. Lucky to have so much love around him. He thought of Molly James, unloved and unwanted all those years. He knew the truth about Mal James, even if Molly wouldn't face it. Mal had barely had time for the girl, and he'd sent her away so he wouldn't be bothered. Without his love and support, she'd toughened up, all right. She was one hard lady. But her kiss told him something he'd suspected all along. Molly had her love bottled up inside her: Sam could sense it, just waiting to be tapped. It would take someone special, someone willing to put out the effort . . .

But the real question was, did Sam want to be that someone? He'd never been willing to make that kind of commitment before. But then he hadn't met Molly James.

"Sam! Come quick." Emmet's husky voice jolted him from his thoughts. "Hurry! We got trouble!"

# *Chapter Eight*

MOVING QUICKLY THROUGH the door, Sam glanced at his brother's worried face, then followed the line of his gaze to the snorting black beast dancing a few feet away.

"Won't let me git near him," Emmet said, then spoke softly to the animal. "Whoa, son. Steady now. We ain't gonna hurt you."

"Let me, Emmet." Sam felt his chest tighten as his glance leveled on the small red-haired woman who fiercely clutched the animal's mane.

"The horse knows me. Maybe he'll let me get close."

Sam approached the big gelding cautiously, worried the animal might bolt or hurt the girl in some way. "Easy, True. Let me have her, boy. I'll take care of her, I promise." He stroked the sleek neck and felt the horse tremble. True's eyes rolled up, exposing the whites, but he didn't back away.

"It's all right, True," Sam soothed. "Molly, it's Sam." He edged closer, started to lift her from the horse's back, then realized her fingers were locked so tight they wouldn't come free. Her thick red hair, matted with blood, hung down to the horse's knees.

"By the saints!" Sam cursed. "What kind of animal would do this?" His glance took in the girl's bloody back, the bruises on her face, her cut and swollen lip. Swallowing a second string of oaths, he pried the small hands free and scooped her into his arms.

"Sam?" Her voice was a croaking whisper.

"I'm right here, Molly." Her small face rested against his chest. He could feel fresh blood from the wounds on her back begin to seep into the sleeves of his shirt as he carried her toward the house, and knew a helpless rage he hadn't felt since his father had died. Emmet and Peter trailed behind him, their features pale and grim.

"Emmet, send one of the men to fetch Doc Weston," Sam instructed.

"No doctor!" Molly cried, raising herself up.

"Molly, don't be foolish."

"No doctor, Sam." She licked her dry lips.

"Or . . . or I'll get back on that horse, I swear it."

Sam took a deep, steadying breath and spoke to Emmet, who stared at Molly in utter disbelief. "We can probably do anything the doctor could, anyway. Let it be for now." He sidestepped Peter's bags and headed up the stairs, opening a bedroom door with his booted foot. Peter rushed in to turn back the sheets. Sam placed Molly on the bed facedown, then carefully began pulling off her boots. "Tell Lee Chin to mix up some chamomile and lard and bring me a pitcher of water and some towels—and a pair of scissors and some bandages."

"Who is she?" Peter asked as Emmet left the room.

"Molly James," Sam answered stiffly, removing her second boot.

Lee Chin rushed in with the water and towels. His dark, slanted eyes grew almost round when he saw the bloodied figure on the bed. "I get chamomile."

Sam just nodded, and the little Chinese fled the room.

"What the hell do you suppose happened to her?" Emmet asked, walking back up to the bed.

"I don't know, but I intend to find out."

"Patience is over at Mrs. Colby's, Sam," Emmet said. "Looks like you'll have to do the doctorin'—unless you want Lee Chin to do it."

"I'll do it," Sam said flatly. Even if he hadn't had a sneaking suspicion the girl's beating had something to do with him, he wouldn't have allowed anyone but himself to tend her. The thought disturbed him more than a little.

"We'll wait downstairs," Peter said. His slightly green expression said Molly looked even worse than Sam thought. Again he nodded, and Emmet led Peter away. When the door closed, Sam turned his attention to the girl lying quietly on the bed. Her eyes were open, staring straight ahead, and he wondered what she was thinking.

"You're going to be all right, lass. I'm going to get you cleaned up and put some medicine on your back."

"Could I have some water?" she asked, swallowing with a bit of difficulty.

"Of course." He raised her head, placed the cup against her lips, then tipped it up gently, allowing the cool liquid to refresh her.

"Thank you," she whispered, then closed her eyes and slipped into blissful unconsciousness.

Sam said a prayer of thanks, wanting her to suffer as little as possible. Deftly, he cut away the pieces of bloody fabric that had once been her shirt. He tried to remain businesslike, but his hand shook slightly as he worked. When he lifted her to remove the remainder of her shirt, his eyes locked on her two full, perfectly formed breasts. Luscious pink nipples blossomed at each crest, and no matter how hard he fought it, his mind kept conjuring the image even after she once more rested comfortably on her stomach.

He slid her heavy denim breeches over her hips and tried not to notice the rounded curves of her bottom. Deciding to leave her dignity intact as much as possible, he left on her lacy cotton drawers, but noticed that in several places the whip had sliced through the tender flesh beneath.

It was all he could do to keep his temper under control, even though he knew for the time being he had no choice. But when he discovered her assailant's identity, he intended to beat the man senseless.

Sam washed away some of the blood from Molly's back, carefully rinsed out the sticky ends of her hair and set the mass aside, then continued until the water in the bowl ran red. Anticipating the problem, Lee Chin appeared several times with a fresh bowl and more clean towels, then finally arrived with the chamomile mixture, some rubbing alcohol, and a bottle of whiskey. Again he closed the door, leaving them alone.

Molly bolted upright with the first dab of the acrid, stinging alcohol, and Sam caught a second glimpse of her full, round breasts.

"I'm sorry, lass," he told her, pushing her gently back down on the bed.

For a moment, Molly felt confused. Where was she? And why was her back burning like the flames of hell? When she recognized Sam's bearded features, she relaxed a little, feeling safe, but still unsure from what. A bit more strength returned—along with the memory of what had happened. Then, glancing down, she discovered her naked breasts and turned crimson from head to toe. She hugged the pillow tightly against her.

Sam pulled the sheet up to her waist. "I was hoping you'd sleep through this," he told her. "I know it burns like Hades, but I'm afraid we have no choice. We've got to make sure there's no infection. Take a sip of this. It'll help a little."

Molly complied, sipping the whiskey from the cup he held, then grimacing as the fiery liquid burned a trail down her throat. Though her back still burned like holy bejesus, her dizziness had lessened, and the knowledge she was safe helped her to feel stronger.

"Ready?" Sam asked. She noticed the grim set of his features.

Molly nodded. As he dabbed the alcohol into her wounds, fiery pain seared her. With every grimace, Sam flinched as much as she. Clamping her teeth into the pillow, she stifled the cries in her throat.

Molly closed her eyes, fighting against the terrible stinging, and doing a fair job of being stoic—till she felt Sam lower the sheet and slide down her drawers. Forgetting her pain, she shrieked with outrage instead.

"What do you think you're doing!" she demanded.

Sam lifted one corner of his mouth in an amused smile. "I'm putting alcohol on your backside. Now please let me finish. I promise I'll close my eyes."

Knowing she had no choice, Molly hugged the pillow tight across her chest and fought down the tide of embarrassment washing over her. In seconds, the big man was once again sloshing the burning liquid on her back, and all Molly could think of were the angry coals burning into her flesh. Again she stifled the whimper in her throat.

"It's okay to cry, you know." Sam returned the cork to the bottle and set it aside.

"I never cry. I don't even remember how."

"Never?" he pressed, finished with his loathsome task. Unlike the alcohol, the chamomile would only soothe, not burn.

"Not since my mother died." She looked away from him, not wanting to meet his gaze.

Sam felt a tug at his heart.

"This will take away the sting," he promised, dipping his fingers into the chamomile compound. "Then I'll bandage you and let you get some sleep." He began applying the soothing mixture and felt her muscles relax a little beneath his hands. Again rage welled up in him. "Before I go, Molly, I want you to tell me who did this." His hand shook a little as he fought to control his anger.

"No."

"*No!* What do you mean, *no?* I want to know who the hell did this!" Sam clenched his teeth, fighting to remain calm

"It's none of your business, Sam. I'll take care of it myself, as soon as I'm able."

Sam eyed the small woman lying on the bed. She'd take care of it! That was a joke. "Just what in hell makes you think you can handle the bastard any better the second time than you did the first?"

When Molly turned her round blue eyes on him, Sam felt their chilling glare. "Because the next time, I'll have a gun."

Taking a steadying breath, Sam knelt beside the bed. "Listen to me, Molly. Let me help you. Tell me who did this."

"No."

"Well, at least tell me why."

Molly didn't answer.

"It was because of what happened between us, wasn't it?" He cradled her cheek in his palm, forcing her to meet his gaze.

Still no answer.

"Wasn't it?" he shouted.

She closed her eyes.

"Tell me, damn it!"

"Yes," she whispered. "He saw us kissing."

"Who?" Sam asked, his fury threatening to suffocate him. "Who saw us kissing? Joaquin? Surely Joaquin would never do this."

She shook her head. "I can't tell you."

Suddenly Sam knew. "The reverend," he said, his voice so deep and cold that Molly shivered at the sound of it. "He was at the dance. I talked with him for a moment. He's your guardian, isn't he?"

"Listen to me, Sam."

"Jason Foley did this."

"Listen to me!" Molly demanded. "I can't let anyone know what happened. I've worked too hard to gain the men's respect. This would destroy it. They would think I was weak, that I couldn't take care of myself. I can't let them know Foley did this to me!" She was looking at him with such utter despair in her eyes, Sam's fury ebbed a little.

"I've got to think of the Lady Jay," she said.

"Please, Sam, promise me you won't tell anyone, or do anything that might give me away."

"Molly, you can't expect me just to let this go. I'm the one who's responsible."

"You have to, Sam. I can't even tell Joaquin. He might try to kill Foley."

"I don't blame him."

Molly took Sam's hand. "Is there some place I could stay for a few days? Just until I'm feeling well enough to go home. I know it's a lot to ask, but there's no one else I can turn to."

"We're neighbors, Molly. We're supposed to help each other. I know you don't believe that, but it's true."

Molly felt a surge of guilt that almost overwhelmed her. "On second thought, maybe you could take me into Truckee. I could stay at the hotel."

"That's nonsense, Molly. You'll stay right here."

"But you don't understand, Sam. Even if you help me, it won't change things. I . . . I mean about the lawsuit and all. I have to go through with it. I just have to."

Sam looked down at her in disbelief. Her eyes seemed to plead for understanding. Wordlessly, he bandaged her back, then quietly moved toward the door.

"Get some rest, lass," he told her resignedly. "I'll send a rider over to the Lady Jay. He can tell your *guardian* that Patience is sick, so you've agreed to stay with her a couple of days. I'm sure he'll understand."

"Thank you," she whispered.

With a last glance into her round blue eyes, Sam stalked from the room.

Emmet and Peter both rose as Sam descended the open stairway into the front room.

"How is she?" Emmet asked.

"I think she'll be all right. She'll carry those scars for a while, but I don't think they're permanent. She's got a nasty lump on the head; we'll have to keep a close eye on her." Sam sank heavily down in his usual brown leather chair, and his two brothers returned to their places on the couch.

"Who'd she say done it?" Emmet asked.

"She wouldn't say," Sam evaded, fighting a flash of anger.

Emmet leaped to his feet. "Why the hell not?"

"She's afraid it'll undermine her authority with the men. She's more worried about that damn ranch than she is about herself. Worst of all, she's right. She's had a helluva time getting men to work for her. This would just reinforce the fact she's a woman."

"Sometimes I wonder if she really is," Emmet muttered. "Most gals would have been crying and fussin' somethin' awful, but not her. 'No doctor,' she says, 'or I'll get back on that horse.' Darnedest thing I've ever seen. Just like that day you busted her in the jaw."

"What!" Peter leaped to his feet alongside Emmet, turning accusing green eyes toward Sam. "*You* beat her up, too?"

"Simmer down, Peter." Sam sighed wearily,

feeling a surge of guilt. "She was taking pot-shots at us up on James Pass. She was wearing those breeches of hers, and I thought it was a man."

"Woman's got ice water for blood," Emmet said, shaking his head as he sank back down on the couch.

Sam thought of her bloody red back, but didn't bother to correct him. "She needs a place to stay, Emmet. Just for a couple of days. She can't stay here with me. Do you think Patience would mind?"

"Patience was mighty fired up when she heard about that lawsuit. You know how she is about family and all. But I suppose now that Miss James is wantin' our help, the lawsuit'll be dropped, so Patience ought to agree. She don't ever stay mad for long."

"The lawsuit is not going to be dropped," Sam said. "Miss James was insufferably clear about that. But she's still our neighbor; we can't very well turn her out. . . . Besides, it was my fault she got the beating in the first place."

"Your fault!" Peter exclaimed. "This whole episode is becoming more incredible by the moment. How was all this your fault?"

Sam raked his fingers through his thick blond hair. "I went to see her today. To return her comb. At least that was my excuse. I wanted to try to convince her not to continue with the suit. I'm afraid tempers got a little short and I . . . well . . . I kissed her."

"You kissed her?" Emmet grew more incredulous.

"Yes." His gaze met Emmet's slightly speculative one. "And I can assure you the lady does not have ice water for blood."

"I think she's quite lovely," Peter put in.

"I'm warnin' you, Sam." Emmet moved to stand in front of Sam's chair. "That woman's nothin' but trouble. Patience ain't gonna be none too pleased to have Molly James foisted on her."

For the first time, Sam smiled. "You may be in for a surprise on that score. Miss James has a way of insinuating herself before you even know it's happening. Even Patience may find her hard to resist."

"She's trouble, I'm tellin' ya. Look at the commotion she's already stirred up. That ranch is all she cares about. I never seen a body so blasted determined to succeed as that one."

Now Peter grinned. "Unless it was Sam when he came home from the war."

Sam and Emmet laughed aloud. "You've got a point there, lad," Sam said. "I'll try to remember that." He rose and headed toward the door. "Right now, I think I'll see to the lass's horse. I think she'd take a whip to me, if I let anything happen to him." Sam plucked his hat from its peg as he strode through the massive plank door.

"It was awfully nice of you to let me stay here, Mrs. Brannigan." Molly had been staying with Emmet and Patience for two days. Her back was feeling better, and her head throbbed hardly at all. She was determined to return to the ranch tomorrow.

"We're neighbors, Miss James. Neighbors are 'sposed to help each other." The brown-haired woman continued her stitchery. They were seated on the wide covered porch in front of the sprawling log house Emmet and Patience Brannigan called home.

"That's what Sam said."

"Sam's a good man, Miss James. Maybe you ought to pay more attention to what he tells you."

Molly ignored the fair-skinned woman's remark, but her conscience pricked her more than a little. Sam had been good to her, cared for her, and all she'd ever done was cause him and his family grief. Of course, the Brannigans had certainly caused the Jameses more than their share.

"But then, you Jameses never were much good at bein' neighborly," Patience added a bit peevishly, raising her well-rounded figure up from the rocker she'd been sitting in. "I've got preserves boilin' on the cookstove. You'll have to excuse me."

Molly nodded, knowing she was being summarily dismissed. Patience Brannigan had barely tolerated her presence, refusing to call her anything but *Miss James* and preferring to keep their conversations to a minimum if they spoke at all. She was a buxom woman, but more lush than fat, and Emmet, Molly could tell, found his wife's ample figure more than a little attractive. In the past two days, Molly had discovered a married couple with two wonderful children who were still desperately in love. Sometimes, when she watched them together, it was hard not to feel a stab of envy.

Emmet and Patience were well suited. Neither was highly educated, nor did either seem to care. The couple was warm and loving and devoted to their family. And both Emmet and Patience practically worshiped Sam.

It seemed to Molly that each of the Brannigan men had gained exactly what he wanted out of life. Sam had his empire; Peter his schooling and career; and Emmet his home and family.

"H-Hello, M-Miss J-James." Little Emmet Samuel sauntered up beside her on the porch.

"Hello, Emmet. How are you today?"

"F-Fine." Emmet Junior spoke little. At first, Molly could only get him to smile for her, but by the second day he'd been curious enough, and trusting enough, to speak. At seven years old, Emmet looked a lot like his mother. He was fair-skinned, with soft brown hair and gentle blue eyes. He was a bit more frail than his hearty father, but there was no mistaking the straight Brannigan shoulders or the finely shaped mouth.

"Your mama's putting up preserves today. Think maybe we could help?"

Little Emmet grinned from ear to ear and nodded vigorously. "Goo-goose-b-berry." He rubbed his tummy in circles, demonstrating his affinity for the delicious preserves.

"They're my favorite, too," Molly agreed. "Especially when they're warm." She reached out a hand and Emmet accepted it, leading her toward the back of the house, where his mother, humming as she worked, bent over the big black stove. Two-months-old Charity Ann gurgled softly from her cradle in the corner.

Patience Brannigan looked up at the two intruders who entered her domain. She was determined to dislike Molly James, but seeing her there, holding little Emmet's hand, Patience felt her resolve weaken. What miracle had the girl performed to reach her son so quickly? Emmet avoided most people, terrified of their often cruel remarks about his stuttering. But he'd taken to Molly almost from the first. Whatever the reason, the pretty redhead had stolen the little boy's heart.

"Is there anything we could do to help?" Molly asked. "I'm afraid I don't know much about canning, but I'd be more than happy to learn."

Patience looked at Molly, thinking about the mother the girl had never had, and try as she might, she felt a maternal pull at her heart. Molly was only six years younger than Patience, but smiling like that, so guilelessly with those round blue eyes, she looked more like a child. No wonder Sam was so taken with her. Patience had seen it in his eyes when he'd brought her over in the back of the wagon. If the girl had a lick of sense, she'd quit tryin' to act like a man and set her cap for Sam. Patience grimaced at the thought. All she needed was to have a James for a sister-in-law.

"Anybody home?"

Patience recognized Peter's soft voice coming

from the parlor. "Out here," she called. "You might as well come on back—the rest of the world seems to be in here."

Peter strode through the door, tall and handsome in a dark gray tailcoat and navy trousers. His eyes assessed Molly, who wore a soft pink batiste Patience had taken in for her, and his face broke into an appreciative smile.

"Hello, Miss James. You're looking much better today."

Molly hadn't missed his appraising glance. "You mean because I'm wearing a dress, Mr. Brannigan?"

Peter's smile turned sheepish. "I . . . I meant no offense."

"All three of you scat outa my kitchen," Patience said, waving a wooden spoon. "Unless . . . Emmet, you want a bowl of these preserves?"

Emmet Junior nodded enthusiastically and moved to the kitchen table as Molly and Peter walked into the parlor.

"Sam took care of sending that note you wrote to Joaquin," Peter told her.

"You've all been very kind." Molly sat down on the settee. She'd written to Joaquin, since Angel couldn't read. The note confirmed Sam's message that Patience was ill and needed Molly to stay with her. Molly knew the couple would wonder at the fact she was helping a Brannigan, but the Sanchezes had given up trying to understand Molly years ago.

"May I?" Peter indicated the place beside her.

"Of course."

"Miss James, I've come to ask you to reconsider your suit. James Pass has been used by both families for years. If you go to court, the whole sordid feud will be dug up. The gossip will hurt both of our families."

"I have no family, Mr. Brannigan."

"But surely you don't want to suffer all the social stigma again?"

"I want what is mine, Mr. Brannigan." She leveled her gaze on him.

"But we have just as much legal claim as you."

"I guess we'll have to let the courts decide that."

"Is there nothing I can say to make you see reason?" His sincerity pierced her armor but only strengthened her resolve.

"Your idea of reason and mine are different. Try to remember that."

Peter eyed her boldly. "As lovely as you are, Miss James, in your presence it's difficult to remember one's own name."

Incredulous at the young man's words, Molly turned to face him, feeling at a disadvantage for the very first time. "Why, Peter, I . . . I'm afraid you've taken me quite off guard."

"I like the way you say my name, Miss James. May I call you Molly?"

Molly hadn't meant to refer to him so intimately, but now she had no choice but to allow the privilege in return. "Of course." Peter Brannigan was an extremely attractive young man. Molly guessed him to be only a few years older than she. He was tall and whipcord-lean. His light brown hair framed smooth, arching brows and intelligent green eyes.

"How much longer will you be staying with us?" Peter asked.

"I'm leaving tomorrow." Though she dreaded facing her uncle, she hated the thought of being indebted to the Brannigans even more. Her back still hurt but the pain in her head was gone; it was time to go home.

"So soon? I was hoping we might get better acquainted. How would you feel about my visiting you at the Lady Jay?"

"I . . . "

Sam's deep voice, echoing from the open doorway, interrupted her stunned reply. "Speaking from experience, lad, I can assure you your greeting will be none too welcome—that is, unless you can manage to get Miss James to stand still long enough for a kiss."

Sam eyed the young woman sitting on the settee. Her face flamed red, and Sam knew she was quietly fuming inside. He didn't really blame her. He hadn't meant to goad her. In fact, he'd been eager to see her today—too eager. Seeing his brother beside her, clearly professing his intention to court her, had unleashed a jealous demon that surprised even Sam.

"Once more, Mr. Brannigan"—Molly turned her furious blue gaze on Sam—"I'll remind you to stay out of my affairs. However, Peter, your brother is right. I don't think it would be a good idea for us to become too friendly. I'm already in your debt. I just want matters settled between the Lady Jay and Cedar Creek. When that's done, maybe we'll all be able to live in peace."

"Peter," Sam said sternly, "I believe Emmet wants some company on the trip into town."

"But today's Saturday. You always go to Truckee on Saturday."

Sam's hazel eyes darkened at his little brother's unfair tactics. It was obvious Molly well understood the meaning of his words, so he decided to address the issue straight on. "Mrs. Rose is in San Francisco for a few weeks, if that's what you're wondering."

He didn't mention the startling sense of relief he'd felt upon receiving Lilly's note. He'd already decided not to see her, not with Molly so close. His mind would have been occupied with thoughts of the pretty little redhead. Even the widow's skillful lovemaking couldn't have swayed him now, and he needed some time to sort out his feelings.

Peter rose from the settee. "Good-bye, Molly," he said deliberately, and Sam didn't miss the implication. Peter headed toward the door without a backward glance.

When he heard the wagon pull away, Sam approached the young woman sitting stiffly on the settee. "Would an apology make you stop looking at me like that?" Sam asked teasingly. But underneath her furious gaze, he sensed the hurt she hid beneath her anger, and cursed himself for a fool. She might be a Brannigan, she might wear breeches instead of a dress, but inside, Sam felt certain Molly James was a lady.

"You needn't bother, Mr. Brannigan. I'm sure

your family's already low opinion of me couldn't possibly sink any lower."

Sam sat down beside her and lifted her stiff fingers in his hand, brushing them gently against his lips until he felt them relax. "There are so many obstacles already between us, I just didn't want my little brother to be one more."

"And just what is that supposed to mean?"

"It means, *Molly,*" he said, deliberately using her Christian name, "that I want some time to find out what's going on between us."

Molly felt stunned. Was Sam Brannigan trying to tell her he felt something for her? Surely that couldn't be—not when he already had the beautiful widow in his bed. "I'm afraid I don't understand your meaning, Mr. Brannigan. There's absolutely—"

"Sam," he corrected.

"There's absolutely nothing between us, Mr. Brannigan."

"Am I supposed to believe you always let men kiss you like that?"

"I refuse to discuss this any further." Molly clutched her skirt and fought to control her pounding heart.

"All right, Molly. For now, we'll play it your way. Emmet says you're leaving tomorrow. Are you certain you're up to it?"

"I have a ranch to run." Molly refused to look at him, afraid of what he'd see in her eyes. He had a way of spotting the truth. He had a way, all right, a way she found nearly irresistible.

Damn him! Damn him to hell! Why did he have to be a Brannigan?

"I brought something," Sam said, fishing into the front pocket of his snug blue denims.

Molly caught the flash of sunlight on metal as he placed a tiny derringer in her hand.

"It's a three-shot Marston pocket pistol. Thirty-two caliber. If you're half the shot I think you are, you'll only need one of these barrels, but your guardian may be tougher than he looks."

Molly accepted the weapon gratefully and felt her tough veneer slip another notch. "Thank you, Sam."

"How's your back?" he asked, and Molly felt the color rush to her cheeks a second time.

He'd seen more of her than any other man, and made no attempt to disguise the hungry look in his hazel eyes.

Using her favorite tactic, Molly pretended not to notice. "Much better, thank you. I think your salve is a miracle drug."

"My mother's own special concoction." The minute the words were out, he looked as if he wished he hadn't said them. He glanced down at his large hands, then back to her face. "I think I'd best be going. There's plenty to do this time of year. Tell Patience good-bye for me." He moved toward the door.

"I will."

"I'll see you before you leave tomorrow."

Molly nodded, but knew no matter how early he came, she would already be gone.

# Chapter Nine

✦◆✦◆✦

Wearing her jeans, now washed and mended, and one of Emmet's old shirts knotted up around her waist, Molly arrived back at the Lady Jay to find Jason Foley waiting on the porch. A trickle of fear snaked up her spine as she slid off True's back and brushed past him into the house. As much as she despised him for what he had done to her, Foley was just another obstacle she'd have to overcome in order to achieve her goals: reviving the Lady Jay and extracting retribution from the Brannigans.

"Molly," Jason said, following her inside. "We need to talk."

"I have nothing to say to you, *Uncle* Jason." The word left a bitter taste in her mouth.

"Please. At least give me a chance to explain."

Molly turned to face him, her shoulders rigid. "You're my guardian for the next two years, Jason. Unless I want the world to know what you did to me—and I don't—I'll have to tolerate your presence in this house." She'd do anything to keep Jason's beating a secret. With her age and sex already against her, it was imperative she keep things running smoothly and keep the respect of the ranch hands. "I'll listen to what you have to say, but I'm warning you. If you ever lay a hand on me again, I'll shoot you."

Foley paled. "I understand your anger," he said contritely. "I know my punishment was harsh, and in truth I never meant it to go that far. You do something to me, Molly. Make me feel the kind of sinful things I've fought against all my life. You make other men feel them, too—like Mr. Brannigan."

Color flooded Molly's cheeks, forcing her to glance away.

"It's those clothes you wear," he told her. "Your hair. The way you display your body. It's a sin, Molly. Can't you see that? I'm a preacher. It's my job to save souls. Underneath, I believe you're a good girl. I just want to help you."

Molly watched her uncle's face, felt the conviction with which he spoke. He looked a little haggard. His eyes held a hint of remorse.

"I can't forgive you, Jason. What happened between Mr. Brannigan and myself was . . . an unfortunate occurrence that won't happen again. But what you did was wrong. Maybe your intentions were good, I don't know. I'd prefer you leave the Lady Jay, but I don't suppose you'd consider that alternative."

"No. I'm your guardian. I'll not shirk my duty to you."

Molly released a long, slow breath. "Then I guess we'll have to come to some sort of truce."

"I think you should sell the ranch. Move to the East."

"This is not the way for us to start, Jason. I'm a grown woman. I intend to run my life exactly as I see fit. Understand that, and we'll get along. Try to interfere, and I'll stop you—one way or another."

Jason Foley stiffened. "Is there nothing I can say to make you change your mind?"

"No."

"Then at least try to see why I turned to force."

Molly's eyes locked with his. "Beating someone half your size is hardly excusable under any circumstances."

"Have it your way, Molly. At least for the present. I won't give up hope of reaching you. That's my duty as God's servant." He rose from his chair. "Until supper, I bid you good day."

Molly watched him as he strode from the room. Automatically, her hand strayed to the tiny derringer lodged in her pocket. She wondered what Sam would have said to the good Reverend Foley.

As for Molly, she would never trust the man again. She would carry Sam's weapon wherever she went. Just the feel of the cold metal against her fingers gave her a measure of comfort.

In the days that followed, she said nothing of her ordeal to Angel or Joaquin and, true to his word, Sam didn't either. Molly successfully avoided him for the rest of that week and all of the next. Sam stopped by the ranch several times, but Molly had cautioned Angel to tell him she was gone, not that she thought he'd believe it.

By Saturday she was packed and headed for Denver, on her way to negotiate a timber contract with the Denver and Rio Grande Railroad.

"Well, that's it," she told Joaquin, checking the straps securing the lid of her Saratoga trunk. "Let's get going. I don't want to miss my train."

The railroads were building at an incredible

pace, and lumber was at a premium. Obtaining the contract to supply railroad ties was a crucial part of her plan to reestablish the Lady Jay financially. Molly hadn't mentioned her trip to Jason Foley, and he hadn't asked where she was going. It seemed her beating had at least gained her some measure of freedom. Her back, though still lightly scarred, had healed with no complications, but Molly would never forgive or forget the incident.

Standing beside her at the wagon that would take her to the train station, Joaquin frowned down at her and shook his head.

"I still do not like your traveling alone," he said, repeating Angel's words almost verbatim. "Why can I not go with you, or at least you could take Angel. Who will be your chaperone?"

"This is a business trip," Molly said. "I don't need a chaperone. Besides, I need you two here to keep things running smoothly. We can't afford to be any more short-handed than we already are."

"I still do not like it, *hija*." He shoved his huge black sombrero to the back of his head and grabbed one end of the trunk. Willie Barnett, a tall, rangy cowhand, grabbed the other. The trunk was quickly loaded, and with Willie's assistance Molly climbed aboard the high seat of the spring wagon.

She tucked the skirt of her light-brown traveling dress out of the way, and straightened the matching bolero jacket which partially covered the cool ivory blouse beneath. The blouse's muslin fabric was lightweight enough to be comfortable in the hot desert temperatures after the train left the high altitude of the Sierras, yet the color would help disguise the soot and dust the long train ride would guarantee. A narrow-brimmed dark brown hat that matched the trim on her dress covered much of her thick red hair. The rest was pulled into a tight chignon at the nape of her neck.

They arrived in Truckee with little time to spare, and Molly quickly boarded the train. She loved the bustling mountain town with its strange mixture of people: the miners—some who still worked the played-out streams; the timber men who had come to be the lifeblood of Truckee since the decline of the mining industry; a scattering of cattlemen; and the dozens of merchants it took to keep the little town running.

Molly waved to Joaquin, who stood on the platform, his worried frown crinkling the lines of his weathered face, stoically refusing to leave until the train pulled out of the station. One glance at Willie Barnett's wily expression said he was anticipating the hours he would spend in the nearby saloons.

As the train slowly pulled out of the station, Molly watched the town disappear in the distance. The two-story buildings with gay-colored placards advertising their wares that lined Front Street became smaller and smaller as the train ran alongside the crystal-clear Truckee River. Houses dotted the steep hillsides—everything from miners' shanties to three-story Victorian mansions.

Molly observed the town, wondering which of the stately residences belonged to the beautiful Lillian Rose—and just how much time Sam Brannigan spent there. The thought disturbed her more than a little. She sighed as she drew her attention away from Truckee.

Though she was loath to admit it, she'd missed Sam these past two weeks. She couldn't forget that morning beside the barn, the feel of his hands, so big yet so gentle as he cupped her breast and brushed her nipple. His kiss had stirred feelings she hadn't known she could have. When she'd pulled away, she'd felt almost bereft.

Sam made her feel like a woman. But more than that . . . he made her yearn for love. Molly felt a tightening in her chest at the thought. All her life she'd wanted someone to love her. Yet, after the lonely years she'd spent without love, she'd hoped she'd rid herself of the need.

Resigned to the long journey ahead, Molly leaned back against her dark green tapestry seat, forcing thoughts of Sam aside. She was traveling first class, riding the luxuriously appointed Hotel Express. She'd paid a lot of money for this trip, so she might as well relax and enjoy herself.

Her fingers played over the heavy velvet draperies that covered the windows. The Express boasted elegant Silver Palace cars and comfortable Pullman coaches that made into berths at night. The train had its own dining car, serving exquisite multicourse meals. On her trip home from Chicago, Molly had ridden the train west from Cheyenne. East of there, the Union Pacific provided equally luxurious cars.

Relaxed at last, Molly began to enjoy the first leg of her journey. The scenery outside Truckee was spectacular: winding trestles suspended over deep-plunging gorges, green forested hillsides, and grand panoramic vistas from the towering Sierras out over the flatlands of Nevada. The train was roaring along a steep mountain pass when a tall, blue-eyed man entered the car and stopped beside her seat.

"Well, Miss James." Michael Locke smiled warmly. "It seems our paths cross again."

Surprised, Molly turned to face him. "Why, Mr. Locke. What brings you on this journey?"

"May I?" He indicated the place beside her on the brass-trimmed seat.

"Of course."

"I'm on my way to Denver," he said. "I have a meeting with my employers to discuss the upcoming timber contracts. That wouldn't, by any chance, be the same place you're heading?" Michael Locke smiled knowingly, displaying his dimple and a flash of interest in his bright blue eyes.

"You're very well informed, Mr. Locke." Molly wasn't certain if she felt glad of or disturbed by the handsome man's presence. It was always safer to travel with a companion, but just how safe Michael Locke was, she really wasn't sure.

"It's my job to be informed." Michael looked

out the heavily draped window to the passing landscape. "You know, I usually hate this trip, but now that I find myself in such lovely company, I'm looking forward to it."

Molly didn't reply. Michael looked dashing in his fawn-colored frock coat and dark brown trousers, with his black curly hair, though neatly trimmed, falling casually across his forehead. Molly saw several ladies seated across the way eyeing him with covert glances and seductive smiles. She knew she should feel flattered by his attentions, but felt the same hesitancy she'd felt before. He seemed a little too polished, a little too smooth for Molly's taste. Still, she was thankful to have someone to pass the time with for the next few days.

"I suggest, Miss James, we begin this journey by dispensing with formality. I would be pleased if you would call me Michael. May I call you Molly?"

It was the only sensible thing to do, yet somehow Molly found the idea rather distasteful. "Of course," she answered graciously.

"It's almost noon," Michael said, pulling a gold fob from his pocket and checking the time. "I would be honored if you would join me in the dining car. I assure you the fare is quite sumptuous."

Molly *was* getting hungry. "I'd like that Mr. . . . I mean, Michael."

"Then, afterward, we can play some whisk." He stood up and offered his arm.

When Molly rose, his blue eyes swept her from head to foot, then he smiled appreciatively.

Molly wasn't certain whether to feel complimented or insulted. There was something unsettling about Michael Locke, but he was intelligent—and devilishly handsome. Molly began to worry she'd fall prey to his charming spell.

The trip to Denver was uneventful, and by the end of the journey, Molly had grown to enjoy Michael Locke's sophisticated companionship. He was winsomely captivating, and always concerned with her comfort. Further, he was well educated, able to discuss every topic from Shakespeare's sonnets to the carpetbaggers of the South. Molly wondered why she wasn't more attracted to the man, and why, instead, her thoughts kept drifting to Sam.

She went over their last conversation a thousand times, wondering what he could have meant. *I want to find out what's happening between us.* At night as she lay in her berth, the train wheels clacking beneath her, Molly would hear those words spoken in his deep, resonant voice, and fall asleep with them echoing in her ears.

Sam was right—there was something between them—something she was determined to ignore at all costs. Sam was a Brannigan—her adversary. Why, Sam's father had murdered her mother! Was she just supposed to forget that? Then there was the lawsuit, the land the Brannigans claimed that belonged to the Lady Jay. And finally, there was Lillian Rose. Molly wanted no part of Sam Brannigan, yet she couldn't rid her mind of Sam's words, or the feelings he aroused in her.

Her dreams were filled with shameful thoughts of Sam holding her, kissing her, touching her—everywhere. She'd relived every moment of his kiss every night for weeks. She cursed him, vowed to forget the way he made her feel, tried to get interested in Michael Locke. And for a time, she'd succeed.

Then night would fall, sleep would come, and Sam Brannigan would be holding her again. Molly couldn't wait to get to Denver, where she could focus on business, keep her thoughts squarely on the Lady Jay.

After leaving the train in Cheyenne, Molly and Michael boarded the Denver and Pacific and completed the last four-hour leg of the trip. Never having been to Denver, Molly found the bustling city fascinating.

"Denver was founded in 1859," Michael explained on the ride from the station, "at the junction of the South Platte and Cherry Creek. Gold was discovered here in '58, silver in '64. Now it's one of the richest communities between San Francisco and St. Louis."

"It's certainly a busy place," Molly commented as they wove their way through the crowded streets, passing everything from freight wagons to elegant black carriages.

Pulling up in front of the Grand Denver Hotel, Michael jumped down from the hansom cab and, holding her around the waist, swung Molly down to the street. Since the business meetings would be held in the downstairs rooms of the hotel, both she and Michael were taking rooms there. The hotel was touted as offering Denver's finest accommodations. Though Molly felt a little guilty staying in such a luxurious place, it was important the railroad owners see her as a prosperous timber owner.

As the bellman loaded her trunk onto his brass-trimmed cart, Michael took her hand. "You'll be in the session this afternoon?"

"Yes. I'm to meet with the owner, William Jackson Palmer. He already has my proposal. If all goes well, this meeting may be just a formality."

"For your sake, Molly, I hope so. I'll be in the meeting, too, so I'll see you there. Meanwhile, I believe I'll shed some of this dust."

Molly nodded. "A bath sounds wonderful. And I could use a nap as well."

Michael smiled. "Until this afternoon."

Molly luxuriated in the deep copper tub, set in the corner of her luxurious hotel room. Her bath water was scented with orange blossom, and the warm, sudsy water felt wonderful against her thirsty skin. She washed her hair, then added a few more drops of orange-scented fragrance to the water and soaked a little longer.

Finally, resignedly, she climbed from the tub and dried herself with a thick cotton towel. Wrapping it around her, she headed toward the high double bed, which, like the room was decorated in subtle shades of mint green. The bed had a brass head and footboard and a thick satin comforter. In the corner was a fireplace topped by a marble mantelpiece.

Stopping beside a tiny Queen Anne settee that nestled beneath a wide bay window, Molly watched the bustling city traffic, particularly fascinated by the horse-drawn street cars. Michael had mentioned them on the train, saying the horses towed the cars up the hill, but rode down the hill on the platform along with the passengers. It was a fascinating sight.

Yawning, Molly donned a light cotton nightgown, then climbed into bed, determined to catch a quick nap before her meeting just a short while away. Several hours later, she awoke groggily and hurriedly began to dress. Combing out her hair, she drew it back on the sides but let the long tresses curl down her back. When finished with this part of her preparation, she rang for the chambermaid, who brought in her freshly pressed garments. Looking critically at her clothing, Molly chose a very proper navy-blue day dress trimmed with simple white piping. The dress fit snugly in the waist, and the simple gored skirt fell gracefully over her hips to the floor. As she slipped into the round-collared crisp white blouse and tailored jacket, she felt pleased with her appearance: feminine yet businesslike.

Once dressed, Molly summoned her composure and headed downstairs, praying the meeting would run smoothly and there would be no problems. She knew her proposal was a good one, beneficial to railroad and lumberman alike, and the price she was asking was better than fair. But would the railroad company believe she could deliver the timber according to the terms of the agreement? Would they trust the Lady Jay now that it was run by a woman?

Arriving downstairs, Molly raised her gloved hand to knock at the imposing mahogany door of the conference room, but it opened before she had the chance.

Michael Locke smiled down at her in welcome. "Miss James. We've been expecting you."

She appreciated that he was treating her in a businesslike manner, even though they had become friends on the train. Sweeping into the room, Molly moved to stand beside Michael, and he introduced her to the other five gentlemen in the room: William Jackson Palmer; Spencer Whitcomb, the Denver and Rio attorney; Warren Jacobs; and Clarence Webb. When the last man approached, Molly's blue eyes rounded in surprise.

"Hello, Miss James." Sam Brannigan's deep voice was unmistakable. He looked devastatingly handsome in his cream-colored frock coat and navy-blue breeches. The light-colored coat somehow made him seem even taller than he was, and his hazel eyes, today a smoky green, twinkled with a hint of mirth. Noticing the way his blond hair curled above his collar, Molly's heart began to pound. Damn him! She needed all her wits about her to win the men's confidence—the last person she wanted to see was Sam.

"Mr. Brannigan," she said. "I didn't realize you were interested in the railroad contracts. I thought your timber was already spoken for."

"Our production has increased considerably in the last six months. We find we have enough to expand our markets."

"I see." Molly groaned inwardly. Not only would she have to convince the railroad she was capable of producing and supplying the lumber they needed, but she would have to compete with Sam Brannigan. And she knew from experience that Sam Brannigan was a tough opponent.

As Molly took her seat, the men returned to theirs. William Jackson Palmer, an attractive man with thinning light brown hair and a bushy mustache, began the discussion.

"First of all, Miss James, let me assure you the Denver and Rio has plans for expansion that will require, as you rightly surmised, a great deal of timber. Besides our own track, we're planning to subcontract with small feeder lines, which will also need ties and beams for tunnels and trestles. Second, my attorneys and I agree that your proposal is more than fair, and Mr. Brannigan has vouched for your reliability."

Only Molly's years of self-control kept the stunned expression from her face. She merely shifted a little in her chair and wondered why in the world Sam would help her get the contracts when he himself was a contender.

"In fact, Miss James," Palmer added, "our timber needs are great enough to award contracts to both you *and* Mr. Brannigan."

Molly breathed a sigh of relief.

"However," Palmer continued "there is a problem involving the two of you we find insurmountable. Mr. Whitcomb, since you're our legal counsel, I think you'd better be the one to explain." Palmer sat down, and Spencer Whitcomb, a balding, spectacled man with a slight paunch and fretful eyes, rose in his place.

At the end of the long walnut table, Sam leaned nonchalantly back in his chair. His expression remained unreadable, but it was obvious he'd already been told the problem, and Molly wished she'd left Truckee in time to beat him to Denver. Then it would be she, instead of Sam, who would know what in blazes was going on. Damn! How did he always manage to be one jump ahead of her?

"Our records indicate, Miss James, that you and Mr. Brannigan are involved in a land dispute over a portion of your timber land. We believe the dispute could wind up involving lumber we might be purchasing. There could be doubt as to whom the lumber belonged, doubt as to whom we should be paying, etc. As counsel for the Denver and Rio Grande, I cannot allow the company to enter into contracts that might lead to a lawsuit. You must understand our position, Miss James."

Again Molly registered no emotion, though inside she was seething with anger. Sam Brannigan would win again. She would have to drop the lawsuit in order to get the timber contracts, and she had to get the contracts in order to make the Lady Jay profitable. Otherwise, she would be forced to sell out.

Determined not to let him guess her sense of defeat, Molly smiled as if humoring a child. "Then, gentlemen, we have no problem. I shall simply withdraw my suit. I'm certain Mr. Brannigan will also find no problem in that."

Sam smiled lazily, but made no reply.

Spencer Whitcomb removed his spectacles and laid them on the table, creating a momentary echo in the elegant but sparsely furnished room. "I'm afraid it's not that simple, Miss James. You see, the ownership of the land has never been settled. Even if you drop the suit now, there could be other questions raised at a later date. Either you or Mr. Brannigan could have grounds against us for payment to the wrong party. No, Miss James, until the matter is settled in court, I'm afraid the Denver and Rio Grande is prohibited from doing business with either of you."

"Settled in court!" Molly jumped to her feet. "But that could take years!"

"I'm sorry, Miss James. There's really nothing we can do."

Molly felt sick at heart. By bringing the lawsuit against the Brannigans, she had unleashed a monster. It was her own fault, and yet hadn't Palmer suggested that it was not solely her lawsuit which had decided them? She sank back down on the high-backed red leather seat, fighting a wave of despair. Her only consolation came from knowing Sam Brannigan would get no contract either.

"I'm sorry, Miss James," William Palmer added, beginning to gather his paperwork. "If we'd uncovered the problem sooner, we could have saved you both the trip."

Michael Locke looked across at her sympathetically. He shoved back his chair, the sound grating against the marble floor, and moved to stand beside her. "I'm sorry, Molly. Truly I am." Solicitously, he captured her hand, then helped her rise from her seat. Molly found the concern in his bright blue eyes comforting. She allowed him to settle her hand on his arm and started to follow him from the room. Although defeat seemed certain, she hadn't given up completely. Her only chance was to gain some time to think. Maybe by tomorrow she could come up with a solution.

From the other side of the room Sam noticed the familiarity between Molly and Michael Locke. Since she'd entered the room, she'd barely looked in his direction. Now, she was leaving on Locke's more than eager arm. Sam felt the heat at the back of his neck. When the hell did Locke get so friendly with Molly? The man was a smooth-talking rogue. Definitely not the kind of man for a girl like Molly James, yet she certainly seemed to know him well enough!

"What if both ranches were owned by the same person?" Sam asked, raising the question he'd pondered all morning. As soon as he'd been informed of the problem, he'd thought of the wild solution, then spent hours talking himself out of it. Part of him couldn't believe he had spoken the words aloud.

Molly stopped short, her expression for once clearly discernible—pure, unadulterated rage.

Sam ignored her anger. "It seems to me, gentlemen, that if the ranches were owned by the same person, there'd be no question whose timber belonged to whom."

Spencer Whitcomb answered for the Denver and Rio. "That's quite correct, Mr. Brannigan. Are you proposing Miss James sell out?"

"The Lady Jay is not for sale!" Molly stormed.

Sam smiled with amusement, enjoying the fiery look in her large blue eyes. Her bosom heaved with anger, and her shoulders were set as if she were about to do battle.

"No, Mr. Spencer," Sam said, purposely continuing to ignore Molly's outburst. "I'm proposing *marriage*."

The room fell silent. Molly's eyes were so enormous, they looked like clear blue lakes. She clutched Michael Locke's arm as if he were the only thing saving her life, then sank back down into her chair.

Michael Locke broke the silence. "That's quite preposterous, Brannigan. Miss James has no intention of marrying you. Why, you two hardly know each other."

Sam raised his eyebrows disdainfully. "Since when, Mr. Locke, did you receive authority to speak for Miss James on matters of such importance? Up until now, I've found her quite capable of speaking for herself." He turned his attention to the stunned men in the room. "I understand you gentlemen will be in Denver until tomorrow, is that correct?"

"Yes," William Palmer confirmed.

"Then I believe Miss James and I have some talking to do." He moved to where she sat motionless in her chair. "We'll give you a decision at that time." Reaching down, he took her arm and none too gently drew her to her feet, placing her hand through the crook of his arm. Woodenly, she let him lead her from the room. Her other hand clutched her reticule so tightly her skin paled.

"Until tomorrow, Miss James," Spencer Whitcomb called after them, but Molly seemed not to hear him.

Sam guided her into the elegant dining room and seated her at a small table in the corner behind a towering potted fern, where she finally found her tongue.

"You . . . you can't be serious!"

"You want those timber contracts, don't you?" He ordered her a sherry from a black-clad waiter.

"Why, yes . . . but . . . but . . . "

"You want to be safe from your oppressive guardian, Jason Foley, don't you?"

"Yes, but . . . what about you? Why should you want to marry me?" The sherry arrived, and Molly lifted the long-stemmed glass to her lips with a shaking hand. She hoped the sweet-tasting liquid would soothe her ragged nerves.

"Because I want that timber contract as much as you do, and because I want this damned feud between our families settled once and for all."

Molly didn't believe a word of it. "You mean you want to control the Lady Jay. That's it, isn't it?"

"I'll have Spencer Whitcomb draw up all the documents necessary to give you complete control of the ranch. You give me written and irrevocable permission to use James Pass. You can have fee title to the land."

Molly felt as if the wind had been knocked from her sails. He was offering her everything she wanted, yet she was giving up everything—her name, her independence, her chance for love and happiness.

"Don't look so sad, Molly." He reached across the marble table and took her cold fingers in his hand. "Surely being married to me couldn't be all *that* bad."

His hazel eyes caressed her, lingering on the swell of her breast, and Molly's face flamed red. "But surely this is to be a marriage of convenience, Mr. Brannigan?"

"Sam," he corrected.

"Sam," she repeated in a whisper, beginning to sense another defeat.

"Not a chance," he said. "I'm not cut out for celibacy, Molly. Nor do I believe a husband should cheat on his wife, no matter what reason they have for marrying. If you agree to this marriage, you'll act as my wife in every way."

"But we hardly know each other. What if we find out we hate each other?"

Sam sat quietly a moment, pondering the lovely face across from him. Worry lines marred her smooth forehead, and a pulse throbbed nervously at the base of her slender throat.

"All right, Molly. If we hate each other after a year, we'll dissolve the marriage."

"But we're both Catholic. We're not allowed to divorce."

"Then we'll be married by a judge, if that'll salve your conscience. Personally, it doesn't matter to me either way."

"You've got an answer for everything, don't you?" Her voice was so low, Sam could barely hear it.

"Not quite everything, Molly. I don't have *your* answer yet."

"I . . . I have to have some time to think," Molly said evasively, desperately searching for some way out. She couldn't marry a Brannigan—even if she did harbor some sort of feelings for him. And what about Sam? He certainly didn't love her. She searched his eyes. "What about Lillian Rose? Don't you want to marry her?"

"Miss Rose and I have an understanding. I don't wish to marry her any more than she wishes to marry me."

Molly took another sip of her sherry, buying time. Her father would spin in his grave if he knew she'd married a Brannigan—no matter what the reason. The thought of her disloyalty made her feel slightly ill. She felt guilty and trapped, and for a moment she hated Sam Brannigan.

"I suppose it's only fair to tell you"—she eyed him with a boldness she didn't feel—"there have been other . . . gentlemen before you."

For the first time, Sam felt his composure slip. "Are you telling me you're not a virgin?"

Try as she might to fight it, Molly's face again flamed red. Why the devil had she told him that?

Because she was tired of him intruding in her life, tired of him always getting the best of her. Tired of being defeated by the Brannigans. She'd found his weakness, she could see it in his eyes.

"Yes. That's exactly what I'm saying. I can tell by your expression, that changes everything. I hope you'll be noble enough to keep my secret." She rose to leave, but he caught her arm.

"That changes nothing. It just makes things easier. You've had enough experience to understand the advantages of my proposal."

Molly swallowed hard. As usual, Sam was right. She had to think of the ranch. Nothing mattered but the Lady Jay. If she didn't marry Sam, she'd wind up losing the ranch. Time was running out.

"All right. I'll marry you. But only on the condition that I spend five nights a week at the Lady Jay."

"Three." His eyes had turned a dusty brown, and Molly knew she'd scored a slight victory.

"Four or the deal's off."

"Agreed. I'll make the arrangements, and we'll get married tomorrow."

"Tomorrow! Why, I couldn't possibly marry you tomorrow!"

"You forget, Molly, we have no choice. If we want those timber contracts, we'll have to sign them by tomorrow. Palmer isn't going to wait around for us to get married some other time."

Molly felt a wave of nausea. "I . . . I suppose you're right."

Sam called for the check. "I think you'd better get some rest. You look a little pale. I'll call for you at eight. We'll have supper here in the hotel. That'll give us a chance to get better acquainted. After all, you *are* going to be my wife."

Molly nodded and, thankfully, he guided her up to her room. She felt as if she were sleepwalking. Her arms and legs moved, but only by force of habit. Tomorrow her whole life would change, all her hopes, all her dreams again destroyed by a Brannigan. Why did it have to be this way?

"Get some rest," Sam told her gently. "I'll see you at eight."

# Chapter Ten

MOLLY UNDRESSED AND lay down on her bed, but she couldn't fall asleep. Thoughts of her childhood, her mother's death, and the lonely years she'd spent at boarding school spun through her head. Now she would marry a man she was determined not to love. A man who didn't love her. But Sam wasn't just any man. He was special, and Molly knew it. She felt more for Sam Brannigan than she'd felt for any other man in her life. Except, of course, her father. Maybe whatever she felt for Sam would be enough to get her through the coming year. Her conscience wouldn't allow her to consider the marriage permanent. After a year, they would quietly dissolve the marriage and return to their separate lives. And the Lady Jay would have been saved.

Though her guilt was eased by the knowledge that she was saving the ranch, her stomach was not. Marrying a man, living with him as man and wife, then leaving him, went against everything Molly believed in. She had been raised a Catholic, though she hardly considered herself devout. Still, the institution of marriage was sacred, not something to be engaged in lightly and then cast aside. God, what a tangled mess! The only sensible way to approach the problem was to take things one at a time. First she'd get through dinner, then the wedding—then the wedding night.

Molly groaned inwardly. Just thinking about that made her palms damp. She knew nothing of a man and a woman. Even Angel had never discussed those things with her. Molly knew only what she'd learned by watching the animals on the ranch and listening to the stories she'd heard whispered among the girls in Mrs. Finch's finishing school.

The stories had been terrible—about pain and blood and the degradation of having to submit. But she hadn't felt that way when Sam kissed her. She hadn't felt that way in her dreams. Still, kisses and dreams were a far cry from actually making love. Molly felt chilled by the thought.

Forcing herself to brush the feeling aside, she determined again that the best way to handle the matter was to take things one at a time. Somehow she would get through all this. She had to think of the ranch.

Sam checked his gold pocket watch. Eight o'clock straight up. He rapped lightly on the door to Molly's room and was surprised when it opened immediately. Lilly would have kept him waiting for at least fifteen minutes.

"Good evening, Sam."

"Good evening, Molly." His eyes swept over her, taking in her gown of palest ice-blue silk. The back of the dress was cut high, and Sam knew she'd chosen it to hide the traces of the wounds that he was sure still marred her skin. He felt a sudden surge of temper at the thought. Fighting it down, he offered his arm. "Shall we go?"

Molly accepted graciously, though Sam detected a tiny tremor in her hand.

"You look beautiful," he told her, noticing the artful way her thick red hair had been gathered at the side of her neck and arranged in tiny ringlets. His gaze drifted to the sweeping neckline at the front of her gown. A less than modest display of full white bosom conjured heated memories of her luscious pink nipples.

"Thank you," she replied."You look quite dashing yourself." They moved down the wide, carpeted hall, passing several elegantly garbed ladies and gentlemen. Sam had dressed formally in black evening clothes. The toes of his shiny black shoes glistened in the soft light of the crystal gas lamps.

"I want you to promise me something, Molly."

She looked up at him with those blue eyes of hers, and though she fought to hide it, he read her apprehension. She had never seemed the least bit fragile to him before, but now he saw her in a whole new light.

"Promise me just for tonight you'll forget about the ranch. You'll forget about tomorrow; you'll just be Molly and I'll be Sam. Two people in a beautiful city sharing a wonderful evening."

Molly looked up at him, her ruby lips parting in a slightly timid smile. It was a side of her he'd never seen before, and he found it enchanting.

"That sounds lovely, Sam. I promise I'll try. And . . . thank you."

He squeezed her hand as he led her down the sweeping staircase, through the luxurious lobby with its lofty ceilings and gilded furniture, into the dining room. The Grand Salon was everything it promised: Pink marble columns rose two stories into the air; tiny panes of rose-colored glass crowned the room; and the pink marble floors were lined with tables, each covered by a rose-colored cloth. A pink rosebud graced the intimate table Sam had requested near the harpist. Soft strains of music drifted over the table, setting a romantic tone for the evening he had planned.

Sam pulled out Molly's chair and moved to his own, ordering champagne from their waiter.

"Do you come to Denver often?" Molly asked.

"Once or twice a year. I have several friends in town, and some business acquaintances. Is this your first trip?"

"Yes. I think Denver's lovely. Although I've gotten to see little of it." The waiter arrived with their champagne, and poured some for Sam to taste. At Sam's nod, he filled both their glasses, then departed.

Sam lifted his champagne glass. "To Denver, a beautiful city. And to Molly, a beautiful woman."

"And to Sam," she added with a smile, "a formidable opponent."

But Sam wouldn't drink. "No, lass. Not an opponent anymore." His gaze held hers. "To Sam, Molly's new partner."

The crystal goblets chimed together. Molly took a long, slow sip of the bubbly liquid and felt the sparkles tickle her nose. After the first few sips, she began to relax. She'd been surprised by Sam's thoughtfulness; but then, he always seemed to have a knack for putting her at ease, and she was determined to prove herself worthy of his concern.

She continued to feel the effects of the champagne, but didn't really care. Tonight she was just Molly. She didn't have to worry about tomorrow; she could do anything she damn well pleased!

Sam ordered dinner for both of them. The first course, chilled watercress soup, was followed by salmon aspic, both dishes served on the finest porcelain. Molly ate lightly, enjoying the feel of the champagne, and forgetting her troubles, at least for a while.

With the main course, baked filet of trout in madeira sauce, Sam ordered a second bottle of champagne. By the time she finished several more glasses, Molly found herself laughing at some clever remark Sam made and really enjoying herself.

"Would it be all right if I asked you something personal?" she said. He smiled and ran a finger along the line of her jaw. Molly felt a shiver run the length of her.

"We're going to be partners, aren't we?" he said.

"How did you . . . hurt your leg?"

Sam's smile faded, and his eyes took on a glazed, faraway expression.

"Maybe I shouldn't have asked," Molly said, not wanting to spoil the evening.

"It's all right. It was a long time ago." He straightened in his chair and smiled at her as if her question bothered him not at all, but his eyes had lost their twinkle, and his voice took on a husky note that Molly didn't miss.

"I was seventeen when the war broke out. I was young and foolish and determined to make my own way in the world. I believed war was glorious, that battle brought men honor. I told my father I wanted to fight for the North. He forbade it. It was the only real disagreement we ever had. He said California was a long way from the South. We Westerners had our own wars to fight. But I believed in the cause. I didn't think men should be kept as slaves. In abolishing slavery, I believe some good did come of the war. But . . . "

"Go on," she encouraged softly when he didn't continue.

"But there was no honor. No glory. There was just blood and death and destruction. I was in South Carolina when two of my friends got pinned down on a bridge under heavy artillery fire. I went in to get them out. One made it; one didn't. I nearly didn't.

"I took a musketball in the chest and one in the knee. The chest wound healed without complications, but the knee was more serious. The doctors were sure I'd lose my leg. At best, they said, I'd never walk again." This time Sam grinned. "But I showed them a Brannigan doesn't accept defeat easily."

She laid her hand over his and smiled up at him. "If there's one thing I've learned about you, Sam, it's that you don't accept defeat. Ever."

He laughed good-naturedly, and she was happy to see the sparkle back in his hazel eyes.

"How about lady friends?" she teased. "There must have been scores of Yankee women looking to keep you handsome soldiers happy."

Sam smiled down at her. "There were women. I can't deny that. Not as many as you might think. I didn't really have time to get involved with anyone in particular."

"Until Lilly."

Sam looked her straight in the eye. "What Lilly and I shared was a casual relationship. We never had any intentions of making it permanent."

"Sam?"

"Yes, lass."

"I know I promised, but . . . Do you think we're doing the right thing?"

"What do you think?"

"I don't know."

"Everything will work out, Molly. I promise."

The delicious meal ended, and Sam insisted he and Molly take a carriage ride through the city. The air was brisk and clear, and the stars twinkled in the heavens like sparkling jewels. Sam took her up to Brown's Bluff for a view out over the town.

"It's beautiful, Sam."

"Not nearly as lovely as you." He watched her closely, feeling suddenly overwhelmed by the thought that tomorrow the beautiful woman beside him would be his wife. He still found it difficult to believe. His actions had been so out of character, he staunchly refused to examine them. He was committed now. He'd abide by that commitment.

As Molly turned to look at him, moonlight danced across her pretty blue eyes, and any doubts Sam might still have been harboring fled with the gentle evening breeze. Pushing several thick strands of hair from her cheek, he tipped her chin up and captured her mouth in a feather-soft kiss. Her lips felt warm and full, and his heart pounded. He tasted the cherries they'd shared for dessert and deepened the kiss.

Molly didn't fight him. The champagne had done its job, leaving her feeling warm and languorous. She felt Sam's hands cradling her face, felt the softness of his beard against her cheek. He was nibbling her lips, tasting them, exploring the corners of her mouth. It seemed so right somehow, so natural. She shivered and pressed against him, allowing him to continue, wanting him to. When he kissed her again, she parted her lips, and he slid his tongue between her teeth, searching her warmth, delighting her with the sensation. She could taste his breath, tinged with a trace of brandy. She moaned softly and kissed him ardently in return.

Sam struggled to maintain his control. He could sense her passion, feel it in the tension of her body, the fiery heat of her kiss. When she slipped her arms around his neck and laced her fingers through his hair, it was all he could do to keep from taking her right on the floor of the carriage. Her full breasts thrust against him, each peak hard against his chest. He remembered their size and rosy fire and groaned aloud, the force of his desire staggering. With a shaky hand, he tore himself free.

Molly swayed against him, pressing her small hands against his chest, her eyes uncertain. If he hadn't known better, he would have sworn she had no idea of the effect she was having on him—nor did it seem she understood the response she herself was feeling.

"I think we'd better be getting back." He could hear the ragged timbre of his voice, and wondered if she could hear it, too. But there was no privacy in the open carriage. The driver sat on his seat just a few feet away. Tomorrow would be soon enough, he told himself. Tomorrow she would be his.

Molly nodded her understanding and moved away from him, swaying unsteadily. "I . . . I think I drank a little too much champagne."

Sam took a good look at her, noting the slightly glazed look in her eyes. "It's still early," he said, his voice more normal. "I think you'll be all right if you get a good night's sleep. You're probably a little tired from the trip." He instructed the driver to return them to the hotel, and the carriage moved off toward the city.

"I had a wonderful time tonight, Sam. Really wonderful."

"So did I, lass."

The cool air seemed to refresh her, leaving her more drowsy than drunk. "I used to dream about my wedding day," she told him wistfully as the carriage rolled along. "How I'd walk down the aisle in a beautiful white gown on my father's arm, and he'd tell everyone how proud he was of me. Afterward there'd be a big reception with a six-tiered wedding cake and an orchestra, and we'd dance until midnight."

Sam felt a tug at his heart—and a twinge of guilt. He shrugged it off. He was doing Molly a favor, saving her precious ranch—and saving her and his family from the hurtful gossip she was determined to stir up.

"And did you live happily ever after?" he asked.

"Of course." She smiled forlornly. "After all, it was only a dream."

The carriage rolled up in front of the hotel, and Sam helped Molly down, his large hands nearly spanning her tiny waist.

"Feeling better?" he asked as they mounted the wide staircase to her room.

"Yes. Much better. I'm really not used to champagne, but it was fun, wasn't it?"

"More than fun, lass." He couldn't help thinking how innocent she looked. Different here than she was on the ranch. There she was in control. Here, for the first time, she seemed vulnerable; she almost seemed to need him—and Sam was enjoying every minute of it.

"Well, here we are," he said as they reached her door. He wasn't going to kiss her. The night would be long enough without adding to the ache he already felt. But she closed her eyes and tipped up her face, offering her full red lips, and he just couldn't resist.

This time he was careful not to let himself go. There'd be plenty of time for that tomorrow night, in the privacy of the suite he'd taken for the occasion. He brushed her lips with a light kiss, then backed away.

"The wedding's set for six o'clock. I'll call for you a little before."

"But the groom's not supposed to see the bride before the wedding! It's bad luck." Her luminous round eyes looked so appealing, Sam felt he might drown in their depths.

"All right, I'll send someone for you." He watched her a moment, then weakened and pulled her into his arms, kissing her soundly.

"Good night, lass."

Slightly breathless, she backed inside her room and quietly closed the door.

Molly's thoughts swirled—and not from the champagne. She'd shared a wonderful evening with Sam. And although she felt guilty about it, she'd have to come to grips with her conscience sooner or later. What bothered her was the way she had felt when he kissed her. As if she were drowning in . . . something hot or cold . . . But the feeling was too nebulous for words. It was as if, for that moment, she had no mastery of her body or her thoughts—or just about anything at all. She felt entirely out of control, and despite the pleasant sensations Sam stirred, Molly didn't like it one damned bit.

She called for a ladies' maid to help her undress, then brushed her hair with a little more energy than necessary. After donning a nightdress, she slid between the sheets. What was he after? And why was he being so nice to her? Was he looking for a way to cheat her out of her share of the ranch, or maybe just wheedle control away from her? Surely he must be after something more than he'd told her.

Molly punched her pillow and tried to fall asleep, as angry with herself for responding to his kisses as she was with Sam for what she guessed were dubious intentions. And what of tomorrow night? Would she feel as warm and trusting as she had tonight, wanting something from him but not understanding what it was? Or would she feel sick and repulsed and yet be forced to submit?

Refusing to dwell any more on the matter, but with uncertain thoughts as to what the morrow would bring, Molly drifted into a fitful sleep.

The sun was bright in the Colorado sky when Molly awoke to a banging at her door. Donning her light silk wrapper, she stretched and yawned and opened it a crack. A tiny, dark-haired Oriental woman stood beside a thin-faced bellboy whose arms were piled high with boxes.

"Mr. Brannigan send these," the woman said in her Pidgin English. "Say I come, fix for you."

The bellboy dropped the boxes on the bed and left, closing the door behind him. Wondering what Sam could possibly have sent, Molly lifted one of the lids to find a snow-white French lace negligee along with a pair of white satin mules. She spread the revealing negligee out on the bed and surveyed it with awe. It was beautiful, what there was of it. Glancing toward the little Chinese woman, whose face bore a knowing smile, Molly felt the color rush to her cheeks.

"Mr. Brannigan nice man, yes?" the woman said.

"Yes," Molly said. But looking at the nightgown and knowing he expected her to wear it for him, she wasn't really so sure.

With a sense of trepidation, Molly lifted the second lid. Her hand began to tremble and a lump formed in her throat as she carefully lifted out the beautiful white silk wedding gown. Simple and elegant, with a high neck and long, sheer sleeves, its only trim was the tiny tucks from neck to waist and the row of pearl buttons down the front. The fabric was exquisite, the sheerest tulle over silk. Miniature pearl buttons closed up the sleeves at each wrist.

By the time Molly pulled out the matching tulle veil gathered beneath a band of pearls at the crown, her heart thudded against her ribs so loudly she was sure the little woman could hear it. Molly spread the dress out on the bed and was about to put the lid back on the box, when she spotted a tiny white envelope at the bottom.

Struggling to control her trembling fingers, she pulled out the card and read the few simple words scrawled in a man's bold hand. *Sometimes dreams come true, Molly.*

Beneath the message, a single stroke of the pen curled in the shape of an *S*. Molly clutched the card to her heart, feeling the lump swell tighter. Sam. He always seemed to know her heart. Searching through the rest of the boxes,she discovered lacy petticoats, silky white hose, and satin garters, along with several more decidedly revealing nightgowns. The wedding dress turned out to be a little long and slightly large in the waist, but Wen, as the slender woman was named, assured Molly she could have the dress ready in just a few hours. For the first time in two days, Molly felt a sincere desire to smile. Maybe dreams *could* come true after all.

# *Chapter Eleven*

BY FIVE O'CLOCK, Molly was so nervous she was sure she'd never survive the ceremony. Spencer Whitcomb had stopped by at four with all the necessary documents to secure her retention of the ranch. Now she paced her room in corset and petticoats, wishing the time would go faster. If she had to go through with this wedding, the sooner it was over, the better.

Wen was her only comfort. Sam had sent her to help Molly dress, and Wen, it appeared, had plenty of experience. The little Oriental coiffed Molly's hair in a crown of elegant ringlets to which she would secure the veil. The rest was left to curl in a thick mass down her back, but wispy strands of flame-red hair escaped to curl beside each ear.

"Time to dress, Miss James," Wen said, and Molly nodded. Her heart thumped dully, and tiny tremors shook her hands. Wen fastened the gleaming pearl buttons, then, insisting Molly not sit down and wrinkle the dress, climbed on a chair to set the veil. After donning her satin slippers, Molly let Wen lead her in front of the full-length oval mirror at the end of her room. With a trembling hand, Molly reached toward the ethereal creature in the mirror. Was it really Molly James whose blue eyes stared back?

The gown showed off her tiny waist, and the simple, clean lines enhanced the beauty of her face. Molly refused to acknowledge the smattering of freckles across the bridge of her nose, which seemed somehow undignified against the stark loveliness of the gown. But her skin looked smooth and healthy, and her lips and cheeks, heightened by a bit of rouge, glowed prettily. There was no denying she looked lovely. She only wished she felt as good as she looked.

A light knock on the door set her pulse racing.

Wen's thin lips curved in a satisfied smile. "You make beautiful bride for handsome groom."

"Thank you, Wen." Molly nodded her readiness and tried to maintain an air of confidence she didn't feel.

Wen opened the door, and Molly was surprised to find William Jackson Palmer standing in the hallway holding a bridal bouquet of white roses in a cone of silver lace. Silver lace streamers hung nearly to the floor. He handed the flowers to her with a soft light dancing in his dark brown eyes.

"I'd be delighted if you would allow me the honor of giving away the bride."

Molly smiled, feeling a little better already. She liked William Palmer. He seemed like an honest, forthright, and sincere man. Drawing a little strength from his comforting presence, she accepted his arm and swept into the hall.

It turned out the wedding was to take place in the Rocky Mountain Suite on the top floor of the hotel. William Palmer patted her arm encouragingly as he opened one of the heavy double doors leading into the luxurious interior. Her shoes echoed a moment against the glistening wooden floor, then sank into the thick blue carpeting. Entirely furnished in ice blue and silver, from the heavy blue velvet draperies to the delicate Louis XIV furniture upholstered in blue brocade, the suite was sumptuous.

In front of a spray of white roses that lightly scented the air, a man somberly clad in black held a book of prayers open to the marriage ceremony. In a half circle around him, Molly spotted Spencer Whitcomb, Warren Jacobs, and Clarence Webb, the men who'd been in the meeting the day before. Another man stood beside two elegantly dressed ladies, and Michael Locke stood beside them with a sober, worried expression on his darkly handsome face.

As she moved across the room still clinging to William's arm, she spotted Sam's tall, broad-shouldered figure striding toward her, and her heart increased its tempo. He wore well-tailored black evening clothes over a crisp white shirt, and his thick blond hair curled a bit willfully along his collar. His eyes, today a light shade of green, glowed with approval. His broad smile, a flash of white against his tanned skin, should have been a comfort, but Molly felt only apprehension. Her smile was fixed in place, and her hands were cold and stiff as she allowed William to release her into Sam's gentle custody.

"You're even lovelier than I imagined." With her thick hair gleaming in the glow of the crystal scorces, her blue eyes hesitant and looking to him for assurance, the fiery little redhead looked breathtaking. Sam thought about his night of ragged sleep, the self-doubt, and the guilt he'd felt about luring the girl into marriage, yet this instant knew he'd done the right thing. Her fingers felt brittle and cold as he laced them through his and guided her toward their guests, but later he was sure they'd be warm and eager, as they had been the night before.

"Molly, meet William and Elizabeth Byers," he told her, introducing her to two of his dearest friends. "They own the *Rocky Mountain News*. And this is Mary Palmer." He indicated a short, rotund brunette who was William Palmer's wife. "I believe you know everyone else."

"Yes." She knew them, all right, but could scarcely remember their names. Sam guided her toward the man who stood at the head of the circle.

"And this is Judge Barton." The judge, a thin, graying man with a bristly mustache and kindly blue eyes, smiled warmly.

Molly forced a smile. "Hello, Your Honor."

"Are you ready?" the judge asked.

Molly could only nod. She gripped Sam's arm as if he were her lifeline, and the judge began to intone the words every woman knew nearly by heart.

"Dearly Beloved: We are gathered together in the sight of God and in the presence of these witnesses to join together Molly James and Samuel Shamus Brannigan in the bonds of holy matrimony according to the ordinance of God and the laws of the territory of Colorado. . . ."

Molly heard little of the next few sentences. Her mind struggled with the name that conjured horrible memories of violence and murder. Shamus Brannigan, the killer whose son she was marrying. Molly felt a swelling in her throat at her own treachery. How could she be marrying into this enemy family? How could she go against everything she'd ever been taught? Ever believed in? Yet how could she *not* save the Lady Jay?

It's only for a year, she told herself. Only to save the ranch. But as she glanced to the tall blond man beside her, catching the virile line of his jaw and the sensuous curve of his lips, she wondered at the truth of her words.

"Do you, Samuel, take this woman, Molly, to be your wedded wife? Will you love her, comfort her, honor and keep her, for better, for worse, for richer, for poorer, in sickness and in health, to love and to cherish, and forsaking all others, for as long as you both shall live?"

Sam's voice rang clear and strong, but held a note of tenderness that belied some inner emotion. "I do." He squeezed her hand as if he sensed her uncertainty.

"Do you, Molly, take this man, Samuel, to be your wedded husband? Will you love him, comfort him, honor and obey him, for better, for worse, for richer, for poorer, in sickness and in health, to love and to cherish, and forsaking all others, for as long as you both shall live?"

Molly worried her bottom lip and swallowed hard. Was she doing the right thing? "I do," she whispered.

The judge looked up at Sam. "You may place the ring on her finger."

Sam slipped a glittering diamond band on her

third finger and smiled reassuringly. Molly tried to smile in return.

"Repeat after me," the judge instructed. "With this ring I thee wed."

Sam repeated the words, then the judge went on, "Let this ring be a symbol of your true wedded love and a seal of the vows you have made."

Molly felt faint. *True wedded love . . . vows you have made.* She'd agreed to be Sam's wife, not for a year, but for as long as they lived. She was a liar and a cheat and a traitor to her family. A hard lump swelled her throat, but as always, no tears came. For once, she was grateful.

"By the authority vested in me by the territory of Colorado, I now pronounce you man and wife. What God has joined together, let no man put asunder. You may kiss your bride."

Sam lifted her veil; she felt his strong fingers beneath her chin, then the softness of his beard and the warmth of his lips. He swept her into his arms and kissed her soundly, leaving her breathless and in no doubt as to just whose wife she was.

The guests in the room came forward to offer their best wishes for the couple's happiness, and Molly accepted their light kisses on her cheeks. Only Michael Locke kissed her boldly on the mouth. He drew her into his arms and captured her lips, smothering them until she felt lightheaded. When he released her, Sam glowered down at them ominously.

"Make that the last time you kiss her like that, Mr. Locke." Sam's tone was light, but all three knew the warning it held. Sam had been watching Michael Locke since before the ceremony. The man was obviously none too happy about the event, and seeing the possessive way he eyed Molly now, Sam wondered just how well the man knew his pretty, red-haired wife. Molly had warned him of her indiscretions, and Sam had vowed not to hold them against her. He wasn't pure himself, by any means.

Lack of virginity on their part hadn't bothered Sam with the other women he'd known. In fact, it had been a relief. Somehow with Molly he felt different. He would have enjoyed teaching her the delights of love. Thinking of her in the arms of Michael Locke—or any other man, for that matter—sent him into a fit of temper. He fixed his gaze on Molly. She seemed to be watching him warily, and he wondered if his suspicions about her and Locke were right. Not that it really mattered. From now on Molly belonged to him. He was eager for their guests to depart so he could make damn certain she understood that fact as clearly as he.

Molly felt Sam's arm around her waist. Glancing up, she caught the curve of his smile—and the look in his eyes she'd been dreading. The hungry look that told her he was thinking of the night to come. Molly felt sick with fear. The stories she'd heard rose up to haunt her. She thought of the marriage ceremony just ended. She'd made it this far; somehow she'd get through the rest of the night. Pasting a smile on her face, befitting a bride, she moved with Sam toward a table laden with food.

Silver platters rested on white linen tablecloths, and the aroma of spicy pickled meats and rich, dark cake drifted from the table. A white-gloved waiter popped the cork on a bottle of champagne, then filled and passed crystal goblets around.

William Jackson Palmer, standing beside his wife, lifted his glass in a toast. "To the bride and groom. May their marriage be as successful as their new partnership with the Denver and Rio Grande!" Everyone smiled good-naturedly except Michael Locke, who barely raised his glass and didn't drink at all. Molly noticed Sam's frown as he caught Michael's hostile gesture.

Waiters bustled about the room, refilling glasses, removing empty trays, and bringing in a constant array of delicacies: everything from smoked salmon to Russian caviar. The smell of fresh-roasted quail filled the air, and the tinkle of crystal mingled with soft laughter and good wishes. Sam had spared no expense. And despite her trepidation, Molly delighted in his extravagance on her behalf. There was even a tiered white wedding cake. Only three layers, not six, but lovely just the same. Spencer Whitcomb insisted the bride and groom cut the cake and feed each other, and Molly fought the mischievous urge to rub a little of it in Sam's smiling face.

As if reading her thoughts, he chuckled. "I wouldn't if I were you," he whispered in that husky voice of his. "Remember, lass, you'll be at my mercy after they've gone." Feeling his strong, suntanned finger along the line of her jaw, Molly's smile slipped just a little.

She wished he hadn't reminded her. Suddenly the sweet taste of the cake turned bitter in her mouth, and she had to force herself to swallow. Glancing away from Sam, she turned just in time to catch Wen and several bellboys enter the room with her trunk and discreetly head for the bedroom. Remembering the lacy French negligee, Molly trembled inwardly and took a large gulp of champagne.

The evening wore on slowly, each minute an agony of anticipation as Molly envisioned the tortures ahead. Yet when the last guest departed, it seemed as if the hours had raced past.

"Well, Mrs. Brannigan. At last we're alone." Sam swept her into his arms and kissed her thoroughly, the kind of kiss that usually made her hot and weak. This time, she felt only fear.

"I believe we've both had quite enough champagne," he told her. "I'll wait for you out here." His hazel eyes had changed to the smoky green that betrayed his desire, and Molly's stomach knotted in growing terror.

She nodded and fled the room. Closing the door behind her, she leaned against it in an effort to remain on her feet. How would she get through this? What should she expect? What would he expect of her? "Mother of God," she whispered aloud, "what am I going to do?"

Woodenly, Molly seated herself at the delicate spindle-legged bureau and pulled the fluffy tulle veil from her head. In the mirror, the reflection of the huge four-poster bed with its blue satin comforter loomed ominously. In minutes she'd lie naked beneath the sheets. Naked and quivering with fear beside a man who cared little for her except as a business partner and an object to satisfy his desires.

Her cheeks were flushed from the champagne, yet Molly felt strangely sober. With trembling fingers, she pulled the pins from her hair, then stroked the long red tresses over and over with her mother's silver-handled brush. Colleen James's dark-haired, blue-eyed face loomed in her mind's eye, infusing her with a fresh surge of guilt.

The lacy negligee had been spread out on the bed and her clothes neatly put away—a gentle reminder that this was now her room. Hers and her husband's. If only she'd married a man she trusted enough to let him show her the ways that would please him. Instead, she was entangled in a loveless marriage that was no more than a business arrangement.

The clock on the wall ticked ominously as long minutes passed. She'd had more than enough time and she knew it, but still she couldn't seem to get up. Trancelike, she dashed a bit of orange scent behind each ear and continued to stroke her hair.

Sam's light rap at the door seemed as loud as gunfire, setting her heart hammering against her ribs.

"Molly?" He opened the door without waiting for permission, and she felt a cool gust of air against her heated skin. He'd removed his shirt, but left on his breeches. Bare to the waist, his tanned skin glowed in the lamplight as he strode into the room. Molly remembered the power in his huge arms, the strength the man commanded, and shivered. Taking a deep breath, she forced herself to rise and face him.

His gazed swept her accusingly. "You're still dressed," he said, and she sensed his change of mood.

"Sam, please listen to me."

"Why are you still wearing your wedding dress?" His voice sounded harsh; the lines of his face had deepened, making him appear hard and remote. He worked a muscle in his jaw, and his eyes bored into her. "You've kept me waiting too long already." A heavy pulse pounded at the base of his throat, and she could not guess what thoughts he struggled to control.

"Sam, I . . . " She couldn't finish. There was nothing she could say.

"You're not thinking of breaking your agreement, are you?" When she didn't answer, he balled his hands into fists, and his eyes darkened till they looked like blackened pits. "We're married, Molly. And you agreed to uphold this marriage in every way. Now undress and get into bed."

Molly had never seen this side of him. Quietly calm, deadly serious, and so furious he could barely speak. "I . . . I can't," she whispered.

He seemed incredulous. "You can't!" The words echoed in her ears. "*Can't*, Molly? Or *won't*? You're married to me, by God, and you'll start acting like my wife. So get out of that dress right now!"

Molly backed away from him, shaking her head, unable to speak and deathly afraid. She had never seen Sam so angry, and right now he looked menacingly large. His fists were doubled at his side, and she knew his restraint was slipping.

Sam was mad with rage. He'd done everything in his power to please her, helped her get the timber contracts, given her a wedding, even bought her the dress she was wearing. And now it seemed he'd been a fool to marry her—none of her other lovers had. He stalked her, until she backed against the wall. Her eyes looked huge, her face stricken and pale. The sight of her withdrawal sent a fresh wave of fury the length of him. He could bet she hadn't acted that way with Michael Locke!

"You're mine, Molly. You sold yourself to me to save the Lady Jay. You're mine, and I'm going to have you—willing or not!" Her head moved from side to side as he reached a hand to the front of her wedding dress. He gathered the soft material in a bunch beneath his fingers and ripped it to her waist, the sound of the rending fabric muffling her tiny cry of fear. He clutched her lacy chemise and tore it away, leaving her full pink-tipped breasts spilling over the top of her corset, naked to his gaze, and rising tantalizingly up and down with her labored breathing. He ached to fill his hands with them—and he intended to do just that. She'd thought to make a fool of him—it was a mistake he'd teach her never to make again.

Grabbing her arms, he hauled her against him; he could feel the rigid set to her shoulders, the tension that betrayed her feelings. His mouth came down hard over hers, bruising her soft lips, slashing them against her teeth until he tasted a faint trace of blood.

He filled his hands with her breasts and pressed his stiff manhood against her, daring her to push him away, wanting to punish her for rejecting him. He tangled his fingers in her thick red hair, pulling her head back brutally, forcing his tongue between her teeth. He heard her whimper, felt her hands pressing feebly against his chest, and knew a pain in his own that pierced like a blade. She didn't want him. He sensed her aversion, her hesitancy, and knew an anger unmatched by anything he'd known before. She was his, by God! He'd bought and paid for her. He wouldn't keep her—he didn't want a woman who didn't want him. But with or without her consent, he'd bed her just this once—and she would never forget it!

Ruthlessly, he stroked the soft fullness of her nipple, and, even in her aversion, he felt it harden. A vicious stab of satisfaction coursed through him at the traitor her body was, and he moved to the side of her neck to nibble her ear and force a response.

He heard her whimper again—and then he felt her tears.

A blow to the stomach would have hurt him no more. The breath escaped his lungs; his stomach knotted into a hard, tight ball, and a buzzing filled his ears. Had he lost his senses completely? Nothing was worth causing another human being such pain. Shaky but resigned, he pulled away to stare at her tear-stained cheeks, the wetness in her eyes.

"Your uncle beats you till you're bloody and you have no tears, then you cry because your husband wants to love you. Do you hate me that much, lass?"

She shook her head, denying his words.

"Why, then? Why? You've been with other men, so it's not—"

She whispered the words so softly, he almost didn't hear them. "I lied," she said, then stared at the floor.

"You what?" He cupped her face in his hands while her body shook with quiet sobs. "What did you say?" His heart was beating so fast and hard he was sure she could hear it.

"I . . . I've never . . . there's never been anyone. . . ." Once she got started, the words tumbled out in a series of unfinished sentences. "I . . . I don't know what to do . . . I don't know anything about . . . about . . . " She looked so small and vulnerable. "And . . . I'm so . . . afraid."

Sam's chest tightened till he could barely breathe. He looked at the tears streaking her cheeks, the wetness spiking her lashes. A cry of remorse caught in his throat as he pulled her against his chest, cradling her, holding her and squeezing his eyes shut against the terrible image of himself ripping away her beautiful wedding dress.

"Forgive me, lass," he whispered, stroking her hair, letting her cry, kissing the top of her head. "Please. I never meant to hurt you. I just wanted you so damned much." She wrapped her arms around his waist and sobbed against him, clinging to him. Had he stopped in time? Would she be able to forgive him? Somehow he'd find a way to mend things. A way to make things right between them. Somehow he'd find a way for them to love.

Then he thought of her lie, and his temper sparked again. Holding her away from him, he forced himself to look at her sternly, though part of him longed to kiss away her tears.

"No matter what the reasons, lass, we're married. That makes us partners, and partners don't lie to each other. Promise me you'll never lie to me again." She sniffed and looked up at him, but didn't answer. "Promise me," he said, shaking her gently.

"I promise," she whispered. He drew her back into the circle of his arms, crushing her soft breasts against him. Feeling their silky warmth, he fought a fresh surge of desire. It was all he could do to still the throbbing in his loins.

"And you have my promise as well," he told her. "You don't have to be afraid, lass. I'll not bed you tonight." Another round of sobs shook her. "Do you hear me, Molly?" The up-and-down motion of her head rippled her thick curls and tickled his chest.

"If only you'd told me the truth, lass, none of this would have happened. I want to make love to you, but not until you're ready." She seemed to relax a little, and he felt the tug of a smile. "But I *am* going to sleep with you. There's nothing to be afraid of. Just let me take care of everything. All right?" Again he felt the movement of her head.

He set her away from him, all business, and slid the torn dress down over her hips. Next went the petticoats, then he unlaced her corset. When he slid her soft, lace-trimmed drawers down to her ankles and instructed her to step out of them, it took every ounce of his willpower not to take her right there on the bedroom floor.

She was all sweet curves and ivory skin with a tempting triangle of deep red curls to mark her womanhood. But he'd already come too close to destroying the tiny, tenuous thread of hope that was all they had. He'd wanted a virgin for a wife. Now, he had one. The thought that she hadn't really scorned him lifted a burden from his heart.

He left her only for a moment, to fetch the lacy French negligee. He grumbled beneath his breath, wishing he knew where to find a thick cotton nightgown, which wouldn't leave him hard and frustrated the rest of the night. But the truth was, now that he'd glimpsed her high full breasts, luscious curves, and shapely bottom, he wouldn't be able to sleep no matter what she wore.

"Raise your arms," he commanded. Molly obeyed him as if he were her jailer instead of her husband. When he finished dressing her, he lifted her into his arms and carried her to the deep four-poster bed, placing her carefully in the middle, treating her as if she were a china doll. She moved as close to the edge as she could get, and Sam chuckled at her valiant effort to protect herself. He removed his own clothes and lay down beside her, pulling her carefully against his hard length, knowing she could feel his erect manhood pressing determinedly against her hips, but knowing, too, the sooner she got used to him, the better for them both.

"I won't hurt you, Molly," he told her, "but you may as well find out what a man is like." He chuckled, a soft rumble in his chest. "I promise you, lass, soon you'll look forward to this as much as I do."

Molly was sure he was wrong.

# *Chapter Twelve*

MOLLY AWOKE to find Sam gone. She'd slept little, finding it nearly impossible in the arms of a naked man. She wondered if Sam had slept at all. During the hours she'd lain beside him, he'd stroked her hair, spoken soothing words, and several times, when he was sure she was sleeping, kissed her gently on the cheek. She found the sensation strangely disturbing. Now, as she stretched and yawned and saw the sun's yellow rays spreading across her pillow, she felt the tiniest twinge of disappointment in finding him gone. In a few short hours she'd grown to like the feel of him beside her, the warmth of his breath against the side of her face.

Molly rose and pulled the lacy peignoir over her nightgown, blushing a bit as she thought of the way Sam had undressed her. Moving to the window, she saw late-morning traffic bustling on the streets below—farmers' wagons piled high with hay, freight wagons carrying bricks, even a colorful red Overland stagecoach. Most of the traffic consisted of hansom cabs or carriages, hauling the rapidly growing population of city-folk on their myriad errands around the town. Businessmen in bowler hats and frock coats, along with ladies in bright silk tie-back walking dresses, parasols, and plumed hats, passed miners in grubby overalls and cowboys in wide-brimmed felts and denim breeches.

All in all, Denver was an exciting city, if a bit overwhelming to a woman traveling alone. Maybe that's why Molly had felt so out of her depth. Back home, she'd never have felt so helpless, so utterly defenseless. She'd never have allowed herself to depend so much on Sam. Just the knowlege that she'd be returning soon to the Lady Jay gave her a surge of spirit. She'd lost control last night, become fearful of something she didn't understand, then let her fears run away with her.

She rarely allowed her self-control to slip so, and she vowed never to let it happen again. Molly thought about the events of the evening, the terrible scene with Sam. He'd very nearly raped her, but she couldn't really blame him. She'd given her word, then broken it—something a

James didn't do. She'd lied to him, told him she'd slept with other men, hoping to upset his cocksure nature, and she'd succeeded—far beyond her expectations.

Wen's familiar singsong voice accompanied a knock at the door. "Bath for you, Missa Brannigan."

Donning her wrapper, Molly opened the door, allowing a blond youth and a tall, skinny boy to bring in steaming pails of water to fill the beautiful marble tub that regally monopolized one corner of the dressing room. Steam roiled in puffs off the surface as the tub filled up.

"You need me scrub your back?" Wen asked.

Some other time Molly might have enjoyed the luxury. But right now she needed some time alone. "No thank you, Wen. Maybe you could stop back by in an hour and do up my buttons."

Wen shook her finger in rhythm to her wizened head. "Not need Wen then. Husband say he take care, real good." She grinned knowingly, and Molly felt a blush spread to her toes. The old lady shuffled from the room, closing the door softly behind her. Molly could hear her cheerful humming as she moved through the salon and out the front door of the suite.

Even the little Chinese woman seemed nonplussed by what was supposed to have occurred last night. Her wedding night. Molly groaned with remorse. Last night she had botched things up and broken her word. Tonight she would set things right. The words Sam said about her selling herself for the Lady Jay still stung bitterly, but if that was what she'd done, then now was the time for her to pay. Molly felt better just knowing she was in control again. As long as she stayed that way, nothing could hurt her. Nothing could be as bad as it seemed last night. Other women married men who didn't love them and survived. She wasn't even sure her mother had loved her father, though Molly was sure Mal had loved Colleen.

In any event, other women submitted to their husbands, and so would she. Molly smiled at her decision and climbed into the tub. After all, Sam wasn't an ogre. As soon as he'd discovered her fears, he'd been gentle and understanding. She could trust Sam. He'd always been there for her. He wouldn't hurt her, not as long as he knew she was trying to do what was right. And perhaps the stories she'd heard at school had exaggerated matters. Perhaps a man's love was a good deal less terrifying than she had imagined.

Sinking into the tub, Molly felt lighthearted for the first time in days. She allowed herself to remember the feel of Sam's kiss, how warm and pleasant it had been. Maybe she would even learn to enjoy making love—just as Sam had said. Then another thought rose up to shake her. By then, she probably wouldn't be married to Sam.

Molly raised her arms above her head, struggling into her rust-colored silk plaid walking dress when Sam entered the room, again without permission. She guessed husbands were supposed to do that and found herself liking the idea.

"Here, let me help you." He tugged the dress down over her shoulders, and she settled it around her waist. Then he lifted her heavy mass of hair away and began working on the buttons. When he finished, he turned her to face him and kissed her soundly. This time the sensation sent warm shivers along her spine. How much easier this all seemed, now that she'd come to her senses.

"Well, Mrs. Brannigan," Sam said, "don't you look pretty." Her new name sounded strange to her and conjured a stab of guilt, but she liked the way Sam looked when he said it.

"And you, kind sir, cut a handsome figure yourself." His dark brown tail coat fit perfectly, accenting the width of his shoulders and his narrow waist and hips. Light brown trousers covered his muscular legs. When Molly recalled exactly what those long legs looked like—and how hard they felt pressed against her—a crimson blush warmed her cheeks and spread all the way to her toes.

"I thought we'd take in the city this afternoon," Sam told her, "and maybe the theatre this evening. The Faye Simonsen Opera Company is putting on *The Gods Grown Old.*"

"A perfect choice," Molly said, and didn't try to disguise the twinkle in her eye. Standing in the center of the room with sunlight glinting off his close-cropped beard and thick golden hair, Sam could have passed for Thor himself. All he needed was his magic hammer and a bolt of lightning in his hand.

Sam eyed her speculatively, wondering what she was thinking. An impish smile curved her luscious ruby lips, her neck and cheeks were flushed, and her tone seemed almost playful. The ease with which she had regained her good humor pleased him.

"I'm glad you're feeling fit this morning. You see—having a husband in your bed has improved your temper already." She blushed prettily but made no reply. He didn't tell her the rest of what he was thinking: that if she'd let him make love to her, her humor would be greatly improved on a daily basis. But after a sleepless night and a long, cold shower at the bath house down the street, he'd come to a decision: he'd court her awhile before consummating their marriage. He wanted it to be right for both of them, and a romantic side to his nature he hadn't known he possessed wanted to woo her in leisurely fashion, despite their hasty marriage.

"May I have the pleasure of escorting the prettiest lass in all of Denver on a tour of the city?" With a slightly mocking bow, he offered his arm.

"I assure you, kind sir, the pleasure is entirely mine." She rested her gloved hand in the crook of his elbow, and together they swept through the double doorway.

Molly knew she should be exhausted. She'd had the most wonderful day of her life. They'd seen Denver from top to bottom, been to a marvelous light opera, and shared a late supper in the most luxurious suite in the city. She'd slept little last night; she should be tired. Instead she felt strangely restless. Besides, she'd made up her mind to submit to her husband tonight, and submit she would.

Seated beside him on the blue brocade settee, Molly leaned over and kissed Sam's cheek. He'd been fidgeting for the past half-hour. And Molly found herself wondering at his thoughts.

"If you'll excuse me, Sam, I think it's time I made ready for bed." Just the sound of the word on her tongue flamed her cheeks scarlet.

Sam eyed her uncertainly. "Molly, I think I'll sleep out here tonight. I've got to get some rest, and I won't be able to sleep if I lie in there with you." He wound his finger in a lock of her hair, and his eyes turned smoky in that unmistakable way.

"I don't want you to sleep out here," she told him and noticed the pulse quicken at the base of his throat. Her own heart thudded uncomfortably.

"Do you know what you're saying, lass?" His finger moved absently along her cheek, and Molly's stomach squeezed into a hard, tight ball.

"I was wrong to do what I did last night," she said. "I was afraid, and I let my fear run away with me. I'm not afraid anymore." At least not terrified, she added to herself, but more than a little nervous.

The words constricted an iron band around Sam's heart. Molly was offering herself to him, wanting to please him. The thought made him light-headed and a little fearful at the same time. Was it too soon? Despite his earlier vow to court her, he longed to make love to her. He looked into her face and saw the certainty there. She'd thought this through and was ready for him. Sam wasn't about to let her misgivings return to haunt her again. Drawing her into his arms, he captured her lips in a warm, soft kiss, wanting to assure her he wouldn't hurt her. Making love was nothing remotely connected to what she'd experienced last night. He wanted her to know he'd help her through this first time, wanted her to sense his gentleness, know that he'd take care of things. When he released her, she didn't back away, just lifted her eyes to his and smiled.

"I'll wait here until you're ready," he said.

"No," she told him, determined to remain in control. If she closed the door between them, she'd never be able to open it again. "Come with me now. You can unbutton my gown."

Sam swallowed hard. He had never taken a virgin, had never wanted the responsibility. He was a little uncertain just how to proceed. With a slightly hesitant stride, he followed Molly into the bedroom. He unfastened her buttons, then sat on the edge of the bed while she moved into the dressing area to remove the gown and slip into one of the negligees he'd purchased. The ivory satin did little to hide her charms as she moved to the bureau. Sam's chest tightened.

Molly sat down in front of the mirror, intent on stilling her trembling hands. Sam was her husband, at least for the time being, a man who'd seen every part of her, held her next to him through the long hours of the night, a man who'd broken through her defenses and even made her cry. She'd been stunned at the time, but in a way she was grateful to be in touch with that part of herself again. After thinking things through, her fear had receded, replaced with a determined calm that surprised even her. She pulled the pins from her hair and brushed it a few quick strokes. The soft thud of Sam's boots hitting the carpet, then the slippery sound of his breeches being tossed away sent a tiny tremor the length of her.

Rather than let her uncertainties build again, Molly rose from the tapestry seat and moved toward the huge four-poster bed where Sam sat propped against the carved headboard, the covers pulled to his waist. She noticed the way the lamplight played against the muscles of his chest, the shadows it created beneath the taut skin over his ribs.

Molly climbed up on the bed beside him, her actions carefully controlled. Sliding beneath the sheets, she rested her head against the soft down pillow, pulled the covers to her chin, and closed her eyes, snuggling into the mattress until she was comfortable.

"I'm ready," she whispered, then waited tensely for Sam's next move. She heard a deep chuckle instead.

"Oh, you are, are you?"

Her eyes flew open. "Am I doing something wrong?"

"I suppose not." Sam slid down beside his

lovely young bride. What a picture of the virginal wife she presented. Stoic, resigned, determined to suffer what she supposed to be an indignity with as little complaint as possible. He felt a knot of disappointment curl in the pit of his stomach, but ignored it. Lots of brides were timid at first. Somehow he just hadn't expected it of Molly James.

Molly felt the touch of his lips and parted her mouth to receive his tongue. It felt sweet and warm but not insistent. Maybe this wouldn't be so bad, as long as she kept her mind occupied with other things. She concentrated on the ranch, on the timber they'd need to cut. Was Jumbo making progress with the timber crew? Was Joaquin able to hire more men?

She felt Sam's hand on her breast, his thumb brushing her nipple through the soft fabric of her nightgown, and a tiny tremor shook her. She tried to ignore it. Was Angel working too hard as always? Was her uncle giving the poor woman fits about her cooking? Sam's lips moved along the line of her jaw to nibble on her ear. She'd need to send a wire tomorrow, telling of her marriage and impending return to the ranch. She wanted to ride out to Pitch Camp as soon as they got back. Molly hardly noticed when Sam stopped caressing her.

Cursing beneath his breath, he ran a shaky hand through his thick blond hair and sat up in the bed. "Damn you, Molly Brannigan. Damn you for the little witch you are!"

She bolted upright, stunned at his words.

"But, Sam, what did I do? I thought this was what you wanted. You said I should fulfill my part of the bargain."

Sam was pulling on his breeches, fumbling with the buttons at the front. "I should have taken you last night, when you were soft and loving. At least I'd have known you were a woman."

Molly felt her temper flare. "And just what does that mean?"

"It means if I wanted to make love to a corpse, I'd have married someone who wasn't breathing!"

"How dare you say such a thing!" Molly came to her knees, hands on her waist, glaring up at him. "I let you kiss me, didn't I? I let you put your hands on me!"

Sam held his tongue and strode fiercely toward the door, carrying his boots and shirt in his hand. As he reached for the doorknob, a tiny voice nudged the back of his mind. *Don't be a fool, Sam. She's a virgin. She doesn't understand.* Sam grunted. Frigid was more like it. He should have known a woman in breeches would be cold and unresponsive.

Then the voice said, *She's a woman, Sam, not a china doll. Start treating her like a woman, and you'll get what you want.*

He turned to face her. Breathing hard, with her flame-red hair tumbled around her shoulders, covering the gleaming satin that outlined the points of her breasts, she looked furious and beautiful, and he wanted her more than ever.

Maybe the voice was right. His eyes roamed

over her; then a slow smile curved his lips. Molly was a virgin, all right, but she was also a woman. And where women were concerned, Sam Brannigan didn't doubt his capabilities. He watched the way the soft light played on her hair, the way her curves filled out the negligee.

He tossed his shirt and boots onto a chair as his long, sure strides carried him to the place beside her. Without a word, he tipped her head back and kissed her soundly, demandingly, sliding his tongue into her mouth to claim the sweetness within. As he wound his hand into the thick mass of her hair, he glimpsed her stunned expression. He could taste the gooseberry cake they'd shared, smell the orange blossom scent she wore.

As her breath quickened, he felt her heartbeat pounding against his hand. Moving his fingers downward, he cupped the fullness of her breast. He plundered her lips, nibbled the corners of her mouth, and knew a tightening in his groin and an inward smile as he heard her tiny moan of pleasure. With a single quick movement, he drew the negligee over her head, leaving her bare to his gaze.

Her eyes were closed, and he knew without a doubt he had her attention now. Her lashes fluttered open the moment before he kissed her again, her soft expression betraying her desire. When she slid her arms around his neck and laced her fingers in his hair, Sam let his tongue probe deeper, seductively exploring her mouth, and her tongue met his.

His hand lifted her soft full breast, caressing it,

kneading it. His thumb stroked the bud of her luscious pink nipple, and it hardened against his hand. He heard her gasp and felt her shiver, and continued his loving assault.

Again, Molly had lost control but this time, she didn't care. She cared only for the heat of Sam's kiss, the wetness of his tongue in her mouth, the warmth of his skilled fingers as they circled her breasts or stroked the flat spot below her navel. He left her only long enough to shed his breeches; then he was beside her, pressing her softly into the feather mattress, kissing her lips, her cheeks, her eyes, nibbling her earlobe, maddening her with his passion. She could feel the prickly hairs of his chest against her smooth skin, and warmed to his hardness pressing insistently against her. No longer frightening, his maleness seemed to complement her femininity, and she was aware of a lush wetness deep inside her.

When he lowered his head and took her rigid nipple between his teeth, Molly cried out at the delicious sensations. His lips were everywhere, arousing her, tasting her, making her want to do the same to him. And Molly did. She kissed his face, his cheeks, the curve of his mouth . . .

His massive neck intrigued her—the corded muscles, the pulse throbbing at the base of his throat. She nibbled his earlobe and made him groan, then felt thrilled by the power she held.

By the time he rolled on top of her, Molly was trembling all over, begging him for something, but uncertain what it was. "Please, Sam," she whispered. "Please." A surge of desire flooded her veins, and she felt strangely yet wildly on fire.

Sam groaned, moving his hands along her thighs, his fingers stroking her secret womanly place. She was wet there; how or why, she didn't know, but she could feel the liquid spreading down her legs, smell the musky odor. As Sam's fingers caressed that intimate place, all rational thoughts fled, replaced by dizzying sensations of pleasure.

Sam spread her legs with his knee and positioned himself above her, his throbbing manhood pushing urgently between her legs, then sliding tentatively inside her. She wanted it to go deeper. She didn't know why, but, God, she wanted it to.

"Please, Sam," she pleaded, still not understanding the sweet sensations. She clutched her arms around his neck, stroked the width of his shoulders, the corded muscles along his ribs.

"Soon, lass. Soon you'll get what you need." He claimed her mouth again, thrusting his tongue deeply, moving his body above her.

She writhed against him, wanting him, seeking him, glorying in the feel of him on top of her, thinking of nothing but her burning need. Sam clutched her tightly, lifted her buttocks, then penetrated her silken flesh. Molly cried out as a fiery pain tore through her.

He paused a moment, still deep inside, fighting for control. "It's all right, lass, the worst is over. From now on only pleasure." He held her a little longer, but remembered the lesson he'd learned. Molly was a woman—not some delicate child—with a woman's wants and needs. Slowly he began to move again.

Tears slipped down Molly's cheeks, but the pain wasn't repeated. Instead she felt a throbbing ache building between her legs that cried out for release. Molly felt Sam's hardness driving into her, felt her own tension mounting. Some instinct told her he was holding back, restraining himself on purpose, using every effort to control his movements. He thrust deeper and deeper, and the feelings he aroused drove her to frenzy.

"Please," she begged, and the sound of her voice, low and hot with desire, drove him on. He plunged into her, filling her, lifting her—until she knew not where she was, knew not what she wanted, saw only a fierce light in her mind's eye, and burst with such joy she cried out Sam's name, sobbing with relief and pleasure and glowing with a happiness she could not name.

Sam followed her to release, shuddering, his muscles bunching beneath her hands. Finally he relaxed against her. As their breathing calmed, he rolled to a place beside her and curled her in the crook of his powerful arm.

For the longest time, no words were spoken. Sam traced a light pattern in the fine sheen of perspiration on her shoulder. The air from the open window fluttered the silken draperies and cooled their heated skin.

"Sam?"

"Yes, lass."

"Was I . . . ? Were you pleased?"

"You were glorious and wondrous and lovely and beautiful. Yes, I was pleased. I think we both were." He looked down at her for an answer, and she smiled impishly up at him.

"It was the most wonderful thing that's ever happened to me," she told him candidly, then frowned. *Too wonderful.* So wonderful it could destroy her resolve, destroy her well-laid plans. The thought darkened her lighthearted mood.

Sam smiled down at her, a lock of his thick golden hair falling across his brow. "That's the nicest thing you could have said to me." He kissed her lips, still slightly swollen from his kisses, moved his mouth to her neck, and then back to her lips. A tiny gasp escaped when she felt his shaft against her, hot and hard again.

"Sam! Can people . . . do it twice?"

"Why don't we find out?" With a gleam darkening his hazel eyes, he leaned over her and covered her lips with his.

Molly felt a sharp flicker of conscience, but in moments it was lost to the heat of her passion, the wants and needs he soothed. With only a niggling suspicion of the guilt she'd feel tomorrow, she gave herself up to Sam's tender loving skills.

# Chapter Thirteen

✦✦✦✦✦

MOLLY SLEPT LATE. There was no warm sun to awaken her, only drifting clouds and blustery breezes. Glancing out the window, her mind on their abandoned lovemaking of the night before, Molly thought the weather fit her mood perfectly. Grim and dismal—like the traitor she was. Again Sam had risen before she awakened and left her alone. Today, she was glad he was gone. She needed time to think things through, to regain control. It seemed she'd been trying to do that a lot lately, with very little success. What was there about Sam Brannigan that kept her constantly at odds with herself?

Molly slipped into her cream-colored silk wrapper, lifting her tangled mass of hair out of the way and snugging the sash around her waist. How could she have let this happen? This was supposed to be a business arrangement, not a real marriage. So why did she feel so much like a wife? Sam's wife. No. Sam Brannigan's wife. She mustn't forget that. She'd gone to California to settle an old score, to repay the Brannigans for all the misery they'd caused her and her family. Instead, she'd fallen prey to Sam's charms. She felt like a fraud and a Judas. Her father wasn't even cold in his grave and here she was, pleasuring Sam Brannigan. Worse—letting him pleasure her!

She knew what Malcolm James's reaction would have been. Her father would have disowned her, thrown her off the ranch and out of his life for good.

"I want you packed and out of here," he'd once said to one of the hands. "I saw you drinkin' with Emmet Brannigan. As far as I'm concerned, that makes you a traitor to the Lady Jay. Get off my land and don't come back."

Molly twisted the folds of her wrapper. All the cowhand had done was *drink* with Emmet. She'd made passionate love with Sam.

Breathing a long, discouraged sigh, Molly untied her wrapper and slipped into the beautiful marble tub, which had been readied for her. She soaked for a while, then completed her toilette, donning a dove-gray traveling dress. Thank God they were going home. Maybe back at the ranch she could put things in proper perspective, get her priorities straight. The Lady Jay came first, of that she had no doubt. The rest she'd resolve day by day.

*It's only for a year,* she repeated to herself for the umpteenth time, but she felt a tremor of doubt as she remembered the feel of Sam's hard body pressing against her, the way his lips and hands caressed her, bringing her pleasure she hadn't dreamed existed. Somehow, some way, she had to remain as remote as possible, had to live up to her agreement but go not one inch beyond.

Sam's light knock distracted her. As he stuck his head through the door, she noticed his smile, warm and sensuous. Tiny butterflies fluttered in the pit of her stomach. She knew what he was thinking. She flushed and looked away.

"What do you say we get something to eat while Wen and the bellman ready our bags?" Sam suggested.

"That sounds wonderful. I'm starving."

His lips curved in a soft, teasing smile. "It's amazing what a little *exercise* will do for the appetite." He watched as a second wave of color touched her cheeks. She looked enchanting this morning, all somber and staid in her tailored gray dress, her flame-red hair in a tight chignon at the nape of her neck. Remembering the wanton lover beneath her proper facade, it was all he could do not to bed her again as he damn well wanted to. He would have, but he was afraid she might be a little sore, and he didn't want to press her too hard. There was much he intended to teach her, and now that they were married, he had all the time in the world.

He wished they could stay in Denver another week and have a real honeymoon, but neither of them could afford the time away from their ranches. At least not right now. When things settled down, he'd take her somewhere. Someplace elegant and extravagant, where he could shower her with gifts and make love to her endlessly. In the meantime, Peter could move in with Emmet until he opened his office in Sacramento. That would give them plenty of privacy and time to get to know each other.

But before they got home, there was still the long train ride, which he knew would leave him frustrated and moody. Just sitting across from Molly without being able to touch her would test his patience sorely. God, he'd be glad to get home.

Molly enjoyed the train ride back to California more than she imagined. Sam was wonderful company—most of the time. In the evenings he seemed distracted and often a little ill-tempered. She wondered if it was because they slept in separate berths. In the daytime, they played cards and checkers and dominoes. Sam was surprised when she beat him at chess. He said he'd never met a woman who was worth a damn at the game, then apologized for swearing. Molly just smiled. Of course, he'd beaten her the next two games in a row, which was typical of Sam. Where his wife was concerned, Sam seemed determined to let her know just exactly who wore the breeches in the family.

The sun was low in the afternoon sky when the train rumbled into the Truckee station. The breeze, stiff and cool, felt wonderful after the long desert crossing. Emmet and Peter were waiting for them as they descended the iron stairs to the platform. Having received a wire of Sam's marriage, each man gave his brother a congratulatory hug, then turned his attention to Molly.

Emmet swept his black felt hat from his head and nervously twirled the brim in his hand. "Welcome to the family, Miss James . . . er, Molly."

Peter was less formal. He drew her into his

arms and kissed her squarely on the lips, though with obvious brotherly restraint. "I hope Sam will forgive me for paying court to you, Molly." He grinned at the bigger man. "If I'd known his intentions were honorable, I'd never have tried to stand in his way."

Sam clapped his tall, lean brother on the back. "You never had a chance, lad. But then again, neither did she." Sam smiled down at her, and Molly noticed that his eyes held an unmistakeable hunger. The other brothers noticed it, too, and Molly blushed profusely. Was nothing sacred among these Brannigan men?

"C'mon," Emmet suggested, "Peter and I will get your bags. Patience is anxious to see if Molly has cost you your senses completely—no offense, ma'am."

Molly simply smiled. "I believe it is I who may have lost my mind."

"I hope you've lost your heart a little, too, lass," Sam whispered.

Molly straightened, ignoring the remark. Tonight she intended to perform according to her agreement. She would never put Sam through the horrors of just lying there—she wasn't even sure she could—but she certainly didn't intend to let him drive her to distraction as he had before.

"Hello, Sam." Judge Egan, Lilly's father, a stocky man with bushy brows and lines around his mouth, strolled up beside them.

"Hello, Judge." Sam glanced at Molly, and she wondered at his thoughts. He started to make the introductions, but the judge cut him off.

"This must be your lovely bride," he said, a bit dryly. "My daughter told me about your wire."

Molly hid her surprise. Thinking about it, she guessed Sam had little choice. He would have had to let the widow know before anyone else.

"You know Peter and Emmet," Sam said as the brothers returned with the baggage, "and this is my wife, Molly." She extended her gloved hand, and the judge brushed it against his lips, his eyes assessing her.

"My pleasure, Mrs. Brannigan."

"Pleased to meet you, Judge Egan," Molly said.

"Congratulations, Sam," the judge added. "You certainly picked a beauty."

"Thank you."

"Don't let me keep you," the judge said. "I know you've had a long trip, and I'm sure you have important matters to attend to." His knowing glance was tempered by the coldness in his eyes.

"Tell Lilly I send my respects," Sam added, but the judge seemed not to hear him. Instead, the somberly dressed man stepped back against the building and watched them depart.

Molly felt Sam's large hands surround her waist to lift her atop the wagon. She wondered at the judge's attitude, but guessed she couldn't blame him. Lilly should have been Sam's bride. It would have been better for all of them.

The image of the beautiful widow standing next to Sam wearing Molly's wedding gown flashed across her mind, and Molly felt a tightening around her heart. Glancing at her new husband, she found he was watching her curiously, as if he wondered what she was thinking. She forced an uncertain smile and channeled her thoughts in another direction. As the wagon rolled down the dusty streets, she pondered the evening ahead. She was tired and grimy and looking forward to getting some rest. She owed it to Sam to stay with him tonight, but tomorrow she'd return to the Lady Jay.

Sam knew something was different about the ranch house even before the wagon rolled to a stop. Below several of the windows, there were flower boxes filled with yellow chrysanthemums, and daisies lined both sides of the walk. Lifting Molly down, he moved into the house to find several bouquets of pink and red roses, and a banner above the stairs that read WELCOME HOME MOLLY AND SAM.

A warm smile lit his face. How like his family to put aside their biases and wish him well. His heart swelled with warmth as he turned to gratefully clasp his brothers' hands.

"I'll be staying with Emmet," Peter told him, grinning slyly. "My things have already been moved, so you'll have the whole place to yourself. We even gave Lee Chin some time off."

"I suppose this was Patience's idea," Sam teased. "Neither of you two are smart enough to know when you're not wanted." He squeezed Molly's hand, hoping his brothers would take the hint and leave them alone. Three days to a new husband was far too long without the comfort of his bride.

He turned his attention to the delectable little redhead who clung shyly to his arm. She always seemed reserved when reference was made to the marriage bed, and Sam found her modesty endearing. A delightful change from the other women he'd known—especially since he knew he could make that modesty disappear as soon as he closed the bedroom door.

Molly smiled and nodded and made as little idle conversation as possible. Her mind rested on the long minutes that remained before Sam took her into his arms. Half of her longed for the time to hurry by. The other half dreaded the moment they did.

"You say Lee Chin's gone, too?" Sam said to Peter.

"We thought Molly would rather cook than give up her privacy."

Sam looked at her with a teasing light in his eye. "The only problem with that logic is that Molly may not know how to cook. Maybe we'll just have to live on love."

"Of course I can cook!" Molly replied indignantly. "Angel taught me."

"Angel?" Sam hoped his uncertainty didn't show.

"She happens to be a very good cook."

"We'll haul your bags upstairs," Emmet said,

"then be leavin'." Sam smiled. Molly looked down at the floor as if searching for some lost object.

"I'd better warn you," Peter told them as he helped Emmet drag Molly's trunk upstairs. "Patience has a get-together planned for you two a week from this Saturday. Half the county's invited."

Sam groaned. Molly felt the blood drain from her face. She had been hoping to keep the marriage as quiet as possible; then, when the dissolution came, few would be the wiser. Now that would be impossible. She guessed it didn't really matter. In a community as close-knit as Truckee, nothing stayed secret very long.

As soon as his brothers were gone, Sam scooped Molly into his arms and carried her upstairs to the huge master suite. With a booted foot, he opened the heavy plank door and carried her, "over the threshold" as he called it. Threshold of what, Molly couldn't say. The Cedar Creek Ranch was not her home, could never be her home. The thought strengthened her resolve.

Too soon, she found she needed every ounce of her self-discipline. Sam's mouth came down hard over hers, insistent and cajoling at the same time. She felt a wave of heat surge through her veins. His tongue moved between her lips to taste the warmth of her mouth, and Molly knew all the promises she'd made to herself weren't worth the time she'd spent making them.

"I was going to let you bathe," he whispered

in her ear, "but I can't wait that long. Besides, that womanly smell of yours drives me insane."

Molly knew exactly what he meant. Even dusty and grimy from their trip, Sam's masculine scent only made her heart beat faster. There was something primitive about it, something elemental that stirred an ache between her legs before she even had her clothes off.

She let him strip her dress, corset, and petticoats, then helped him shrug out of his shirt and breeches. She felt his arms beneath her knees, as he carried her to the huge tester bed that dominated the center of the room. The puffy quilted comforter felt soft against her skin as Sam deposited her on the feather mattress.

He lowered his mouth to her nipples, which were already hot and hard, and she laced her fingers through his thick blond hair. God, how she wanted him. What a fool she'd been to think she could control her responses.

Sam tasted Molly's round pink nipple and groaned at the pleasure it gave him. She writhed and arched against him, demanding he take her, wanting him but afraid to let him know it. He'd been right about her all along. She was all woman, not fragile and gentle and careful like Lilly, but passionate—giving all she had, yet demanding something in return. And he wanted nothing more than to give it to her.

Feeling her wet and ready for him, he mounted her and guided himself inside. He felt her tight heat all the way to his loins. With a groan of pleasure he drove into her, penetrating her with his hard length again and again.

Molly met each of his thrusts with a parry of her own. She drew him deep into her warmth, deeper than she'd thought possible. He filled her completely, then withdrew, torturing her, teasing her until she could stand the sweet agony no more. With a tiny moan of pleasure, she burst upon the silver horizon. Tiny pinpricks of delight exploded in her blood.

Sam followed her to release, then held her gently in his arms. When their breathing calmed, he propped himself on an elbow.

"Turn over."

"Why?" she asked, suddenly hesitant.

"I want to look at your back."

Molly did as she was told. His fingers lightly brushed the surface of her skin, examining the tiny ridges and valleys that were left from her beating.

"By the saints," he swore softly, "I'll have that bastard's hide for this one day." He pressed his lips against a scar near her waist.

"It's still important to keep the matter secret," she cautioned. But then she smiled. "Someday, I'll help you have the bastard's hide.' "

For a moment Sam looked surprised by her casual use of his swear word, then he laughed in that deep rumbling way of his and pulled her into his arms. "One thing's for certain, lass. Being married to you will never be dull." Then he kissed the top of her head and drew her to her feet. "I'll put the water on for your bath, milady." He bowed formally. "But only if you'll let me join you."

Molly accepted defeat graciously, nodding her

head and moving toward the big hammered brass tub that rested in one corner of the room. Sam headed for the door. It would take several trips to fill the tub, but he seemed more than willing, and Molly looked forward to being clean, even if it meant sharing the tub with Sam.

Making love to him again had shown her the futility of trying to control her body. The bedroom seemed to be Sam Brannigan's ultimate domain. The trick was to keep him from getting her there as much as possible. She'd agreed to spend three nights a week at Cedar Creek. If she played her cards right, Molly could limit their lovemaking to the same number of times. Sam wouldn't like it, to be sure. But Molly had to soothe her conscience. And it would help her remain uninvolved—or at least less involved.

They finished the bath, and Molly pleaded a headache. Sam grumbled, but politely respected her wishes. Donning a prim cotton nightshirt, she slid between the sheets. She was sound asleep seconds after her head touched the pillow.

Sam was downstairs, cooking eggs and bacon by the smell of it, before Molly came fully awake. Freshening up quickly, she dressed in her breeches and shirt. Since she'd gotten so used to wearing them, she'd packed them along on her trip just in case—and now she was glad she had. She could go straight to the ranch, saddle True, and get to work. After a brief stop to see Joaquin she'd go up to Pitch Camp.

Heading downstairs, Molly hummed a light tune. She pushed open the kitchen door to find Sam standing over the cookstove with a spatula in his hand. Pervading the air with its rich aroma, coffee sputtered onto the hot iron, so Sam carefully set the big black pot aside.

When he turned to greet her, the smile on his face faded to a narrow, unfriendly line. "What in blazes are you doing in those?"

Molly stiffened. "I'm doing exactly the same thing I've been doing every day since my return to the Lady Jay. I'm going to work."

"I hoped you'd stay here a few days. I was bringing you breakfast in bed." His smoky green eyes said he also planned on making love to her.

The idea intrigued her more than a little, but she pushed the thought away. "I'm afraid I have too much to do. I'll be back tomorrow night, just as I promised."

She turned aside, wanting to ignore the disapproval in his eyes. His gaze roamed the length of her, coming to rest on the seat of her breeches.

"I was also hoping you'd be smart enough to know a married woman can't go running around the countryside in a pair of men's breeches. Go put on a dress."

Molly's temper fired. "Do you know what you're saying? Now who's breaking their commitment? You said I could run the ranch. That's exactly what I intend to do, and I certainly can't do it in a dress!" She stormed toward the door. "You knew what I was like when you married me. Don't try to change me now!" She dragged open the heavy door and shoved open the screen, letting it fall back against the wood with a loud bang as she moved across the porch and down the wooden stairs.

Sam raced after her. "Come back here, Molly. You're my wife, damn it!"

Molly kept on walking. "I'm borrowing a horse. I'll return it when I come back—*if* I come back!"

The blood rushed to Sam's face, his fury igniting a pounding in his head. Damn her! She was without a doubt the most stubborn, pigheaded woman he'd ever met! He couldn't believe she still intended to wear those breeches. Why, he'd be the laughingstock of the whole damned county!

Sam sniffed the air, groaned inwardly and raced back toward the house. As he opened the door, smoke billowed from the kitchen. Striding across the room, gritting his teeth, he picked up the skillet full of burnt eggs and bacon. What the hell! He'd lost his appetite anyway.

Sam had plenty of time to contemplate his marriage, for Molly didn't return that night or the next. He was torn between anger at her impertinence and despair that he missed her so much. How quickly she'd inched her way into his heart. The nights without her seemed endless. He'd had plenty of time to think things through, and he didn't like his conclusions one little bit—he was thinking maybe Molly was right!

She'd only agreed to marry him in the first

place because she wanted to keep the ranch. She loved that place, and Sam knew it. How could he expect her to give it up for him?

He had spent the last two days checking on the timber operations and helping Emmet with the cattle. Today, he decided, he'd ride over to the Lady Jay. Maybe he could talk some sense into his pretty little wife; maybe they could reach some sort of compromise that would leave his pride intact and convince her to come back home.

Emmet rode up as Sam strode to the barn. The wry grin on his brother's face told Sam he was well aware of Molly's departure.

"Your lassie fightin' the bit?" Emmet asked.

Sam just grunted and kept on walking. "Don't you have some fence to mend?"

"That bad, is it? Should have married a sweet woman like my Patience, but knowin' you, all that good treatment would have bored you in a week's time. At least this one'll keep you interested."

Finally Sam grinned. "I'll try to remember that when I feel like wringing her neck."

"Like now?" Emmet teased.

"Exactly." Sam led Gil from his stall, saddled him, and mounted. Emmet waved over his shoulder as Sam set out for the Lady Jay to fetch his headstrong wife.

When Sam reached the ranch house, Angel stood in the kitchen, preparing the evening meal, something she was rarely allowed to do anymore, she told him. She also told him how happy she was to have him in the family.

"You will be good for Molly, Señor Sam. Maybe you keep her in line. Joaquin and I, we do not have a prayer."

Sam grinned down at the charming little woman whose girth nearly matched her height. "She's a handful, Angel. I'll tell you that."

"She's pretty mad at you, Señor Sam. She say you make a deal, then break it. I tell her Señor Sam would never do that, but she just storm out the back door. She did not even eat her *chile con queso.* I don't think she get much sleep, either. I saw her walking around out back way past midnight."

Sam felt the pull of a smile. Maybe he wasn't the only one who was miserable. Either way, until he could think of a solution, he'd decided to let her wear the breeches—so long as she understood it applied only to hers, not to his.

"Where is she now, Angel?"

"She rode up to Pitch Camp this morning. Something about a new section of timber."

"Thanks." Sam touched the brim of his hat.

"You want some *chili con queso?*" Angel asked. "I make it fresh this morning."

Sam shook his head, his stomach roiling at the thought of the spicy Mexican food he found so hard to digest. "Maybe next time." He moved out through the kitchen door, mounted Gil, and headed toward the high country, hoping Molly's temper had cooled as much as his own.

* * *

"I tell you, this here goose-pen tree is gonna fall six degrees right a' yonder." Beefsteak Marlowe leveled his arm and pointed in the direction of the late afternoon sun.

"Yer as wrong as wrong can be," Joey Mavis disagreed. "This ponderosa's gonna land four feet left of that ol' sawed-off white pine."

The two men stood eye to eye as Molly approached. "What are you boys arguing about?"

Beefsteak, the shorter of the two, a middle-aged logger with a bald spot at the back of his head and a thick handlebar mustache, answered, "Joey here thinks this burnt-out ponderosa we're fellin' is gonna land one way; I believe she'll go t'other."

"What do you think, boss lady?" Jumbo Reilly, all 270 pounds of him, sauntered up beside her.

Molly had ridden in two hours ago, checked on the camp, spoken with Torger, then headed up to the new section to find Jumbo. She smiled warmly, liking the big logger a little more every day.

Molly walked around the two deep notches that had been cut at the front and back of the goose pen—what the loggers called a dangerous, partially burned-out tree. They were hard to predict, their weight being unevenly distributed along the trunk, but Molly thought this one more easily discernible than some she'd seen.

Pleased with the loggers' progress, and feeling a little playful as the day neared its end, Molly pursed her lips. "Tell you what I'll do. I'll bet all three of you a five-dollar gold piece I can set the wedge and make this tree fall on the spike I'll lay."

Jumbo guffawed. "You never cease to amaze me, little girl. I got a fiver says you can't."

Beefsteak and Joey grinned. "We'll take your action, boss lady."

"Jumbo, will you drive my wedge for me?"

"Sure thing."

"Then all bets are on." Again Molly moved around the great trunk of the pine. She knelt and examined every inch of the tree, climbed up on the springboard—the plank notched into the tree that provided a work platform—and checked the inside portion that had been destroyed by fire. When she was satisfied, she climbed back down, picked up a steel spike, and moved away from the tree in a direct line along the path she believed the tree would topple. About forty feet out, she rechecked the tree, knelt, and began to hammer the spike into the ground.

As he approached the men in the clearing, Sam spotted his wife kneeling some distance away. "What in blazes is she doing?" he asked as he dismounted and walked up beside Jumbo. The big logger chuckled and explained about the bet Molly had made. Sam felt his heartbeat quicken.

"It's too damn dangerous, Jumbo. Those goose pens can jump backward and cut a man in half. I won't stand for it!" Sam started forward, but Jumbo caught his arm. Sam stiffened against the big man's powerful grip, and a wave of anger hit him at the logger's affront.

"Don't do it, Sam," Jumbo warned. "She's worked too hard to gain the men's respect."

Sam tensed even further. Jumbo still held his arm, a gesture indicating he meant to back up his words.

"Besides," Jumbo added, "I'm gonna drive her wedges in. Even I wouldn't let her do that."

Sam took a deep breath and relaxed, and Jumbo let go of his arm.

"You're a smart man, Sam. Smart enough to know a damn fine woman when you see one. She's already a legend up here. She pulls this one off, they'll be talkin' about her for years."

Sam grinned at the bigger man. "Thanks, Jumbo. Where that woman is concerned, sometimes I don't think as straight as I should."

"I don't blame you. She's somethin'. Treat her right, and she'll make you a good wife—that is, if you can keep her home."

Sam just nodded.

Molly finished pounding the spike into the ground and turned to take a last look at the tree. Even from a distance, she recognized Sam's blond beard and wide shoulders. Her heart began throbbing with a uneven beat. How could he have such a maddening effect on her? Walking purposefully toward the loggers, who by now numbered most of the men in the camp, she noticed Sam stood taller than all of them except Jumbo. A gentle breeze ruffled his thick golden hair, and Molly felt like rushing into his arms. God how she'd missed him! To her chagrin, the days without him had seemed like years.

"Hello, Sam."

"Hello, Molly." His eyes lingered on her shirt-front, and she wondered why he'd come. He didn't look angry, but she sensed something was on his mind.

"Ready, Jumbo?"

The logger grinned and picked up a sledge-hammer. Molly leaned over and picked up four heavy metal felling wedges. She pressed one into the backcut, marking the spot where Jumbo should drive the steel. As Jumbo began his powerful strokes, she felt Sam's arm gently but firmly drawing her back a safe distance from the tree.

When the wedge was far enough in, Molly did the same with the second wedge, then the third, and the fourth.

Even hammer strokes, metal ringing against metal on each of the four wedges, started the cracking rumble that accompanied the log as it began to topple toward the earth.

"Timber!" one of the loggers yelled, and a cheer went up among the men. The huge tree groaned with the massive force of its weight, strained and teetered, then careened through the air. A *whoosh* followed by a heavy crashing thud set the ground atremble beneath their feet. The men rushed forward to locate the spike, and for a few heartstopping seconds, Molly was sure she'd missed.

"Here it is!" Beefsteak cried out, pointing to a place beneath the trunk of the tree.

Molly was jumping up and down, shouting with the others when she felt Jumbo's huge hands circle her tiny waist and her feet lifted off the ground. He rested her daintily on one of his massive shoulders and carried her toward the camp. Sam scowled only for a moment; then, caught up in the excitement, he let himself be swept along in the throng of loggers who surrounded his redheaded wife.

"You'll have to stay for supper," Jumbo told him. "Your little girl's just been declared the guest of honor!"

# *Chapter Fourteen*

SAM WASN'T SORRY he had to stay. With Lee Chin gone, he hadn't eaten a decent meal since he'd left the train. And the loggers' home-cooked meals were delicious, even taken in the stuffy quarters they called home.

Jumbo set Molly back on her feet and pushed open the bunkhouse door. The familiar, stuffy smell of drying woolen socks and shirts, sweat, snuff, and coal oil was disguised by the pungent aroma of meats and fresh-baked bread. Mountains of golden corn, beans, and potatoes steamed on the rough-hewn planks as the loggers unlaced their corks—the spiked boots they wore—and bellied up to the table.

After helping Molly to a place between himself and Jumbo, Sam dug in, as hungry as the lumberjacks. He noticed Molly eyed him rather suspiciously, but her temper seemed to have cooled, and now was not the time for the discussion he had in mind.

Used to eating in a hurry, the men bolted down their food, and Molly tried her best to keep up. Sam grinned when she'd finished less than half her plate by the time the others were through.

"I . . . I guess I was too excited to eat," she lied. Watching the way her tongue touched the corner of her mouth as she eyed the last few pieces of apple pie being taken back to the kitchen, Sam smiled good-naturedly.

"Think you could get the gut robber to send home that pie for Molly?" he asked Jumbo. "I'm afraid she hasn't learned to eat quite as fast as we have."

"That little girl's gonna have to learn she don't have to be a man all the time."

"That's a lesson I'm doing my best to teach her, Jumbo."

Jumbo chuckled and clapped Sam on the back. "Good luck, Sam. If any man can, it'll be you . . . only . . ."

"Only what?"

"Only, I ain't so sure any man can!" Jumbo laughed uproariously. He pulled the cork from a bottle of Who Hit John and handed it to Sam, who took a long draw. Thinking of Jumbo's words, he glanced toward Molly, then passed the bottle to her. Several of the loggers watched for her reaction. Molly glowered hotly, grabbed the bottle, and took a long pull equal to Sam's.

Sam knew he had her. Lesson time, he said to himself. I'll teach her who wears the breeches in this family once and for all. After Molly passed the bottle back, Jumbo motioned them outside. Sam smiled at the big logger's perceptions. Molly was Jumbo's boss, and he didn't want her to look like a fool in front of her crew, but he was a man first, and men stuck together. Molly James Brannigan needed a lesson in femininity, and Sam Brannigan and Jumbo Reilly were about to give her one.

"So, little girl," Jumbo taunted, "you like a little whiskey after a meal?"

"Not exactly," Molly hesitated.

"Well, you must like it a little," Sam chimed in. "I noticed you didn't even blink when I offered it to you."

Molly clenched her fists, beginning to get angry. She'd only accepted the whiskey because Sam had put her on the spot. Even then, she would have said no, but her temper was still sore from the fight they'd had two days ago, the sleepless nights she'd had—and the ache in her heart from missing him so much.

Forcing herself to be calm, Molly shrugged. "I just wanted to see what the great attraction was. Now that I've tried it, I can see there's nothing to it at all. For years, you men have been acting as though it were some secret male potion, when in truth it's just like drinking hot cough medicine."

Jumbo held out the bottle. "You have to have a few more sips before you understand the *attraction*, as you call it."

Molly looked from Jumbo to Sam and back

again. So that was the way of it. Sam was still mad at her for wearing her breeches, and Jumbo obviously took his side. She jerked the bottle from the big bullwhacker's hands and took a long swig. Again she was able to control the cough that swelled her throat, but she couldn't keep the burning tears from her eyes. Watching each man fight to hide a knowing grin, she tilted the bottle up for another long draw. This time Sam's brows drew together, and his hazel eyes darkened.

He lifted the bottle to his own lips and emptied a goodly portion of the amber liquid down his throat. Jumbo accepted the bottle and repeated the process, his Adam's apple bobbing with the motion.

Another swig from the bottle, and Molly felt a surge of warmth and a wave of dizziness. It was no longer unpleasant. In fact, she felt wonderful. "You know," she said, after a few more draws on the bottle, "maybe you men have something, after all." She graced Sam with a lopsided smile, her vision a little fuzzy and her words beginning to slur.

"I've never felt so . . . so . . . absolutely free! I know I should be worrying about the ranch, but I don't even remember *why* I should be worrying." She giggled and slapped Sam on the thigh. "How about some more?"

Sam's jaw clamped shut, and he scowled furiously, but Molly didn't care.

Jumbo left momentarily and returned with a bottle of Simmond's Medicated Nabob Whiskey. "We don't keep much whiskey in camp. This'll have to do." He pulled the cork with his teeth, took a swig, and passed the bottle to Sam.

Molly found the taste of the second bottle less repulsive than the first. In fact, she could barely taste it at all, but she loved the warm glow she felt—from the top of her head to the very tip of her toes.

"Sam," Molly giggled, "why didn't you give me some of this before?" When she laced her fingers through his hair, Sam glowered down to her, and Jumbo rose from the log they sat on.

"I hope this works out the way you planned, Sam."

"We're going home," Sam announced. "Loan me the rest of that bottle. She started this little game; now, I intend to finish it."

Jumbo tossed him the bottle. Sam offered Molly a drink, which she accepted, giggling, then he tugged her toward her horse. "Can you ride?" he asked.

"Don't be silly. Of course I can ride. Why? Can't you?" She grinned drunkenly up at him, and Emmet's observation that at least she'd keep him interested rang in Sam's ears—because he definitely felt like wringing her neck.

She tried to mount and after two unsuccessful attempts, Sam swung her up into the saddle. "Thank you," she told him. "You are truly a gentleman."

Sam just grumbled. Forcing her to ride ahead of him, he followed her down the trail. Periodically he stopped to pass the bottle to her. Each time she grandly accepted a drink, and Sam was amazed she could still sit her horse. He almost wished she'd pass out so he could sling her across the saddle and jounce some sense into her. He hit the bottle a few times himself, just to keep his temper under control.

By the time they reached the ranch, Molly was singing and swaying precariously on her horse. By this time, Sam could barely keep his fury in check. He hauled her off her mount, left both horses to one of the stable boys, and carried her into the house. When he reached the master bedroom, he pulled off her clothes and tossed her naked onto the bed. She fell back against the pillows with a giggle. Sam tugged off his boots and shirt, temper high, then worked the buttons on his breeches. He fully intended to pleasure himself with his young wife's luscious body; he'd thought of nothing else for the past two days.

"Sam?"

"What?" he snapped.

"I'm not feeling"—she hiccuped—"too well."

Sam's fury surfaced. "Damn you, Molly. Don't you dare get sick!"

But it was already too late. Molly slid from the bed, holding her hand over her mouth, and ran for the chamber pot behind the screen in the corner. He could hear her retching and moaning, and felt an unwelcome stab of guilt.

Sighing resignedly, he poured water into the pitcher on the bureau, wet a cloth, and walked around the screen to where the little redhead leaned over the pot and moaned pitifully. He'd get no comfort from her tonight, that was for sure. He just hoped she'd learned a lesson. He wanted a woman for a wife, damn it! Not some hoyden who played at being a man. Holding her head as she heaved again, he almost regretted his role in her drunkenness. Almost, but not quite. Sam intended to turn Molly Brannigan into a wife one way or another.

Molly was on a ship, the waves crashing over the bow, the ocean rolling beneath her. Her head pounded in rhythm to the sea, and her stomach tossed and turned. God, she felt like she was dying. She opened her eyes but immediately snapped them shut again. Blinding sunlight streaked into the room, causing her stomach to roll over again and splitting her head apart with pain.

"Good morning." Sam's deep voice held a note of triumph she didn't understand.

"Sam?"

"Yes, lass?"

"Where are we?"

"If you open your eyes, you'll see you're right where you belong. Home—in our bed."

"What happened?"

He strolled to her bedside. When he sat down on the mattress, the slight movement shot another wave of nausea through her. She swallowed hard and fought the bile in her throat.

"You don't remember?" he asked.

"I remember being at Pitch Camp. Then you came."

"And we had dinner—"

"God, don't mention food!"

"That bad, huh?"

Molly just covered her eyes with the back of her hand and groaned. Sam pulled her to a sitting position. "Here. Drink this." He handed her a mug half full of something thick and smelling a bit like the whiskey she'd consumed the night before.

Another bout of nausea threatened. "I can't."

"Yes, you can. It'll make you feel better, I promise."

"I don't trust you anymore."

So she did remember some of it, after all. "Molly, I didn't make you drink the whiskey."

"No, I suppose not."

"You know, lass, women are made to be different than men. That's the way God planned it."

"I'm just as smart as you are, Sam! I work just as hard, and I want the same things you do."

Sam laid a damp cloth on her forehead. "I never said we weren't equal, Molly. I only said we were different. It's okay to be a woman."

"Women are dependent. I can't afford that, at least not right now. I have to make the ranch work. I have to, Sam. It's the most important thing in the world to me."

Sam released a long breath and raked his fingers through his hair. "I know, lass. I know." How he wished he didn't. How he wished *he* were the most important thing in her life—he and the family they would raise. He wondered if she even wanted children. They'd never discussed it. Maybe she hated the idea. Maybe that's why she avoided making love as much as possible. It certainly wasn't because she didn't enjoy it.

There was so much about each other they didn't know, so much they disagreed on. Still, underneath, Sam felt he'd found his perfect mate. Somehow he'd make her change, make her love him and want to stay with him. Somehow he'd find a way.

The week progressed uneventfully. Sam said nothing more about her clothing, and Molly kept her word scrupulously. She spent every other night with Sam, making love only once each time, then returning the next morning to the Lady Jay. On the day before the wedding celebration, Molly stood in Sam's kitchen watching the late afternoon sun. She had arrived at the ranch ahead of Sam and, since Lee Chin would not be back until Sunday, was determined to cook Sam's supper. She was chopping onions to stir into a simmering pot of chile verde when Sam pulled open the screen door.

His face looked drawn, his eyes bleak.

"Sam?" Molly's heart went out to him. "What is it? Are you all right?"

Sam's heavy footfalls carried him across the steamy room. He pulled out one of the high-backed kitchen chairs, the sound scraping across the wooden floor, and slumped wearily into the seat. "There's been an accident. Down at the mill. The bearfighter was hurt pretty bad."

Molly knew a bearfighter was a man who separated strips from boards in the sawmill. "What happened?" She moved to stand beside him.

"One of the blades came loose, cut him up pretty bad."

"Is he going to be all right?"

"Yes, but he'll be off work for quite a while. I'll provide for the family, of course. But the worst part is, I'm not sure it was an accident. I looked at the equipment; it appeared to have been tampered with. Who in blazes would do a thing like that?"

"I don't know, Sam." Molly walked over to stir the bubbling concoction on the stove. "At least the man will be all right. Maybe it was just some sort of mistake."

"I hope so."

"You know," Molly told him, "I've been meaning to stop by your mill. I'd like to see how you operate. Someday maybe we could build one of our own."

Sam stiffened, knowing that *we* and *our* meant the Lady Jay. "*We* have a sawmill, Molly. You're welcome to use it any time you like. Matter of fact—" He reached into his pocket, then opened his palm.

Molly picked up the tiny round leather button. "You found it!"

"It is yours, then?"

"Why yes, off my high-button shoe. I lost it last week. Where did you find it?"

Sam watched her carefully. "Not far from here," he evaded. He'd found it beside the saw at the mill. Why had she said she'd never been there? Had she just forgotten? Sam refused to allow his mind to come to any other conclusions.

"What's for dinner?" he asked, changing the subject and sniffing the air. "Something smells awfully good."

"Chile verde and tortillas. Angel says mine are even better than hers."

Sam groaned inwardly. He should have known if Angel taught her to cook, he'd be eating spicy Mexican food. "I'll go wash up and be down in a few minutes."

Molly nodded and left to set the table. She waited anxiously for Sam's return, eager to please him, then set a steaming bowl of chile verde in front of him. She handed him a tortilla, then did the same for herself. Ravenous after a long day in the saddle, Molly was halfway through her meal, sopping up the juice with the tightly rolled tortilla, before she glanced up to see Sam had eaten little of his food. The tortillas were gone, even the ones steaming beneath the folds of a dish towel, but the spicy pork and chile stew remained nearly untouched.

Sam caught Molly watching him. Hefting a forkful of stew, he took a big bite, chewed, and swallowed. Tears came to his eyes, and his face turned red.

"It's very good," he said.

"You don't like Mexican food." Molly looked disappointed.

"Oh, but I do." He ate another heaping spoonful. "See? And yours is the best I've ever eaten." In fact, it was only the second time he'd tried the spicy food. Lee Chin had certainly never prepared it, and he'd passed up Angel's occasional offerings, knowing he wouldn't like it just from the smell. The first time he'd tried Mexican cooking, he'd gotten deathly ill. This time his throat burned and his eyes watered, but he finished every bit on his plate. God, he'd be glad when Lee Chin came home.

"You want some more?" Molly asked, jumping up to serve him.

"No! I mean, no thank you. I'm really very full. It was delicious. Thank you, Molly."

"You're welcome."

Later that night, Molly had one of her famous headaches, and Sam wondered again if she worried about getting pregnant. Knowing the headache was a ruse, he let her get away with it only because his stomach was feeling queasy. But he was determined to have her in the morning. She always looked delectable when she woke up: red hair mussed across her pillow and a languorous smile on her face.

Having slept fitfully, Sam awoke before dawn, rose and freshened up, then returned to bed. Molly opened her eyes and yawned. She'd worn her cotton nightdress, and Sam hadn't protested. It was hard enough for him to sleep beside her when she was fully clothed, let alone half-naked. She tried to slide from the bed, but Sam caught her around the waist and pulled her against him.

"Not this time, you don't." He lowered his head and kissed her soundly, but Molly pulled away.

"No, Sam. I have to get back to the ranch." She tried to roll free, but Sam forced her back down.

"Damn you, Molly. You like this as much as I do. Why won't you let me make love to you?"

"I . . . I have too much to do. Let me go, Sam." She jerked away and slid from the bed.

"You're not going anywhere until I'm through with you!" Grabbing the back of her nightshirt, he hauled her back on the bed. Molly rolled to her knees and grabbed one of the massive bedposts. Her flame-red hair fanned out across her back as she looked over her shoulder and waited for his next move.

Sam just chuckled. He grabbed her slim ankle and tugged her none too gently down on her stomach, sliding her across the covers toward him. The nightdress bunched beneath her arms as her body slid from beneath it, exposing her round ivory buttocks to his view.

Molly clung to the post tenaciously. "Leave me alone, Sam. I'm not going to let go, so you can just forget it."

This time Sam laughed aloud, the sound a hearty rumble in his chest. "Have you never seen a stallion mount his mare, lass?"

Molly sucked in a breath. "Surely people can't . . ."

Naked and aroused, Sam climbed back onto the bed."I can see it's time for another lesson, lass." He nibbled her ear and kissed the curve of her neck. His hands slipped beneath her breasts, caressing the peaks of her nipples until they grew hard. He heard her tiny gasp of pleasure, but she didn't let go of the post. He trailed his fingers along her back to stroke her bottom, kneading the smooth flesh, caressing it, then he leaned down to kiss the tantalizing roundness and felt her quiver. He slipped his hands between her thighs to tease her womanhood and found her wet and ready.

Smiling to himself, he returned to the back of her neck, fitting himself against her, spreading her legs with his knee.

Molly felt his hardness pressing between her legs, felt his loins against her bottom, and the feeling sent a surge of fire through her veins. She knew she was ready when she felt him slip inside her, then surge to fill her completely. The feeling drove her to frenzy. As tall as he was, his chest hairs brushed her back with each stroke, exciting her even more. She could feel his muscles rippling, plunging against her, and couldn't stifle the moan of excitement that broke from her lips. She was trembling all over, arching her hips in the air, meeting him thrust for thrust, and beckoning him to take her. Heat enveloped her, and she cried out Sam's name. Fierce chills of pleasure consumed her as she reached her climax, and Sam followed in her wake.

Relaxing against her, his lips brushed her neck. "Now was that so terrible, lass?"

How could she tell him it was never terrible? Making love with Sam was always wonderful. So wonderful it threatened her very existence.

Each time they made love, he captured a tiny part of her. What would be left of Molly James by the end of the year? What part of her would not be in love with Sam? The forbidden thought both startled and tortured her. She rolled away from him.

"I have to go now," she told him. He didn't miss her change of mood.

He sighed resignedly. "Yes. I'm sure you have much more important things to do than keep your husband happy."

"That isn't fair, Sam, and you know it."

Sam ignored her defense. "Tonight's our wedding celebration. I hope you'll be able to fit it into your busy schedule."

"I'll be back in plenty of time." It was all she could do to keep the terrible lump in her throat from filling her eyes with tears. Since her wedding night, she'd found crying no difficult task at all.

Sam rose from the bed, pulled on his breeches, and left the room without so much as a terse good-bye. It was all she could do to convince herself not to run after him.

# *Chapter Fifteen*

✦✦✦✦✦

THE WEDDING CELEBRATION, held at Emmet's place, was well under way by the time Sam and Molly arrived. The sprawling redwood home, overflowing with guests, echoed with laughter and gaiety. When Sam opened the door, a bandy-legged fiddler accompanied by a fat guitarist held the guests' attention, allowing him and Molly to slip in unnoticed.

Sam's smile widened as he caught the delicious aroma of fresh-baked bread. Wetting his lips with anticipation, he eyed the table laden with foodstuffs Patience had prepared: everything from platters of meat to succulent stews and mounds of steaming corn and beans, topped off by cakes and pies of every variety imaginable.

Molly felt a pang of jealousy. Patience Brannigan was the epitome of the perfect wife. Molly didn't miss the warmth in Sam's eyes as he pressed a kiss to his sister-in-law's rosy cheek.

"Everything looks wonderful," he told her.

Molly had to agree. "You've done a beautiful job, Patience. Sam and I appreciate all your hard work." Molly kept her eyes fixed on the dark-haired woman instead of turning away as she wished she could. She always felt a little inferior to Patience, who kept a home, raised two beautiful children, and pleased her husband as easily as she threw a party for half the county without even mussing her skirts.

Patience smiled dutifully at Molly, then warmly at her brother-in-law. "Never been a man who deserves to be happy more than Sam." Patience's cornflower-blue dress emphasized the rounded swells of her bosom. Molly noticed they jiggled seductively every time she moved. She was a sensual woman in a voluptuous sort of way, and Emmet and Sam both adored her. It was obvious the feeling was mutual.

Emmet clapped his brother on the back before his dark-haired wife had a chance to continue. " 'Bout time you two showed up! We was just about to give up on you."

Sam smiled down at Molly, but the smile never touched his eyes. "Molly had to work late, something about a sick heifer."

"I . . . I'm sorry if I've caused any trouble," Molly said, feeling slightly hurt by Sam's obvious disapproval. Those things happened when you tried to run a ranch the size of the Lady Jay on a nickel and a penny. She didn't have enough help, and couldn't afford to hire more men if she could find them. Sam should understand.

"You're here now," Patience put in, sensing Molly's discomfort. "That's all that matters."

Molly felt a surge of affection for her new sister-in-law. "Did you make the punch?" Molly asked. "It looks delicious."

"Sam?" Patience said pointedly.

Sam's hazel eyes danced with amusement. "My pleasure," he said, accepting her light rebuff. He turned toward the cut-glass punchbowl, but Peter handed Molly a glass before Sam could take a step.

"Allow me." Peter smiled boyishly, passing her the cup and leaning over to kiss her cheek. He was always so cheerful, so open and honest. Molly found herself drawn to his sincerity a little more each time they met.

"Thank you, Peter."

"You look beautiful, Molly." He eyed her cream-colored silk gown. "You'd better be careful, or you'll give Sam a taste of that green-eyed monster he swears he's immune to."

Molly hoped she looked as good as Peter said. She hadn't had much time to dress. Sam had been standing out on the porch, angry and grumbling, when she reached Cedar Creek. Still, she'd taken a few extra minutes to arrange her hair in soft curls beside her neck, and had chosen one of her favorite gowns. It displayed her shoulders and the swell of her bosom, but no more than considered proper. And the narrow waist and flaring skirt did wonders for her figure.

Sam was dressed in a black frock coat and breeches. As always, Molly admired the handsome figure he cut. His golden hair and beard set off his tanned features, and the coat emphasized the broad width of his shoulders.

"Well, if it isn't the happy couple." The crystalline voice rang with a sweetness few could have discerned as false. Lillian Rose clung to Jason Foley's arm with a casual assurance that hit Molly like a blow. Judge Egan strolled along beside them.

"Congratulations again, Sam," the judge said, but the hard line of his bushy brows and the tiny lines around his mouth proclaimed that his words, too, were false. "And, of course, best wishes to you, Molly."

Molly felt Sam's arm go around her waist, and a tiny place in her heart thanked him for the comfort he gave.

"I see you all have something to drink," Sam said, avoiding an equally false greeting and smiling thinly. "Is there anything else I can get you?" It was obvious he'd expected none of the hostile group who stood before him to attend the party. But Molly had. There'd been no choice for any of them—not if they expected to continue the ruse they'd been living for the past two years. Lillian Rose and Sam were "just good friends." Judge Egan had also been Sam's friend. As for Jason Foley, he was Molly's loyal and loving guardian —at least he was until she married Sam. Of course he would come to wish her well.

Jason leaned down to place a chaste kiss on Molly's cheek. She didn't miss the heat trapped behind his eyes. Sam's arm tightened protectively around her waist.

"All the best to you both," Jason said simply, then he returned his attention to the beautiful widow.

Molly felt a surge of relief and a longing for the party to end. They made quite a pair, she thought as she sipped her lemony punch—Lilly with her lovely pale features, Jason with his handsome dark ones. In a different way, they were nearly as striking as Lilly and Sam had been. Judge Egan also eyed the couple with interest, and his daughter in particular with what could only be called protectiveness. Molly wondered what would happen to Jason Foley if he ever took a buggy whip to the judge's daughter.

The heavyset man kept his gaze carefully blank when he looked at Sam and Molly, but it was obvious the judge heartily disapproved of their marriage. According to Sam, he and Lilly had had an understanding: Neither of them wanted to wed. But from the judge's cool demeanor, it was clear *he* hadn't felt that way.

"Molly, dear," Lilly said sweetly, just loud enough for Molly and Sam to hear, "Sam explained about the timber contracts. I think it's wonderful to see a woman who thinks of marriage in such practical terms."

Molly's heart wrenched. Sam had gone to town to speak with Lilly as soon as he returned to Truckee. Molly had known Sam would have to say something to the woman he'd been sleeping with for the past two years, but she hadn't allowed herself to imagine what it would be. Now, she felt sick at heart to think he'd made light of their marraige, though she tried to do the same to herself every day.

"Yes," Molly agreed tightly. "I heard you felt that way too, Mrs. Rose." She wondered if Sam had also told the widow he'd be free at the end of the year. The thought knotted her stomach and swelled a hard lump in her throat.

"If you'll excuse us," Sam said, urging her toward the men's bar at the back of the room, "there's someone I'd like Molly to meet."

As they moved out of earshot, Molly looked up at him uncertainly.

He squeezed her hand as if to reassure her. "I didn't think they'd be here."

"I did," was all she said.

"*Óla, chica* . . . and Señor Sam." Angel and Joaquin crossed the room to stand beside them. Joaquin hugged Molly and extended his hand toward Sam. Molly noticed several men from town whispering to each other as Sam accepted Joaquin's handshake and clapped him on the back.

"I'm glad you could make it," Sam said.

"We cannot stay long," Joaquin said, and Molly despaired at the prejudice that discouraged *Californios* from mingling with whites. "But we wished to give you this." Joaquin handed Sam a large, heavy box. Sam lifted the lid to find a pair of matching bridles, finely worked and trimmed with silver. "For your wedding," Joaquin added.

Molly felt tears behind her eyes. "They're beautiful, *Padrino.*" She hugged the crinkled neck of the old vaquero, then again hugged Angel's ample girth.

Sam shook Joaquin's hand a second time and planted a warm kiss on Angel's pudgy cheek. "They're magnificent," Sam said. "Thank you both."

"We must go now," Joaquin said.

"At least have something to eat," Sam offered, "and a bit of cheer. Come on, I'll get you a drink." Joaquin's weathered face broke into a broad smile and, setting the box aside, the two men moved to the bar.

"He is so handsome, your Señor Sam." Angel patted Molly's cheek. "From the very first day, I know you think he is special. He *is* special, no?"

"Angel," Molly said, suffering a terrible guilt in accepting the gift, "when we get a chance to talk, there's something I want to tell you about our . . . marriage."

"You are happy, yes?"

"I'm afraid it's not that simple. But I'd rather talk to you about it some other time."

"Of course, *chica*. Tonight is fiesta! Joaquin and I, we just come by to wish you well."

Molly hugged her rotund friend. "I love you both."

"And we love you, *hija*," Joaquin added as he and Sam rejoined the women. The couple stayed only a few minutes more, then quietly left the party. Molly hated the way the ranchers treated the *Californios*, but there was little she could do.

"H-He-llo, M-Miss M-Molly." Emmet Junior rushed up between the folds of her skirts, and Molly bent down to give him a hug.

"Hello, Emmet. I'm so glad to see you."

Sam watched Molly with fascination. He hadn't missed the way her face lit up the moment she'd spotted the brown-haired boy. If she didn't like children, she certainly had a funny way of showing it.

"Molly's your aunt now, Emmet," Sam said. Molly looked up with a stunned expression that showed she hadn't yet figured that out. Sam wasn't surprised. Molly still hadn't accepted their marriage. Sam was beginning to wonder if she ever would.

"C-Can I c-call you Aunt M-Molly?" Emmet asked, tugging her skirt and watching her with a shy smile that brightened his cheeks.

"Of course you can."

Sam didn't miss the flash of despair in her eyes. Her obvious regret in marrying him squeezed his heart like a noose. It was all he could do to keep from turning on his heel and striding from the room. *Give her some time,* he told himself. She'll come to care for you if you just give her time. But he wasn't convinced. And he wasn't about to spend the rest of his life with a woman who didn't want to be his wife.

The party continued late into the evening. Sam was immersed in conversation with Emmet and Peter, so, fanning herself with her kerchief, Molly strolled out on the porch for a breath of air. The waning moon rode high over the jagged mountains, lighting the rim of trees along the crest with a silvery glow. The gentle breeze felt cool against her skin.

She was lost in thought until muffled voices coming from beside the house drew her attention. Recognizing Emmet Junior's soft stutter, Molly moved to the edge of the porch.

"I-I c-can too s-say it. I-I j-just d-don't f-feel l-like it."

"Can not!" an unseen deeper voice taunted. "Emmet can't say his own name!" The boy kept repeating the words, and another voice chimed into the singsong rhythm as Molly stepped down off the porch and rounded the corner of the house.

"What's going on here?" she asked, her temper high. "You boys leave him alone."

"We didn't mean no harm, Mrs. Brannigan," a string-bean youth told her, shuffling his toe in the dirt.

"We was only funnin'," a second tall boy with limpid eyes said contritely.

"You're having fun at someone else's expense. You get out of here and leave him alone. If I ever catch you bothering him again, I'll take a broom to your hides. You hear me?"

"Yes, ma'am," the boys called out as they backed away, then bolted toward the barn.

Molly caught the gleam of tears in little Emmet's eyes before he dashed around the corner of the house. She wanted to go after him, but decided she'd caused him enough embarrassment already. Still, she felt a painful ache in her heart for the little boy. Sighing resignedly, she turned to see Emmet and Patience standing beside Sam on the edge of the porch. No one commented on the scene, but she could have sworn an approving smile curved Sam's sensuous mouth.

In the end, the party was a smashing success. The newlyweds were showered with gifts, which Emmet promised to deliver to the house the next day. By the time the last gift was opened, Molly looked drawn and pale. The despair in her eyes might have gone unnoticed by the others, but Sam hadn't missed it. For the first time, he admitted the possibility that Molly might call off the marriage at the end of the year. The thought filled him with bitterness and more than a little regret. Why had he ever married a woman who didn't want to marry him?

The gray light of dawn shone on the porch by the time Molly and Sam returned to the big house. Sam reined the wagon up and, circling her tiny waist with his hands, helped her down. One of the stable boys took care of the rig while Sam followed Molly inside.

She seemed distracted, as she had been most of the way home. "Sam, I've been thinking."

Considering the train of his thoughts, he felt apprehensive. "Oh?" was all he could manage to say. Maybe she wouldn't even wait out the year.

"Did you see the way those boys teased little Emmet? They were ruthless. I can't stand to see him hurt like that."

Sam released a long, relieved breath, then cursed himself for letting Molly insinuate herself so deeply in his affections. "We've tried to help him learn to speak," he replied, keeping his voice carefully even, "but nothing seems to work. Patience has spent hours with the boy. The more she tries to help him, the worse he gets. I'm surprised he took to you so quickly."

But he really wasn't surprised. There was something about Molly that seemed to draw people to her. A sense of caring and concern. Even

Emmet and Patience were beginning to weaken. He'd seen it in their eyes when Molly rushed to little Emmet's defense against the taunting bigger boys. She'd threatened to take a broom to them, and, though the youths were taller than she, Sam had no doubt she would.

"Well, there ought to be something we could do," she was saying. "He can't even say his own name."

"I know."

"He's such a sweet little boy."

Sam put an arm around her shoulder and led her up the stairs. "And I thought you didn't like children."

Molly looked stunned. "Why would you think a thing like that?"

Sam halted in front of the door, his gaze suddenly cold. "Or maybe it's just *my* children. Is that it Molly? You don't want to have *my* children?"

Molly blinked back tears. She shook her head numbly. "Your children would be beautiful, Sam."

He pulled her into his arms. "Then why do you hold back from me? Why can't you let yourself go? Why can't you give us a chance?"

Molly glanced away. "I don't know," she lied. She had to stay a year, that was the deal she'd made. She wouldn't make things worse by telling him the truth—that she could never stay married to a Brannigan.

Sam stared at her for a moment, then his mouth came down hard, his kiss demanding. He slid his hands beneath her knees and lifted her into his arms, shoving open the bedroom door with his booted foot. His impatient strides carried them to the big tester bed, where he hurriedly began to undress her. Molly didn't resist. She needed him to make love to her. Needed him to make her forget, to numb her to the pain she carried most of the time now. Numb her to the thoughts of family his words had stirred.

They made love passionately, driving each other to frenzy, demanding responses more powerful than each had given before. Whatever else there was between them, there was also this hunger, this craving each had for the other. Molly gave herself up to it and let him carry her away.

She awoke several hours later to find the sun already high in the sky. The rich smell of bacon frying stirred a gnawing in her stomach. Dressing hurriedly, she headed downstairs. Sam was making a second valiant attempt to feed her. This time Molly was determined to let him succeed. Hoping to make amends for the night before, she walked up beside him and kissed his cheek above the line of his short-cropped beard.

"That smells delicious," she told him. "I'll set the table." She gathered up plates and flatware and went into the dining room. A large, gaily wrapped box rested on the long oak table. Molly picked up the card. *For my feisty redheaded wife.* A big blue *S* was scrawled beneath.

"You can only open if it you promise not to get

mad and leave," he said, strolling up behind her.

"What is it—a photograph of Lillian Rose?"

Sam laughed heartily. "Do you promise?"

"I probably shouldn't, but . . . all right, I promise." Molly tore off the wrapping paper and lifted the lid. She pulled out the contents to discover a split skirt made of heavy reddish brown suede. Brass rivets held the skirt together, and fringe trimmed the bottom. Deep pockets rested on each hip. Molly held the skirt up, still unable to believe what she was seeing.

"Well," Sam asked, "do you like it?"

Molly wasn't sure. She'd grown used to her breeches, but there was always a chance she'd meet someone who thought of them just as Sam said—as an invitation.

"Where did you get it?"

"I saw a photograph of a woman wearing one in a Bill Show. Pawnee Bill or Buffalo Bill, I don't recall which. I had Dan Wiggins down at the saddle shop make it. I thought maybe it might solve our . . . problem. How about trying it on for me?"

It was the least she could do. She ran her hands over the rough-out leather then dashed upstairs to put it on. The skirt fit perfectly. Sewn with fine stitches, the leather rested comfortably on her hips, then flared in a slim, A-shaped line to her ankles. The split legs of the skirt would allow her to ride astride and protect her against brush and undergrowth even better than her denim breeches.

Returning downstairs, she hurried to his side. "I have to admit, I love it."

Sam assessed her, noting the curves the skirt enhanced and the slim, booted ankles that peeped from beneath the fringe. "Damned if you're not as fetching in that skirt as you were in your breeches. I guess I'll just have to accept the fact I have a seductive wife and let it go at that."

Molly threw her arms around his neck. "Thank you, Sam. It's a wonderful present." She smiled at him, then sniffed the air. "Do I smell something burning?"

Sam groaned and raced for the kitchen. This time he was able to save the meal, though the bacon was a little extra crunchy and the eggs were solid all the way through. They both ate heartily. After they finished, Sam broached the subject he'd been thinking about all morning.

"Molly, there's something I've been wanting to speak to you about."

Molly straightened in her chair.

"It's about the nights you spend at the Lady Jay. I want you to let me speak to Foley. I don't like the way he looks at you. I want him to know if he bothers you again, he'll have to contend with me."

"No."

"Molly, I want to talk to him about something else. I want to offer to buy him out. Once you're free of him, no one can make you sell the ranch. You'll be able to take your time, build it up slowly. We can do it together, if you'll let me. You wouldn't have to work so hard."

Molly fought to control her temper. "Are you quite finished?"

"Molly, please, I only want to help you."

"You've never listened to a word I've said. The Lady Jay is *my* ranch. It's my business, and I'll run it exactly as I see fit. I don't want your help. I don't want your interference. You agreed to those conditions before I married you, and I expect you to abide by them now."

Sam shoved his chair back, the legs grating on the heavy plank floor. His temper hot, he glowered down at her. "I never agreed not to buy Jason Foley out. There isn't a damn thing you can do to stop me. You're my wife, Molly. I want Foley off that ranch and out of your life!"

Shaking with anger, Molly stood up and faced him, defiance darkening her eyes. "You're so used to running things around here, you think you can run me, too!" She unbuckled the riding skirt, let it fall to her feet, then kicked it aside. "That skirt is just one more attempt to control me, and I won't have it!"

Fire leaped at the back of Sam's neck. Molly stood facing him, wearing only her blouse and soft cotton knee-length drawers. He felt like strangling her with his bare hands. Instead, he turned and angrily strode toward the door.

"Sam!" He kept walking. "Damn you, Sam Brannigan!" Molly picked up a plate and hurled it above his head to crash against the wall. Sam stopped for a moment, his fists balled at his side, then he started walking again. Molly picked up a second dish and hurled it against the door, narrowly missing his head.

Sam spun to face her. "Stop it, Molly!"

"You're . . . you're an arrogant, dominating bully!" She threw an empty coffee cup. Sam ducked and stormed in her direction. Molly raised another cup, sent it crashing to the floor, then picked up a saucer. Sam caught her wrist, and hauled her against him.

"I swear by the saints, Molly Brannigan"—his eyes, dark now, snapped with fire as he glowered down at her—"if you break one more dish in this house, I'll . . . I'll . . . turn you over my knee and paddle your luscious little bottom till you can't sit down for a week!"

Molly felt the color drain from her face. She'd seen him this mad only once before, on their wedding night. It was easy to believe he meant every word he said. Swallowing hard, fighting a desire to turn and flee, Molly let her shoulders sag in defeat. When Sam released her arm, she set the saucer carefully back on the table.

"If you'll excuse me," she said with as much dignity as she could muster, "I'll put some clothes on and finish doing the dishes."

Head held high, Molly turned and walked back upstairs. She returned wearing her denims and set to work clearing the table. Sam leaned nonchalantly against the door watching his tiny wife work; her single thick braid swished just above her bottom as she marched indignantly into the kitchen. She was a handful, all right. Willful, stubborn, determined—and more exciting than any woman he'd ever met.

Molly pushed open the swinging door to the kitchen and traipsed to the washtub, her arms filled with the remaining dishes. Setting them down with a little too much force, she cursed Sam beneath her breath and sent a greasy platter against the side of the empty tub with a loud crash, shattering the platter into a hundred pieces. Heavy footfalls rang out, then Sam shoved the door open, his eyes dark with fury.

Molly's heart pounded, Sam's threat ringing in her ears. Unconsciously, she took a step away from the giant man who advanced on her from across the room. "It . . . it was an accident, Sam," she stammered. "I . . . I swear it!"

Sam just kept coming, his expression unreadable. Before she could flee, he caught her wrist and pulled her up short.

"Don't you think I can see that, lass?" Tugging a dishcloth from a nail beside the tub, he wrapped it around her wrist. "You've cut yourself."

Molly released a slow breath and relaxed against him, allowing him to wipe away the blood for a closer look.

"It's not serious." He plunged the pump handle several times, sending a surge of water into the tub. After dipping her wrist to cleanse it, he tore the dishcloth into strips and wrapped it around her hand.

"Thank you," Molly whispered.

"Lee Chin will be back today. Somehow I think we'll both be better off if we leave the kitchen duties to him."

"Sam?"

"Yes, lass?"

"The Lady Jay. I have to make it on my own. It's something I just have to do. I'll buy Foley out as soon as I earn enough money. Please, Sam. Let me do it my way."

"I'll think about it," was all he said.

The next morning, Molly set off for the Lady Jay wearing the leather split skirt Sam had bought her, after Sam had agreed not to buy Foley out. Sam chuckled to himself as he watched her ride away. Maybe they were making some progress, after all. When she didn't return that night, but stayed at the Lady Jay the extra day she was entitled to, Sam wasn't so sure.

# *Chapter Sixteen*

MOLLY SPENT THE days away from Cedar Creek doing some heavy soul-searching.

She might be a little naive when it came to men, but she wasn't a fool. The nights she spent without Sam were miserable. She was lonely and restless, and she thought about him until she fell into an exhausted slumber. Only her pride—and her conscience—kept her from making the long ride back to Cedar Creek every night after work. After two days away, she had dark smudges beneath her eyes. The only real rest she got was in Sam's bed. Nestled in the curve of his arm, she felt protected, as if her troubles were unimportant, her future secure. In Sam's arms, she was home—even at Cedar Creek.

In truth, Molly realized, she was in love with Sam Brannigan. The knowledge, which up until now she hadn't fully admitted, came upon her swiftly, in the long hours before dawn of the second night. She'd been lying awake, thinking about her riding skirt and smiling to herself as she remembered their fight and the threat Sam had made. He'd meant every word, and maybe that was one of the things that attracted her to him. He was man enough to handle her. It didn't matter about his arrogance and his domineering ways. Besides, she'd been able to manage him so far; surely he'd quit trying to change her and come to see reason eventually.

Molly mulled over the way he'd cooked for her and tended her cut wrist. She always sensed his concern, though he was proud, with more strength than any man she'd ever known. Just thinking about him made her heart beat faster, her body glow with a tender ache. A tender *loving* ache. With a blinding flash of clarity, Molly knew for certain she was in love with Sam. Dangerously, unwillingly, hopelessly in love. But did she love him enough to put aside her prejudice, her guilt, her need for revenge? Molly wasn't sure.

She returned to Cedar Creek the next evening, then spent every other night with Sam. She still wouldn't allow herself to stay more often than they'd agreed There was too much at stake. But like it or not, fight it or not, Molly found herself falling a little more under Sam's spell each day.

On Monday, Trueno threw a shoe and bruised his foot. Molly tied him to the buckboard and led him back to the Lady Jay. She and Joaquin were in the barn, seeing to a bar shoe to protect his injury, when Judge Egan and Father Fitzsimmons rode into the compound.

"Good morning, Molly," Judge Egan greeted her. He heaved his thick frame down from the sorrel mare he rode and strolled up beside her.

Molly wiped her hands on the leather apron she was wearing. "Welcome to the Lady Jay."

Father Fitzsimmons, a lean, gray-haired priest with warm blue eyes and a kindly smile, climbed down from his buggy and walked up beside Judge Egan. "The judge and I crossed paths on the way out of town. It seemed our destination was the same, so we joined forces."

"I came to speak to your uncle," the judge said. "Is he at home?"

"He's in the parlor," Molly told him.

"Beautiful animal," he remarked as he watched Joaquin ready the black's left hind hoof for the shoe.

"Thank you."

"You say Jason's in the parlor?"

"Yes, go right on in."

"Nice to see you again, Molly," the judge said, tipping his expensive black bowler. He shuffled off toward the main house, leaving the priest to speak with her in private.

"We've missed you at mass, Molly." Father

Fitzsimmons looked sternly down the line of his nose. Molly removed her apron and motioned him toward the garden.

"I . . . I've just been so busy."

"Are you certain that's all? The rest of the Brannigans seem to find time for church. All except you and Sam. If you discussed it with him, I'm certain he'd find a way to make time. Emmet and Patience are always there and even little Emmet asks after you. He sings in the choir, you know."

Molly stopped short. "He sings?"

"Like an angel."

"But, Father, how could he possibly sing in the choir? He can barely speak."

"As strange as it may seem, when he sings he doesn't stutter at all."

"I can't believe it."

"Why don't you come and see for yourself? He'll be there this Sunday."

"Father, there's something else. I've been meaning to go to confession, but now is as good a time as any to tell you."

The priest turned to face her. "Are you certain you wouldn't rather wait?"

"No, Father. What I wanted to confess was that Sam and I . . . well, we weren't married by a priest. A Judge Barton married us."

For a moment, the thin priest looked surprised. Then he smiled. "I'll speak to Sam about it immediately. I must say, I'm surprised he would ask that of you. But don't worry, Sam's a good man. He'll do what's right. We'll have a small, private mass, just the family—"

"It wasn't Sam's idea, father. It was mine. It's a long story. One I'd rather not tell you now."

The priest studied her thoughtfully. "Molly, you and Sam must rectify this situation for your own immortal souls, but although I must deny you the Eucharist until you're married in the Church, at least come to mass." He patted Molly's cheek. "I'll expect to see you both on Sunday."

Molly glanced up to see the judge and Jason Foley striding toward them.

"Dinner's at eight," the judge was saying, and Jason smiled delightedly.

"I'm looking forward to it. Give my regards to your lovely daughter."

The judge nodded. With a bit of difficulty, he pulled his stocky frame into the saddle. "Say hello to Sam for me," he said to Molly.

"I'll do that, Judge." The judge waited until the priest climbed up in his buggy, then followed him back down the road toward town. It was a long ride to deliver a dinner invitation, and Molly wondered if perhaps Judge Egan was grooming a new suitor for his daughter. Maybe the good judge wanted to put an end to the town's wagging tongues once and for all.

Ignoring her uncle, who walked beside her, Molly strode back into the barn.

Joaquin was just finishing. "He will be fine now." He surveyed the shoeing job, then let True's hoof down. The big gelding stomped several times as if to test the shoe, then nickered softly.

"You work too hard, Molly," Jason told her, eyeing her dirty clothes and the strands of red hair escaping her thick braid. She glimpsed something heated in his clear black eyes, then it was gone.

"I must see to the bay stallion," Joaquin said, leaving them alone.

Molly turned her attention to the taut-featured man beside her. "I work as hard as necessary to make the Lady Jay profitable. This is my ranch, Jason. You're just along for the ride."

"You're a married woman now, Molly. You belong with your husband. Surely he wants you home."

Molly's head came up. "What Sam Brannigan wants is not important. It's what's best for the ranch that counts. I fully intend to buy you out just as soon as I'm able. Until that time, our peaceful coexistence is a necessity." Molly brushed past him. "Now if you'll excuse me, I have work to do." Without a backward glance, she left him standing in the barn.

Jason watched her go, feeling the now-familiar desire. Though he'd tried to fight it, he felt more and more attracted to her. He wished he could leave this place, return to the East where he belonged, but he had God's work to do. Heading back toward the house, he vowed he would ignore the lust she stirred in him and achieve the goals he had set.

* * *

Molly spent the night at the Lady Jay. As usual, she worked till well after dusk, then retired to her room. At the end of the next workday, she tied True to the buckboard she'd driven over and headed home to Sam. As always, thoughts of him waiting for her urged her on, and she clucked the team into a trot. Molly was smiling to herself, eagerly anticipating the night of lovemaking ahead, when she spotted the folded slip of paper wedged in a crack at her feet. Gathering the reins in one hand, she leaned down and picked the paper up, then opened it and read the elegant script in the paling light of the dusk.

> *My darling Sam:*
> *Last night was wonderful as always.*
> *I look forward to our next meeting*
>
> *All my love,*
> *Lilly*

Molly felt sick at heart. She checked the date at the top of the note, written in the same beautiful script. July 18, 1875. Quickly Molly counted backwards on her fingers. It was the first day she and Sam had fought about her clothes. She hadn't returned to Cedar Creek that night or the next.

Molly reread the note, a lone tear slipping down her cheek. She'd always trusted him. Always. Even in the beginning. How foolish, how naive she'd been, to think he'd meant the words he'd said about fidelity.

Molly felt a chill, though the late summer

evening was still warm. Her hands trembled on the reins, and the road ahead began to blur as the tears came in earnest. For the first time, she realized exactly how much she had come to love Sam. The thought of him in another woman's arms tortured her. The crushing ache around her heart left no more doubts, no more uncertainties. She loved Sam Brannigan unfailingly, totally.

But Sam didn't love her. At least not the same way she loved him. He couldn't love her and lie to her, or cheat on her with Lillian Rose.

Molly pulled up the wagon and brushed the tears from her eyes. Sam had made a fool of her. That much was clear. He'd duped her and used her. Molly felt the first stirrings of anger. Soon anger turned to white-hot, blinding rage. She read the note one last time, shredded it into tiny pieces, and tossed it into the wind. The sane part of her warned she should turn the wagon around and head back to the Lady Jay. The other part wanted to kill Sam Brannigan.

Molly felt the tiny derringer in the pocket of her skirt. She wouldn't really shoot him, she loved him too much to hurt him; but then, he wouldn't know that. She would make him beg for her forgiveness, then she'd ride away and never go back.

By the time Molly reached the ranch, her cheeks flamed, and her eyes were round with unsuppressed fury. She pulled the team to a halt in front of the porch and called Sam outside.

His smile of welcome thinned to a line of

worry as he looked at her face. "My God, Molly, what's happened? Are you all right?" Long strides carried him across the porch.

"Stop right where you are, Sam."

Sam clenched his jaw and kept on walking. "If Foley's done something to you, I swear I'll kill him."

"I said stop, Sam, and I mean it!" Still seated on the buckboard, Molly held up the derringer and leveled it at Sam's heart. With him standing only a few feet away, she couldn't miss blowing a hole in his broad chest.

"What the hell's going on! Put that thing away before someone gets hurt!"

"The only one who's going to get hurt is you! Now put your hands up and keep them there."

"Molly, tell me what's wrong." Sam lifted his hands in an attempt to placate her, but uncertainty darkened his eyes. He edged a little closer.

Molly pulled back the hammer. "I'll shoot you, Sam, I swear it."

Sam took several deep, controlled breaths. "All right, Molly. We'll play this your way. What do we do now?"

"What *you* do, Sam, is admit you lied to me. Admit you cheated on me with Lillian Rose. Then you beg me to forgive you—which I have no intention of doing. After that, if I'm feeling benevolent, I might ride out of your life and leave you alive."

Sam reached out a hand, edging closer. "Molly, I've never lied to you. I've never cheated on you, and I certainly don't need your forgiveness."

"I know you're lying, Sam. I found the note."

"What note?"

"The note Lilly wrote thanking you for such a *wonderful night*."

"I've only seen Lilly once, to tell her about our marriage. That was in the daytime. You knew about it at the time."

He sounded sincere. God, how could he sound so sincere? Molly felt the sting of fresh tears, but held them at bay. She wouldn't let him make her cry. Sam inched closer.

"Get back, Sam, I swear I'll shoot you. God, you must think I'm a fool. All that balderdash about how partners never lie to each other. You couldn't even be faithful for a year." Molly raised the tiny derringer, aiming it even closer to Sam's heart. "Beg me, Sam. Beg me to forgive you. If you don't, I swear I'll pull the trigger."

Before she knew what was happening, Sam thrust his arm out, knocking the gun from her hand. Her cry of alarm was muffled by the gun's loud report, and Molly felt herself jerked none too gently from the seat of the buckboard into Sam's iron grip.

"Let me go, damn you! I should have shot you when I had the chance!" She fought against him, struggling in his arms but unable to tear free. "Let me go!"

"I'll let you go after you listen to what I have to say and not before." She squirmed again; then, making little headway, she rested her hands against his chest in furious resignation.

"That's better."

Molly tried to ignore him, but his powerful

thighs pressed against her riding skirt, and she felt their heat even through the folds of the heavy leather.

"First of all, I've never lied to you. Not ever."

"I don't believe you."

"Because of some note you read?"

"Yes."

"Let me see it."

"I threw it away."

"Molly, I'm telling you the truth. I've never lied to you. And I've never cheated." For the first time he allowed himself a smile. "I've never had the faintest desire to be with another woman since I met you. Surely you can tell you please me. I don't need to look elsewhere, Molly."

"It . . . it was the night of our fight. You were mad at me."

"It didn't happen, lass. I've been a true husband to you in every way. But I can only give you my word. You'll have to look to your heart to find the truth."

Molly felt his pulse beating against her hand, saw the tenderness in his eyes. Every shred of her reason told her he was lying. He *had* to be. The note said he'd been with Lilly. He tilted her chin up and captured her lips in a gentle kiss that spoke more than words ever could.

"Look to your heart, lass," he whispered.

And Molly did. "Oh, God, Sam." She threw her arms around his neck, and only the tiniest doubt kept her from speaking her love. Warm tears rolled down her cheeks, and Sam brushed them away with the tip of his finger.

"It's all right, lass. Trust me, and I promise

you won't be sorry." He lifted her into his arms and carried her into the house.

"Lee Chin!" The little Chinese stuck his head through the swinging kitchen door. "Have one of the men see to the horses. Mrs. Brannigan and I will be dining in our room tonight." He moved with quick strides up the stairs. "We won't be ready for a while yet. I'll let you know when."

Lee Chin smiled knowingly and let the door fall closed. Sam closed the door to the bedroom.

The rest of the week passed uneventfully. Sam never mentioned the note and Molly didn't either. They both just pretended the incident never happened. It was easier that way. Molly continued to work long hours, but an idea had been formulating in the back of her mind, so she took a day off on Saturday to act on it. Instead of going to the Lady Jay, she rode over to see Emmet Junior. He was playing quietly in the yard when she rode up and dismounted.

"H-Hello, Aunt M-Molly."

"Hello, Emmet." She moved to stand on the soft grass beside him. The sun felt warm against her back, the breeze clean and fresh. "What are you playing?"

"C-cup and b-ball."

"May I try it?"

"S-sure."

Molly reached down and took the hardwood stick from his hand. A wooden cup sat at the end of the stick, and a string with a hard round ball attached hung from the end. The object was to swing the ball and land it in the cup.

It wasn't as easy as it looked.

After several tries, Molly handed the stick back to Emmet, who proudly landed the wooden ball with a rhythmical thud, time and time again.

"You're very good," Molly said, pressing for the opening she'd been seeking. "I hear you're also good at singing."

Emmet beamed proudly up at her, the wind ruffling his shiny dark brown hair. "I-I l-love to s-sing."

"How about singing something for me?"

"R-right n-now?"

"Why not?"

"W-what s-should I s-sing?"

"Do you know 'Clementine'?"

With a broad grin, Emmet began to sing: "Oh, my darlin', oh my darlin', oh my darlin' Clementine. Thou art lost and gone forever, dreadful sorry, Clementine." His voice, usually soft and shy, boomed out across the yard, bringing Patience to the door. Molly smiled and waved, but made no move to join her. Emmet waved too, but kept on singing, never missing a word.

Molly smiled down at him. "That was lovely, Emmet."

He glanced at the ground and shuffled his feet. "Th-thank you, Aunt M-Molly."

"Do you think you might learn one especially for me?"

"S-sure."

"It sounds just like 'Clementine,' but it's a special song about you."

"M-me?"

"Uh-huh. It goes like this. 'Oh my name is Emmet Samuel, Emmet Samuel Brannigan. I live here on Cedar Creek, I'm Emmet Samuel Brannigan.' "

"That's s-silly."

Molly smiled and felt a twinge of disappointment. "I suppose it is. I'm afraid I'm not a very good songwriter. But I thought maybe if you learned to sing your name, the next time someone asked you, you could sing it. I thought it might be worth a try."

Emmet stood quietly beside her. When he looked up, his face seemed a little older somehow. "N-no one ever j-just s-says it r-right out l-like th-that. Th-they always t-try t-to f-fool m-me into s-saying it r-right."

"But it doesn't work."

"N-no."

Molly shrugged her shoulders. "It was just an idea. I didn't like the way those boys were teasing you at the party."

"If I-I w-was older I-I'd have p-punched th-them!"

"I bet you would have. But you know there's always somebody bigger."

Emmet just nodded, as if he'd figured that out long ago.

"I guess it was a pretty silly idea. Singing your name, I mean."

Emmet watched her closely. First he hummed softly, then a little louder, then finally he began to sing. "Oh, my name is Emmet Samuel, Emmet Samuel Brannigan. I live here on Cedar

Creek, I'm Emmet Samuel Brannigan." He stopped and looked up at her with an expression of pure joy lighting his face. Realizing he'd said his whole name for the very first time, he dashed into her arms.

"It w-worked, Aunt M-Molly! I-I s-said m-my n-name!" He turned toward Patience, who stood quietly watching from the porch, tears glistening on her cheeks.

"M-mama!" Emmet called out. "D-did you h-hear?"

Patience only nodded, opening her arms to the scruffy little boy who bolted to her embrace. "Yes, honey. I heard you." She hugged him hard, then set him back down. "Maybe Aunt Molly could teach you some other songs, so you could learn to say some more words. What do you think?" She looked up at Molly with what could only be hope shining in her eyes. It was the first time Patience had ever referred to her as a member of the family.

"I'd like that," Molly said, striding toward the porch. "I'd like that very much. But I could sure use some help making up the words." Both women laughed aloud, and again little Emmet began to sing his name. It came out clear and faultless, and Molly felt a sudden mist of tears in her own eyes.

"Let me get you some lemonade, Molly," Patience said, turning away. "Why don't you sit a spell?"

And Molly did. She sat listening to the soft refrains of Emmet Samuel's newest song.

# *Chapter Seventeen*

SAM WAS PACING the porch waiting for Molly, who as usual was late, when Charlie Corwin, one of the mill hands, came racing down the road at a gallop. He swung from the saddle before his horse slid to a stop.

"There's been an accident, Sam. Up on Big Bend curve. A break in the flume. I'm sorry, Sam, but Emmet's been hurt."

Sam tensed. "How bad is he?"

"Broken ribs, some internal bleeding. I'm afraid it doesn't look good."

Sam reached inside the door and jerked his broad-brimmed hat from its peg. Pulling it low across his brow, he set his jaw and was halfway to the barn before the screen door slammed shut behind him. "What was Emmet doing up at Big Bend?"

"Guess he'd spotted a group of strays at the base of the flume." Corwin, a wiry little Texan with a shaggy mane of hair, shook his head and ran along beside the bigger man in a futile effort to keep up. "He just happened to be in the wrong place at the wrong time. We've sent down for a wagon, but I figured you'd want to be there."

"Thanks, Charlie." Sam led Gil from his stall, saddled him quickly, and mounted. "Let's go."

The men rode off in a cloud of dust, then left the road for a narrow trail that climbed the rise.

It was the shortest way to reach the Big Bend portion of the flume.

Along with the rest of the timbermen, Sam had found the flume to be the most efficient way to transport logs. The V-shaped flume used a small amount of water to carry the logs swiftly across ravines and mountains to the sawmill seven miles below. Flume riders rode the length of the wooden transporation system checking for any weak seams or areas of stress, but still accidents were not uncommon.

As they reached Big Bend, Sam looked past piles of timber strung along the ground below the break in the flume. At least fifty logs were heaped like broken sticks on the soft earth below the wooden structure that loomed some thirty feet overhead. Several riders huddled around Emmet's still form on a blanket near the base of a fir.

Sam knelt beside him and grasp his calloused hand. "How you doin', brother?"

"Not too good this time, Sam." A tremor shook him and more color drained from his already pale face. "I was ridin' below the flume when the damned thing broke. Beat a trail, but not quite quick enough. One of the logs knocked my horse down. Just barely hit me, or I'd be dead now."

"Don't try to talk," Sam cautioned. "Save your strength."

"Somethin' I gotta tell ya, Sam. In private."

The others stepped quietly away.

"What is it?"

"Weren't no accident, Sam. Saw somebody

ridin' away just . . . just—" He covered his mouth to cough and frothy blood trickled from between his fingers.

Sam's grip tightened. "Take it easy, Emmet. There's a wagon on the way."

Emmet pulled him closer. "Had long red hair, Sam. I'm only tellin' you 'cause I don't want you to get hurt. Whoever it was didn't know I was around. Don't think they planned on hurtin' anyone. I just happened to get in the way."

Sam's mouth had gone dry. "Are you trying to tell me it was Molly?" First her shoe button at the sawmill, now this. Still, there were other people with red hair.

"Can't say for sure, Sam. But you know how them Jameses feel about us." The wagon crested the hill, then rumbled off the road to the place where Emmet rested.

"I'll take a look around, Emmet. You just rest easy. I'll do whatever needs to be done."

"I know you will, Sam. Just be sure you get all the facts." The wagon arrived and the men carefully lifted the blanket, laid Emmet in the back of the wagon, then covered him with another blanket to keep him warm.

"I'll be over to see you just as soon as I'm finished here. Just take it easy. Patience will have you back on your feet in no time." Sam forced a reassuring smile he didn't feel. Emmet smiled weakly in return, and the wagon rumbled away.

Sam stayed behind until everyone was gone, then he set out to discover the truth. He felt sick at heart over his suspicions, and was worried to distraction about his brother. Trying to keep his mind on his search, he climbed the hill next to the flume, his stiff leg bothering him as it always did when he was upset. Walking along the catwalk that ran beside the flume, he came to the break. It was obvious his brother had been right. A small charge of explosive had detonated the boards, leaving the edges ragged and covered with a trace of gray powder.

Sam climbed down the wooden trestle and scoured the ground below the break. A single set of hoofprints rode away from the flume into the cover of the underbrush. A single set of hoofprints—and on the left hind hoof the animal carried a bar shoe. Sam studied the print closely, feeling as if his blood had turned to ice. A cold knot of dread curled in the pit of his stomach. True was wearing a bar shoe. Molly had told Sam about it when she came back from the Lady Jay. Sam wasn't sure which hoof the shoe was on, but he intended to find out before this night was over.

With a despair heavier than any he had known, Sam mounted Gil and headed toward Emmet's house.

Molly arrived at the ranch expecting to find Sam waiting for her as usual. She felt a twinge of disappointment as she called his name through the huge living area, then ran upstairs to their bedroom. When she came back down, Lee Chin stuck his head through the kitchen door.

"Mr. Sam ride off with other man. He not say where."

"When did he leave?"

"Just befo' dark."

"Something must have come up," Molly said, wondering what could have caused Sam to leave in such a hurry. She hoped it was nothing serious. Lee Chin went back to work in the kitchen, and Molly used the time to freshen up. On her way over tonight, she had decided to ask Sam if he wanted her to stay with him every night. If he said yes, which Molly fervently hoped he would, she would tell him she'd decided not to seek an annulment of their marriage in a year's time, but to make it a permanent commitment—that is, if that was what he wanted, which she fervently hoped he did.

It was all so confusing, and more than a little upsetting. She'd be letting him know she cared, taking a chance he would come to love her as she loved him. She'd been working up her courage for days, wanting his love so badly it almost made her ill. Now that the time had come, she hoped she had the strength to go through with her plans. All her life she'd yearned for someone to love her. She prayed Sam would be that someone.

Molly donned a soft green muslin dress and brushed her hair till it gleamed. When Sam still didn't come home, Molly began to worry.

"Missa Molly," Lee Chin called out as the evening lengthened, "you want eat now?"

"No, thank you, Lee. I'd rather wait for Sam."

Molly waited. Still no Sam. As the hour grew late, she finally gave up. She was more than a little worried as she dressed for bed, climbed between the sheets, and tried to fall asleep. She listened for his footfalls till just before dawn, but heard only the ominous ticking of the big oak clock downstairs.

By morning Molly was frantic. What could have happened? On a ranch the size of the Cedar Creek, there were a million possibilities, most of them distressing. She wasn't about to return to the Lady Jay until she knew Sam was all right.

With worry tensing her nerves, she dressed in her riding skirt, a blue cotton blouse, and her kidskin boots. She brushed and braided her hair, letting it fall to her waist. She was headed down the staircase when she heard heavy footsteps and the sound of the wide plank door scraping open. Sam stood in the doorway, his expression unreadable.

"Sam!" Molly raced down the stairs. "Where have you been? What's happened?"

Sam removed his hat and hung it on the peg beside the door. Every movement seemed an effort. He brushed past her as if she weren't even in the room.

"Sam, tell me what's wrong."

"Emmet's been hurt," he told her as he pulled a decanter of whiskey from the sideboard in the dining room. He looked dusty and tired, and dark smudges marred the tanned skin beneath his eyes.

"Hurt? How? Is he all right?"

"There was an accident. As to whether he's all

right, it's too soon to tell. He's been hurt pretty bad."

"Oh, God, Sam." She walked up beside him, but he recoiled from her touch as if he'd been burned.

"Happened up at the flume. On Big Bend curve." He watched her closely. "You been up that way lately?"

"Why, no."

He lifted the glass of whiskey to his lips and downed the contents in a single long gulp. Then he turned to face her, his face a tightly controlled mask. "I spent the night thinking, Molly. About Emmet and Patience, and about you and me."

Molly felt her stomach tighten. Something was wrong. Terribly wrong. "I've been thinking about us a lot lately, too," she said softly. His face looked haggard, beaten. She saw none of his usual warmth or affection, none of the gentleness she had come to love.

Again he spoke as if she weren't there. "I think our marriage was a mistake. Neither of us wanted it. I practically forced you into it and—"

"That's not true!" she interrupted. "I made the final decision."

"And I'm sure you were resentful," he went on in the same monotone. "It was a mistake then—it's a mistake now."

"Sam, please, you can't mean that."

"I've never meant anything more in my life." He turned to the sideboard and refilled his glass.

"You're in love with Lilly," she whispered, her voice now nearly as flat as his.

"Maybe. Maybe not. The important thing is to

end this marriage before . . ." *Before someone gets killed,* he wanted to say. He decided against it. More antagonism, more scandal and injury would be the only result. All he wanted, all he had ever wanted was for the Brannigans and the Jameses to live in peace.

"Before what, Sam?"

"Before either of us gets too involved."

Molly fought a sickening wave of despair. A hard lump swelled her throat and tears threatened, but she held them at bay. If she let go now, she'd lose control completely. Sam was telling her he didn't love her, had never loved her. Sam was saying the words she'd said to herself a hundred times, but never really believed. She'd always loved Sam. Always. And he'd never loved her at all.

"I think it would be best if you left today," he was saying, though Molly could barely make out the words for the buzzing in her ears. "I'll have someone pack your things and send them over to you. Peter can draw up the necessary papers."

"Papers?" She couldn't think straight; her mind refused to function. She clutched the back of the couch and tried to focus her thoughts.

"Annulment papers. We haven't been married long. There are ways. Peter will know what to do." He took another long draw on his drink, then swirled the rich brown liquid in the glass. His gaze seemed lost in the swirls.

"Of course." Still she clung to the couch. Her feet refused to move. She should leave now, before she threw herself at his feet and begged him to let her stay. God, how she loved him. Even after all he'd said, she ached to feel his arms around her, yearned for the warmth of his lips. How could she live without him? How would she endure?

When she looked up at him, she noticed he watched her hesitantly, as if he wondered at her thoughts. If he'd come home last night, he would know. He would know how much she loved him. If he'd come home last night, her humiliation would be complete. Molly lifted her chin, determined to leave with dignity, determined not to show the hurt and despair his words had wrought.

"Then I guess this is good-bye."

"I suppose so."

"It might have been easier if you'd given me a little more warning," she said with a tinge of bitterness. "But then, Lilly didn't get much warning either."

Sam didn't respond to the barb. "Good-bye, Molly."

The lump in her throat threatened to choke her. So easily, he said the words. So easily, he destroyed her life, her happiness. She couldn't speak, could barely see the door for the blur of tears in her eyes. She blinked furiously, but refused to hurry, refused to let him see how his words had crushed her, had devastated her very soul. With a calm she didn't feel, her head held high, she pulled the heavy door open and strode from the room.

She made it almost to the barn before the racking sobs hit her. She led True from his stall and saddled him through a film of tears that soaked her shirt but refused to cease.

Now she knew what a broken heart felt like—leaden, painful, dizzyingly empty. Climbing into the saddle, she rode through the wide double doors of the barn. Sam lounged carelessly on the porch. Before he could spot her tears, she quickly turned her face away. She wouldn't let him see her cry. She'd steel herself, just as she'd done before. Then, she would trust no one, rely on no one. In the future, she'd take care of herself, make her own way. Somehow she'd make things work. She had done it before. But before, she hadn't known Sam.

Against her will, Molly pictured his handsome face, the flash of his even teeth as he grinned at something she'd done or said. She wanted to hate him. She planned to. She had to. It was the only way she could survive without him. And yet as she galloped True up the rise, taking the shortcut to her ranch, she thought only of the soft feel of his golden hair beneath her fingers, the warmth of his hands as they stroked her breasts or cradled her face for his kiss. Her mind replayed the night of their wedding, the way he'd curled her against him, comforted her, assured her things would be all right. She remembered the times he'd been gentle, the times he'd been strong. *Oh, Sam. Why couldn't you have loved me? Why do I need you so?*

The ache in her throat moved to her breast. She couldn't swallow. She could barely breathe. Maybe it was her fault. If only she'd given herself more freely. But now it was too late. She'd never feel his arms around her, never hear the deep timbre of his voice as he whispered passionate words of love, never again see the laughter in his eyes. *Oh, Sam.* How could I have been so wrong about you?

Sam let the screen door slam and moved to the sideboard. He needed some sleep, and the only way he'd get it was to drink himself into a blind stupor. His eyes burned, and his hand trembled as he refilled his glass. He'd spent hours at Emmet's bedside, until his brother had finally drifted to sleep. Then he'd ridden home, taking his time, unwilling to find the answer to the question that burdened his heart.

When he'd finally reached Cedar Creek, graying light washed the distant horizon. He'd gone straight to True's stall and lifted his left hind hoof. The proof of Molly's guilt gleamed in the dawn like the blade of a murderer's ax. The bar shoe. On the left hind hoof.

He'd sat in the barn, propped against a wooden stall, until a crowing rooster had awakened some of the hands, and they drifted in to begin their daily chores. At least he'd had time to decide what course of action he would take. He wouldn't press charges, not as long as Emmet recovered. That would only arouse more gossip, and the proof he had was far from conclusive, at least in the eyes of a jury.

But not in Sam's eyes. There was no mistake. Molly James Brannigan had caused the accident at the sawmill, then sabotaged the flume. Her hatred was all-consuming, her need for revenge was a madness. He wondered if she'd made up the story about the note so she'd have an excuse to shoot him.

Sam slugged down his drink, refilled the glass, then carried it over to a place before the empty hearth. The ashes lay cold and grim against the gray stone. That was the way his heart felt: empty and cold, like the ashes in the burned-out fire. Molly had come to be the fire in his heart, the all-consuming object of his feelings. Her radiance made him feel whole, kept him happy and content. Just thinking about her could brighten his day. He'd known he cared for her, but until today, he hadn't known how much. Without her, the world seemed dimmer. Life had lost its luster, its magic. For Sam, life without Molly would be as lonely and dreary as the long night had been.

How could he have been such a fool? He'd been in love, that was how—in love with Molly James since the day he'd seen her up on Live Oak Ridge. He could still remember the determined way she'd pushed that old bull. She'd have gotten him out sooner or later, with or without Sam's help. Maybe that was the problem. Sam had wanted Molly to need him, and she never really had. He almost wished he'd told her he loved her; maybe she would have forgotten her need for revenge.

It didn't seem likely.

Sam crossed his booted feet on the table in front

of the fireplace. He felt sick at heart. *Bleak.* That was the word for it. Bleak and vacant. And terribly, terribly alone. From now on, loneliness would be his companion. Of that, Sam was certain. No one would ever take Molly's place. Sam was a man who could love only once. There would be other women. He was a man, and a man had needs. But there would never be another woman he *loved.* He'd given his heart to Molly James, and she'd crushed it beneath the heels of her dainty kidskin boots. Maybe it served him right. He'd sworn he'd never make a fool of himself the way his father had over Colleen. His father had died for love of a James. At least Sam was still alive; in that he counted himself lucky.

But as he thought of the lonely years that stretched ahead, years without the woman he'd come to love more than life itself, he wasn't so sure.

# Chapter Eighteen

NEEDING SOME TIME alone, Molly didn't return to her ranch right away. She wanted to compose herself—before she faced Angel and Joaquin, and, more importantly, before she saw her uncle. Jason Foley had been seeing Lillian Rose on a regular basis. The last thing Molly wanted was for Jason to tell the widow how desperately hard Molly had taken Sam's loss.

Molly rode up to Live Oak Ridge, near the mud bog where she'd found old Satan. She probably shouldn't have, she later decided. All the place did was remind her of Sam. But then, there was no place she could go and not think of him. Somehow, she'd have to learn to blot him from her mind. The mud bog was as good a place as any to start.

After several hours, and numerous unsuccessful attempts to purge herself of her feelings, Molly gave up the notion. She couldn't forget him. She'd have to learn to live with his loss just as if she'd been widowed. She might just as well have been, for Sam was irretrievably lost to her now. The thought only made her feel worse.

Molly returned to the Lady Jay well after dark. Angel was in the kitchen, a worried expression lining her heavy-jowled face.

"Where have you been, *chica?* We have been worried.

"I had some work to do up on Live Oak Ridge." It was a lie and Angel knew it; Molly could tell by her eyes.

"You had better sit down, *chica,*" Angel warned. "You do not look well."

Molly nodded and pulled out a chair, deciding the truth would be better for everyone. "There's no easy way to say this, Angel. Sam doesn't want me anymore. He's annulling our marriage. He asked me to leave."

"I cannot believe it!" Angel stormed to the

table. "Señor Sam would not do such a thing!"

Molly felt the sting of tears. "He doesn't love me, Angel. It's as simple as that."

"I do not believe it. What have you done to make him so angry? Surely he will forgive you if only you ask him."

Molly just hung her head. "I wish it were that simple. I haven't done anything. He just doesn't want to be married to someone he doesn't love."

"*Querida,* I do not believe this. I have seen the way he looks at you. So much pride in his eyes, so much love. There is some mistake."

"No mistake, Angel. Would you mind if I skipped dinner? I . . . I'm afraid I'm not very hungry."

"You go lie down. I will bring your supper on a tray. You must keep up your strength until we can find out what has happened."

Tears slipped down Molly's cheeks. "Please, Angel. Just leave things alone. There's nothing you can do. Nothing anyone can do." With that she turned and headed through the door, determined to avoid her uncle, which fortunately she succeeded in doing.

Angel watched her walk away, noticing the sad slump to her shoulders, as if all her hope had been taken away. Angel had seen her young friend like that only once before—just after her mother died. Her father had left Molly alone for days on end, forcing her to conquer her grief alone. Even after that, he'd paid her little heed. Though Molly learned to hide it, Angel knew she had always been lonely. Then she met Sam.

Angel had seen the subtle change in Molly,

the warmth in her eyes whenever she looked at her handsome husband. She loved him—of that Angel was sure.

And winning Molly's love was quite an accomplishment for the big gringo. For Molly James, loving didn't come easily.

Maybe in time they would work things out. Angel hoped so—for everyone's sake, but especially for Molly's. Whether she would admit it or not, Molly needed Sam's love.

Molly worked as if in a dream. Days came and went, endless hours in the saddle. She rode from dusk till dawn, trying to occupy her mind, trying to blot out the painful memories, trying to discover the clues she'd missed that might have kept her from falling in love. Surely there were things he'd said or done that should have told her he didn't love her. But try as she might, Molly could find none. In every way, Sam had acted the part of husband, lover, and friend.

In every way his actions said he loved her—except for the note from Lilly. The note she'd destroyed in her fury. She wished she could see it again. Wished she could reread the words, use them to convince herself he'd been unfaithful. It seemed so hard to believe. Every time she thought of Sam she pictured his sincerity. Every word, every phrase, every action seemed unrehearsed and deeply sincere. Obviously, the man was a consummate actor. Either that, or he'd just searched his soul as he'd said and discovered he didn't love her.

Either way, Molly was the one who was suffering for his actions now. She couldn't eat. She couldn't sleep. She'd lost weight, and her hair no longer shone with its previous coppery luster. Jason Foley had made little comment. She'd told him she and Sam had agreed to the annulment, that the marriage had only been a business arrangement in the first place. Jason seemed uninterested. Much of his time was occupied by the widow. Even if Sam was in love with Lilly Rose, it appeared the widow's interest lay elsewhere. Well, Molly thought, if she were going to pine away for her lost love, it was only fair Sam should, too.

The idea of Sam Brannigan pining for Lilly's love brought on another fit of weeping, as did just about everything of late. She was standing in the barn, immersed in self-pity and currying True's glistening mane and tail, when she heard her uncle's footsteps crunching against the bits of straw that littered the stone floor. What was he doing out here? What day was it? She could barely keep track anymore.

Jason walked up beside her. "Molly, dear, I've been worried about you." Dressed in a pair of gray trousers and a blue sack coat, Jason looked as handsome as ever.

"What do you want, Jason?"

"I want to know what's wrong. You haven't been yourself lately." He moved to her side. Molly could smell his dewy scent, but the cloying odor only sickened her.

"Nothing's wrong. I . . . I've just been working a little too hard." Jason traced a finger the length of her arm and Molly felt a sudden chill.

"You always work too hard. I would have thought your husband would have insisted you stay home. Maybe that was why he left you. You should learn to be a woman, Molly."

The bite of his words stirred her anger. "That's none of your business, Jason." His glance settled on the hills of her breasts, and Molly saw the lust firing the black pits of his eyes. She thought of the last time he'd caught her alone in the barn, and a second tremor shook her. Backing away, she rested her hand on the derringer in her pocket, and the cold metal reassured her.

He watched her closely, and she noticed the subtle change in his bearing, as if he had been fighting some inner war and finally surrendered.

"Maybe you need some attention," he said, his voice soft, his meaning clear.

Molly pulled the gun from her pocket. She'd worn her breeches today, meaning to stay close to the house and tackle some heavy cleaning in the barn.

Jason Foley's eyes raked her from head to toe, then settled on the derringer. "I admire your spirit, Molly. You're no ordinary woman."

"Get out of here, Jason. I won't hesitate to shoot you."

"I told you once before, you stir something in me. Something I can't fight anymore. I want you, Molly."

"You've got the widow. Isn't that enough?"

"Lillian is a gentlewoman, a woman of status and position. You, Molly, are all fiery heat.

You're the devil's own spawn, Molly, but, God forgive me, I want you more than life itself." Jason stepped closer.

Molly cocked the hammer on the gun. "I let you near me before, Jason. It won't happen again. One more step and I shoot."

Jason Foley paled. For a moment he seemed uncertain, then his eyes glittered with the same dark violence she'd seen before.

"I won't hurt you, Molly. That was a mistake. I should have loved you instead. Come to me, Molly. Let me hold you. I can show you God's love."

Molly held the gun steady. "You're sick, Jason. Go away and leave me alone."

"All right, Molly," Jason conceded, taking a step backward. He moved as if to turn away, pretended to stumble but instead lunged forward. The gun clattered to the stone floor of the barn. Jason pulled her into his arms and shoved her backward, into a thick pile of straw, his weight pressing her down into the scratchy stems.

Molly screamed once, then his lips silenced her cries. Jason's hand groped her breast through the fabric of her blouse, his manhood thrust stiffly against her. Molly struggled beneath him. Freeing one arm, she groped above her head, searching for some weapon she could use to defend herself. His hand moved down her body to fumble with the buttons of her breeches. She tried to thrust her knee into his groin, but he blocked the move. He tugged her shirt free of her breeches, then unbuttoned them, his hand moving inside across the flat spot below her navel.

Molly felt the bile rise in her throat. She groped the wall beside her until her hand touched a hard metal object. Her fingers closed around it and she poised to strike, but Foley's weight left her before she had the chance.

She heard the sound of a fist connecting with flesh, then Foley's agonized moan. Sam Brannigan towered above him, his face a mask of blind rage. Again his fist smashed into Foley's face. A blow to the stomach sent the preacher to his knees.

Sam hauled him to his feet and hit him again, hurling him across the stone floor to sprawl against the pine boards of the stall. Foley didn't move.

As she gained her feet, Molly's heart filled with such joy she could hardly believe the man before her was real. She wanted to rush to his arms, but when he turned to face her, he wore the same empty expression he'd worn before.

"I was working the ridge," he told her. "I heard you scream. It's Thursday. Angel's day off." Still he spoke in a monotone. "I knew you were alone." He delivered his speech without feeling, without expression, as if it were by rote.

"Thank you," was all she said.

"I don't think he'll bother you again." Sam raked his fingers through his thick blond hair, then glanced around for his hat, which had come off in the tussle. He found it, slapped it against his powerful thighs, and settled it on his head. "Where's the gun I gave you?"

"I . . . I . . . even with the gun, I couldn't stop him. I guess I needed your help after all." She wished she hadn't said it, wished she could call back the words, but it was too late.

At least she'd pierced his shell. She hadn't missed his flash of surprise before his mask fell back into place.

"I'd better be going." He brushed past her toward his horse, the touch of his arm against her breast sending a ripple of sensation the length of her. He mounted his big buckskin and turned a last glance in her direction. "I warned you about those breeches," he said, but his voice sounded gentle.

Molly smiled sadly. "Yes. Yes, you did."

"You might button them up before he wakes up."

Molly glanced down to the open front of her pants, then felt hot color flood her cheeks. By the time she had finished with the breeches Sam was gone. She refused to acknowledge the cold trail of tears that dampened the front of her shirt.

It was all Sam could do to leave her. He'd been riding the ridge overlooking Cedar Creek every Thursday for weeks. He'd tried to stop himself, told himself she wasn't his responsibility anymore. But when Thursday rolled around, he'd find himself overlooking the Lady Jay. Only if Molly rode out with the hands did he leave. Today, when he saw Foley heading toward the barn, he'd descended the rise. Molly's scream had done the rest. He thanked God he'd been there to help her, though, just as on that day at the bog, she'd probably have been all right without him.

Her comment about needing him disturbed him more than a little. And the tender look in her eyes was clearly meant for him. But he couldn't be married to her. He couldn't afford the risk. Emmet was healing, but he could just as easily have died. Sam didn't trust Molly, could never trust her again. But it didn't keep him from loving her. He'd keep seeing that soft look, keep falling asleep each night remembering it and wondering if maybe after they'd parted, she'd discovered she loved him, at least a little. Maybe she even regretted what she'd done.

One thing was certain: He'd never know one way or the other. It was imperative he stay as far away from Molly as he could. He couldn't afford to weaken. Not ever. Cresting the ridge, he dropped down the other side, heading toward Cedar Creek. By careful planning, he wouldn't get home until dark. The less time he spent alone in the big empty house, the better.

Straightening in the saddle, Sam rode back to the house he'd once called home. Now it felt more like a prison. He wished he could take comfort in a woman. Not Lilly. Lilly no longer held an appeal for him. Just some woman who could comfort him for the night, then let him go. But he wasn't ready even for that yet. Memories of Molly still burned too brightly in his heart.

* * *

Molly and Jason silently agreed to a stiff truce. Neither mentioned his cut and swollen lip or the blue-gray color around one eye. But every time Molly noticed his distorted features, a tiny smile lighted her eyes and warmed her heart. A present from Sam. That's how she thought of it. Just one more present besides the one that rested in her belly. The most precious gift of all.

A child.

At first Molly refused to believe it. She was just a little late. It wasn't the first time. But as her usually flat abdomen developed a slightly rounded curve, Molly felt pretty sure. She was even more certain when bouts of nausea forced her to leave for work hours later than usual. But Molly didn't mind. She had something to live for again. In her mind, she imagined how beautiful their child would be. She'd told Sam that once. Now she would see for herself.

Molly was humming in her room, feeling lighthearted for the first time in weeks, when Angel knocked on the door to see if she was ready for the ride to town. She opened the door just as Molly raised her arms above her head to slip into a pink muslin frock. It was Sunday, and Molly was going to church.

"It is good you are coming to church today, *chica,*" Angel said, smiling. "You can pray that things will be better for you and Señor Sam. Now there is the child to think of."

Molly's head came up. "You know?"

"I was not sure until today."

"It doesn't matter. The baby will have a home here on the ranch."

"It does matter," Angel insisted, her smile disappearing. "A child needs a father. You of all people should know what it is like to be raised with only one parent."

Molly's temper flared. "I survived. So will he! Or she."

"Do you really think Señor Sam will not take you back when he hears about the child?"

Molly turned on her friend. "He isn't going to hear about the child. At least not until it's far too late. I don't want to return to a loveless marriage where I'm not wanted. Would you stay with Joaquin if he didn't want you?"

Angel brushed a strand of thick red hair from Molly's cheek. "I might, if I had a child to think of."

Molly glanced down. "I'm not you, Angel. I'm going to do this my way."

It was Angel's turn for anger. "Not this time, *chica*. The child is his, too. You tell Señor Sam, or I will!" Her heavy breasts heaved with determination.

"Angel, please. Listen to me. It's better this way. Better for everyone."

The heavy woman only shook her head. "Tell him, *chica*. It would be better coming from you. I will give you some time. But I mean what I say."

Molly groaned. Angel rarely went against her wishes; she only did that when she felt strongly about something, and then she never backed down. Molly would have to tell Sam. What would he say? What would he do? She didn't think he would want her back. Angel was wrong about that. Sam Brannigan had severed her from his life as cleanly as if he'd used a knife. But she would tell him; she would even allow him to spend time with the child after it was born—if he wanted to.

Maybe Sam wouldn't acknowledge the child's existence. It didn't seem likely. But then, nothing he'd done since the day of the accident had been like him.

"Hurry up, *hija,*" Joaquin urged as he pushed open the door. "We have a long ride into town, and I do not wish to be late."

With a heavy heart, Molly gathered her reticule and, along with Angel and Joaquin, headed into Truckee to attend morning mass.

The mass was held at St. Mary's, a small country church frequented by the locals and a few stray travelers, miners, and timbermen. Molly enjoyed the gentle camaraderie of the parishioners and the quiet time contemplating the spiritual side of her life, and confiding in Father Fitzsimmons had been a comfort. Now, sitting on the hard wooden pew, she spotted Emmet, and Patience, who carried little Charity asleep in the crook of her arm. Emmet Junior was busy with the choir. Molly planned to avoid them. She wasn't ready to face them just yet.

As she moved through the door of the church after mass, she spotted Michael Locke standing on the narrow whitewashed porch. He captured her hand as she walked by.

"Molly, it's good to see you."

He looked handsome as always in his immaculate dark brown coat. "I didn't know you were Catholic, Michael."

"Not a very good one, I'm afraid. Actually, I came hoping to see you."

Molly glanced down at her gloved hand in Michael's. "I'm flattered, Michael, really I am. But I . . ." What could she possibly say?

"You what, Molly? I know you're not living at Cedar Creek. Your marriage—or lack of one—has caused quite a stir. I was hoping you might let me call on you from time to time."

Molly pulled her hand away. "I'm afraid that's quite impossible. I appreciate your friendship, Michael. But I've just got too much to do, what with running the ranch and all."

"You mean you don't have time for *me*. Isn't that more like it?"

"No, of course not." She looked him in the eye, then sighed resignedly. "The truth is, I'm just so confused right now. I need some time, Michael. Maybe in a few months . . ."

"I could help you, Molly. Make things easier."

"I appreciate your concern, but this is something I have to get through alone." *Like everything else that's happened in my life,* she thought.

"All right, Molly. I'll let things stand for now. Just remember I'm here if you need me." He kissed her lightly on the cheek.

"Thank you, Michael."

Molly crossed the porch, heading toward the wagon.

"Molly!" Patience Brannigan's voice rang with clear authority, stopping her midway there. Joaquin and Angel continued on toward the wagon, leaving Molly alone as the round-faced woman approached. "I want a word with you."

"I . . . I would have spoken with you before," Molly told her. "Only I thought it would be better for everyone if . . ." She let the sentence trail off.

"If what, Molly? If you left Sam to wither away up in that big house by himself? If you left him lonely and desolate and so in love with you he can barely survive it?"

Molly felt a rush of stunned disbelief. Sam had told his family *she'd* left *him!* Was he trying to protect her? Or was he just unable to stand their disapproval? Well, either way, she wanted Patience to know the truth. "I didn't leave Sam at all. Sam left me. He threw me out."

It was Patience's turn to be stunned. "*Sam* left *you?*"

"Please, Patience. I know you're trying to help, but—"

"You can't be telling the truth."

Molly lifted her chin defiantly. "Sam didn't want me. He asked me to leave. If he's pining away for anyone, it's Lillian Rose." She picked up her skirts and walked toward the wagon, Patience following in her wake.

"Something's not right here, Molly."

"This is none of your concern, Patience."

Molly turned to face her. "I wish things were different. I miss you all very much. More than you'll ever know." Hearing the slight quiver in her own voice, she swallowed the hard lump in her throat and started walking again.

Patience's clear voice rang over her shoulder. "I'm going to find out what's going on, Molly."

Without looking back, Molly climbed up to the bed of the wagon, leaving Angel and Joaquin the seat. She appreciated Patience's concern, but it was clearly a case of misunderstanding. She was sure Sam would set his sister-in-law straight, tell her that he felt nothing for Molly at all. The thought swelled another dry lump in her throat.

"Aunt M-Molly! Aunt M-Molly!" Little Emmet's plaintive voice echoed in her ears as he burst from the doors of the church. Running as fast as his slim legs would carry him, he climbed up in the wagon beside her. Molly hugged him tight.

"Aren't y-you going to c-come over anymore?"

She heard the slight improvement in his speech and her heart thrilled at his small measure of success. "Not right away, Emmet. I'm awfully busy at the ranch." Seeing his forlorn expression, she had to glance away. "Maybe a little later." She turned to face him again. "You just keep singing with your mother. She makes up really good songs."

Emmet just nodded. "I-I miss you, Aunt M-Molly."

"I miss you, too." She brushed a tear from

beneath her lashes. "Go on, now. Your mama's waiting."

He hugged her again, then slid down from the back of the wagon. Joaquin slapped the horses lightly on the rump, and the wagon rolled away.

Sam Brannigan leaned against the batt-and-board wall of the livery stable across the street from the church. He'd come to town with Emmet and Patience, then had seen Molly sitting primly in a pew and decided against attending mass. Instead he'd gone for a walk through the quiet streets of the town, returning within the hour to wait outside the church for mass to end. He'd seen Michael Locke and Molly in quiet conversation, and try as he might to ignore it, felt his jealousy flare. It was none of his business, he told himself. What Molly James did was none of his concern. He wished he could convince himself.

A few minutes later, he'd watched Patience approach, then caught the exchange between Molly and Emmet Junior. Though he couldn't make out the words, he wasn't surprised when Patience stormed up beside him.

"You left *her?*" she said accusingly, her blue eyes dark with suppressed anger. "You told me *she* left *you!*"

"It's a long story, Patience."

"It's a long ride back to the ranch. I've got plenty of time."

"Not in front of the boy."

"Fine. He can ride your horse, and you can sit with me."

Sam shifted against the wall, smiling faintly. "You always get your way, don't you?"

"Most of the time. Now let's get going."

Emmet pulled the buggy up next to the livery and watched them with an uncertain expression on his face. All were amazed at his remarkable recovery.

Sam sighed resignedly. He probably should have told Patience the truth in the first place. He'd just wanted to keep things as simple as possible. He lifted his broad-brimmed hat, raked a hand through his hair, then settled it back on his head.

"All right. I'll tell you what happened. But you aren't going to like it." On the way home, he told Patience the truth about Emmet's injury and the "accident" at the sawmill, leaving out nothing, including the way he'd asked Molly to leave.

"You're a fool, Sam Brannigan!" Patience told him, making no attempt to disguise the contempt in her voice.

"There's no other possible explanation. Don't you think I prayed a thousand times I might be wrong?"

"Well, I don't believe it!" Patience straightened in the buggy seat, her shoulders squared, her chin jutting forward.

"Why the hell not?"

"Because she loves you, that's why! No woman's going to hurt the man she loves. Not for some ancient feud that means nothing to her now."

"How do you know she loves me?"

"Sometimes I don't believe what a fool a man can be. If you can't see it, I certainly can't make you."

"Well, I can't afford to take the chance. Emmet almost died. I can't ask people to risk their lives on your female intuition. If it were just me, I might give it some thought. But it's not. Molly was responsible for those accidents, and that's the end of it."

Patience just stared straight ahead, obviously unconvinced. Since when had Molly James wheedled her way into Patience's heart as well as his own? Sam wondered. It really didn't matter. Emmet was sure about Molly—he didn't bat an eye when he confirmed the truth of Sam's words—and so was Sam. He'd think no more about it, he promised himself for the hundredth time.

And during the busy workday he didn't. But during the lonely hours of the night, a nagging suspicion he'd been wrong began to drive him crazy.

Peter compounded the problem. Though he'd moved to Sacramento City and officially opened his office, he made a special trip to the ranch to rail at Sam. Apparently Patience had written to Peter, explaining the situation in no uncertain terms.

"Why didn't you tell me!" Peter stormed, his lean frame pacing up and down the great room of the ranch house. "I'm a member of this family and a partner in the ranch. I had a right to know!"

"Yes, I guess you did." Sam leaned against the heavy oak mantel above the fireplace. "Now that I think about it, I probably didn't tell you out of some misplaced loyalty to Molly. I thought it would be better if you believed she was the one who wanted out of the marriage. I knew how much you thought of her. I didn't want to tarnish your image."

"Well, I hate to disillusion you, Sam. But I agree with Patience. I don't believe Molly is capable of committing those crimes. Did it ever occur to you someone might have wanted you to believe Molly did it?"

"Frankly, no. At least not at the time." Sam shoved his hands into his pockets and walked over to look out the window. Heavy clouds rolled across a gray sky, and a stiff breeze pushed dust and a few dry leaves across the road in front of the house. Fall would be upon them soon. Without Molly's laughter to warm the big house, the winter would seem longer than ever.

Sam turned to face his brother. "And just who do you think would want to lay the blame on Molly? For that matter, who besides Molly would want to sabotage the ranch?"

"Jason Foley might," Peter replied. "Or have you forgotten the beating he gave her? I, for one, will never forget it."

A muscle tightened in Sam's jaw as he remembered the bloody bundle he'd carried upstairs to his room. Hoping they'd keep an eye on Foley and after swearing them to secrecy, he'd finally told his brothers the truth.

"I haven't forgotten," he said softly. "But it doesn't make any sense. How would Foley get True up to the flume? He certainly isn't horseman enough to ride him."

"I don't know. I just don't believe Molly's guilty."

"I wish it were that simple, Peter. Unfortunately, I can't afford to take the chance of being wrong. There are lives at stake. Emmet could just as easily be dead right now, and the bearfighter still hasn't been able to return to his job."

"What about Molly, Sam? Have you thought about her feelings? If you are wrong about her, can you imagine the pain you've caused?"

Sam could well imagine. If Molly felt a fourth of what he felt for her, she would be in an agony of despair, just as he was. But the odds were against it.

"Molly didn't want to marry me in the first place. I doubt she's lost much sleep over the annulment." He spoke calmly, but his eyes had taken on a haunted look as he thought of the papers he'd served.

"That's not what Patience says," Peter replied softly. He moved to a place beside the window and laid a gentle hand on his brother's shoulder. "Think about it, Sam. You owe it to both of you to find out the truth."

Sam's control snapped. "Don't you think I've tried? I've done everything in my power. I've asked the hands where she was during the time of the accident, praying someone was with her. She was off by herself, supposedly chasing strays. Emmet said he saw someone with long red hair. Her horse has a bar shoe on his left hind hoof. I found the button from her shoe at the mill. What more evidence do you need?"

"I know it looks bad, but I still don't believe it. Why didn't you at least give her a chance to tell her side of the story?"

"I didn't ask her," Sam replied, his voice husky, "because I knew no matter what she told me, I'd believe her."

"You really love her, don't you?"

Sam pulled away. "Look Peter, you're only making things tougher. I just can't risk people's lives."

In the end it was Molly who made Sam's decision for him. She rode up to the main house late one evening. Sam had just ridden in tired and dusty, his mood as sour as the taste on his tongue. Taking the stairs two at a time, he then freshened up. Finally, shirtless, a damp towel looped around the back of his neck, he returned downstairs to answer a knock at the door, which Lee Chin was apparently too busy to notice. The last person he expected to see was Molly James.

"Hello, Sam." Just the sight of her nervous smile melted away his fatigue.

He pushed open the screen and welcomed her inside, feasting on the sight of her. "Hello, Molly." He took in her leather riding skirt and glistening red hair with a sweeping glance, but noticed an uncommon pallor to her cheeks. "Let me run upstairs and grab a shirt."

"There's really no need. This will only take a second." *Why in the world had she said that?* She could barely take her eyes off his chest, keep her hand from reaching out to stroke the mat of pale hair that curled across the dark skin beneath. She remembered the tickling feel of it against her nipples, and warm color rose to her cheeks. "On second thought, maybe you'd better." Sam's mouth curved in a lazy, amused smile, and Molly wished she could call back those words, too.

"I'll be right down," he told her, but she didn't miss the heat in his eyes as he mulled over the import of her words. "Make yourself comfortable. Have Lee Chin bring you something cold to drink."

Molly nodded, watching him ascend the staircase to what once had been their bedroom. She wondered if another woman—or women—had shared the room with Sam since she'd been gone. The thought seared her heart like a branding iron.

Sam returned to find her seated on the couch. "Sure you don't want something to drink?"

"No, thank you. I just want to get this over with."

Sam's guard came up. "You want to get what over with?"

"I'd rather you sat down. You're too damn tall when you're standing up."

"I don't remember you complaining before,"

he reminded her as he moved to stretch out in his favorite leather chair.

"That—was before." Molly watched him closely and noticed he was observing her as well. "What I came here to tell you . . ." She wrung her hands nervously and turned to face the empty hearth. "I only came here because Angel made me. She said if I didn't tell you, she would."

Sam straightened in his chair. Was she going to admit her part in the accidents? Beg his forgiveness? "Go on," was all he said.

"I didn't want you to know. I didn't want you to feel responsible, but you would have found out sooner or later, so I guess it might as well be now."

"What are you getting at, Molly?" Sam leaned forward, his hands resting on his knees.

"I guess there's no easy way to say this." Molly steeled herself. "Sam, I'm going to have your child."

Sam heard the air escape from his lungs. Of all the things he might have guessed, this was clearly not among them. For a moment he couldn't speak.

Molly watched him hesitantly. Of all the reactions she had anticipated, cold acceptance seemed the worst. Somehow it hurt more than anything he could have said. Wordlessly, she rose from her place on the couch. "I'd better be going now."

The emotionless tone of her voice seemed to snap Sam from his trance. "Go? Do you actually think I'm going to let you leave?" He rose from his chair and intercepted her before she reached the door.

"But it's obvious you don't care. You seemed so—"

"*Stunned* might be a good word for it." He caught both her hands in his, and she felt their strength and warmth, just like before. Memories crowded her thoughts, and it was hard to keep her mind on what he was saying.

"I'll have the annulment stopped. You'll move back in. You can work for a while longer. But I won't have you jeopardizing our child's life."

The way he said *our child* sent tiny shivers down her spine. He wanted the child, after all. She could see the proud expression in his eyes. It made her heart swell with warmth. Then she remembered he used to look at her like that and some of her warmth faded. She pulled her hands away.

"You're awfully certain I'll come back, Sam. What do you plan to do if I refuse? You didn't want me before. Now, because I'm carrying a Brannigan, everything's changed. I'm supposed to live in the same house with you, knowing you don't care for me, wondering every day if you're going to come home and ask me to leave." She fought the tears that suddenly welled in her eyes, but several slipped down her cheeks. "I can't do it, Sam. I just can't live like that."

The sight of her tears tore at his heart. If that was how she saw it, maybe Peter and Patience were right. Maybe someone *had* made it look as though Molly were at fault. If that were the case and Molly was innocent, he'd destroyed everything he'd worked to build between them. She'd never trust him again. But then if she had been the culprit, how could he ever trust her? It was a tangled web—one that wouldn't be unraveled easily.

"If you'll come back, lass, I promise you I won't put you through that again. You'll be my wife in every way." Sam ached to pull her into his arms. Instead, he lifted a tear from her cheek with the end of his finger.

Molly shook her head, denying his words, his touch. "No, Sam. If I come back, it will only be for the sake of the child. I want a separate bedroom. I won't sleep with you, Sam. Not when I know how you feel about me."

"You have no idea how I feel about you, lass." He tilted her chin up to review the blueness of her eyes. "No idea at all."

He looked as if he might kiss her, and though she wanted him to with all her heart, she broke away. "I . . . I have to go home now. Angel will be worried. I'll think about what you've said."

"I want you and our child here at Cedar Creek. You're my wife, Molly."

"I believe you were the one who forgot that, Sam."

Turning away, Molly strode to the heavy oak door, shoved it open, and walked away, leaving Sam to face another night alone—this time, with a heavier heart than before. He was beginning to believe he had wronged Molly James.

# Chapter Nineteen

✦✦✦✦✦

MOLLY RODE HOME the long way, taking the extra time to think. Of all the possibilities she'd considered, returning to Cedar Creek had seemed the least likely. She'd given it little consideration: Thoughts of renewing a life with Sam always conjured hurtful memories of things that could not be.

Now that he'd asked—no, practically commanded, which was typically Sam—she didn't quite know what to do. She no longer doubted her love for him, but what about Sam? He obviously cared little for her. He'd asked her to leave and never looked back.

But there had been a time when he cared, Molly was sure of it. Something had changed between them, suddenly and drastically. Something Molly didn't understand. If Lilly Rose was the cause, why hadn't Sam set out to win her? It wasn't like him not to pursue something he wanted. As far as Molly could discover, he'd never even called on Lilly. But then, maybe it wasn't Lilly he loved. Maybe there was another woman involved. The thought brought a bruising ache to her heart.

Molly rode True into the barn and dismounted. The evening had turned chilly. She heard one of the cows lowing in a stall, heard the chickens' timid clucking as they settled on their perches for the night.

As she unsaddled True and slung the heavy

leather across the boards of a stall, Molly wondered if there was really any decision to make. Though part of her said the risk would be too great, the pain unbearable a second time, the other part said, *You're Molly James. You fight for what you want.*

And this time Molly knew exactly what she wanted: She wanted Sam Brannigan, wanted him to love her as much as she loved him. Wanted the two of them to raise their child together, give him or her the kind of home Molly never had. But could she win Sam's love? She'd come close once, she was sure of it. Something had happened. If she moved back in, she'd have a chance to find out what it was.

Molly rode to Cedar Creek the following night, arriving just as the orange-red glow of dusk lit the sky. She waited in the great room of the ranch house for an hour, pacing up and down, the fringe on her leather skirt rustling with every turn. Lee Chin had let her in, brought her a cup of tea, then left her alone, a happy smile lighting his smooth-skinned face. He always knew everything that went on in the house, and Molly had no doubt he knew she was carrying Sam's child.

Sam shoved open the heavy door and hung his felt hat on its peg before realizing her presence. His tanned face, dusty and lined with fatigue, broke into a wide smile when he found her waiting.

"Quite a change," he said. "You waiting for me."

Molly ignored his remark and jumped right into the topic she'd come to discuss. "There's something I need to know before I make my decision." She held her head high, set her shoulders determinedly.

"All right." He moved to stand before the fire Lee Chin had made in the hearth.

"I want your word that what you say will be the truth."

"I won't lie to you, Molly."

She digested the statement and continued to look him squarely in the eye. He didn't flinch. "I want to know if you're in love with Lillian Rose."

Sam regarded her closely. "No."

"Were you?"

"No."

Molly's heart pounded. Sam met her searching eyes with a cool look all his own. "Are . . ." She swallowed hard. "Are you in love with another woman?"

Sam ran over his options. He'd given his word. Now she wanted an answer. "Another woman?" he stalled.

"Someone other than Lilly."

*Yes,* he wanted to answer. *I'm desperately in love with my wife.* But if he did she'd want to know why he'd asked her to leave. If he told her the truth and she was innocent, she might be so angry that he'd lose her forever, and their child as well. And on the other hand, if she *was* guilty, being found out might make her react like a cornered animal. He tried to sound casual. "If you're asking me if I'm in love with someone outside our marriage, the answer is no."

It seemed an odd answer to her question. Molly wondered why he'd phrased it that way. Then the impact of his words sent her head spinning. He wasn't in love with someone else! That meant there was still a chance for their marriage to work.

"What about our agreement to end the marriage after a year? Are you still planning on taking that action?" She tried to sound businesslike, but a tiny tremor shook her hand. She was standing in Sam's house. Just a few feet from the man who was her husband, the man she'd missed every day and every night since she'd been gone. She wanted him desperately, ached at the thought of his arms around her, the warm feel of his lips.

"I never intended to end the marriage after a year," he told her. "That was your idea, remember?"

Molly just nodded. He looked so handsome, so rugged. His skin was darker, the lines around his eyes a little deeper. They didn't detract from his good looks.

"Then why did you want an annulment?" she asked and noticed he stiffened. His eyes took on a hooded look that cloaked his expression.

"That's a question I'm not ready to answer, Molly. Let's give it some time."

He'd conceded as much as he was willing; Molly could sense it in his change of mood. "All right, Sam. I'll come back—but I want my own room." She was lying to herself and she knew it. She wanted to be back in his bed. Wanted to be there this minute. If she didn't leave now, he would see it in her eyes. How in God's name would she be able to resist him once they were living under the same roof? But then maybe she wouldn't have to.

Sam seemed to ponder her words. "I'll agree to that for now, Molly. But not for long. I've told you before, I'm not good at playing the monk. It's all I can do to keep from taking you right now."

Molly sucked in a breath. At least she still had some hold on him. The thought infused her with a surge of hope and a quiet resolve. She would win Sam Brannigan's love, no matter what the cost. No matter how long it took. "Then I guess I'd better go."

"It's too dark for you to travel alone. I'll send one of the hands along, just to be on the safe side."

"I really don't need—" His glowering expression stopped her cold. She'd forgotten how protective he was. Before, she would have found his interference meddlesome, a threat to her independence. Now she found it strangely comforting. "That's probably a good idea," she conceded, and caught Sam's mild surprise.

He only nodded, then escorted her through the door and out into the yard. "I'll send a wagon over tomorrow to pick up your things."

"You're not wasting any time, are you?"

"Now that we've made the decision, I think it's best for everyone if we get on with it." He lifted a wild strand of her flame-red hair. "Besides, the sooner you're here, the sooner you'll be back in my bed. I won't lie to you, lass. I've missed you. More than you'll ever know."

Warm heat burned her cheeks. She should play hard to get, be more aloof, but it was hard to play games with a man like Sam Brannigan.

As they left the house, Molly's heart swelled with happiness. He still felt something for her. She was more certain than ever. Sam seemed to watch her reaction closely, and even in the dark she was sure he caught her smile.

She walked quietly beside him a few paces, till she reached True's side. When she turned to face him, she realized how close he was, and her heartbeat quickened.

When he spoke, his voice sounded low and a little uncertain. "Molly?"

"Yes, Sam?" She tilted her head back to look up at him. In one sure movement, she felt his hands circle her waist, saw his mouth descend to cover hers, then felt the warm, demanding pressure of his lips. She heard him groan, and the kiss deepened, his tongue searching, then finding entrance to her mouth. A surge of warmth nestled in the pit of her stomach; tiny particles of desire seeped through every inch of her body. He was nibbling the corner of her mouth, tasting her, sampling and tempting her beyond endurance. Again she felt the once-familiar ache between her legs. She knew she should stop him, but she hadn't the will. Instead she slipped her arms around his neck and laced her fingers through the thick strands of his golden hair. She could feel his hardness pressing against her, and it fanned the flames of her desire.

When he moved his lips to nibble the place beneath her ear, she whispered his name, softly, over and over, with all the love she'd kept hidden for so long. She couldn't stop herself. Dear God, she could barely think. She clung to him desperately, wanting to make him stop, wishing she had the strength. Knowing the stakes were too high to give in.

"Sam, please," she whispered, her voice ragged.

"You want me as much as I want you," he told her as he continued to trail warm kisses along the side of her neck. She could smell his woodsy scent as his fingers worked the buttons on her shirt, his mouth warm against her throat. His wide hands slipped beneath the fabric and he filled them with the fullness of her breasts. His thumb teased the peak of her nipple until it hardened and felt just a little achey.

"I'll never be able to let you go again," he whispered, and Molly felt her knees go weak. Sensing her submission, he lifted her into his arms and with long, powerful strides carried her into the house and up the stairs.

Sam's heart was pounding so hard he could scarcely think. Every instinct told him to beware. Molly could be a threat to everything he'd worked for—his home, his family, his very existence. He should stop now, take some time to think things through. Withdraw before he succumbed to her magic again. But try as he might, he couldn't stop himself. Nothing mattered without her. Nothing mattered except loving her.

He nudged open the door to his room with a booted foot, crossed the room quickly, and placed her on the bed. Slightly swollen with passion, her ruby lips beckoned him, and he captured them in a deep, urgent kiss. He tugged her blouse from the waist of her leather skirt, pulling it off her shoulders, then fumbled with the buckles that held the skirt around her waist.

"Here," she whispered, her voice husky, "let me do it."

Sam could barely suppress the tremor in his hand as he stepped back to light a coal-oil lamp, turning the wick down low. He turned to watch just as she shed her skirt and chemise. Her soft cotton drawers slid down over her hips, leaving her ivory skin bare to his gaze. His throat went dry. The downy triangle of red curls at the base of her thighs captured his attention, drawing his eyes and thoughts to the pleasures ahead. Ignoring the heat in his loins, he quickly shed his clothes.

Molly seemed to be watching him with the same eagerness he had shown. When he reached the bedside, she laid a hand on the mat of pale hair curling against his chest, then circled a flat copper nipple with her finger. His hand slipped through her hair to loosen the single thick braid and spread it like a mantle across her shoulders.

"I'd forgotten how beautiful you are," he said.

"Tell me everything's going to be all right."

"We'll make it be all right, lass." His powerful arms circled her as he made room for himself on the bed. His lips brushed her cheek, then burned the hollow of her throat. He pressed her body down into the soft feather mattress, moved his lips along her shoulders, then surrounded the erect peak of her nipple. Molly moaned and writhed against him, sliding her hands over his body, loving the feel of his corded muscles, the smoothness of his skin. Sam trailed kisses lower, his tongue probing the hollow indentation of her navel, sending shivery sparks racing through her veins. Molly tensed as she realized his intentions.

Moving his head even lower, his tongue traced patterns along the slightly curved flesh of her abdomen, his lips gentle on the silken triangle above her womanhood.

"Sam?" Molly whispered, a little uncertain. She tried to move away from him, but he caught her hands in his and pinned them against her hips.

"You're mine tonight. I mean to let you know it."

He kissed the inside of each thigh, and Molly squirmed with the delicious sensations. When his tongue, warm and moist, circled the bud of her womanhood, Molly thought she would die of sheer pleasure. His mouth followed his tongue as he nibbled and tasted, carrying her to a heated frenzy that ended in rippling waves of climax. Before her pleasure ceased, Sam mounted her, driving his thick shaft inside her, thrusting powerfully, dominating her and leaving her breathless. She met each of his thrusts with equal abandon, mindlessly responding, loving the feel of his hard body pounding against hers. She clutched his neck, felt the fine sheen of his effort mingled with her own, and arched her hips against a second series of powerful thrusts. His hands cradled her buttocks, giving him access to the farthest recesses of her womanhood. Another climax shook her, the wild tremors forcing her to buck against him and wrenching his name from her lips.

He whispered soft words of passion as he followed her to release, but Molly wasn't certain what they were. She wanted to believe he'd used the word *love,* but maybe she'd only heard it in her mind. Maybe her pleasure had driven her to the brink of sanity. That was the way she felt, as she spiraled back into the real world and her heartbeat slowed to normal. Neither of them spoke for a time, and Molly began to wonder at the foolishness of her actions.

He'd only taken her back because of the child. He wanted her in his bed, that much he'd proven. But Molly wanted more. She wanted Sam's love. Whether letting him make love to her would win his heart, Molly didn't know. Like her decision to return, she'd really had no choice.

"I have to go home, Sam," she whispered softly.

"No."

"Joaquin will be worried."

"I'll send one of the men to tell him you're spending the night with your husband." The way he said the words filled her heart with warmth and again left little choice.

"Sam?"

"Yes, lass?"

"Why is it always so good with us?"

*Maybe because we love each other.* But he didn't say the words. He'd already said too much. He prayed she hadn't heard him. He couldn't grant her any more power than she already had. "Maybe we should try it again and see."

Molly sucked in a breath, then heard Sam's hearty chuckle. The sound was as dear to her as rainfall after a drought.

"First I'll send Hank Withers over to the Lady Jay." He sat on the edge of the bed and pulled on his breeches, then shrugged into his shirt. "When I get back, we can discuss the matter at length." He kissed her mouth and left the room.

As soon as the door closed, Molly succumbed to her doubts. Nothing was going the way she'd planned. Sam was already drawing her back into his grasp. Surely if he found out how much she loved him, he'd take advantage of the situation in every way. He might even tire of her again, discard her as he had before. Molly felt a wave of despair that threatened to drown her. Then her courage surfaced to buoy her spirits and give her the strength to go on.

She loved Sam. Somehow she would make him love her. Hearing his impatient footfalls, the unmistakable halting step of his limp, Molly stifled the balance of her fears. She wondered if she'd ever truly rid herself of her doubts, wonderful if she'd ever be able to put her trust in him as she had before. But just to be near Sam again was worth the uncertainty. At least that was what she told herself. She hoped she'd feel the same tomorrow—or this time next year.

The balance of the week went nowhere near as well as that first night. Distrust loomed as a constant barrier between them. Having decided to spend as much time with Sam as possible, Molly returned each night to Cedar Creek, but no matter how hard she fought against them, doubts and fears crept into her heart.

Would he walk through the door and ask her to leave as he had before? Would he wait till the child was born, then ask her to go? Was he just putting up with her because he wanted someone to warm his bed? And the most nagging fear of all—would he try to take the child away? Sam Brannigan was a powerful man. He had friends in high places. His brother was a lawyer. Molly had no one. Maybe Sam could do it.

Sam seemed equally uneasy. He rarely relaxed in her presence, rarely conversed for more than a sentence or two. No matter what they spoke of, the conversation seemed formal, stilted. Only at night, when they retired to their room, did their relationship improve. They were passionate people, Molly decided. Their bodies took over, allowing their minds a respite from the thoughts that tortured them daily. In Sam's arms she found peace for a time, peace and affection. She refused to call it love. Love was something two people gave each other without restraint. The *affection* she and Sam bestowed on one another was given grudgingly, as if neither could stop, though he would, if only he were able.

At the end of the week, Molly made a decision: She had come back to win Sam's love; come hell or high water, she would give it her best shot! She would be the kind of wife he had always wanted her to be.

Molly wiped her hands on the apron tied over her muslin dress. She'd gotten home early, pampered herself a little, then waited for Sam to arrive. Instead, Patience, with little Emmet perched on the wooden seat beside her, rolled up in a heavy spring wagon laden with boxes of crisp green apples.

Molly ran out the back door to greet thm, unmindful of the screen door that banged loudly behind her. She hadn't seen her sister-in-law since their meeting at the church.

"Aunt M-Molly!" little Emmet called out. He climbed over the seat to the back of the wagon, jumped from the tailgate, then rushed to greet her on the porch. Molly bent down and hugged him close.

"I'm so glad to see you. Let me look at you." She held him at arm's length. "I bet you've grown two inches this summer."

"M-Mama says I'll be as b-big as P-Papa someday."

"I'm sure you will." She turned to Patience, who had strolled up to the porch and, on impulse, reached out to hug her. "It's good of you to come."

"Emmet told me you were back. I'm glad you're here." She looked as though she wanted to say something more, but instead turned her attention to the wagon. "Let's get these boxes unloaded. Got a good crop this year. Figured you might want to do some cannin'."

Molly hadn't the heart to tell her that she didn't have the faintest idea how to can. Even with all her years of schooling, many of the basics of homemaking were still a mystery to her. All she'd ever really wanted to do was learn how to manage the ranch.

"That's kind of you. I'm sure Sam will be pleased."

"Having you home, Molly, is the thing that will please him most."

"Patience. I told you before, I didn't leave Sam, he left me. He asked me to move. I worry every day he'll come home and do the same thing again."

"Sam loves you, Molly. Give him some time. Things will work out."

"I hope so, Patience." If Sam loved her, why didn't he say so? And why had he wanted to end their marriage? "I'm determined to make him happy this time," was all she said.

"Why don't you bake him a pie?" Patience suggested. "Apple's his favorite."

"I've never . . . Do you think you could write down the recipe for me?"

"I'd be happy to. Meanwhile, let's get these

boxes unloaded. We can stack them on the porch."

The first box Patience picked up contained a small, blanket-wrapped bundle with a pink nose and soft blue, dark-fringed eyes. Charity Ann Brannigan had the look of constant wonder on her face, but she rarely fussed or even made a sound. Sometimes she would coo softly, and almost always she had a big smile for her aunt.

"She's the most beautiful baby, Patience."

"I think so, but then mothers are always sure their child is the most beautiful child in the world."

Patience set the box down on the porch, and Molly leaned over and kissed the baby on the cheek. She wondered if the child she carried was a boy or a girl. It didn't matter to Molly, though for Sam's sake she hoped it was a boy. Every man wanted a son; she was sure Sam would feel the same. It appeared he hadn't told Patience. She wondered if he were waiting to see how things worked out between them. She hoped not, but she wasn't so sure.

Molly joined Emmet Junior and Patience at the back of the wagon. Each hoisted a box of apples from the bed and carried it the short distance to the porch. Molly spotted Sam across the barnyard just as she hoisted a second box. Instead of entering the barn, he whirled Gil on his hind legs, dismounted before the big buckskin slid to a halt, and strode angrily up beside her. Furious, he snatched the box from her hands.

"Don't you have a lick of sense, Molly Brannigan! If you won't think about yourself, think about the child!"

Molly stood rooted to the spot, bright color firing her cheeks. "How dare you talk to me that way! I'm pregnant, not bedridden! Lots of women work right up until the day the child is born."

Sam's fury ebbed. He glanced from Molly's hostile face to Patience's stunned one, then back again to Molly. "I'm sorry, lass. You always did have a way of making me a little crazy. I just don't want anything to happen to you." He smiled down at her, and Molly couldn't miss the tenderness in his eyes.

"Congratulations," Patience put in. " 'Bout time you made me an aunt. As for you, Sam, you big bully, Molly's right. From the looks of her, she can't be too far along. At this point, exercise is good for her." She glared pointedly at Molly. "But Sam's right, too. Be careful about lifting anything heavy. These boxes are all right for the time being, but you'd best git in the habit of being careful."

Molly nodded. "I'll be careful. I promise."

"Good," Sam said, then bent to brush a light kiss on her lips. "You two go on inside. I'll finish up here and join you."

Molly smiled. As usual, Sam would have his way. Somehow his overprotectiveness seemed encouraging, and Molly's spirits lifted. Tomorrow she would bake him a pie.

# *Chapter Twenty*

✦✦✦✦✦

"See you after work," Sam called out as he swung into his saddle using only the horn. "You'll be home the same time as usual?"

Molly hesitated. She was coming home early—to bake Sam's pie. Lee Chin had gone to Truckee for supplies. He had a brother there he wanted to visit, so Sam had given him the night off.

"I . . . ah . . . yes. Same as always. See you then." It was only a tiny lie—a white lie, they called it. Still, it was the first she'd told since the promise she'd made on their wedding night, and it didn't sit well with her. She just hoped he liked the pie.

Sam waved back over his shoulder and headed out with some of the hands. He needed to check the stock in the upper meadow, start moving them down to lower ground, but his mind remained on Molly. He was certain she had lied to him, and he intended to find out why. Surely she wasn't going to stir up more trouble. The thought tightened his gut, and his mouth went dry. He needed to find out. He couldn't afford another "accident."

As the men rounded the first turn from the ranch house, Sam motioned them on. He whirled Gil around and rode behind one of the outbuildings. Tying the big horse out of sight, Sam sat down to wait for Molly. He didn't have long to wait. She was no more than fifteen minutes behind him, heading up the road toward the Lady Jay. Careful to keep his distance, he trailed along behind her.

Molly seemed to be doing exactly what she did every day. She rode over to the Lady Jay, spent time in the main house, then either worked outside or set out to rendezvous with Joaquin and the hands. Some days she headed up to Pitch Camp, but today she looked as though she'd be staying closer to home.

Nothing unusual happened, and Sam began to feel like a meddlesome fool. Maybe he'd imagined the slight inflection in her tone. Deciding he might have been wrong but still determined to find out for sure, he spent the morning mending a fence line along the ridge overlooking the ranch. Molly spent the time working in the barn, but shortly after noon she resaddled True and rode off at a brisk pace. When Molly turned True in the direction of Cedar Creek, Sam wasn't so sure he'd been wrong.

He mounted Gil, pulled his hat low over his brow, and with a grim expression that betrayed all the uncertainty he felt, followed Molly home.

Molly reached Cedar Creek, unsaddled True, and put him away. After changing into a dress, she quickly set to work. Humming softly, she carefully laid out Patience's recipe, along with various and sundry implements and pans, then sat down to peel the apples. When she finished with the fruit, she took out a sack of flour, a bag of sugar, and some lard. She reread the recipe:

*2 cups of flour*
*⅔ cup lard plus a smidgen*
*A pinch of salt*
*½ cup of cool water*
*¾ cup of sugar*

So far, the recipe didn't look too difficult. Surely she could make something as simple as pie crust! But as she eyed the words *plus a smidgen* and *pinch of,* and the phrase at the bottom—*before adding sugar, taste the apples to see how tart they are*—she realized there was plenty of margin for error. Just how much were a *smidgen* and a *pinch,* anyway?

Determinedly, and with meticulous care, Molly mixed the concoction together. It was no easy task. While the crust fought to remain in a doughy wad, the sack of flour stood open near the sink, and the bag of sugar, nestled in a neat white pile, trailed granules from one end of the kitchen to the other. Molly's apron was covered with flour; her hands, smeared with lard as far as her elbows, were gritty with sugar. Even her red hair wore traces of white. Catching a glimpse of her reflection in a shiny metal pan, Molly figured she now had a pretty good idea how she'd look when she got old. She was busy with the rolling pin, trying to keep the doughy crust together on the flour-covered board, when Sam burst through the back door.

Molly shrieked and jumped at the same time. More than a little off balance, her shoe hit a spot of lard, and down she went. She tried to catch herself, but only succeeded in knocking over the bag of flour and pulling the flattened crust from the board to land on top of her bosom.

Sam knelt beside her. "Are you all right?"

Molly was covered from head to foot in flour. Her crust lay in broken pieces, and her backside ached from landing so hard on the floor. She sat up spitting flour and sputtering, "No, I'm not *all right*. What are you doing home so early? This was supposed to be a surprise!" She knew her tone sounded accusing, but she couldn't help herself.

Sam helped Molly stand up, then began brushing flour from her face with the tips of his fingers. Molly shoved his hand away, but accepted the cloth he handed her. He felt more than a little guilty. He'd been spying on her all day, his temper heating up, sure she was up to no good—and all the time she'd been coming home early to bake him a pie.

"Well?" Molly pressed.

"Well, what?"

"Well, why on earth did you barge in here like that? Why aren't you out working like you're supposed to be?"

She was mad at him, furious, in fact. Her eyes flashed blue fire, and Sam thought how utterly desirable she looked. He probably shouldn't tell her the truth; she'd be more angry than she was already. But then he didn't want to lie to her, either.

"I followed you," he said simply, as if it were an everyday occurrence, which, if things had turned out differently, it might well have become.

"Followed me? But why?"

"Because I knew you were lying to me this morning and I wanted to know why."

"It was only a white lie, Sam," Molly said sheepishly. "I . . . I just wanted to surprise you. It's the only one I've ever told you . . . except for that one other time."

Sam's head came up. "What other time?"

Molly finished wiping away the flour, but her hair and clothes were still covered and she knew she looked frightful. Damn! Did nothing ever turn out right with Sam? "You know," she told him. "The time I told you about . . . about . . ." Molly fought a bright flush, but lost the battle. "About all the other men I'd made love to."

Sam laughed aloud. "Oh, that lie." He tried to scowl, but Molly could see he was fighting a grin. "You see, this is the second time telling tales has gotten you in trouble."

Molly brushed more flour from her skirt and apron. "Just tell me how I'm ever going to surprise you."

Sam pulled her into his arms. "Surprise me by going upstairs and taking off those clothes."

Molly didn't miss the smoky green of his eyes. "In the middle of the day?"

He kissed her soundly, thoroughly, then turned her around and smacked her behind. "Go on. I'll be right there. I'd rather have *you* for dessert than apple pie any day."

Smiling to herself, Molly removed her apron

and hung it on the peg beside the door. Upstairs she would be on familiar ground. When it came to making love, Molly trusted her abilities completely.

After a night of heated lovemaking that left both of them satiated and content, Molly decided to make a second attempt at pleasing Sam. His birthday loomed only a week away. If she hurried, maybe she could sew a shirt for him. At least she knew how to sew—a little. She decided she'd work on the shirt at the Lady Jay; that way maybe she could surprise him. She was making fairly rapid progress when she tore a sleeve on the arm of her chair. Since she had no extra material, a trip into town became a necessity. Returning to Cedar Creek an hour after dark, she found Sam pacing the front room floor.

"Where the hell have you been?" he accused, storming up to her before she got two feet into the room.

"I had to go into town for . . . for supplies."

"You're lying again, Molly. I can hear it in your voice." His eyes were dark with suppressed rage.

"Why are you so all-fired upset? It's only a little late. I didn't think it would take this long."

Sam seemed not to hear her. He grabbed her arm and hauled her up short. "I asked you a question. Where have you been?"

Molly felt the sting of tears. "You're hurting me, Sam," she whispered.

He eased his hold, but didn't let her go. "Tell me damn it!"

Molly blinked hard. "Damn you! You always spoil everything!" She jerked her arm away. "You're not my jailer, Sam. I don't have to explain every move I make. I'm not going to tell you where I've been. You'll just have to trust me. Now get out of my way and leave me alone!"

She brushed past him, furious at him for his obvious mistrust. How would they ever build a relationship if neither could learn to trust the other? Growing angrier by the minute, Molly raced up the stairs and slammed, then bolted the door to their room. Sam's heavy footsteps followed close behind.

"Let me in, Molly," he demanded, pounding his fists on the door. "I want to know exactly where you were today. Joaquin was looking for you, and so was Jumbo. Nobody knew where you were. Now I want to know, damn it!" He pounded on the door again.

"Go away and leave me alone. I don't have to report to you. You're my husband, not my boss!"

Sam wedged a broad shoulder against the door. Three hard thrusts and the latch splintered, propelling him into the room. "Don't ever lock a door between us, Molly. By the saints, I'll break it down, I swear it!"

As angry as Sam was, Molly refused to back down. She'd done nothing wrong. He was acting like a madman—all because she'd ridden into Truckee without telling anyone.

"Where I was is none of your business. Get

out of here and leave me alone." She stood facing him, with only inches between them. His face burned scarlet, his chest heaved, his powerful legs were planted in an angry stance.

"You'll tell me, by God, or I swear I'll beat it out of you!"

Molly felt the first trickle of fear. His fists were clenched at his sides, and he looked as though his control could snap at any moment. Would he really beat her? Would he harm their child? Nothing was worth the risk.

Molly swallowed the hard lump in her throat. All this anger over a trip into town. She lifted her eyes to his, and tried to be strong, but salty tears rolled down her cheeks.

"I went into Truckee. To the Whitehouse Mercantile. Mr. Higgins waited on me. He can prove I was there." Her throat was so tight, she could barely choke out the words. "I needed some cloth to finish the shirt I was sewing. For your birthday. It's this Sunday, remember?"

She had to get away. She couldn't let him see how his mistrust had crushed the tiny bud of hope she'd been nurturing. It would never work between them. Sam didn't trust her. Maybe he never had. He'd threatened to beat her—knowing she carried his child. Her heart ached so badly she thought she might die of the pain.

"I'm sorry if I upset you," she told him, her voice barely a whisper. "Now if you'll excuse me, I think I'll go out to the barn and check on True." Her shoulders straight, Molly brushed past him and headed toward the door, tears glistening on her cheeks. He could hear her soft steps on the stairs, then the sound of her weeping as she pulled open the heavy front door.

Sam fought a wave of despair that threatened to engulf him. What had he done? He'd seen it on her face, the tortured look, the disillusionment. She'd forgiven him before, returned to him though he'd practically thrown her out. She'd put aside the past, tried to overlook the heartache he'd caused her, but she wouldn't forgive him again. Not this time. Not only had he mistrusted her, he had threatened her—threatened their child. He hadn't meant one word, but Molly couldn't know that. He'd only done it as a last resort. He'd had to know.

There'd been a fire up at the sawmill. No damage, only a bit of old lumber had gone up in flames. But the fire could have been set. Molly had disappeared, and Sam had to know where she was.

His heart thudded miserably. Molly had been telling the truth. He was sure of it. He'd discovered what he needed to know, but the price was too high. He'd lost Molly for good . . . unless he did something about it. She'd come back to Cedar Creek, put aside her pride, tried to please him in every way. It was obvious she wanted their marriage to work; she'd gone out of her way to show him just how important it was.

Sam headed downstairs and pulled the door open just as Molly mounted True and headed down the lane at a gallop. Sam raced across the yard, bridled Gil, and swung up onto his back without taking time for the saddle. It took awhile for him to catch her. True was nearly as fast as

Gil, and Molly had a head start. She had crossed the first ridge and was riding through a meadow before she realized he was behind her. Though she urged True faster, Gil had sensed the race and had drawn alongside, neck and neck.

Grabbing True's reins, Sam slowed the big black to a trot and finally to a walk. When he let go, he circled Molly's waist with his arm and pulled her across his thighs onto Gil's back.

She fought him fiercely, sobbing, crying, scratching at his face, trying to twist free. Sam captured her wrists in one hand and, holding her tightly, threw a leg over Gil's neck and slipped to the ground. He carried her beneath a pine and settled himself against the trunk, keeping her firmly surrounded in his arms.

"Can't you just leave me alone?" she pleaded. Her tear-filled eyes wrenched his heart.

"No."

"All you ever do is hurt me. Go away and leave me alone." She said the words, but her arms circled his neck and her head rested against his shoulder. Sam could feel the thick strands of her hair, wild and tumbled free, against his cheek.

"I can't."

"Why not?" she asked between ragged breaths.

"Because I love you too much."

"What?"

"I can't leave you alone because I love you too much."

"Oh, God, Sam." Molly's tears began anew.

Sam squeezed his eyes shut. She was so much

woman. Yet she was small and sweet—and he loved her so.

Molly sniffed and looked up at him; the pain in her eyes broke his heart.

"If you loved me, you wouldn't hurt me."

"I didn't mean to. Sometimes things get mixed up. It should be easy to love someone, but it isn't."

"No," she conceded, "it isn't." Molly straightened in his lap but didn't let go of his neck. He'd said the words she'd waited so long to hear, but did he mean them? Or would he continue to doubt her? But then, she understood his doubt a little. She felt the same doubt about him. She still wasn't sure she could trust him. Not after the way he'd acted before. "Would you really have beaten me?"

Sam's hold tightened. He kissed her eyes, her cheeks, her nose. "I could never hurt you, lass. If I ever threaten you again, you have permission to beat *me*."

Molly smiled inwardly, believing his words and feeling safe in his arms. Her heart felt light for the first time since her return to Cedar Creek. "You threatened me once before, you know."

He didn't remember. "When?"

"When I broke all those dishes."

For the first time Sam smiled, a flash of brilliance in the moonlight. A coyote howled on a distant knoll and the wind rustled leaves in the rocks beside them. "That was a threat I meant. Your beautiful backside belongs to me. I wouldn't damage it unjustly, but a husband has to have some rights."

Molly laughed softly and snuggled against him. "Sam?"

"Yes, lass?"

"Are you sure? I mean, absolutely sure you love me?"

"I'm sure."

"Then show me how much."

"Here?"

"Here."

Sam tilted her face and captured her lips. The kiss was feather-soft, a show of his love. He'd make it up to her for the way he'd treated her. He'd make her happy if it took the rest of his life. He loved her. He wished she'd told him she loved him. But after the way he'd acted, he could hardly blame her.

"Don't move." He settled her against the tree, stood up, and walked to her horse. Untying the bedroll behind Molly's saddle, he spread it beneath the pine on a soft bed of needles. Molly joined him on the blanket.

"I remember the first time I saw you in those clothes," Sam said, referring to her breeches and red-checked shirt. His large hands deftly worked the buttons up the front as they sat facing each other on the blanket. "Up at the mud bog. I wanted to do just what I'm doing now."

Molly smiled, unbuttoned Sam's shirt and tugged it free, then slid her fingers through the silky mat of hair on his chest. "Go on," she whispered, and Sam felt a surge of heat in his loins.

"I wanted to strip off your blouse and fill my hands with your breasts. Your shirt was wet, and I could see them even through the cloth."

"Sam!"

"You were beautiful. Like some water nymph." He nibbled the hollow of her throat and popped open the buttons of her breeches. Pulling the shirt free, he drew it off her shoulders, leaving her bare to the waist. Moonlight gleamed on her hair and across her satiny flesh; dark shadows cloaked the skin beneath each breast. "God, I love to look at you."

Molly pulled Sam's shirt off. His wide shoulders and narrow waist beckoned. The muscles over his ribs flexed and strained as he moved, and Molly felt a shiver of anticipation. When Sam lowered his mouth to circle her nipple, she moaned aloud, unconsciously arching her back to give him access. Tingly heat flooded through her. His hands cupped her breasts, and her hands played over the surface of his muscular torso. When he stopped his gentle suckling, Molly surrendered to a sweet ache that only Sam could still. He paused a moment to slide the rest of her clothes down over her hips, did the same with his own, then returned to finish the pleasant task he had set.

His lips went to her mouth, warm and moist and seeking. His hands stroked her breasts, her hips, her thighs, then a finger slipped inside her, and Molly moaned Sam's name. She reached for him and found him hard, his thick shaft demanding release. Molly was more than ready to meet his demands.

Sam pressed her gently down on the blanket, containing himself, it seemed, by force of will. "I love you so much it hurts." He spread her thighs with his knee and guided himself inside her; then the last of his control fell away, and he drove himself fully inside her. Molly rose to meet each driving thrust. As he plunged into her, she arched and surged beneath him. He rode her, claimed her, branded her. She clung to his neck, wanting all of him, accepting all he had to give, and giving all she had in return. She heard nothing but the soft sound of his love words, saw nothing but the red and black swirls of passion, felt nothing but the fiery strokes of his shaft.

Swept to new heights, Molly surged upon the glittering sands of climax, and Sam followed her to release.

Her breathing, labored and ragged, slowed to a soft, contented purr as Sam nestled her in the curve of his arm.

The following week was the happiest Molly had known. Sam fairly doted on her. She knew he was trying to make up for his lack of trust and his harsh words, and Molly basked in the luxury of his attention.

Only one thing dampened her spirits. She still hadn't told Sam how she felt about him. He hadn't asked her, but a sixth sense told her the question lay on the tip of his tongue. She wanted to tell him how she felt—and she would. But telling him she loved him would forfeit the last of her security. She would be at Sam's mercy, just as she had been before. Not that she wasn't already. But at least for now he wasn't completely certain of the power he held.

Molly liked having an edge. With a man like Sam, a woman needed all the help she could get. But she also knew Sam wouldn't wait long. Having hidden her feelings from him in the first place might have been at least partly responsible for their problems. If she wanted to keep his love, she'd have to tell him sooner or later.

While continuing to work up her courage, Molly made small concessions to him. They talked of things they'd rarely spoken of before: his plans for Cedar Creek, work she was doing at the Lady Jay. One evening after a delicious meal of roast quail Lee Chin had prepared, Molly brought up a subject she'd been thinking about for some time.

The fall weather had set in: Rain clattered noisily on the roof and beat against the windows. The ground was muddy, and a sharp wind whistled through the pines. Sam had built a fire in the great hearth, and the dining room felt cozy and warm. Molly's fork clattered noisily against her empty porcelain plate as she shoved her dish away. The succulent aroma of roast quail still hung in the air. Molly breathed deeply, expelling a contented sigh.

"God, that was good. I wish I could cook half as well as Lee Chin does."

Sam wiped his mouth with a coarse linen napkin and leaned back against his chair. "There are things Lee Chin can do, and things you can do. Personally, I'd almost rather go hungry." He smiled wolfishly, and Molly gave in to a rippling burst of laughter.

Lee arrived with coffee, and Molly fiddled with her cup, trying to find an opening. "How's that new section of forest coming?" she asked.

"The splash dam's near overflowing," he replied. "We'll be opening the dam and floating the timber down to the mill day after tomorrow. The men have outdone themselves. We've got quite a tidy profit in those logs, but the river's getting high. We've got to go now, before it's too late. It'll take some careful rafting to get them down, but the river pigs we've hired are as good as they come."

"Would you like some help from Jumbo and the crew at Pitch Camp?"

"I don't think we'll need them." He covered her small hand with his big one. "But thanks for the offer. It's nice to feel that we're on the same team."

Molly smiled up at him. When he looked at her like that, her heart nearly stopped.

"By the way," he added, "when are you putting your logging road in?"

"Now that it's started raining, I've decided to wait. We can do without it for a while longer. The ground's just too soft right now."

"I think that's a wise decision."

"Sam?"

"Yes, lass?"

"There's something else I've been wanting to talk to you about." She forced herself to look him in the eye. "It's about Jason Foley."

Sam straightened in his chair. Molly didn't miss the angry pulse that began throbbing at the base of his throat.

"Is Foley bothering you again? I swear, Molly, I'll beat him senseless this time."

"Foley hasn't come near me since you taught him a lesson last time. But I still don't trust him. What I wanted to say was . . . now that . . . our marriage is . . . is . . . now that there's going to be no annulment . . ."

Sam brought her fingers to his lips, his short beard soft against her fingers. "Yes?"

"What I'm trying to say is that if your offer to buy Foley out still stands, I'll accept—but only as a loan. I . . . I couldn't forgive myself if something happened to our baby."

Sam came out of his chair to stand behind her. He kissed the top of her head. "I know how hard that was for you, Molly, and I just want you to know how much it means to me. You and the baby are more important than anything else. I'll have Peter start the negotiations. As soon as we reach an agreement, the better off we'll all be."

Molly rose from her chair and stood in the circle of his arms. The words *I love you* crowded her tongue, but Molly couldn't say them. They were blotted out by memories of lonely nights without Sam, by words on an ivory slip of paper written in Lilly's hand. Once she understood why Sam had cast her aside in the first place, she would tell him how much she cared. Until then, Molly would be the only one to know.

* * *

The rains continued throughout the night and into the next day. Sam tried to dissuade her from going to work, but there were things she had to do. There were things Sam had to do as well. He had to go into Truckee to make final preparations for the log float the next day—unless the downpour forced a postponement. As he drove the team into town, Sam prayed the weather would let up.

As usual, Truckee was bustlng with travelers, miners, and timbermen. When Sam rolled the big spring wagon to a halt in front of the Whitehouse General Mercantile, Judge Egan, with Lilly on his arm, was scurrying down the boardwalk seeking cover from the rain. Seeing Sam, they stopped beneath a striped canvas awning and waited for him to join them.

Sam tipped his hat to Lilly, then extended a hand to the judge. "What brings you two out in this weather?"

"Daddy promised to take me shopping," Lilly told him in her soft, crystalline voice. "I wanted to go into Sacramento City, but with the weather, I had to settle for Truckee. Besides, I was about to go out of my mind in that house." Lilly laid a silky, slim-fingered hand on his arm. "I've missed you, Sam."

"The way I heard it, Jason Foley's been keeping you occupied lately."

"Reverend Foley's a good man," the judge put in. "At least his intentions are honorable." The judge put a little more emphasis than necessary on the last word. Sam wondered how honorable Judge Egan would think Foley was if he could see the scars on Molly's back. The thought sent a surge of temper through his veins.

Peter had been out of town, so there'd been no offer tendered as yet for Foley's portion of the Lady Jay. It was a loose end Sam was eager to tie up.

"If he does marry Lilly," Sam said, "I'd suggest you keep an eye on him. See that he keeps that temper of his under control."

Judge Egan bristled, but Lilly seemed unconcerned. A stagecoach rolled by on the street, splashing mud in their direction. The judge gallantly stepped in front of his daughter, protecting her skirts from the muck.

"You still planning on runnin' your logs tomorrow?" the judge asked.

"If the river's passable. It's high, but so far not too high. Haven't got much choice. My dam's near to overflowing. I can't afford to have those logs go over."

"Too bad the rain didn't hold off a little longer."

"Tough to outguess Mother Nature." Sam turned to Lilly. "Take care of yourself, Lilly. And don't let that father of yours push you into something you don't want."

Lilly smiled knowingly and touched a hand to Sam's cheek. "He's been trying to do that for years, but he hasn't succeeded yet." Nearly as tall as Sam, she leaned toward him and whispered softly in his ear, "You're *sure* you're happily married?"

Sam smiled. "Quite sure. Have a nice lunch." He started to leave, but Lilly stopped him. "Don't you want to join us? Or wouldn't your little *wife* approve?"

Sam grinned broadly. "You're right about that, Lilly. My little wife would definitely not approve. And for reasons I couldn't begin to explain, I'm happy she feels that way. Good-bye." Sam left Lilly staring after him and the judge muttering to himself.

He strode into the Whitehouse, needing some extra length of rope, some heavy-gauge chain, and some extra pike poles and cant hooks to maneuver the logs on the run.

"Howdy, Sam." Lester Higgins, a skinny man with liver spots on his forehead and a thick mustache, waited behind the counter. "What kin I git fer ya?"

Sam told him what he wanted, and two young boys loaded the goods into the wagon, covering them against the rain with a heavy canvas tarp.

"Thanks, Lester. See you next trip."

"Oh, by the way, did your wife git that dynamite she needed?"

"She's decided to put off the logging road till the rains stop." Sam turned to leave.

"That's funny. Message I got said she had to have it today. Said it was a must. I had it delivered over to the freight office. They was supposed to take it out this afternoon."

Sam's heart pounded. "You got a message from her today?"

"Yeah. It was waitin' for me when I got back

from lunch. You might check over to the freight office, if you've a mind to. If they haven't left yet, you could save them the trip."

"I'll do that. Thanks, Lester."

"Good luck with yer run."

Sam just nodded. It seemed just about everyone in Truckee knew about the big timber run. He tried to blot the nagging suspicion there might not be a run, and headed toward the J. W. Irving Freight Office. As he walked the wide board sidewalk, he forced himself to remain calm. He'd jumped to conclusions too many times before; this time he had to be sure. There'd be no second chance.

"Hello, J. W." Sam wasted no time crossing the room. "Do you have a shipment of dynamite here for the Lady Jay?"

"Did have," J. W. said. He scratched the thin gray hairs combed evenly across his balding head. "Somebody picked it up 'bout an hour ago."

"Who was it?"

"Didn't see 'em, Sam. Wilbur Jensen was workin'. He's gone over to Tahoe City with a load."

"Thanks, J. W." Pulling his hat down low, Sam headed into the rain. He climbed atop the wagon, drawing his slicker around him, and rolled the wagon down the muddy streets of Truckee toward home. He wasn't sure if he should go straight to the Lady Jay or head back to the ranch. Either way, he was likely to miss her. Finally, he decided to wait for her at Cedar

Creek. She should arrive shortly after he did. If she didn't show up on time, he'd head up to the splash dam.

The two-hour trip home seemed an eternity. Thunder cracked and roared and lightning flashed, making the sky more threatening by the minute. The downpour remained steady. Sam hoped it wouldn't get worse.

Several hands ran out to the wagon as he rolled into the yard. He climbed down, wet, tired, and weary, and headed for the house. Lee Chin pushed open the door.

"Mr. Sam, you come in quick. I bring nice cup of hot coffee while you get dry clothes."

"Have you seen Molly?" Sam asked, knowing it was a senseless question.

"Lee Chin no see, but man bring note, say Miss Molly work late. Be home after dark if she can."

The words stirred a shiver of dread. "How convenient," was all Sam said. "Bring me that coffee, Lee. And a handful of jerky. I'm going back out."

"No, Mr. Sam. It getting dark. Too dangerous."

"I think Molly's going to blow the splash dam. Another 'accident.' Just like before. Someone could get hurt, to say nothing of the money we'll lose."

"No, Mr. Sam. Miss Molly not do that. You wrong."

"Sorry, Lee, I don't think so."

Shaking his head, Lee Chin left, returning in

minutes with the coffee and jerky. "You catch man this time. Not Miss Molly. You see."

Sam didn't bother to answer. Downing the coffee in several scalding gulps, he strode through the door into the rain.

# Chapter Twenty-one

MOLLY RETURNED TO Cedar Creek bone-tired, but earlier than she expected. Lamplight beckoned through the windows, and she urged True faster, eager to see Sam. As she rode the big black into the barn, Jack Tucker, one of the hands, offered to unsaddle and rub him down. Molly accepted gratefully. She was almost to the front porch, rainwater pouring off her hat brim and trailing down her slicker, when Lee Chin opened the door.

"Is something wrong, Lee?"

The little Chinese looked old beyond his years as he held the door open, his eyes cast down. Molly felt a stirring of unease.

"Where's Sam?" she asked, her worry building. "Isn't he home yet?" Rainwater pooled at her feet.

When Lee still didn't answer, Molly fought a surge of temper mingled with the sharp edge of fear. "Damn it, Lee, I want to know what's going on!"

Lee Chin wrung his small hands and refused to meet her gaze. "Mr. Sam go up to splash dam."

"What! In this weather? Why in God's name would he do that?"

Lee Chin looked away. Molly grabbed the front of his quilted blouse. "What's wrong, Lee? You've got to tell me."

Again he glanced away, then looked back as if making some momentous decision. He took a long, steadying breath and rolled his eyes skyward. "I pray to ancestors I do right thing."

"Damn it, Lee, tell me what's going on!" She let go of his blouse, her hands shaking with the cold and now a shot of fear.

"Mr. Sam, he think you try to blow up dam. He go to stop you."

"But why would he think that?"

"Mr. Emmet. No accident. Flume blown up. Mr. Sam think you did it. He find tracks. Match your horse's. Find your shoe button at sawmill. Tonight he think you up at splash dam. I tell him he wrong. Now pray I am right."

"Foley!" Molly shrieked. "Foley's the only one with reason to cause trouble. He wants me to sell the ranch. He's capable of doing anything to get what he wants. I don't understand exactly what he's up to, but I intend to find out." She leaned down and kissed Lee's smooth-skinned cheek. "Thanks for trusting me. I promise you won't regret it." She started to turn, but he stopped her.

"Mr. Sam love you. He die inside when you leave. He worried about the others. He feel responsible if something happen to them. You forgive?"

Molly wasn't sure, but at least she understood what was going on. "How long ago did he leave?"

"About hour."

"Everything's going to be fine, Lee." She moved through the door into the rain.

"Saddle him again, Jack," Molly instructed, rain dripping from the brim of her hat.

"You going back out?"

"Something's come up." She wished she could take the man along, but until she straightened things out, the fewer people who knew about the incidents, the better. She was certain Sam would feel the same.

"You sure you don't want a fresh mount?"

"Not in this storm. I want a horse I can count on. He's tired, but he's had a lot tougher days."

Jack Tucker just nodded. Molly realized with a rush of satisfaction the men were beginning to accept her as the "boss lady." Tucker saddled True quickly, then handed Molly the reins.

"I think I'd best go with you. Don't think Big Sam would approve a' me lettin' you go out there alone."

"Sorry, Jack, not this time." She swung into the saddle and pulled her hat low.

"Sam ain't gonna like this."

"He'll be waiting for me," she told him. "I'll be all right." She spun True on his hind legs and headed into the storm. At least the big horse had been grained, and had a few minutes rest. She could have used a little rest herself.

By the time Sam reached the splash dam, the rain was falling in sheets. He'd thought about Molly all the way, his gut twisting tighter with every passing minute. She'd made a fool of him again, duped him into loving her, all the while planning to destroy him. Of course Jason Foley could be behind the incidents, and a tiny part of him prayed it was so. But his rational mind began to blot even that tiny ember of hope. Sam cocked his head against the wind, and pulled up the collar of his slicker. Rage seethed inside him, more powerful than the storm.

If he found Molly at the splash dam, he wasn't sure what he would do. Woman or not, wife or not, Molly James Brannigan was out to destroy him, destroy his family. Already, she had very nearly succeeded in killing his brother.

Sam spent the better part of an hour circling the area around the dam, trying to flush out whoever might be trying to sabotage his operation. He saw no one. But as he descended into the depression that housed the lake, he spotted a tiny flickering light, glowing on the ground in the darkness. There was no mistaking what it was.

Sweat beaded on his forehead as he urged Gil forward. If he reached the fuse too late, he'd be blown to kingdom come along with his logs.

The big horse covered the ground as swiftly as possible, given the mud and the rain. As Sam neared the burning fuse, which was well protected beneath a fallen log, he calculated he had only seconds to spare. He swung from the saddle and rushed to the log, pulling the fuse from the dynamite pack just before it set off the charge.

Even in the raging cold, Sam was sweating. *Close. Too close.* And somewhere equally close, Molly Brannigan waited to see the deadly results of her work.

Sam lifted his hat and blotted the sweat from his brow with an elbow, deciding he'd make one last pass before heading home. He wanted to catch her. Leave no shred of doubt about her guilt.

Blue eyes, round with tenderness, came unbidden to his mind; thick red hair cascading over full, creamy breasts with luscious pink nipples. The knot in his throat threatened to choke him. How could she have fooled him so completely? How could he still love her so?

Scarcely able to see the trail, Molly was glad of her surefooted mount. Even slowed by the storm, she'd made good time by taking a dangerous shortcut through Simmon's Pass. She'd forgotten it existed until tonight, but the pass had served her well. She calculated she'd gained at least half an hour on Sam.

Molly crested the rise and began searching for her husband. It didn't take long to spot his big buckskin across the lake, but Sam was nowhere to be seen. Molly cupped her hands against the wind and called out to him, but the sound died in the storm. She began to circle the lake, fighting the stinging wind, letting True pick his way cautiously along the narrow, steep trail. She spotted Sam some distance away, standing beside a fallen log. When he turned toward her, she waved an arm above her head and again called his name.

It was easy to see by the set of his shoulders, the fury in his stride, how angry he was. It didn't matter. He was safe, and the dam was still intact. She'd make him listen to reason once they got home. Better yet, she'd make him confront Jason Foley. Sam could get the truth out of Foley if anyone could.

Sam stalked past Gil and continued striding toward her. The path was steep, the drop deadly. Much of the trail had already washed away, and Molly felt an uneasy tingling down her spine.

"Watch the trail, Sam!" she called out to him, but again her words died on the wind. Lightning crackled against the black sky and thunder roared in its wake.

Molly waited for Sam to approach, torn between fury at his mistrust and terror that he still wouldn't believe her. If only she could have caught Foley at the dam. Sam would have had to believe her then. She scanned the hillsides in a vain effort to spot him, knowing it was probably a fruitless quest, until another bolt of lightning lit the sky. Molly look back at Sam just as the heavy thunder rolled and the trail turned to mush beneath his feet. A dark wall of mud swept him from her sight.

"Sam!" Molly screamed. She rushed toward him, fighting down her terror, close to hysteria and blinded by tears. "Oh, God, no!" Only a gaping hole in the trail remained. Molly scanned the darkness below, trying to see where he could have been carried. She saw no sign of him. Blinking to clear the wetness in her eyes, she climbed down the muddy embankment to a place several feet below the trail. Terror clutched her. *Please, God, don't take him from me now.* Then she saw him. He was hanging from the slender branch of a shrub that protruded from the side of the muddy cliff.

"Hang on, Sam!" she called to him, then frantically raced to get True. She untied her rope and shook out a loop with numb, trembling fingers as she led him down the path to a point just in front of the washout and as close as she could get to Sam. Tying one end of the rope to the saddle horn, she dropped the other end down the side of the mountain.

"Put the rope under your arms, Sam! I'll pull you up."

"Don't do it, Sam," came a man's warning voice. "She's trying to kill you." Sitting astride his rain-soaked horse, Judge Egan hurled his own rope over the edge of the trail. "She's tried before—she'll do it this time, if you let her." The judge sat astride his horse, rainwater dripping from his bowler onto the canvas duster he wore.

Molly could scarcely believe his words. "He's

lying, Sam!'' Why would he say such a thing? Then it all became perfectly clear: *It wasn't Jason Foley—it was Judge Egan.* Molly looked down at Sam. The roots of the shrub were beginning to show. In minutes the shrub would be washed away, and with it, its precious burden.

"Sam, you've got to trust me! There isn't time! Grab hold of the rope!"

"Take my rope, Sam. You'll die if you don't."

Molly squinted hard against the rain. The judge's rope was looped around, but not tied to the horn. A cry of despair lodged in her throat. What words could she say to make Sam believe her? Another flash of lightning cracked and the sky opened up.

"Take my rope, Sam! I'm not behind the accidents—he is!" Half the shrub pulled free, leaving just a last slender root. In seconds, he would be gone. "Look to your heart for the truth, Sam! Look to your heart!" The clap of thunder muffled her final words: "I love you, Sam!"

The mountain crumbled away, and Molly shrieked in terror. She closed her eyes, fighting a wave of nausea. There was no way he could survive it: If the fall didn't kill him, he'd be buried beneath tons of mud.

Then she heard True's soft neigh and felt the heavy weight on her rope. Molly stifled the sob in her throat and set to work, carefully backing True down the trail, hauling his heavy burden slowly up the side of the mountain.

Mud-covered, scraped, and bloodied, Sam hauled himself over the edge. Molly hurled herself into his arms.

"How touching." The judge's voice penetrated the raging wind. He'd moved around the mountain to a position near where they stood. "Now raise your hands and step away from each other."

"Why, Judge?" Sam asked, his arm still tight around Molly's waist. "Why?"

"You disgraced my daughter. You made us both a laughingstock. Everyone in town knew what was going on. You should have had the decency to marry her."

"Lilly didn't want to marry me," Sam told him. "She was happy with things the way they were."

"You ruined us both, and you're going to pay." The judge cocked the hammer on his rifle.

Sam inched forward, easing Molly's hand away from where it clutched his arm. "At least tell me how you did it. If I'm going to die, I think I have a right to know."

The judge lifted a corner of his mouth in a watery smile. "It all started that day at the train station. Molly's shoe button fell off and I picked it up. I'd been thinking how I could get even. The button gave me the idea about the sawmill accident. The day I rode over to the Lady Jay, I saw her foreman using a bar shoe on that big black of hers. I had the left hind hoof of one of mine shod with the same kind of shoe."

Sam moved closer, but the judge only smiled and backed away. "Stay where you are, Sam."

"It isn't worth it, Judge. You'll hang for this."

"Not a chance. Everyone will think Molly did it. Even your brother believes it. When they find you both dead, they'll believe you killed each other."

"Please, Judge Egan," Molly pleaded. "Sam didn't mean to hurt anyone. Marrying me was just a business proposition."

"Who do you think you're kidding? The man's in love with you. That's why I left that note in your wagon. Did a nice job on the writing, don't you think? I figured if I couldn't make him leave you, maybe I could make you leave him. When that didn't work, I planned more 'accidents.' I didn't mean to hurt Emmet, but I did want that red wig seen." He laughed coldly and lifted the rifle, sighting the barrel toward the middle of Sam's chest.

Molly's voice stopped his finger on the trigger. "There's one more thing I think you should know."

The judge seemed amused. "Go ahead."

"Sam and I are ending our marriage at year's end. He could marry Lilly then if she still wanted him." She felt Sam stiffen and hated herself for the words she forced herself to say. "You're wrong about loving each other. We never have. We just married to get the timber contracts. Sam thought you and Lilly would understand. No one's been killed yet. It isn't too late. Sam loves Lilly. And I love Michael Locke. We've been seeing each other all along. You can ask him yourself." For the first time the judge seemed uncertain, giving Molly a surge of hope. "You see, Judge, everything can still work out the way you planned."

He pondered her words a moment more. Then his face hardened. Even through the downpour, Molly could see the vicious set to his jaw. "You through?" he said.

Another flash of lightning formed a jagged pattern across the sky. Thunder clapped, followed by a different, quaking roar—and the sound of grinding timber. Sam heard it and so did the judge. Molly screamed; Sam shoved her to the ground as the judge pulled the trigger. A wall of mud and debris muffled his terrified cry and washed him over the brink of the ravine. His eerie wail echoed and faded, leaving only the roar of the rain.

For a moment, neither of them moved. Molly's heart knocked against her ribs. Sam gently caught her arm, pulling her up and away from the edge.

"It's over now," he whispered. "It's over." He pulled her into his arms and held her while she sobbed against his chest. She could still feel the tension in his body.

"It isn't safe here," he said. With his arm protectively around her waist, he guided her back down the trail to safety.

"There's a line shack down the draw a ways," he told her. "We'll have to ride double. Gil's on the other side of the washout. He'll find his way down to the ranch eventually."

Molly nodded. Sam lifted her into the saddle, then swung up behind. They rode the short distance in silence, shivering from the cold, Molly shaking from the gamble she'd taken and the uncertain consequences. Sam hadn't trusted her before. Would he believe the words she had spoken were only an attempt to save their lives?

They reached the cabin. Sam tied Gil in the lean-to beside the cabin and unsaddled him while Molly started the fire. Warm flames crackled in the hearth by the time Sam shoved open the splintery pine door.

"Take off those wet clothes," he instructed, tossing her bedroll on the floor. Several drops of water dripped from the roof to sputter on the hot rocks of the fireplace as he unfurled the bedding and tossed her a dry wool blanket. "You can wrap up in this. Our clothes should be dry by morning. Anything to eat in this place?" His tone was all business, and Molly feared her words had taken their toll.

"A couple of tins of beans and peaches."

"You get undressed," he said. "I'll start getting the grub on."

It was the first time she ever took her clothes off in front of him without stirring his interest. The situation was worse than she thought. Wrapping herself in her blanket, she took over the kitchen duties so Sam could undress. She had the beans on the fire in plenty of time to watch him shed his slicker, boots, shirt, and breeches, and wrap himself in a blanket. His gaze rested in the flickering flames of the fire.

"Sam?" She sat down beside him on the bedroll, the warmth of the fire thawing her and giving her a little courage. Sam didn't seem to hear her.

She ran her hand through the thick strands of

his golden hair. "Why do you think I came after you tonight?"

Sam looked up. "I don't know."

"Because I was worried sick about you, and because Lee Chin told me about the sabotage. He also said you believed I was responsible."

A flash of regret darkened his eyes. "I'm sorry."

"Don't be. Under the circumstances, I would have believed the same as you." She traced the line of his jaw, and he turned away. The defeat in his eyes tore at her heart. "Why do you think I said what I did to the judge?"

"Because you were trying to keep us from getting killed."

"You're sure about that?"

He winced. "Fairly sure."

"But not completely, one-hundred-percent sure?"

He didn't answer.

Molly had never seen him so resigned. Half of her wanted to shake him, the other half wanted to cradle him in her arms. "Remember when I found the note from Lilly?" she asked. He kept his gaze fixed on the fire. "You told me to look to my heart. When I did, I knew you were telling the truth." She turned his face with her hand and forced him to look at her. "Tonight I said those words to you. You're alive because you listened to your heart. Now I'm asking you to listen to your heart again."

He watched her closely. With a silent prayer she willed the right words to come. "I love you, Sam. I've loved you from the start. At first I didn't tell you because I was afraid of losing my independence and because I felt guilty for loving a Brannigan. I was going to tell you the night of Emmet's mishap, but you didn't come home. After that, I was glad I hadn't." She brushed his lips with a feather-soft kiss.

"I love you, Sam. I've never loved another man. I never will."

Sam felt a tightening in his chest and a tender ache that wrapped around his heart. "Are you sure?" he asked softly.

"I've never been more sure of anything in my life."

"God, Molly. I love you so damned much." He pulled her into his arms and crushed her against him. His mouth came down hard. As always, the spark ignited and the kiss became demanding, his lips tasting, touching, searing. There were no secrets left to keep them apart, no unspoken truths, no mistrust. He loved her and she loved him. He intended to leave no doubt as to where she belonged.

Wanting to protect her from the hard floor beneath them, he rolled her on top and settled her astride him, his heart feeling light for the first time in weeks.

"Tonight, Mrs. Brannigan, it is the mare who shall ride the stallion."

Eyes round, Molly smiled impishly, enjoying the power she held. With deliberate slowness, she moved her body lower until she felt his hardness pressing against her, demanding entrance. "And I thought you weren't interested," she teased.

"I'm more than interested, now that I'm sure of your love."

"Be sure, my darling," Molly whispered. "Never doubt it again." She slid onto his shaft, and he groaned with pleasure. With a fire warming her blood, she lowered her mouth to his and began to ride in earnest. She smiled to herself, deciding she'd discovered another of man's pleasures she would not be denied. Then she felt the slow heat in her loins burst into a white-hot flame and gave herself up to the fiery sensations.

They made love passionately, unmindful of the storm, each delighting in the other, content in their mutual love, and determined to put the past behind them.

# *Chapter Twenty-two*

THE WINTER RAINS were only a memory, the meadows deep with summer grass when Molly decided to make her final break with the Lady Jay. She planned to give the big house over to Joaquin and Angel, so she and Sam set out at first light to begin the job of packing and sorting her things.

As usual, they'd both been working hard, so the ride over brought an interlude of closeness.

"I really feel good about this, Sam," Molly

said as the buckboard jounced into a deep rut on the hard-packed road. "I should have done it as soon as Foley left."

"Everything happens in its own good time, lass." Sam had bought out Foley's interest right after the storm—and sent him packing. He'd moved to upstate New York, where he began construction of the church he'd always wanted to build. Later, word reached Cedar Creek that a scaffolding loaded with bricks had toppled over, crushing his pelvis and leaving him partially crippled.

"*'Vengeance is mine, saith the Lord,'* " Molly had quoted when she read the wire. Sam could only agree.

"*Óla, chica* and Señor Sam!" Angel called out as the wagon rolled up in a cloud of dust. "It is good to see you."

Molly spent less and less time at the ranch house, though she still worked with Joaquin and the hands, or Jumbo up at the logging camp.

"Where is *mi niño?*" the big woman cooed, scooping the red-haired bundle from his cradle in the back of the wagon. The baby, Samuel Peter, had arrived in the spring, and with him, the end of Molly's guilt about marrying a Brannigan. She could never be ashamed of marrying the man who had given her such a beautiful child.

"I swear, Angel," Molly scolded as Sam's hands surrounded her once-again tiny waist to lift her down. "You spoil that boy something awful."

"No worse than his papa, *verdad?*"

Sam winked at her and Molly smiled. "You're right there," she said. "Sam thinks his son walks on water. Being completely unbiased, I'd have to agree." All three laughed heartily.

"Padre Fitzsimmons stopped by," Angel said. "He say should have christened the little one long before now. He will speak with you on Sunday." Molly and Sam had repeated their vows in the church, though each felt that in a sense their real wedding had taken place in the dirty old line shack in the middle of the rainstorm.

"The baby can wear my christening gown," Molly said. "I'm sure my mother kept it. I'll probably run across it while I'm packing."

"Speaking of which," Sam said with a twinkle in his eye, "we'd better get at it. The sooner the last of my wife's things are out of here, the sooner I get her back home where she belongs."

It was obvious to both Angel and Molly he meant *back in bed where she belongs,* and both ladies blushed. Sam was determined to make up for the months they'd been unable to make love while they waited for the baby's arrival, and Molly found the idea more than a little appealing.

"Sam's right," Molly said. "Besides, I want to get finished as soon as possible so you and Joaquin can move in."

"You are sure about this, *chica?*"

"Of course I'm sure." They moved toward the house.

"Good." Angel's wide girth filled the doorway. "This way you no leave your husband again."

Molly shook her head, having heard the words several times before. "I never left Sam in the first place, Angel, and you know it." Sam cringed a little at the words.

Angel just grunted. The old woman refused to believe that Sam would ever throw Molly out. She thought he was too much of a gentleman, and besides, no man could possibly resist Molly's charms.

"That's right, Angel," Sam teased, "Molly will be stuck with me for good."

"Like I say before, you good for her. Keep her in line."

"I'm not sure it isn't the other way around," Sam mumbled beneath his breath.

Once inside, Angel set to work in the parlor while Molly, babe in arms, headed for the bedroom. Joaquin joined Sam, and they began loading the furniture she'd be taking back to Cedar Creek.

Her own room long ago emptied, her things moved to the home she shared with Sam, Molly headed down the narrow hallway to the closed door at the end. Her mother's room.

Steeling herself for a job she should have done years ago, Molly turned the knob and marched across the room to the wide feather bed, laying the baby on a soft blue blanket. There was little breeze, so Molly removed the baby's clothes, and he gurgled happily, kicking his feet as Molly readied herself for the task ahead.

For thirteen years, the room had remained the same: the beautiful rosewood bureau, the delicate blue porcelain pitcher on the stand beside the bed. The carved mahogany armoire still held the fancy silk dresses her mother had so loved to wear. Her father had left it just as it was the day her mother died, treating it as if it were a shrine. The room was always kept clean and tidy, as if awaiting her mother's return; Molly hadn't had the heart to trespass, though the room was far nicer than her own.

Molly ran her hand lovingly along the smooth grain of the bureau and a lump swelled in her throat. Since her father had bought the piece as a wedding gift and her mother had always loved it, Molly had decided to move it to Cedar Creek.

Thinking of the past, Molly's gaze moved over the bureau to the silver-handled mirror on the top. A heart-shaped silver box rested beside it. With trembling fingers, she lifted the lid, the soft tinkle of the Viennese waltz drifting to her ears. Her mother's hat pins still gleamed against the red velvet lining. Molly closed the lid and turned away. The past was behind her now. She wouldn't allow it to intrude on her happiness again.

Taking a deep breath, she set to work, sorting through drawers and boxes, packing things away, deciding which she would keep, which Angel might want, and which would go to charity. The baby fell asleep, the quiet immersing Molly deeper in the past and her melancholy mood. She thought of all the things she and her mother should have shared, the days together they'd missed. Although she tried to blot the memories and the sadness, she finally gave up and continued with her task.

"You want to take your mother's dresser home, don't you?" Sam asked, poking his head in the door. His expression softened as he read her forlorn expression. "The past is behind us, lass," he said softly. Long strides brought him to her side, where he held her close.

"I know."

"You'll feel better when we get home."

Molly nodded.

Wishing he could absorb some of her pain, and wanting to finish the unhappy job as quickly as possible, Sam shoved the dresser into the center of the room, the sound a lonely wail that reflected Molly's solemn mood. Glancing down, he saw the back of the bureau had broken loose, scattering yellowed pieces of paper on the floor. He bent to scoop them up and felt a cold shiver run down his spine.

Molly turned in Sam's direction to find him kneeling behind the bureau, several faded letters in his hand. The expression on his face drained the color from her cheeks.

"Sam? What is it?" Hurriedly, she knelt beside him, trying to read his troubled look.

"They're from my father. I'd know his handwriting anywhere. They were hidden in the back of the bureau. Moving it must have unseated them." He handed her the letters.

Molly's mouth went dry. Should she read them? Would they open old wounds just recently healed? Part of her wanted to crumple the letters up and toss them away before they could hurt anyone else.

"Open them," Sam said softly.

"I . . . I'm not sure we should."

"Open them, Molly." Sam's expression looked bleak, his eyes hard. Molly's hand shook as she pulled the yellowed stationery from its time-worn envelope.

*My darling Colleen,* the letter began, and Molly stiffened. "This doesn't mean a thing," she said as she finished reading the words, but a haunted look darkened her eyes.

Sam read the letter. "Open the others," he said softly.

"I don't want to, Sam."

"Do it, Molly! We both need to know."

Molly sensed the demons he was fighting were as terrible as her own. "I don't want to know. I've put it behind me. You have, too. Let's leave it alone."

Sam just shook his head. "Open the letters," he said, his quiet tone a command.

Reluctantly, Molly opened several other letters written in the same bold hand. Again Shamus Brannigan professed his love for Colleen. He spoke of passion and the future. He talked of the guilt he felt in loving another man's wife. He talked of the happiness they would share once they were together. Molly's vision blurred. A single tear darkened a spot on the paper.

Why would her mother have kept them—unless they meant something to her? Her father had said Shamus tried to rape Colleen, that he'd killed her when she wouldn't have him. Would

Shamus have murdered the woman he loved? If he didn't, who did? There was only one other person who could have.

"Now the last," Sam instructed.

Molly shook her head. "I can't." She held the last letter, different from the rest, as if it might burn her, deathly afraid of what it might say. The once pink-hued paper displayed a delicate and lacy handwriting that Molly knew to be her mother's. The envelope was addressed to Shamus, but the letter had never been mailed.

"Read it, Molly," Sam said, his tone flat.

"No," she whispered.

"Read it, damn it!"

Molly brushed away a tear and unfolded the faded paper, her hands trembling so hard she could scarely read the writing. Her mother's words hardened the lump in her throat.

*My dearest Shamus,*

*I am fearful of our next rendezvous. Even as I write this, Malcolm grows suspicious. I am afraid, yet nothing can keep me from you. Only your love and that of my daughter sustain me. I await our meeting with trepidation and abiding thoughts of your love.*

*Now and forever,*
*your Colleen*

Molly was sobbing softly by the time she finished reading the letter. Sam pulled it from her hand. For a moment, he stood transfixed; then he closed his eyes against the moisture that threatened to spill onto his cheeks. Molly felt his arms surround her, cradling her head against his chest as he smoothed her hair with his hand.

Needing his comfort, Molly turned in the circle of his arms. "All those years, Sam. All those years I blamed you and your family when it was *my* father who was the murderer, not yours."

Sam tightened his hold. "He was a lonely, bitter man, Molly. But he's through ruining people's lives. My father and your mother would have been happy we're together. Glad we found the happiness they longed for."

"It breaks my heart, Sam. She loved Shamus the way I love you. I know exactly how my mother must have felt." She cried for a time, and he let her tears wash away the last of her sorrow. Then the soft, muted sounds of the baby's fussing brought them back to the present.

Molly sniffed and dried her eyes. "I'll be all right now," she told him.

"You were always *all right.*"

Molly smiled, running her fingers through his hair. When she moved to the bed and picked up their son, Sam stepped behind her, cradling them both in his arms.

"The past is behind us now," he said. "Sam Junior—and his brothers and sisters, when they come—are the future."

Molly turned to look into her husband's beloved face. "We'll finish this tomorrow," she said. "Let's go home." She smiled at him with all the love in her heart. "I think it's time we started working on the future."

The sparkle in her eyes told Sam all he needed to know.

A HISTORICAL ROMANCE
TO CAPTURE YOUR HEART!

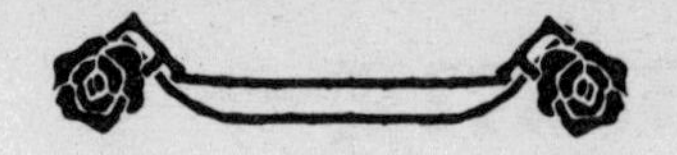

KAT MARTIN

# MAGNIFICENT PASSAGE

Mandy Ashton is fleeing her stifling existence at Fort Laramie and is heading toward California. Travis Langley, a white man raised by the Cheyenne, is hired to escort her, although he mistakenly believes she is the rebellious daughter of the governor. This dangerous deception becomes even more perilous when the two discover they've become captives of a passion as untamed as the wilderness of the American West! Will they be able to overcome their contest of wills and let true love reign?

ISBN: 0-517-00620-0 Price: $3.95

AVAILABLE AT BOOKSTORES NOW!